Praise for

"*A hell of a ride, but heaven to read: eerie, compelling and very funny.*"
**Michael Marshall Smith**

"*Dark, surreal and wickedly funny, Lou Morgan's reimagining of the war between Heaven and Hell mixes angels, alcohol and ammunition to serve up a joy of a read.*"
**Tom Pollock**

"*It's a challenge to take concepts older than the calendar and make them seem new. Louise Morgan has done just that. How to describe this, her debut novel? Bloody Heavenly!*"
**Guy Adams**

"*Dark, enticing and so sharp the pages could cut you,* Blood and Feathers *is a must-read for any fan of the genre.*"
**Sarah Pinborough**

"*A storming debut! Lou Morgan writes with confidence, style and verve. Who would have thought that going to Hell could be so much fun? A must-read.*"
**Mike Shevdon**

LOU MORGAN

# BLOOD
# AND
# FEATHERS

SOLARIS

First published 2012 by Solaris
an imprint of Rebellion Publishing Ltd,
Riverside House, Osney Mead,
Oxford, OX2 0ES, UK

*www.solarisbooks.com*

ISBN: 978 1 78108 019 1

10 9 8 7 6 5 4 3 2 1

A CIP catalogue record for this book is available from the
British Library.

Designed & typeset by Rebellion Publishing

REBELLiON

Printed in the US

*For James.*
*Upside down, on fire, and always.*

"Freely they stood who stood, and fell who fell."
– *Paradise Lost*

"Therefore Hell hath enlarged herself,
and opened her mouth without measure..."
– Isaiah 5:14

# CHAPTER ONE

## Teeth

"Mum! Mum!"

"What?" Iris stuck her head around the shower curtain, listening.

"The toast's jammed again – it's getting all burnt! And there's teeth on the lawn."

"Oh, for crying out loud. Unplug it, then see if you can jimmy it out with a wooden spoon. A *wooden* one!" She stepped back under the running water. "Give me strength… Wait – *teeth*?"

Five minutes later, Iris was wrapping a towel around her head and standing in a puddle in the kitchen, peering out at the lawn. "Teeth?"

"Look." Jack pointed, scattering crumbs on the draining board. Sure enough, there they were – right in the middle of the lawn, a ring of sharp white points that had most definitely not been there the night before. They towered over the shrubs, standing at least as high as a man. Iris stared at them for a moment, then turned and fixed her teenage son with a frown. "Is this anything to do with you, Jack?"

"'snot me," he said through a mouthful of toast. "Ask Addy."

"Don't be ridiculous. Your sister's eight years old – and use a plate, would you? You're getting bits everywhere."

"So what if she's eight? Addy was the one with the cling film last year. You blamed that on me, too."

"That isn't the point. Clean up that mess, please. And don't go anywhere near that... that *thing*." Iris tugged at the edge of her makeshift turban. She left Jack eating his toast, and went back upstairs.

SHE WAS JUST picking up the hairdryer when Jack's voice drifted up the stairs again. "Mum?"

"What is it this time?"

"You'd better come see." Something about his tone made her heart jump, and she dropped the dryer.

When she got to the kitchen, the back door was open, and through it she could see him standing beside the ring of... whatever they were. He looked back over his shoulder at her, and even from this distance she could see how pale his face was.

It was beginning to rain, and the water was soaking into his school shirt, but he did not move.

"Jack? Jack! Whatever's the matter? What are..."

Iris did not finish her sentence. The ground beneath her shifted and lurched, pitching her sideways. "Jack!"

And when she looked up, he wasn't there. There was nothing there except for the rain, and those strange white *things*.

And where was Addy? Jack had called her downstairs, hadn't he, said she had better come into the garden. What had he wanted her to see?

Still off-balance, she half-walked, half-scrambled closer... and all at once she realised why he had been so pale, just why he had been staring back at her.

THEY *WERE* TEETH. You could see it, up close. They looked larger now than they had from the window. Had they grown? A little

10

voice in her head told her that was impossible; how could they have grown? She chose to ignore it, just as carefully as she chose to ignore the other little voice – the one that was telling her there were *teeth* in the *middle* of the *lawn*, and that in itself was pretty bloody impossible, particularly on a Tuesday.

The jagged points, the smoothness of the sides, the ridges of earth below them, like gums. They towered over her, so much taller than she had first thought. And between them, where there had been grass and moss and flowers only yesterday, was a gaping hole leading down into… a mouth.

A throat.

"Jack?" Her voice sounded weak against the rain.

She crept closer to the edge of the mouth that had opened in the middle of their dull, ordinary, suburban garden.

"Jack? Addy?"

The ground shook again, this time knocking her flat on her face and then rolling her sideways, dangerously close to the edge. She slowly, carefully, dragged herself closer and stared down into the dark, calling her children. Not a sound came back – not even an echo. There was only the darkness within, and the noise of the rain on the grass. She leaned as far out as she dared, throwing an arm around the base of a tooth for support. It was cold, slippery to the touch, but she hung on as the world around her tilted again. She might have screamed; she didn't think so, but she couldn't be sure.

The throat had stairs.

Sweeping around it was a narrow staircase; beginning behind the tooth to her left and ending… who knew where?

Iris lay back on the wet grass, feeling the rain on her neck, and she made a choice.

# CHAPTER TWO

## Meet the Family

THE FRONT PORCH smelled like burning ice.

Alice opened the door and squelched her way into the hall, wondering why she'd worn canvas trainers in what was clearly a monsoon – and more importantly, why only *one* of her socks was wet. Dr Grove would doubtless tell her this was 'A Negative Thought,' and instead she should be concentrating on appreciating that one of her socks was dry. Alice mentally told Dr Grove where he could stick his positive attitude. It's hard to be appreciative when you've got one wet foot.

The smell was stronger in the hall: cold and sharp, it reminded her of cigar smoke, if the cigar was made of glass. An odd sort of smell that was somehow familiar. She dropped her keys on the table and switched on the light. Thanks to the rain, it was darker than three o'clock had any right to be, but it was nothing a few lamps couldn't fix. As Alice wriggled her soggy shoe off, she heard voices coming from the back room: some of her father's cronies swung by for a drink, perhaps. It had been a long time since any of his old friends had come to the house, and she had been a little worried about him, but this was promising. Maybe he was finally going to get out again, get a life – get a job. That explained the smell, too: it must be aftershave. Expensive aftershave. There was hope yet.

The voices suddenly stopped, then started up again, their pitch lower and more urgent.

"Ali?" Her father's voice.

"Hi, Dad. D'you want some tea? I was going to put the kettle on."

"We've got guests…"

"Then I'll make a pot."

"Alice…"

"Give me a minute, I've only just got through the door, and it's tipping it down out there." Her words came out sharper than she had intended. That was the sock talking. Rolling her eyes, she pushed open the door to the back room and stepped inside.

IT WASN'T A big room, not even by the standards of all the other houses in the street. Alice had always thought it was rather poky, and her father had often talked about knocking down the dividing wall between the back and front rooms… at least, he *used* to talk about it. That was back in the days when he worked in an office, washed the car on Sunday mornings, mowed the lawn, watched the football with friends and was generally just like everyone else's dad. That was a long time ago.

Despite the gloom, and the fact he had company, he hadn't turned on any of the lights; all Alice could see was her father's silhouette hunched in his chair by the window and the outline of a man standing beside him. She made out the vague suggestion of someone else sitting on the sofa.

"Hey, Dad," she said as brightly as she could, pushing her hair back from her face. "How about some light in here? It's absolutely chucking it down."

She didn't wait for a response, and flicked on the nearest lamp. The bulb flared bright white before going out with a soft pop.

"Oops," said a man's voice.

"Sorry. Hang on, let me try this…" She reached for a lamp on the table. It flared and died. "That's weird. Maybe the fuses have tripped. I'll just go and…"

Her father said nothing; he didn't even seem to have noticed that she was in the room. And when someone answered her, it was the stranger again.

"Not to worry, Alice. A little dark doesn't bother us. It's probably just the weather making the power surge, or something. It *is* still raining, isn't it?" His voice was deep, clear, with a faint accent she couldn't quite place. If anyone could sound like they wore expensive aftershave, it was him. Alice gave a nervous half-smile and headed back out to the hall. Her father still said nothing.

The fuse switches were just as they ought to be. She poked at the cover of the box; clicked the kitchen light on and off, on and off. Fine. As for the tea… the mugs weren't exactly *clean*, but they'd do. And if *they* weren't clean… she opened the fridge with a sinking feeling, picked up the half-full milk carton and shook it gently. The milk inside didn't move. She dropped the whole thing into the bin without even bothering to smell it. Lemon it was.

However much she tried, she couldn't quite make out what they were saying in the room next door. She could hear their voices alright, but somehow the actual words seemed to skitter away from her when she tried to tune in to them.

Five minutes later, she was shouldering her way back through the door, carrying a tray laden with mugs, a teapot, a plate of lemon slices (hacked out of the sad little thing she found at the back of the fridge), a sugar bowl and – miraculously – three clean teaspoons. Balanced on the end of the tray were three lightbulbs, still tucked in their boxes and dug out from the depths of the undersink cupboard. But as she walked into the room, she realised that it was bright and warm.

The lights were on, glowing gently in the corners.

"Can I help you with the tray?"

She realised she was standing in the middle of the room with her mouth open, and it was one of her father's friends – the man sitting on the sofa – who was speaking. Not the same voice as before, which meant it had been the man standing beside her father who had called her by name, asked if it was still raining.

He had told her they weren't afraid of the dark, hadn't he? What an odd sort of thing to say. And remembering where she was, Alice closed her mouth, smiled and handed a cup to her still-silent father before turning to look at their visitors.

They were an unlikely pair. Her eyes settled first on the man beside her father's chair. This was the guy with the money. Money in the sound of his voice, money in the smell of his aftershave. Money in the cut of his suit, the cut of his blond hair. He had a narrow face, and although he was smiling, there was something cool and distant in his eyes. He took a mug from the tray as she held it out to him.

The other, she reflected as she slid the tray onto the table, couldn't be more different. While blondie by the window gave the distinct impression of being uptight, his friend was perched on the sofa, watching her with wide brown eyes.

"You alright with that?" he asked, nodding at the tray.

Alice smiled back. "It's fine, really. Thanks."

Her voice sounded squeakier than she would have liked, and her father laughed quietly. It was the first sign of life he'd shown since he called her into the room. Sofa-Man leaned back against the cushions again, and tucked his boots as far under the sofa as he could. "Fair enough."

What kind of people, wondered Alice as she busied herself with the teapot, traveled in pairs like this? Two suits, she might have understood. Two scruffy looking guys with torn jeans and hoodies under their jackets, well, that was certainly much more her dad's style. But one of each? Something wasn't right.

The blond peered at the plate of lemon slices like she'd just offered him a severed finger, but he eventually took one and dropped it neatly into his mug. The hoodie shook his head at his friend and scooped up three slices, then shoveled seven spoons of sugar into his cup.

"So, Dad...." She sat down on the chair closest to her father, hoping for some kind of response, but all he did was curl his hands around his drink and blow into the mug.

Finally, blondie cleared his throat. "You're Alice. We're... friends of your mother's. My name is Gwyn, and *that*" – he gestured to the hoodie-wearer on the sofa, who half-raised a hand in greeting – "is Mallory. We came to meet you."

"Oh." Alice wasn't entirely sure how to answer that, but was still getting no help from her dad. "You knew Mum?"

"We did. A long time ago."

"That's nice. I don't remember seeing you before. What brings you round this way?"

"I told you. You did. We came to meet you."

"Oh." The conversation wasn't going quite the way Alice had hoped. She felt stupid, and the blond – Gwyn – was frowning at her. Obviously, she wasn't the only one who thought she was being slow. She was rescued by Mallory, who leaned forward and set his mug down on the table.

"What my friend over there is trying to say, Alice, is that we used to know your mother before she met your dad, before you were born. We're not from round here, like you said, but we were in the area and thought it was time to look you up, see how you're doing." He smiled, and the corners of his eyes crinkled.

"How did you know Mum?"

"Worked with her. Sort of. It's complicated. You really do look like her. You have her eyes."

"Thanks. I don't really remember that much about her, you know? I was only six."

"It must've been hard. I'm sorry, if it's worth anything. She was a good friend."

"You've done well, Richard.' Gwyn said to her father. "Not everyone thought you would."

"I did my best." His voice was strained, as though he was holding something back, as though he was afraid. Alice felt her heart rate increase. Something was very wrong here and she had no idea what. Her grip on her mug tightened.

Gwyn laid a hand on her dad's shoulder and continued. "There were some who thought your best would be far from satisfactory. But no matter. *They* are coming. They're coming now. And you appear to have fulfilled your side of the bargain, so now it's time for us to fulfill ours."

Alice met her father's eyes. He was smiling, but tears rolled down his face. He was still looking at her like that when the hands came through the ceiling. The paint bubbled and cracked, and a pair of arms pushed through the ceiling directly above her father's head; the fingers flexing, stretching, reaching for him. They came closer and closer until they were almost level with his shoulders. And no-one but Alice had noticed. Not until they followed her terrified stare. Her father glanced up then and cried out. Mallory swore and leapt to his feet. Gwyn... did nothing. He did nothing, and Alice watched in frozen horror as those hands clamped around her father's head and, with a sudden wrench, snapped his neck.

SHE WAS DIMLY aware of her scream filling the room; vaguely conscious that the mug had slipped from her fingers. She stumbled backwards with the sound of breaking bone echoing in her ears and her father's sightless eyes filling her mind; her hands beating at empty air. She saw Mallory start forward, heard Gwyn's voice as though from far away – but the words were lost, just pieces of noise.

And then hands were holding her, pulling her into focus. "Wake her up," he said, "Wake her up."

Mallory's face filled her vision, leaning over her, and he pressed a cool hand to her forehead.

"Sorry, kid," he muttered, closing his eyes, "This is going to hurt."

He wasn't wrong.

# CHAPTER THREE
## Waking Up

IF ALICE DREAMED, she didn't know it. She was lost in a whirl of pain, and there were *things* in there with her. Not dreams, she thought, not memories. More… ideas. Suggestions. Images that flashed past like they were carried on a storm, and a light so bright it made her skin burn and her teeth ache.

She was afraid, without knowing what it was that she feared. It felt like falling, like flying, like being frozen and scorched all at once. And there with her, always with her, the sensation that a single set of eyes were watching her, and that they saw everything she was.

"COME BACK, ALICE."

The voice was faint, distant. It felt warm, safe. It smelled of home.

"Alice? Alice! Come back." And then quieter, to someone else, perhaps: "Did I ever tell you you're a complete prick?"

"Frequently." A new voice. Harder. A voice that was used to being obeyed. "Open your eyes, Alice. It's time we talked."

SHE WAS IN the back room of her house, lying on the floor. A man stood over her, his blond hair catching the light so it looked almost like a halo. Another crouched next to her, sliding his hand behind her neck to help her sit up, concern in his eyes. They looked familiar, but…

Friends of her father. The lights. Tea.

Her father.

She looked at his chair. It was empty. The room smelled of death – earthen and hard and wrong – and there was a heavy, slow ache somewhere under her ribs.

"I took care of it. He's gone," said Gwyn, moving back as she hauled herself to her feet. "You shouldn't think about it too much. It won't help. There was nothing we could have done to save him." He shrugged, then he said something in another language – one she had never heard before, full of rolling sounds that bled into one another. And yet, it was somehow… It was…

He was still speaking, and she realised that she hadn't moved. She wanted to – she *meant* to, because she needed to get away from…

But his voice filled her mind and crowded her out.

Couldn't move; couldn't think. Alice's feet were nailed to the ground, her hands pinned to her sides, and still he was talking, still he was filling her head, pushing her further and further back into her own mind. But what was truly frightening was that there was something else in her head. Something that was listening, and wanting to stay. And until it was ready, she wasn't going anywhere.

He stopped, at last – and suddenly she could breathe again, could move. Could think. It was all she could do not to slide to the floor again, but she was free. She was free, and her father was gone.

"You. You…"

She couldn't get the words out. He hadn't even flinched. Gwyn had done nothing: he had stood and watched those… *things*, those impossible hands, take hold of her father, and… The words were there but they caught in her throat and burned, and all the time he watched her with an expectant face, as though he knew exactly what was running through her mind.

Even so, he obviously wasn't expecting her to kick him as hard as she could, and then shove Mallory sideways, knocking him off his feet, before stumbling out of the room and into the hall.

She fumbled with the key in the lock, tearing the front door open and running as hard and as fast as she could down the drive. Not knowing or caring that she had left her shoes, her coat, her bag behind; not noticing the rain sheeting down and soaking her to the bone.

She ran until the blood pounded in her ears, and then she ran some more. The pavements blurred and she lost track of street names and road signs, only knowing that she had to put as great a distance between herself and home as she could. At last, her legs and lungs gave out and, gasping, she slumped against a fence.

"How're you doing?" asked Mallory from a garden wall beside her. He sat calm and unruffled, swinging his feet and looking almost apologetic. "Alright?"

Alice tried to back away, but her legs had had enough and they buckled, dumping her into a puddle. Mallory scratched his head "Sorry about Gwyn. He doesn't mean to be such a wanker – he just doesn't understand."

"What do you want? What do you want from me?"

Mallory frowned and hopped off the wall. "We're here to help. I know you don't believe that, but we are. We're here to keep you safe."

"Keep me safe from what? You saw it, didn't you? That was real. You saw it happen! Some*thing* just killed my father. You didn't stop it. Is that how you're going to keep me safe?"

"He never told you, did he?" For a second, Mallory looked surprised. "He honestly never told you. All those years..." He tailed off, and peered up the road, into the rain. "You need to come with me. You need to trust me."

"No."

"Alice."

"No. Get away from me. I'll scream…"

"And a lot of good might it do you." He looked around him again, more anxiously this time. "Alice, whatever you think, something's coming, something bad, and it's coming for *you*. Now, I know this is hard. I know you don't understand, and I know you don't believe me, but you *must* trust me." He held out his hand, but she pulled away.

"I said get away!"

"Alice! We don't have time. They're *coming*." His fingers closed around her wrist, and although she tried to shake him off, his grip was strong. She opened her mouth to scream, but… something stopped her. All she could do was stare at him as the rain dripped into her eyes – and she realised that he wasn't getting wet.

His hair, his leather jacket, his boots: he was perfectly dry. The rain looked like it was falling on him, just the same as it was falling on her, but somehow it seemed to pass through him, or around him.

"I told you. We're here to help you. Can you trust me?"

"I don't…"

"Look at me, Alice. Really look at me." He dropped into a crouch beside her, his face close to hers. "Can you trust me?"

She had no choice but to look into his eyes, which she had been sure were brown. Now, though, she wasn't so sure. They shifted and shimmered like starlight through cloud, and she remembered a warm voice that made her feel safe.

"I swear on my life, Alice, that I will keep you from harm. It's not much, but I can give you that. Your mother trusted me."

"My mother's dead."

"Maybe. But she was my friend, and she would want you to be safe. I can help with that. I will protect you, whatever it takes. I swear."

"Get. Away."

"No."

"I said…"

"And I heard you. But if I leave you here, you'll be dead before sunrise. Worse than dead. Do you understand?"

"My father…"

"Your father made a choice a long time ago, Alice. Things aren't exactly as they seem."

"It seemed pretty straightforward to me."

"Trust me, Alice."

"No."

"Trust me, and I won't let you down."

"No."

"Alice, we're running out of time. Please." He looked over his shoulder, first one way then the other. "Please."

"Why? Why should I?"

"Take it on faith."

"After that?"

"Please, Alice. Your mother would have."

And she knew that it was true. Anyway, what was the point in trying to run? Where was there to run to?

"Alright," said a voice that wasn't quite hers.

"Atta girl. Now, let's get you out of here."

He pulled her to her feet, and with no effort at all he scooped her into his arms. She was about to protest, but there was a sudden wind on her face, and she must have fainted again because the next thing she knew, she was on her own doorstep, with him beside her. The front door stood open, waiting.

GWYN WAS WATCHING the garden through the window, his back to the door. He didn't turn, or give any sign that he knew they were there. Mallory folded himself back onto the sofa, but Alice stayed in the doorway, uneasy. How did the two men know her father? Or her mother? Had her father known what was coming? And why, after she had just seen, was there a little voice in the back of her head that told her she *could* trust them, that she *must*?

"What do you know about your mother?" Gwyn said, and his voice was clear and sharp. It wasn't a kind voice, Alice thought.

She shook her head. "I don't think that's any of your business."

"What you *think* doesn't matter. I asked you a question."

"And I don't intend to answer it."

Alice edged a little further away from him as he turned to face her, and she realised how bright his eyes were: almost turquoise, standing out against the pallor of his skin and the dark of his suit. He opened his mouth to speak, but Mallory interrupted.

"You know what? We should all take this down a notch. It's a big day, everyone's a bit stressed. I know I am, and…"

"I am not stressed." Gwyn said. "I simply asked a question. And I still expect an answer."

"Gwyn, can you just back off? She's not one of your goons."

"No, she isn't, is she? She *thinks* she's something special, something different. Something that doesn't have to follow orders."

"She doesn't think anything. She doesn't *know*." Mallory was on his feet, gesturing at Alice. This was obviously news to Gwyn, who narrowed his eyes, and looked her up and down.

"Doesn't know?"

"No."

"Ah." Gwyn's expression softened slightly, and he beckoned to Alice. "Come here, child."

"No way." Alice planted herself firmly in the doorway. "I don't know who you are, or what's going on, and until I get some answers, I'm not doing anything you say. So you tell me who the hell you are and what you want, and you start by explaining why I shouldn't call the police right now."

"You don't want to do that."

"I really do."

"Oh, for the love of...." Mallory banged his hand on the table, and sighed. "Alright. Why don't we all just sit down and start again? Gwyn, back off and give the girl some space. And Alice, I'm sure this is hard, but like I said, you can trust us." He ran a hand through his hair. "Look, go and get yourself into some dry clothes before you catch pneumonia or something? Then we can talk."

Alice had forgotten that she was soaking wet. Again. It hadn't seemed important, but now he'd mentioned it, the idea of changing into something dry was very appealing indeed. And it would give her time. As she passed her bag in the hallway, she pocketed her phone. It did cross her mind to simply head down the drive and away again, but that hadn't exactly worked last time. She still wasn't sure how Mallory had kept up with her, got ahead of her even, and she certainly didn't know how it was that he had stayed completely dry in the downpour. Both things were going into a small box at the back of her mind, labeled 'Stuff to think about later.' In the meantime, she was going to change her clothes, and call the police.

Peeling off her wet things, she pulled a dry pair of jeans out of the wardrobe, then a T-shirt and a sweater. And socks, dry socks at last! She tossed the wet clothing into the laundry basket and took out her phone. She dialed, and held it to her ear.

"And I thought we were getting past the trust issues," said Gwyn's voice, alarmingly close. Alice whipped round, but he wasn't there. She was alone and, more worrying, she could hear his muffled voice talking to Mallory downstairs. So how....? She looked at the phone in her hand.

"Hello?"

"I told you, you really don't want to call the police."

"You're in my *phone* now?"

"I don't think you understand the gravity of the situation, Alice. The police can't help you. No-one can. No-one except

us. Now stop acting like a silly little girl and come downstairs."
There was a click, and the phone went dead. Not just the line, the whole phone shut down completely. A fizzing sound came from behind the screen, and there was a small puff of smoke from the speaker.

If Mallory realised that she had tried to call the police – or that Gwyn had cut in on the call – he didn't show it when she walked back into the room. Instead, he patted a spot on the sofa next to him and reached inside his jacket, drawing out a small silver flask which he brandished at her, beaming. "Haven't found a drop of booze in the house, so it's just as well I've got this."

"I don't drink," Alice said, pointedly ignoring his gesture and sitting on a chair across the room. Mallory grinned at her. "Oh, I know *you* don't. But I do." He took a healthy swig, watched by Gwyn, who sighed.

"And that, Mallory, is precisely why you...."

"Oh, no. No you don't," Mallory tucked the flask back into his coat. "We're not talking about me. We're here to talk about you." He looked at Alice, who suddenly felt very small and alone.

Gwyn sniffed, and lowered himself into a chair. "Tell me, Alice, what did your father tell you about what happened to your mother?"

"He didn't like to talk about her: she died when I was little. He didn't tell me what happened, wouldn't let me come to the funeral. Never even told me where she's buried. He said she was with the angels, and that's all I needed to know. That much, he was always very clear on."

Alice had the strange sensation that it was someone else talking, as though a stranger had borrowed her voice and was opening up a part of her that had been secret. She wasn't sure whether or not the disconnection was a relief. Gwyn took in her words and steepled his fingers in front of his face, frowning.

There was silence, and then he looked her dead in the eyes and said: "And did he never tell you which angels she was with?"

Alice laughed. "Which angels she was with? Right. Absolutely. I should have thought to ask, shouldn't I? He just didn't think a six-year-old should know too much about how her mother died, and by the time I was old enough to want to know, he'd already decided he was done talking about it. The last couple of years, he hasn't even let me mention her around him. So, no. He wasn't specific about the angels."

The numbness released her, and now she heard the bitterness in her voice. She'd never heard herself sound like that before... what was happening to her? This wasn't how she talked, certainly not to strangers, and above all not to strangers as strange as these. She caught the glance that passed between Gwyn and Mallory: Gwyn raising his eyebrows expectantly and Mallory shrugging. "Totally not my call," he muttered, slouching back against the cushions and focusing very firmly on the toes of his boots.

Gwyn sat forward, his eyes searching Alice's face for just a moment too long, then got up and moved to the window.

"I wish this were easier, Alice." He folded his arms and a chill ran down her spine. She looked sideways at Mallory, but he was still staring at the floor and would not meet her gaze. "You have to believe me when I say this is all far from ideal. It's not at all how I would choose to operate, but we don't always get to make the easy choices. And nor do you.

"We knew your mother, Alice. We knew her better than even your father did. And we know you. Now it's time for you to know us." He closed his eyes, and the edges of the room suddenly seemed sharper, brighter. Everything grew lighter, and there was a sound like the wind in the trees, faint at first, then louder and louder.

As Alice watched, Gwyn unfolded his wings, and every bulb in the house blew out as one.

# CHAPTER FOUR
## Ancient History

ALICE HEARD LAUGHTER. It was light and high, a woman's laugh, and she found herself looking around for its source. It was only when she saw Mallory's scowl that she realised it was her, and she closed her mouth.

The room should have been dark without the lights, but there was another light in the room, one which hummed and throbbed like a heartbeat. It was Gwyn – or rather, it was his wings.

The narrow little room wasn't large enough for him to open them fully, so they sat slightly folded behind him, sweeping down until the tips brushed the floor. They were white and they *shimmered*. All across the surface of the feathers, white sparks glittered and arced.

"He doesn't like it when people do that. Laugh, I mean. Makes him grouchy," said Mallory. "Best act like you're impressed, or you'll never hear the end of it."

"Thank you, Mallory. I think it's time you made yourself useful, don't you?" Gwyn's voice had a slight echo to it, as though it came from far-off, and despite his attempt to hide it, it sounded a little deflated. His wings rustled as he stepped closer to Alice, the light from them casting moving shadows on the walls. Mallory rolled his eyes, then snapped his fingers. There was a gentle tinkling sound, and the lights flared back into life.

Alice knew her mouth was open again, but she couldn't seem to close it. It didn't bother her too much – presumably, said the voice in the back of her head, they were used to it. What with their being *angels* and everything. The laugh threatened to bubble up from inside her again, and she swallowed it down. Something tickled her cheek, and she reached up to brush it away; her fingertips came away wet, and she was startled to find that she was crying. She didn't *do* crying. It wasn't her thing. She looked up, and Gwyn was right in front of her, his wings tucked back. "Alice. This is important…"

"How come I couldn't see them before?"

"I… What?"

"The wings. I couldn't see them before. You can't have had them hidden away, so why couldn't I see them?"

"That's all you have to say? You want to know why you couldn't see them?"

"Well, yes."

Alice wiped her face, hard. Gwyn was frowning at her, and somewhere across the room there was the sound of laughter again, a man's this time. Mallory was laughing so hard that he almost rolled off the sofa, tipping his head back and scrambling to catch his breath. Eventually, he wagged a finger towards Alice.

"She," he said, "is *just* like her mother."

"I very much hope not." Gwyn didn't bother to look over at Mallory, instead keeping his eyes fixed on Alice. They were so very blue, this close. Blue like… well, like nothing Alice had ever seen. And it felt like they were staring straight into her. He was too close, too near – and that smell, that cold smell was overwhelming. She got the feeling it probably wasn't aftershave after all. "You didn't answer my question, though, did you?"

"The wings? Fine. It's a trick of perception. You can't see air, can you, but you don't doubt that it's there. You've woken. You'll find you see a lot of things differently now. That's why we're here. Is that good enough?"

"Not that question."

"I beg your pardon?"

"Who are you, and what do you want?"

"Who *are* we? I don't know if you'd noticed, but... angels?"

Gwyn's eyebrows shot up, and Mallory snorted back another laugh. Alice was warming to him. Gwyn, she wasn't so sure about.

"That doesn't tell me anything."

"Oh, for..." Gwyn backed away and rubbed his forehead with his hand. His wings vanished and the light from them faded. "Do you know how many men and women across the centuries have been visited by angels? No, don't answer. It's a rhetorical question. Let me tell you: thousands. And in all the centuries I've known, never have I been greeted with such arrogance, such... such..."

"I told you, she's just like her mother. She has her eyes, remember? She can see to the heart of things. Even you." Mallory stood up, patting his jacket, feeling for something in the pockets... the flask, perhaps. Evidently, he found whatever it was; a look of relief settled across his face and he stopped patting. "She wants to know who we are, and what we want? I say we tell her. All of it." He turned to Alice and pointed at the sofa he had just vacated. "Sit down. You're going to want to soon enough, so you might as well get comfortable." She sat. Gwyn had retreated to the window, and Mallory smirked at him. "Are you sulking?"

"Watch your mouth. Remember who you're addressing."

"As if I could forget." There was something hidden behind those words, but before Alice could think about it any further, Mallory had perched himself on the arm of the chair opposite her and put one foot on the edge of the table. "Where would you like us to start?" he asked, kindly. Alice stared back at him, and he nodded. "Good point. Anywhere.

"You know our names. And you're a smart girl. You've seen his wings. Mine aren't quite so impressive. It would be a bit of an anticlimax, frankly, if I was to join in with all this, so I won't. But they're there. Buy me a drink, maybe, and..."

"Mallory!" Gwyn snapped.

"Sorry, sorry. You know what we are. And we've already told you we knew your mother."

"Did she know that you were...?" Alice stumbled over the words, although even as they came out of her mouth, she realised how they sounded.

Mallory blinked at her. "Think, Alice. *Think*."

"Oh." She felt cold.

"There you go."

"But that's..."

"Impossible. Yeah. I get that. Almost as impossible as Feathers over there."

"But..."

"If you want to have a conversation, you're going to need to start finishing those sentences, Alice. Otherwise, I suggest you sit tight and listen. When I'm done, you can ask me as many questions as you want. Provided you can actually get them out." He paused, but Alice shook her head and sat in silence.

"So. Angels 101. Real, obviously. Not all harps and haloes. Again: obviously. We're not so big on the sitting around on clouds singing praises, either. We're soldiers."

"Soldiers?"

"Back with the talking again, Alice?"

"Sorry."

"That's my girl. Soldiers. Like I said, you're smart. And if I know your father, you've read the books, haven't you?" He pointed to a tall bookshelf in the corner of the room, stuffed with battered paperbacks. Alice nodded mutely. Satisfied, Mallory continued. "'And there was war in Heaven...' Ring a bell? I bet it does. And you know what? It's all real. The Morningstar, the Fall. *All* of it. They're down there – literally down there. And they want out. They want to be in charge. They've been

34

trying to get out for thousands of years. Our job is to keep them down there, out of the way, by any means necessary."

He reached behind his back, and pulled out a sturdy-looking handgun, which he turned over in his hands before tucking it back into his belt. Alice's eyes bulged.

"You don't smell like he does," she blurted.

Mallory looked a little flustered, and opened and closed his mouth. Obviously he didn't have an answer to that, and he looked towards Gwyn for help. Gwyn folded his arms, enjoying Mallory's discomfort.

"Mallory and I differ in several respects," he said. "Apart from, as you say, our... scent, Mallory has already mentioned the difference in our wings..."

"Compensating!" Mallory coughed into his fist.

Gwyn shot him a dirty look and continued. "What he hasn't told you is that his wings have been clipped. What you're looking at, Alice, is a perfect example of an Earthbound."

"An Earthbound?" Alice asked, glancing from Gwyn to Mallory. He looked uncomfortable, even embarrassed.

"Suspended. You see, if an angel brings disgrace upon himself, his general may choose to exile him. His wings are clipped and he is banished to Earth to serve out his sentence. Such angels are known as Earthbounds. Mallory is one of them."

"And lucky for me, I get *you* to keep an eye on me." Mallory growled, then turned back to Alice. "It's not as bad as it sounds. Honestly. I..." He paused, running a hand through his hair. "I was under a lot of pressure and I made a couple of bad choices." He cocked his head and narrowed his eyes. "I'm sure you, of all people, can understand that."

It was Alice's turn to feel uncomfortable. She didn't like what Mallory was suggesting. It was like he knew things that had happened a long time ago; things she didn't want to talk about. Eager to change the subject, she pointed at Gwyn. "So if you're an Earthbound, what's he, then?"

"'*He*,'" said Gwyn, "is a Descended."

"Which unfortunately means he gets to be the boss of me," Mallory said. He slid further down into the chair, not taking his feet from the table. "All angels, when they come down here, are known as Descendeds. I mean, when you're up there, you're just... angels, so. Every Earthbound – and there's more of us than he'd have you believe, thanks – is assigned to the charge of a Descended. They... supervise, make sure we're behaving ourselves. And I'm afraid that as you get me looking after you, you get him too. It's a twofer."

"Twofer?"

"Two for one. Where was I?" He looked up at Alice, and smiled when he saw the blank expression on her face. "Too much?"

"I'm not sure."

"You got questions?"

"I suppose: what's this all got to do with me?"

"Ah." Mallory pulled out the flask again and took a swig. "You want...? No. You don't, do you?" He screwed the top on and pocketed it. "Your mother was an angel, Alice. What do you think that makes you?"

Alice didn't want to think about that, not at all. It was enough that she had two men standing in front of her talking about angels, and that one of them had a gun and a hip-flask. She had so far, while they were talking, been devoting a great deal of energy to *not* thinking about what any of this had to do with her, or her mother. As it was, she was having quite enough trouble absorbing everything that had been said. It was all so... *odd*. And yet, at the same time, that little voice in the back of her head told her everything would be alright. All she had to do was believe it. Because it was the truth. How ridiculous was that? "I can't be an angel. I'm a librarian. That's absurd."

"You're not an angel," Gwyn said pointedly.

Alice stared at him. "Not... then...?"

"You're only half. It's likely that the angel half is dominant, which is why we're here. But you're still only half."

"Which in and of itself is still a big deal, Alice." Mallory swung his feet down from the table. "You might want to take most of what he says there with a pinch of salt. You're half-angel, which means that you have gifts. You always have done, it's just that you never knew how to use them. Never even knew they were there – not if your dad didn't tell you anything about them."

"Did he know? About my mother, I mean?"

"Not now." Mallory paused. "We don't have time to tell you all of this, not now. There's a reason we're here, and we can't tell you every last detail now, however much you want to know it. We *will* tell you, but it'll have to wait."

"You said something was coming earlier, in the street."

"It is. And it's coming for you. Your father's job was to keep you protected, keep you hidden until we came to find you – until you were ready."

"So I'm ready now?"

"Are you kidding? You're far from ready, but things have changed. They've found you, and we're almost out of time."

"Before what?"

"Before *they* get what they want: ontrol. Forever." He pointed at the floor, and the look in his eyes told Alice everything she needed to know.


"But why me?" Alice asked, throwing clothes into a bag. She was in her room, packing everything she could reach. Mallory hadn't been specific, he'd just told her to pack "stuff."

"Why not you? You've obviously got a talent the Fallen think will be useful to them, or one that they don't want on our side." Mallory was perched on the banister outside her bedroom door. Sitting there, he reminded her of a large, slightly scruffy bird.

"So what now?"

"You come with us. There's somewhere safe we can take you, somewhere they won't be able to get at you in a hurry. Then we can talk. We'll tell you everything, I promise. And we'll see what you can do."

"Like a test?"

"No. No test. But all angels have their gifts, you included."

"What about you? What are yours? Oh… do the Earthbounds still…?"

"I still have my gifts, yes." She could hear the smile in his voice. "I'm a healer. I fix things."

"Like what?"

"Like anything. The lightbulbs, earlier? That was me."

"And people?"

"People too. People are… harder." The smile was gone.

"Time to go." Gwyn's voice drifted up from the hall. There was a finality in it that made Alice stop with her hand halfway to her bag. Until that moment, it hadn't dawned on her that she would be leaving. *Really* leaving. She couldn't stay, she knew that. Regardless of what Gwyn and Mallory said about something "coming," there would be questions.

"We're going. Alice!" Gwyn again.

Mallory stuck his head around the door. "We have to go. Anything else you need, you pack it now. You won't be coming back."

"No. I think I'm done." Alice looked around her room. Her bed, her things, they all seemed so alien now, as though they belonged to someone else.

Mallory held out his hand for her bag. "You travel light. Good. But are you sure that's all you want?"

"Let's just go, okay?"

"If you're sure."

Alice was already at the bottom of the stairs. Gwyn was at the front door, peering out into the darkness of the street.

He looked like he was waiting for something. Listening. All Alice could hear was the rain, but Gwyn obviously had better hearing. He pointed at her shoes. "Get those on, now. They're close." Alice pulled on her trainers and tied the laces as quickly as she could with shaking hands. Mallory was suddenly next to Gwyn, her bag thrown over his shoulder and one hand moving towards the gun tucked into his belt.

"Time to clear up, I think," he said, quietly, and Gwyn nodded. Brushing past her, he opened the cupboard under the stairs. "The fuse box, is it in here?"

"Why?"

"Answer the question."

"Yes. But why?"

"Covering our tracks." Gwyn reached inside the cupboard, and as Alice watched, he placed his palm flat on the cover of the fuse box. There was a horrible hissing, fizzing sound and a wisp of smoke curled out from his fingers.

"Let's go, Alice." Mallory was on the doorstep, beckoning to her. "Let him finish."

"What's he...?"

"Never mind. Keeping you safe."

He took hold of her sleeve and pulled her out of the hallway, marching down the drive and across the road – watching the ends of the street the whole time. They stopped under a tree, and Alice looked back at the house. A white glow was spreading, ever so slowly, from the windows; seeping out into the driveway, reflected in the rain on the tarmac. Mallory muttered something under his breath, and put his hand on her shoulder just as the house exploded.

Windows blew out in a storm of glass. The door slammed shut and then open again, rocking on its hinges. Car alarms sounded and a blast of hot air knocked Alice sideways. Mallory's fingers tightened on her shoulder and held her up. A huge plume of smoke drifted up into the sky, and Gwyn strode out of the fire, straightening his jacket. He looked immaculate. Alice couldn't say she was surprised.

"Let's get moving. Someone will notice that," he said.

Mallory snorted. "You think?" He shouldered Alice's bag again and slid an arm around her, drawing her to him. "Alice?"

"I..." She stared at the flames.

"Alice. Now."

He pulled at her. Suddenly it felt like his arm round her shoulder was not for comfort. He was shielding her from something, hiding her. Gwyn walked off down the road, his blond hair reflecting the light from the fire. Mallory pulled her with him, and Alice saw movement out of the corner of her eye. At the far end of the street, she was sure she had seen someone standing at the end of a driveway, but when she twisted her head and looked again, they were gone. She huddled closer to Mallory, catching the smell of his leather jacket and wondering how it was that he was still bone-dry while the rain was dripping off her nose, and dismissed it. It had been a shadow. It was just... perhaps it had been a trick of the light – a car in the glow of the fire, maybe – but for a moment, it had almost looked like a pair of red eyes: eyes which shone in the darkness, and were fixed upon her...

But there was nothing in the darkness. Only rain and fire, and the past.

# CHAPTER FIVE

## Picking Up the Pieces

"Absolutely not."

"What, Gwyn? You've got a better idea, I'd love to hear it."
Mallory nudged a cardboard box along the floor with his toe;
the box clanked.

"There is no way that I can condone her staying here. It's
appalling," Gwyn looked around him with an expression of
utter disdain. Mallory gave no indication he heard him and
shoveled a stack of books off the sagging sofa and onto the
floor. There was a faint squeak and a scurrying sound that
Alice chose to ignore.

Mallory's home, such as it was, had come as something of
a shock. While she wasn't entirely sure what she had been
expecting, a glorified broom cupboard had not been it – never
mind a glorified broom cupboard at the back of a church. It
was still raining outside, and as Mallory bustled about, clearing
rubbish – and, thought Alice, a quite extraordinary number
of empty bottles – a large, cold drip landed squarely on the
back of her neck, making her jump. Mallory looked round.
"You might want to take a couple of steps to the left. And if
you could scoot that bucket across..." He pointed at a red fire
bucket next to her feet. Alice obliged, and sat down on the
sofa, hoping she was out of the way. It creaked, and a cloud of
dust rose into the air. Gwyn was still taking in the place with a

look of disgust, but now he was touching things: picking up a mug here, moving a newspaper there.

"You're a slob, you know that?"

"Been a little busy, thanks. Or had you not noticed?"

"That's no excuse."

"No excuse for what?"

"For living like this."

"Like what, exactly?"

"Like... this." Gwyn poked at a pile of old pizza boxes. It collapsed, spilling mould-ridden crusts onto his shoes.

Mallory shrugged. "You get used to it. There's been a few things I've had to get used to over the years. But you know that already."

The words were sharp, meant to cut, but Gwyn didn't seem to pay any attention and instead tried to rub a spot of ancient cheese off his shoe and onto a threadbare rug.

Feeling like she was intruding, Alice coughed. "So what happens now?"

"Now," said Mallory, finally giving up on tidying, "we lie low for a while, and try to work out what to do with you."

"What to do with me? You mean you don't know?"

"Well, not exactly."

"I thought there was some kind of plan...?"

"There was," Gwyn cut in. He swept a good inch of dust and muck off a narrow wooden chair and perched on the back of it. Not the seat, but the back. Alice found herself slightly irritated by this, as though it was a deliberate affectation of his. Oblivious, Gwyn smoothed down his jacket. "The plan was that we would come for you when you were ready. Which, as we have already told you, you aren't. We ran out of time, and we needed to get to you before they did."

"Who?"

"Alice, there are more things in Heaven and Earth..."

"Oh, come off it!" Mallory interrupted. "Not Shakespeare. Don't be so bloody pretentious. Or obscure."

"Hamlet," Gwyn said, "is not obscure."

"Whatever." Mallory shrugged again. "He's talking about the Fallen, Alice. The Fallen got wind of who you were, and where you were, and they were coming for you."

"And my father?"

"You saw what they did to him. And this is going to sound bad, but believe me, if they'd taken him alive... I'm sorry, but that's not something I would want on my conscience."

"Taken him where?"

"Where d'you think?"

"No. That's ridiculous. It is. It just... You're kidding me, right?"

"Alice." Mallory crouched in front of her, his eyes level with hers. "Let me be very clear about one thing. I *never* joke about the Fallen." His face was stern; more serious than Alice had yet seen it. She nodded mutely. "This is the way it works. Everyone knows the rules – your father did too. Better than most. In the meantime, you are fair game, so you'll stay here, where it's safe."

"How do you know they won't find me?"

"Find you? They don't need to find you. They already know you're here. But the point is that they can't come in, so they can't get you. As far as you're concerned, right now, this is the safest place on Earth or in Heaven. You don't move from here without our say-so."

"Unless," Gwyn chipped in, "she catches something first. Cholera, perhaps? Dysentery?"

"Would you stop, alright? I'll get the place cleaned up. We can't all live..." Mallory didn't finish his sentence, and instead stared at the floor.

Gwyn raised his eyebrows. "You were saying?"

"Nothing." His eyes were fixed on his boots, and Alice could have sworn she saw something like triumph on Gwyn's face.

"I know it's probably a stupid question," said Alice, "but why here? I mean, what's so safe about this place? Shouldn't we go to the police or something?"

"You're an innocent, aren't you? It's touching. Naive, but touching." Gwyn slid down from his chair. "And what do you think the police would do if you walked into a police station and told them that the Fallen were trying to kill you? That Lucifer had sent his Wolves after you?"

"Wolves?" Alice shuffled on the sofa, making the air even dustier. No-one had mentioned wolves. Angels, yes. But now, the devil? And wolves?

It was Mallory who answered her question. "They're not *actual* wolves. Those wouldn't worry me in the slightest. He means the Wolves of hell, the Twelve. They're assassins, if you like: Lucifer's generals and his personal guard. They're ambitious, and they're only out for one thing: promotion. Nothing else. If any of them had the balls, they'd take on Lucifer himself... not that they'd win. But it's almost certainly the Twelve who'll be on your trail."

"And that's why you're here. To stop them."

"Amongst other things. But that's for another time. For now, I think it's time you got some rest."

"Because that's going to be easy, isn't it?"

"You're safer here than you've been your whole life, Alice. Nothing that would harm you can cross that threshold."

"Don't tell me: hallowed ground?"

"Something like that." Mallory pulled his gun out of his belt pointedly and ejected the magazine, checking it over before reloading.

"Well. That's settled, then." Gwyn was moving towards the door. "I, for one, can't stay here any longer. The smell...." He wrinkled his nose and Mallory sniffed.

"It's not that bad."

"If you say so. Besides, you're right. She needs to rest." He turned to Alice. "Sleep. While you have the chance."

As he laid a hand on the doorknob, he looked back at them. "Keep her safe, Mallory." He made a small gesture with his

44

fingers – something that was too quick for Alice to follow – and stepped through the door, closing it behind him.

Her body suddenly ached, and she shivered. "It's because he's gone," said Mallory from somewhere behind her. "He's so bloody sanctimonious, it's easy to forget he is what he is. But being around a Descended, it makes humans feel… well, *better*. Everything you should have felt – everything since we came – it's all still there. You still felt it, but you didn't know it, not with him around. He protected you. And now he's not here… It's just shock. A good sleep and you'll be fine." He leaned over the back of the sofa and handed her a blanket and a slightly battered cushion. "Not much, but it's the best I can do."

She took them, grateful that they smelled a little better than the rest of the room. "What about you?"

He shook his head. "I don't sleep much. Don't need to. Besides, there's always the floor. I've slept in worse places, believe you me."

Mallory's voice was getting fuzzy, his words muffled and slow. Or maybe that was just her head…? There was something – something she needed to ask. Perhaps if she just rested her eyes for a minute, she could…

Alice was asleep before her head touched the cushion.


WHEN ALICE OPENED her eyes, she felt warm. Sunlight was streaming in through a small, dirty window, puddling on the floor beside her. And despite the sofa being one of the most uncomfortable things she had ever tried to sleep on, she felt like she had slept long and deeply. She couldn't *quite* remember why she was there – not at first, not until the memory of yesterday hit her like a cold wave. Her throat knotted. Her father was dead, her home was gone and she was on the run. With two angels.

Of course.

Sitting up, she looked around for Mallory. There was no sign of him, and it wasn't like there were many places he could be.

In the daylight, the room didn't seem quite so bleak. It was pretty untidy, and the smell was – unfortunately – still there, but it could have been worse. The room wasn't exactly large, either. There was space enough for the sofa and a table in the middle, several ancient, lopsided cupboards and an even more ancient sink against the walls, and that was about it. Two windows, both small and high up – one glazed with small diamond-shaped panes, and one so encrusted with moss and leaves that no light at all made it through. Two doors: one, the door that they had come in through last night and the other, ajar and leading to what looked like a bathroom. Based on the state of the rest of the place, Alice didn't even want to think about the bathroom. She decided she would cross that particular bridge only when strictly necessary.

Books were piled everywhere, great teetering stacks of them. Some of the piles had given way, scattering pages and papers across the floor. Judging by the dirty bootprints across some of them, they'd been that way for a while. She leaned forward and picked up a handful of sheets from the rug, and was surprised to see they weren't in English. Latin, mostly, and some Greek, and, covering pages and pages, a strange, looping handwritten script that she had never seen before.

"See anything interesting?" Mallory's voice came from somewhere behind her ear and, startled, Alice dropped the papers. Mallory hopped over the back of the sofa, landing on the seat beside her and setting more dust free. Alice coughed, and tried to wave it away. "Sorry about that," he muttered and held out a large polystyrene cup. "Coffee?"

"Thanks." She took the cup, not about to tell him that, actually, she didn't really drink coffee. "What's that?" She pointed at the papers that had fallen at her feet. Mallory gave them a shove with his heel. "None of your business. Those are my notes."

"Notes? You mean that's your handwriting? I've never seen anything like that before. It's not shorthand; what kind of language is it?"

"Mine," he said, tersely. "Drink your coffee." He balanced his own cup on his knee, lifting the plastic lid with one hand and unscrewing the cap of his little flask with the other, pouring a generous amount of its contents into the cup. He paused, then upended the flask over his coffee, emptying it altogether. "So."

"So." Alice took a sip of her drink. It was hot and sour. She forced herself to swallow. "What time is it?"

"About ten. You seemed pretty out of it, so I thought I'd get some supplies. I, uh, don't keep much in." He gestured to the bags sitting by the door.

"Oh. And you live here? All the time?"

"Yes, I live here. What's your point?"

"It's just... Nothing."

"You're as bad as Gwyn, you know that? Look, I don't expect you to understand. I was lucky to find this. Do you know how many churches have an extra sacristy just sitting there?"

"Why don't you live in a house or a flat or something, you know, normal?" As soon as she said it, she knew it was a mistake. Mallory looked wounded.

"Because this is the only place that feels like home," he said quietly, and downed the rest of his coffee. "Right," he said after a moment, his tone suddenly brighter as he lobbed the empty cup into the sink. "Let's talk about you, shall we?"

"Me. Yeah, great." Alice's heart sank.

"Well, we certainly aren't going to spend the morning talking about me. I'm boring. Really, really boring."

"What about Gwyn?"

"Nope. Not only is he even *more* boring, he'd kill me. And I might not have that great a life at the moment, but I'd quite like to hang onto it, if it's all the same to you."

"What about my mother?"

"Your mother? Ah. Now there's something we *can* talk about. At least until Gwyn gets here and starts ordering us both around, which I'm afraid is inevitable." He sat down again, this time on the floor beside the sofa. "Your mother was... she was kind. I know. It's a ridiculous thing to say, isn't it? That she was kind. But she was. Kind, and warm." He looked up at Alice, meeting her eyes again. "Not all angels are, you see. I imagine you think you know a lot about us, one way and another, but you don't. Angels are vengeful, or ferocious, or sometimes downright psychotic. Soldiers, remember? So not all that often are we kind. She was, though. She could see the truth in things."

"Was she like you?"

"Like me?" Mallory flinched slightly, then shook his head. "I see what you mean. No. I can't ever imagine her being an Earthbound." There was something missing in his last sentence – Alice could see it in his face. He was saying more than he was telling her, and that was the question she had wanted to ask last night, the question she had forgotten as she drifted. Why were they lying to her?

The knock at the door made them both jump. Alice disentangled her legs from the blanket and stood up. Her feet were sore and her knees shook slightly, but all in all she could have been worse off – especially given the woodlouse that was inching its way across the cushion she had slept on. Oblivious to her close encounter, Mallory was at the door, his palm pressed flat against the wood and a look of concentration on his face. It soon dissolved into a smile and he threw the door open, his arms wide.

The man on the other side was considerably shorter than Mallory. He was younger, too. He pushed a pair of sunglasses up on top of his head and threw an arm around Mallory's shoulder, speaking in a language that sounded familiar, but which Alice could not understand. Mallory cleared his throat and looked back at her. "Sorry. Cantonese. Vin spends most of his time in Hong Kong."

"This her?" The newcomer switched to English, pointing at Alice as he stepped into the room. "Excellent. Pleased to meet you, Alice. I'm Vin." He held out a hand.

"So which kind are you?" Alice shook his hand, and he grinned.

"Gets straight to the point, doesn't she? I like her," he said over his shoulder to Mallory. Turning back to Alice, he pocketed his sunglasses. "You want to know? Why don't you tell me?"

Alice looked him up and down. His jeans were frayed at the hems, trodden down under the heels of his trainers, and his jacket was faded. She pursed her lips. "You're an Earthbound, aren't you?"

He smiled back at her. "Got it in one. He was right, you're just like her. The eyes. So tell me, if you're so good at seeing things: is there anywhere in this dump that's safe to sit?"

"Not you as well," Mallory muttered from somewhere near the sink, where he was unpacking his shopping bags. He seemed to have bought a lot of bread, and even more teabags, and little else. "Alice spent the night on the sofa and appears to have survived. Although a *gentleman* should never sit while a lady is standing."

"Mallory," said Vin, sitting on the sofa and putting his feet up on the table, "You know perfectly well that I have *never* claimed to be a gentleman." He beamed at Alice and patted the seat next to him. "Go on. My arse isn't that big. And I don't bite. Well, not hard."

Alice suddenly couldn't help herself. She laughed. "I'm fine, thanks. And what kind of name is Vin, for an angel?"

"Couldn't very well go around calling myself Vhnori on Earth now, could I? Doesn't exactly blend in. So people call me Vin."

"And by people, you mean…" Alice realised he was smirking at her again, and changed the subject. "So what's Mallory's real name?"

"Mallory." The answer came from under the sink. "Just plain, unambitious Mallory. Told you I was boring." He stood up and rubbed his hands together. "Alice, Vin is a friend of mine. You can trust him as you would me. When Gwyn told me we had…"

"Don't tell me he's around?" Vin cut across Mallory's words. It was becoming clear that Gwyn was not terribly popular among the other angels, or at least, not among the angels she had met. This didn't really surprise Alice. Mallory snorted. "Don't be an idiot, Vin. Of course he's around. You don't think he'd rely on me to take care of her all on my own now, do you?"

"D'you think he ever gets tired of being a babysitter?" Vin asked, ducking to avoid the smack that Mallory aimed at the back of his head.

Alice stared at them both with wide eyes. She could still hear Mallory's voice in her head telling her that angels weren't exactly the most pleasant of characters, and yet these two seemed to be the opposite of everything he had described. As one, they turned to stare straight back at her, and she felt her cheeks flush. "I know what you're thinking, Alice," Mallory said quietly. "But you have to ask yourself why we're down here. Gwyn's a Descended, and we're both Earthbound. Remember that."

"Give the girl a break, Mallory. You're always so serious – lighten up! Besides, I brought you a present."

"Did you?"

"I was a couple of streets away when I picked her up."

"Picked *who* up?" Mallory's hand crept to the back of his belt. Suddenly, Alice wasn't sure she liked the way their conversation was going, but, again, it was almost like Mallory could read her mind. "It's alright, Alice. I've been expecting it. It's one of the Fallen. They were bound to try their luck sooner or later."

"I thought you said it was safe here?"

"I did. It is. But that's not to say it'll stop them from trying."

"And out there, it's one of the Twelve?"

Vin was on his feet. "The Twelve? The *Twelve?* You failed to mention the Twelve were loose. Slip your mind, did it?"

"Oh, stop whining. If it was one of the Twelve who followed you, you wouldn't be standing there getting lippy with me. 'Her,' you say? Who is it? Lilith?"

"The one and only. Haven't seen her for a while, and let me tell you: time has *not* been kind."

"Where'd you leave her?"

"In the churchyard, round the back. She's not going anywhere."

"In that case" – Mallory gestured to the door – "I'll meet you there."

Vin nodded, looking first at Mallory and then at Alice, and with a smile that was just a little less bright than the one he'd flashed when he walked in, he ducked out through the door. Mallory pulled out his flask, shook it and, remembering it was empty, picked up a bottle from the floor. He refilled it carefully, taking a swig and then topping it up again before pocketing it. Alice raised an eyebrow at him. "Do you want to talk about it?"

"No. I don't. And nor do you."

"It's one of the Fallen out there, right? The ones I'm supposed to be avoiding? So what do I do: sit here and wait until you deal with it?"

"Deal with *her*. Her name's Lilith. They may be the Fallen, Alice, but they still have names. We used to know them, all of them. They're not some faceless, formless enemy. Don't forget that. The second you do, you underestimate them... and when you do that, you're lost."

"Cheery. I'll wait here, then."

"Here? Oh, no. You're coming with me. Come and meet Lilith."

# CHAPTER SIX

## Lilith

AT FIRST GLANCE, Alice thought the statue was one of the most beautiful she had ever seen: an angel, its carved wings outspread and hair tumbling over its shoulders. But close up, it seemed out of proportion: the wings were foreshortened and its neck bent at a strange angle. From a few feet away, the angel that had looked so lovely was cold and hard and – there was no denying it – ugly. Alice wrapped her arms around herself, suddenly aware of a chill in the sunlit air.

Mallory stopped right in front of the statue, his arms folded. "Take a good look, Alice. She's one of a kind." He cleared his throat, and Alice could swear she saw a shadow crawl across the surface of the stone. Mallory's eyes narrowed. "Hello, Lilith."

"Mall-ory." The statue turned its head and looked straight at them. So this was one of the Fallen, Alice thought. She didn't seem all that bad. Her voice was a sigh, rolling and breathy.

"Been a while, hasn't it?" Mallory was tossing his flask from hand to hand.

"And here I am," she said.

"You always were a glutton for punishment. And he's right." He jerked his head towards Vin, who was lying on top of a nearby tomb, stretched out in the sun. "Time's not been kind."

"Time? Time is nothing. A heartbeat in hell is forever, and hell is never kind."

"You made your bed. Don't come bitching to me about it now."

"And what would *you* know of my bed, Earthbound?" Lilith smiled unpleasantly; she had too many teeth for it to be pleasant.

Mallory snorted. "More than enough to keep me out of it. But you know that already." He studied her for a moment. "Now then, Lilith. What am I going to do with you?"

"Are they letting you make your own decisions now? How... surprising. Does your keeper know? I would have thought to find *him* guarding such a precious prize." She looked straight at Alice, who shivered and took a step backwards.

Mallory stepped between them. "Maybe – but he's not here, is he? You're dealing with me."

"You? One of heaven's brutes. Unthinking drones, that's all you ever were, and all you'll ever be. A coward who didn't even have the courage to stand with us and Fall. Now look at you! Neutered. A little puppy dog waiting for its master to throw it a scrap."

"Speaking of masters," Mallory said, "how's yours?" He smiled brightly, pulling out his gun, and Lilith cried out as Mallory brought his Colt level with her forehead. "Goodbye, Lilith." He pulled the trigger, and she exploded in a shower of dust.

At the sound of the gunshot, Vin raised his head and peered over his sunglasses, propping himself up on his elbows. "That wasn't at all harsh, was it?"

"What? It's Lilith..."

"I know."

"...and she'll be back again soon enough."

"I *know*. And, boy, will she be pissed."

"By the way, thanks for the help there. Really had her stone-cold stuck, didn't you?"

"That's the thing," Vin sat up, swinging his legs over the edge of the tomb. "She was moving, wasn't she? Shouldn't have been able to. I fixed her, then came straight to you. By the time I was

back, she was almost free. I'm worried I'm losing my mojo."
He held up a hand in front of his face and wiggled his fingers.

Mallory frowned. "You mean, she was breaking loose? That soon?"

"That's what I said. Shouldn't happen."

"But it did. I don't like it." Mallory crouched down and scooped up a handful of the dust that had been Lilith, letting it run through his fingers. Shaking his head, he brushed his palms together and turned to Alice. "So, you've just met your first Fallen. That's what we're up against."

"She was a statue. Are they all…?"

"No! No, that was Vin. Remember I mentioned angels – even Earthbounds – having gifts? That's Vin's. He can turn the Fallen to stone. Which is only occasionally as useful as you might imagine. They break free eventually, of course, but I've never seen one shake it off so quickly, especially not one like Lilith."

"She was… nice. You two have got some kind of history, haven't you?" Alice heard Vin choking back a snigger.

Mallory scowled. "Not exactly. Sort of. It was a long time ago." He leaned around her and pointed at Vin. "And you can stop that. You said you'd dealt with her, and I believed you. I brought Alice, so she could see what's hunting her. So she could understand. What if Lilith really had got loose? What if something had happened to…."

"Hey!" Alice pushed Mallory's shoulder, forcing him to step back. "I'm right here. You stop talking over me, or I'm gone. So far, I reckon I've done really well at all this, bearing in mind this time yesterday, I was still at work…" Her hand flew to her mouth. "Work! I'm supposed to be at work! What am I going to tell them?"

"Nothing. You don't seriously think you're going back there, do you?"

"Well, yes. I have to. It's my job."

"And the first place the Fallen will look for you. From now

on, you don't exist. And from now on, you don't go anywhere without me."

"Wow. Stalker much?" Alice rolled her eyes.

Mallory stared at her. "What? You think this means you get to be clever?" He picked up another handful of stone dust and threw it at her. "This? You think you know what's coming, based on one of the weaker Fallen that Vhnori had already, supposedly, taken care of?"

"Woah, there," Vin interrupted. "First of all, don't call me that. Second, don't you even start trying to blame me for anything. I told you..."

"Shut up, Vin," Mallory snapped at him, then rounded on Alice again. "You need to wake up, Alice. Otherwise you're as good as dead. Worse." It was fairly obvious that there was a lot more he had to say to Alice, who stuck her chin out in defiance. She had had enough. Blowing lightbulbs, dead parents, angels, angels *with a drinking problem*, exploding houses, hiding in churches and now... talking statues in league with the devil. It wasn't exactly *normal*.

Mallory didn't get to finish whatever tirade he was about to launch into. Instead he sighed and stared at a spot somewhere over Alice's right shoulder. She turned – a little reluctantly, as she was really getting warmed up for an almighty fight – and saw what he was looking at.

A tiny, bright point of light was hanging in mid-air not far behind them, sparks crackling about it as it grew larger and larger. Alice heard Vin mutter something under his breath, and suddenly she could see a shape in the light: a man... no, an angel. It was all getting a bit underwhelming, she thought, as Gwyn materialised and the light faded. All the fight went from Mallory and he hung his head, cowed. Alice wasn't surprised. The look on Gwyn's face was the sort you'd expect to see on a rhino that has just been slapped. He strode forward, his finger pointing very firmly at Mallory.

"You. Enough. Move!"

If Mallory was at all startled, he didn't show it. Instead, he spun on his heel and ducked, somehow leaping sideways and drawing his gun at the same time. Alice froze, and would have stayed frozen if she hadn't been hauled aside by Vin. It was a disconcerting feeling: she braced herself to hit the ground, but the ground never came. They were floating... She looked over her shoulder, and saw grey feathers, spread wide behind them. Vin set her down carefully, and pulled her behind the tomb he had been lying on. "Stay here." He stepped back out again, leaving her huddled behind the stone.

There was a noise like the air tearing and then a horrible, hard-edged grating sound: nails on a blackboard. Big nails. Sharp nails. Beyond that, Alice thought she could hear the beating of wings, and she decided to stick her head above the tomb.

What she saw made her grip the edge of the stone plinth until her fingertips went white. Not far away, Vin was rolling across the grass towards the cover of the trees, his wings tucked tightly against his back. As she watched, Mallory hopped onto a gravestone, planting one foot firmly on the top of it and leaping into the air. As he jumped, he slowed, and opened his wings. Somehow, she had forgotten that he had them. Like Vin's, they were a dirty grey – narrower than she had expected, perhaps. He hovered gracefully a few feet off the ground, his gun fixed on something below.

It was a dark shape, hunkered close to the earth; Gwyn stood over it, his own wings outstretched and glowing bright. Sparks shot across the feathers and glistened at his fingertips as he cracked his knuckles. The shape moved, revealing a pale hand inside all the darkness. A hand clenched in a tight fist. Was it a man? It had to be, surely – although it was twisted and wrapped in a mist that made it impossible to see clearly. Gwyn seemed to know what he was looking at and he crouched down, laying a palm flat on what must have been the thing's back. There was a sharp crackle and the shape convulsed, letting out a horrible cry. Gwyn lifted his hand and peered at it. It tightened itself further into a ball, but Alice could still see that fist, creeping ever so slowly forward. Gwyn straightened up and stepped away, turning his back – and then the Fallen made its move.

Alice leapt to her feet. "Look out!"

Gwyn whipped round in time to see the Fallen angel uncurl itself and lurch wildly towards him, fist raised, the darkness that had surrounded it dropping away. He jumped back, his wings easily carrying him out of reach, but then, the Fallen stopped. It drew itself completely upright and cricked its neck… and Alice was horrified to see it had wings of its own. They were black, the feathers sharp and spiny. It opened them out, and not so much shook as rattled them at Gwyn, all the time letting out a terrible cry. Gwyn smiled at it, coldly. And it turned its head and looked straight at Alice.

She found she couldn't look away; no matter how much she wanted to, she simply couldn't. Its face was that little bit too pointed: its chin too sharp, its nose too long, its eyes too close together. Apart from that, she thought, it could have been any man, any passerby in the street – once you got past the wings, of course. It – *he* – had broad shoulders and strong arms which he flexed as he began to turn his whole body towards her. There was a thick bright white mark on his skin, circling one of his wrists, and as she watched, his fingers trailed along it. His eyes turned red. Not just the pupils of them, or the irises, but the whole of them. And as he turned to fully face her, he laughed.

At least, he did until Mallory's boot hit him squarely in the side of his head, sending him tumbling to the ground.

Mallory landed beside him, grabbing him by the shoulders and hauling him to his feet. Vin came scrambling out of the trees, rolling up his sleeves as he ran

The earth shook. Alice was pitched sideways, her head cracking against the stone. She saw stars, shaking her head to clear her vision. Gwyn was airborne, shouting something to Mallory, but Mallory was too busy trying to keep his footing and his grip on the Fallen to listen. Vin took a running jump, clearing the ground, his wings carrying him up above the Fallen just as he broke free from Mallory and made a run for it.

Still blinking back flashes of light, Alice watched as he ran straight at a hole in the ground; one that seemed to have come from nowhere. A gaping maw in the earth where there had been a grave. All three angels lunged for him – two from the air, one from behind – but as they did, the Fallen simply leapt into the void, his wings tucked behind him, and disappeared.

The ground shook again and, unsteadily, Alice stood up.

Gwyn, Mallory and Vin were all standing around the grave where the Fallen had vanished – now nothing but soil and grass and a headstone that said 'Beloved son and father.' As Alice staggered forward, Mallory took her arm. He looked at Gwyn. "Well, that's new."

"They've found something," Gwyn muttered, scuffing at the long grass with a polished shoe. "They're moving ahead. I'd heard rumours, but I was sure…"

"Sure that's all they were? Yeah, me too. Until I saw one of the Twelve base-jump into an open grave." Mallory took Alice's hand in his. "Let's look at you, shall we? Yes, I thought so. Tilt your head up for me?" He lifted her chin gently. "Nasty cut you've got there. Anything else we need to fix?"

"I… don't think so." Her head throbbed; her vision swam and she sagged against him. He caught her easily.

"Let's get you inside. The sooner we can get you sitting down, the sooner I can patch you up."

ALICE DIDN'T REMEMBER much of the walk back to Mallory's little cupboard. Her head was spinning and a creeping darkness seeped in at the edge of her sight. She couldn't hear what

Mallory said – the only sound was a high-pitched metallic scrape. Given the choice between this and passing out, she took the easy option and passed out.

She woke to the smell of dust, among other things. She was on that sofa again. Mallory and Gwyn were huddled in a corner, their voices low, although she wondered why they bothered whispering; she was fairly sure she wouldn't be able to understand them anyway. Mallory seemed to be able to switch between a hundred languages without even pausing, and it probably wasn't a unique talent for these guys. There was no sign of Vin.

She groaned and dragged herself a little more upright. "Ouch."

"Stay there, Alice. Don't try and get up." Mallory passed her a glass of water and she eyed it suspiciously. "I washed the glass. Gwyn saw me. It's clean."

"Thanks." She gulped it down, and promptly fought back a wash of nausea. "Ugh."

"You cracked your head pretty hard on that stone. Probably should be in hospital."

"I should?"

"It'd be sensible. But luckily, you've got me, haven't you?" Mallory took off his jacket and tossed it onto the table, rolling up his sleeves and crouching in front of her. "Let's get you back on your feet, shall we?" He cricked his neck and held out his hands, palm up. Alice stared at him.

"Your hands, Alice. Give me your hands."

"Why?"

"Remember what I told you. Have a little faith."

Alice laid her hands on his; they felt warm. He closed his eyes, and took a deep breath. Maybe she was imagining it, but his hands were starting to feel warmer, and warmer still. Her fingers began to tingle, and the sensation spread to her wrists, her elbows, her shoulders and neck... and finally her head, growing stronger all the time, like a thousand tiny pins were jabbing at her. More: a hundred thousand, a million. Her body began to shake and she was sure she would scream – and then it stopped. Just like that. She snatched her hands back from Mallory, who sagged a little, rocking on his heels. "My head…" she said, blinking.

"Mallory's gift is to heal." Gwyn's voice came from behind her. "But he pays a price for it."

Alice looked back at Mallory, who was still on the floor. He looked pale, his skin shining with sweat. "I think I'm going to be sick," he muttered as he pulled himself to his feet and staggered to the sink, where he proceeded to throw up copiously and noisily. Alice stared at him, and Gwyn spoke again, opening the door.

"I didn't think it could possibly smell any worse in here. Apparently I was wrong. You see, Alice, Mallory can heal anyone, anything, but only if he takes on their pain. Clearly, the worse the injury, the worse the pain and the harder it is for him. But that's his purpose."

"His purpose is to get hurt? That's not exactly fair, is it?"

"That depends on your point of view. After all, you feel better, don't you?"

"Well, yes…"

"And Mallory acted of his own free will to heal you, did he not?"

"I guess…"

"Then how, precisely, can you say that it isn't fair?"

"I just…" She stopped as Mallory let out another loud retch, his head buried in the sink. He looked utterly pathetic. It was very difficult to hold any kind of conversation with someone throwing up, so she gave up and instead decided to test her legs. Half-expecting to land straight back on the sofa, she stood up. She felt fine, better than fine, better than she remembered feeling, well, *ever*.

Gwyn nodded. "It's quite a gift. You might want to thank him later. But possibly not now."

As he spoke, there was another groan from the sink. "Oww. My *head*. You could have warned me about the headache."

"Sorry?"

"Yeah. Because that helps." Another groan.

Vin stuck his head around the door. "It's all clear, nothing else for miles,"

"You're sure?" Gwyn tapped his foot thoughtfully.

"Absolutely. I... oh, I see he fixed you, then? Maybe it'll do him good, get all that shit out of his system."

He mimed taking a drink. Mallory made an obscene gesture towards the door, not raising his head from the sink.

"That must've been some head bump you got," Vin continued. "I've not..." he tailed off, his eyes widening. Alice looked behind her, but there was nothing there besides the piles of books and rubbish. She turned back to Vin, who was definitely still staring. Without taking his eyes off her, he edged towards Gwyn and tapped him on the arm.

"What?" Gwyn glanced up in irritation, then followed his gaze towards Alice. "Well, well." He folded his arms. "Mallory?"

"A little busy here."

"Mallory, get your head out of the sink."

"Piss off."

"Mallory – *look at her*."

MALLORY HALF-TURNED and peered under his arm at her. "What the...?"

"What?" said Alice, not quite sure whether to be afraid or annoyed. And then she looked down, and saw what they were staring at.

She was standing in a pool of fire.

She leapt backwards, but the fire followed. Flames shivered across her feet, snaking up towards her knees, but no higher. And she couldn't feel them, not at all. She swatted at them with her hand, but nothing happened, other than the flames wrapping themselves around her fingers. Should she be screaming, she wondered... and then that little voice at the back of her mind was speaking again, echoing Mallory: *Have faith*.

She swallowed the panic and shakily lifted her hand. Fire danced across her palm and wove between her fingers. There was no pain. Her skin didn't blister, it didn't even feel hot. She looked up, and saw the three of them staring at her – Vin open-mouthed, Mallory still slightly grey, and Gwyn with the strangest expression on his face.

And just as suddenly as it had appeared, it was gone.

Mallory rubbed his face, clearly feeling a little more like himself. Vin nudged him and held out his hand. Mallory pressed his hipflask into it and Vin drained it in one, edging around Alice and slumping down on the sofa. "I didn't just imagine that, did I?"

"No," said Gwyn. "You didn't. And you know what that means."

"But fire?" said Mallory, stretching. "*Fire?* That can't be. It just... can't. Was....?"

"Her mother? Not that I knew, but it seems there's more to this than I was aware of. She's not just another half-breed. She's... something else." Gwyn narrowed his eyes. "I must report this. I'll be back soon." As he spoke, a wind picked up, swirling papers and rustling the pages of books. A bright light filled the room, and then he was gone.

"Would someone," Alice said as calmly as she could, "please tell me what just happened?"

"Fire." Vin was still on the sofa, his head in his hands, muttering to himself. "No wonder they want her."

"Mallory?" She could hear her voice cracking. Mallory

picked up his jacket and pulled it on. "All angels have gifts, Alice. We just found yours. And it means that you're more important than we thought. A *lot* more important."

# CHAPTER SEVEN

## Puddlejumping

HOUSES FEEL SMALLER when it's raining. They might keep you dry, but they close you inside them, wrap you up in suffocating air. After a while, the locks on the doors seem like they're not so much to keep others out as they are to keep you in.

That's why Annabel went for a walk.

She corralled them all in the kitchen: Holly, who put up such a fight that it looked like she might only leave the house if she were allowed to wear her sandals; Rush, determined (as always) to fit both feet into one Wellington boot; Floss, the dog, who didn't mind missing out on a walk if it meant she got to stay dry – thanks all the same. Annabel fought with boots, with hats and waterproof trousers, and wondered whether it might not be more practical to put the lead on the toddlers and the waterproofs on the dog, but sooner than she had expected, they were ready.

ANNABEL USED TO love walking in the rain. She would fold her umbrella, throw back her hood and turn her face upwards until the water ran down her cheeks like tears. Even the hardest rain, the kind that sent everyone else scurrying for shelter, didn't stop her from running out and opening her arms to greet it. Now, it was different. Now, she spent the rainy days tripping over the dog lead and trying to keep hold of both children. Holly would think nothing of breaking away and jumping into the road if there was a particularly promising puddle, and Rush was prone to falling over every time he tried to turn left, as though his feet couldn't quite work out how to avoid each other. The rain that had once been a friend was now a hindrance, streaming into her eyes and pasting her hair to her skin.

No-one had told her how frightening the rain could be.

They inched their way along the pavement – every broken paving slab suddenly a lake, an ocean, a river to be explored. Rush found a cluster of snails hidden beneath a branch and set about flattening them under his boots. He toppled sideways, of course, and landed on the pavement with a flat splash, but this did little to deter him and instead he began to squash them with the back of his hand. Annabel's heart sank and she hauled him to his feet. She wondered whether fifteen months was too young to be a sociopath, and wiped his hands.

Holly was never one to wait for her brother and was ploughing through the puddles up ahead. Or rather, not so much ploughing as kicking, splashing, slicing and jumping – often all at once – up the road. Puddles were drained in her wake, and Annabel smiled despite herself. Moses had nothing on her daughter. She tugged on the lead and on Rush's hand, leading them after Holly and catching her wrist as they reached the end of the pavement. The street was quiet: even cars were few and far between in this kind of weather.

They crossed the road and headed for the alleyway: a narrow cut-through laid with uneven gravel which hid some of the best puddles in the neighbourhood. She had no idea how many hours she'd spent there since Holly could first walk, wasn't sure she could bear to count them. The last year seemed to have been *very* rainy, but perhaps that was her imagination. She didn't like the alley – its sides were too high, its lighting too bleak, but at least it was a change of scene, a different kind of prison.

Holly flung herself at the first puddle, splashing water, scooping it with great sideways kicks that flicked mud and grit onto the walls and the lamppost. She was giggling. An urgent tug on Annabel's hand made her look down at Rush, who was straining towards his sister. "You're right, don't let her have all the fun. But do me a favour and try not to fall over, okay?" Annabel reached down over his shoulder and zipped his jacket up to his neck, letting him toddle unsteadily to the water. For once, Holly was in the mood to share and took her brother's hand, helping him to balance as he hopped about.

There was another tug on Annabel's hand, this time from the dog lead. She had more or less forgotten Floss, and was surprised to see her pressed against the wall of the alley at the extent of her lead, her ears back and teeth bared. She was staring at the children. Annabel's heart leapt. Would Floss ever…? She wouldn't; of course not. But she tightened her grip on the lead and stepped slowly in between the dog and the children. Floss suddenly snarled, barked and then lay down on her stomach, inching backwards.

The alley felt cold. Colder than it should in the rain, colder than it had done in all the times Annabel had walked here. Her breath rattled as she turned her head back to look at Holly and Rush, but there was nothing wrong. They were both still jumping, holding hands, laughing. Relief settled over her. It was just one of those days, the kind where low cloud and a twitchy dog could convince you the world was about to end. There had been more of them, lately, than she was used to. Perhaps it was time to do something about it.

She gathered the lead into her pocket, trying to coax Floss – whose snarling had faded to an unsettled whimper – away from the wall.

She looked back at her children just in time to see the puddle close over their heads, its surface smooth as glass.

# CHAPTER EIGHT

## Preaching to the Choirs

"SO, WAIT. IT'S the clan that determines the gifts, right? No. Other way round? No... Oh, I'm so confused." Alice slumped forward on the sofa, resting her head on her knees.

Mallory ran his hand through his hair and groaned. "One more time. The Archangels head the clans. Which are also known as... come on, Alice?"

"Choirs." Alice's voice was muffled by her legs. They'd been going over this for what felt like hours.

"Correct. Choirs. And the Archangels are the...?"

"Generals. Mallory" – Alice sat up – "do we really have to do this? Now? Or, you know, *ever*? I don't understand."

"You don't understand? Of course you don't. But you need to, so you will."

"It's like being back at school. Only worse."

"Stop whining."

"Can you at least tell me why you're so freaked out?"

"Well, in case you hadn't noticed, you did catch fire there a little bit."

"Thanks, yes. Spotted that." Alice wriggled back into the cushions. They were actually quite comfortable once you got used to them. "What I mean is why are *you* so bothered by it? You've got wings. I'm guessing things like this happen to you all the time. It's all rather new to me."

"I told you: the fire? It's unusual…"

"No kidding."

"I mean it's not as common as you seem to think. Which is why I'm trying to explain how this works."

"I seriously need to know this? Really? Honestly?"

"Yes." He took another gulp from his flask and muttered something under his breath. Alice couldn't quite hear all of it, but what she did make out sounded very rude indeed. Mallory cleared his throat and continued. "Each Archangel acts as the general of the choir: every angel within it reports to him."

"Him? All of them? Not very equal opportunities, is it?"

"No, it's not. Get over it. The choir is made up of angels with gifts that somehow correlate to their Archangel. In my case, that's Raphael, a healer. I was sent to find you because we believed you would also belong to Raphael, like your mother."

"She was a healer?"

"An empath. Like I said, the gifts aren't necessarily exact. Empathy, healing… they belong together. But fire? That's something altogether different."

By now, he was pacing the room. It had dawned on Alice that he did this a lot. There was a dirty grey worn patch on the rug where he walked. Her head was spinning, and he wasn't helping.

She couldn't remember that much of what had happened. She knew there had been fire – *that* she was very clear on – and that Gwyn had left, but everything else was hazy and Mallory had been on edge since.

That had been two days ago.

The first day, he'd just been jumpy: his hand sliding to his gun at the slightest sound. Vin had complained of cabin fever early on and escaped to the outside world, and Alice's heart sank when Mallory firmly bolted the door behind him. "He'll be back. In the meantime…" And he began the most bone-numbingly dull lecture that Alice had ever heard, managing to make even angels boring. He was still going, and none of it made any more sense than it had in the beginning.

Alice sighed. "Alright, I give in. Why's it so important? What's so special about the fire? Or me?"

"I told you, pay attention…"

"Actually," she said, interrupting him, "You didn't. You've been blathering on about how it's a big deal, but you've not managed to get round to telling me why."

"Oh. I haven't?" He stopped pacing. "Are you sure?"

"Yes."

"Oh." Mallory scratched his head, then sighed. "You're right. I'm being an arse. Sorry." He sat down next to her. "Any kind of fire is important. Fire belongs to Michael."

"As in…"

"As in *that* Michael. His is by far the smallest clan. I can't remember the last time I met anyone – Descended *or* Earthbound – who was one of Michael's. To the best of my knowledge, there's never been a half-born with a gift like yours. So yes, it's a big deal. You're a big deal."

"I think I preferred it when I didn't know, thanks."

"You think I'm giving you a headache? You wait till Gwyn gets back. I'm a fluffy kitty by comparison." He tipped his head back against the cushions. "Before you ask, he's gone back up." He pointed to the ceiling with a long, grubby finger. Alice was never sure how or when Mallory managed to get in such a mess. His state was one of almost perpetual-dishevelment. Vin, like Mallory, had been slightly untidy, but Mallory seemed so much more worn down. Rough around the edges, she thought, didn't even begin to cover it, and yet his company was easy – unlike Gwyn's, who made her feel like she was tiptoeing across thin ice.

And she suddenly noticed that Mallory was still talking, and did her best to look attentive. She didn't have a clue what he'd just said.

"…only imagine what he'll have planned for you when he gets back."

"I'm sorry, what?"

"You don't honestly think he's going to be happy leaving you in my hands, do you? You're his ticket up the ranks."

"Promotion?"

"Just the same as any army. You work, you get promoted. You rise. Why d'you think he was assigned to me? For kicks?"

"I thought you were maybe friends or something?"

"Friends? Ha!" Mallory's laugh wasn't as warm as it might have been. "I promise you something, Alice: Gwyn has never been my friend. And when I get home, I want to put as much air between him and me as I can. He's one of Gabriel's, and with one notable exception, I don't trust them as far as I can throw them. They're block-headed, they're ambitious and – mostly – they're bastards. A bit like Gabriel."

"But he's an Archangel. Isn't he supposed to be…"

"Angelic? Yeah, sure. Just like angels are supposed to live in dives and carry pistols. Just like they're supposed to spend their lives scraping…" His eyes were empty, his face blank, and he looked like someone altogether different. But then he rubbed his hand across his face and became Mallory again. "Besides," he continued, standing up, "Gabriel's never been much of a fan of mine. He was all for making my little suspension permanent." He shrugged, rolling his shoulders, and his wings opened behind him. The feathers shivered as he stretched. "Unfortunately for him, he's not the only one with a voice, and I do have a *few* friends."

"Do you miss them?" He clearly did, but Alice couldn't think what else to say.

He smiled. "It's not important whether I miss them or not. What matters is that I do my job."

"You're not exactly what I'd imagine an angel would be like, you know."

Mallory's eyes were already moving towards the bottle standing by the sink, and Alice recognised the signs. Talking about home was not a good idea. "I'd always pictured something, well, *fluffier*."

"I hope that's a metaphor," he said with a laugh.

"I just thought, you know, guardian angels. That kind of thing."

"In my considerable experience, I have to tell you that the only guardian angels you're likely to come across any time soon are me and my buddy here." He waved the gun, setting it down on the worktop and picking up the bottle. He glanced back at her, casually, and he must have seen something in her face because he suddenly looked down at his hands and stopped. He put the bottle back down. "Sorry. I just... Sorry."

"It's no big deal. I'd like to hear more, though."

"About Gabriel? Or the choirs...?"

"God, no. Spare me the choirs."

"It's dull. I get it." He rolled his eyes. "You wouldn't rather I told you about Raphael? He's a good man."

"I'd hope so. Angel and stuff."

"And as I keep telling you" – he sighed – "angels aren't so angelic. Our job is to keep the Fallen down, even if that means breaking them into pieces. They used to be our brothers. That's not an easy job, and if you're a good person, you're probably not going to be doing it very long. Or at least you won't be a good person for very long after you start. Gabriel's been doing it longer than anyone."

"What makes him so different from all the rest of you?"

"He enjoys it."

"Oh."

"Alice, when the lights go out and the world stops, at the end of time, and there's nothing left but dust and ash and embers... Gabriel will still be standing there with blood on his hands."

"He sounds like a piece of work. You're sure he's one of the good guys?"

"He is. He's just a bad one."

"Can't say I've ever seen much of a difference between the bad good guys and the good bad guys."

"Oh, there is one. Namely that he's ours."

"Are you allowed to say things like that?"

"Privilege of being an Earthbound. You get to say what you like. Don't tell them, though. They might think I'm enjoying it too much and make me go home." He winked.

Alice was a breath away from asking exactly what it was he had done that had earned him his banishment, but thought better of it. The only time Mallory's cheery facade slipped was when he spoke about his home – or rather, *didn't* speak about it. His evasion skills were top-class, and whatever he was being punished *for*, it seemed pretty effective. Of course, he wasn't all that bad at punishing himself, either – not if what Vin had told her before he skipped out was true. While Mallory prowled the church, Vin had drawn her close and whispered in her ear, "He's given you the soldier speech, hasn't he?"

"Soldier... yes. Yes, he has. You're not going to, too, are you?"

"Do I look like a soldier to you? I'm a lover, not a fighter, baby." He clicked his tongue and pointed a finger at her, making her smile. Suddenly, he was serious again. "But Mallory, he's right, he's a soldier. He might have a healer's touch, but a soldier is what he *is*, what he does. He sees what a soldier sees: war. And down here, it's in your face, all the time. Every corner of the world is at war – with itself, with the Fallen, with the Descendeds, with the darkness, with hope, with the future, with the past... we can't get away from it. It dogs our footsteps. It seeps into our dreams. And for Mallory – well, you can imagine what that's like."

"That's why he drinks, isn't it?"

"Oh, don't let him fool you. The drinking is the least of his issues." He stopped, laughed when she looked alarmed.

"That sounds worse than it is. By Earthbound standards, he's practically an angel – you see what I did there? – and believe me, if I were you right now, Mallory is the one I'd want looking out for me. Don't get me wrong, I love him, but down here? It's not good for him."

Mallory didn't exactly *look* unhappy. He had perched himself on the edge of the worktop and was flipping through a magazine. Alice peered at the cover. It was dated August 1994. In any other home, this might be surprising. Not here.

"Why *do* you live here, anyway?"

"Why?" He looked up over the top of the magazine. "Because I like it." He followed her gaze around the room, taking in the boxes, the bottles, the junk piled high. "Well, maybe I don't like *that* so much, but I like this place. It reminds me of somewhere. And besides, where else am I supposed to go?"

"That brings me to my next question," Alice said, stretching. "What about me?"

"What about you?"

"Well, I can't go home, can I?"

"Nope. And if you remember, I told you that at the time."

"So, I'll say it again: what about me?"

"And, again: what *about* you?"

"If I can't go home, and I can't stay here... where the hell am *I* supposed to go?"

"What's wrong with here?" He dropped the magazine, and a small plume of dust drifted into the air.

Alice raised her eyebrows. "You mean, apart from that? Mallory, I can't sit around here all day, forever. I've got no home, no... family" – she swallowed hard as her voice cracked – "and you say I can't go back to work. So tell me, please, what I *can* do?"

"You, Alice, can do plenty. But until Gwyn gets back, the topic's closed. Here." He finally picked up the bottle, and handed her a magazine. It had a picture of a woman with red lipstick, slicked-back hair and shoulderpads on the cover. Alice fervently hoped Gwyn wasn't gone too long.

IT WAS DARK by the time he came back, and Alice now knew more about blusher than she had ever thought possible. It was taking her mind off other things, the things still in that mental 'save for later' box; and there were plenty of those. Every time she closed her eyes, something new and unpleasant flashed across them: statues that talked, graves that opened and then closed without warning. Fire. Red eyes that stared right into her. The house, burning. Fire, everywhere fire. Her father – sitting in his chair. Her father – his neck breaking. Her father, who had lied to her, and her father... who had kept his secrets and then left her all alone.

"One thing you are not is alone," said a voice from beside her, and she opened her eyes to see Gwyn. He was reaching out his hands for hers, but almost instinctively, she edged away from him. He dropped his hand. "You fear me. You shouldn't."

"Yes, I should."

"Mallory's been talking. He never can keep his mouth shut." He sighed. "Alice, do you know what will happen to him if he makes another mistake?"

"I..."

"He will Fall. Gabriel will find him, and he will cut his wings and toss him into hell. And he will burn as he Falls, like they always do. And all that is good in him – all his hope, all his heart – will burn with him, and when he's done, do you think they will welcome their new brother, the Fallen? The brother who has sent so many of them crawling back to the pit, time after time after time? The brother who had what they have so long envied... and threw it away?"

"I'm going to say... no?"

"No, Alice. They will take Mallory, and they will turn the Twelve loose on him, and they will torture him and they will *break* him. And the Mallory that you know – that you *think* you know – will be gone. He will be one of them: hopeless, heartless, helpless. For all time."

"Why are you telling me this? Why not him?"

"Mallory knows. Of course he knows. His problem is that he doesn't always understand; and when he does, he doesn't always care. I simply don't want you to be naive. You feel some kind of... bond with him. It's only natural, given his gift, and, I suspect, the true nature of your own. You see me as something altogether different, and I can understand that..."

"You let them kill my dad," Alice blurted out. She tried to stop herself, but the words somehow tumbled out. Gwyn sat watching her for a moment, and then smiled.

"Things are not always as straightforward as you might like them to be. When the time is right, I'll explain. But not now. Until then, you will just have to trust me." He stood up, and the subject was closed. "Everything has been quiet while I was gone?"

"I suppose so. He hasn't let me outside since you went, if that's what you mean."

"And Vhnori?"

"I think he was sick of being cooped up in here. He left, not long after you. It's just been me and Mallory. And the mice." She suppressed a shiver, then looked around. "Where is he?"

"I don't know. But Vhnori isn't far away... and he's getting closer. It seems like there's something he wants to tell us." Gwyn folded his arms and stared at the door.

Alice shook her head. "Whatever."

As it turned out, Gwyn was right. It was only a couple of minutes before Vin banged on the door. He looked startled when Gwyn opened it, but it didn't take him long to pull himself together. "There's been another one poking around," was all he said.

Gwyn frowned at him. "You're sure?"

"Absolutely. Everyone's talking about it."

"'Everyone.' Where, exactly, is this 'everyone'?"

"I was with Mallory. The Halfway."

"Again?"

"Hey, I only went there to try and keep him out of trouble."

"And what did he go for?"

"Answers, he said."

"Give me strength." This, Gwyn muttered under his breath, his jaw clenched. He glared at Vin, who was trying to make himself as inconspicuous as possible.

Alice stared at the two of them. "What now?"

He didn't answer her, and sailed through the door, leaving Vin pressed against the frame. He stayed long enough to say: "Stay here. We'll be back – honest. Just... just stay!"

This was the last straw. Alice had had enough. She would not be left sitting around like some kind of hostage, waiting for everyone to come back and fill her in – or not – on what was happening. She tried the door. It was locked. Of *course* it was locked. But the windows... she eyed them for a moment. They were both small, yes, and one of them was more or less blocked by spreading moss, long-dead leaves and other debris blown into the opening by the wind, but the one above the sink looked like it might just be a possibility. She hopped up onto the worktop and edged across, balancing one foot on either side of the taps. The window was still at shoulder height, even now, but if she could only get it open...

She lifted the latch and gave it a shove. Nothing. Another shove – which nearly sent her toppling back off the sink – and it made a strangled creak and showered her feet with dirt.

"Come on, you piece of crap," she muttered, giving it one final push... and it gave, swinging out and banging back against the wall.

She peered outside. As she had expected, the window looked out onto the graveyard. It was quite a drop on the other side, and there was nothing she could climb onto on the way down, but at least the landing looked like it would be soft: a verge of moss and long grass – and the occasional crisp packet – ran directly beneath her vantage point. She hauled herself up onto the window ledge, and dropped.

Somewhere between letting go of the window and her feet hitting the ground, it occurred to her that she wasn't going to be able to get back inside. Nor, she realised, did she have any idea where Gwyn, Vhnori and Mallory were. This could, she admitted, be a bit of a problem. And the more she thought about it, the darker the churchyard grew; the deeper the shadows became.

"Great plan, A," she told herself. "Way to get yourself killed."

Still, there was no point standing in the shadows, waiting for *something* to come at her. If she headed to the main road, she might get an idea of where they had gone – might even be able to catch sight of them.

She crunched her way down the path running around the church, found the gate, and stepped out onto the pavement.

There was no sign of them. It had been a vain hope, she knew, but one she'd really wanted to hang on to. So, with no clue where they were going, and no way of getting back into Mallory's little room, she was stuck. She kicked her toes against the wall in irritation. What good would these 'gifts' she was supposed to have do her if they couldn't help her find where she was going? She kicked out at the wall again, then stopped. Gwyn had known that Vin was coming, like he could sense him. And hadn't she been able to smell Gwyn – that peculiar cold, clean smell – before she had even opened the door of her house? It was worth a try, at least...

Feeling faintly ridiculous, she breathed in the air of the street. Thankfully there was no-one around to see her sniffing like a lunatic – only a fox, which paused midway across the road to stare at her before moving on. She concentrated, as best she could. She could smell the moss and the wet grass of the graveyard, and the half-empty beer bottle standing further down the wall. That wasn't exactly going to help. She tried again, hoping to catch that same cold scent of Gwyn's and turning her head this way and that. She looked like an idiot, she knew she did, and she was just about to give up when suddenly there was... *something*. It wasn't what she was expecting – and she wasn't even sure what it was – but an instinct she didn't recognise told her she had found what she was looking for.

She took a step to the right and the sensation faded. She stepped back again, and an odd sensation tugged at her, pulling her to the left and up the street. She followed, letting her feet guide her. Alice had never quite understood people who said they followed their heart, or their gut, but now it made perfect sense. She didn't have the faintest idea of where she was going and yet she knew, just *knew*, that it was the right way.

# CHAPTER NINE
## Halfway to Heaven

ALICE STOPPED OPPOSITE a bar. Or rather, the sense that she should keep walking past it dropped away, and the only logical thing to do was to stop. She looked at it from across the street and hoped that was only a temporary glitch. She really, really didn't want to go in there.

The window stretched across the front of the building, and while there were obviously lamps on inside, little light spilled out into the street. Shadows crossed the window from time to time, and voices drifted out into the air.

No, she was definitely supposed to go inside.

Just as she was questioning this newfound gut instinct of hers, two things happened.

Firstly, she looked up. There was a sign above the door of the bar – an old-fashioned pub swing-board. On it was painted the name, the Halfway to Heaven. The words were painted in red across a pair of outstretched angel wings, and hadn't Vin said that Mallory was at 'the Halfway'? That was too much of a coincidence for her to ignore. The second thing was the appearance of a familiar shape in the doorway: Vin. She was about to call out to him when she noticed the figure next to him in the shadows – shorter and slimmer, with long hair. A woman. Alice bit her tongue. They were deep in conversation, and she found herself wondering whether Vin had a girlfriend.

Whether Mallory did, for that matter; whether either of them – any of them – had friends, lovers... *lives*. She had no idea. It hadn't even occurred to her to wonder, and it was as she thought this that Vin turned and looked at her.

"What the...? Alice?"

"Hey." She raised her hand and waved, feebly.

"What are you doing here? How did you even find us?" He hurried across the road to her, his eyes wide.

"I don't know, I just sort of..."

"You can't just stand out here. Not, you know, with the Fallen looking for you." He dropped his voice to a whisper and bundled her towards the entrance. "You better get inside, but I tell you now, Mallory is not going to be happy. At least, he won't be, later."

"Later?"

"You'll see."

The doorman gave her a once-over as Vin hustled her past, but Vin turned and hissed something incomprehensible at him. There was no sign of the woman she had seen earlier. Alice couldn't be sure what the interior of the Halfway to Heaven normally looked like, but when she stepped through the door, the first thing that struck her was that it had been totally, utterly and completely trashed. Tables were lying on their sides, chairs strewn about the room – several of them broken into pieces – and shattered glass littered the floor. There were people about the edges of the room, but Alice's eyes were drawn to the two in the midst of the mess. One was a short, stocky man in a dark coat. A nasty cut ran down the side of his face, dripping blood, and he had the beginnings of a black eye. The other was Mallory. They edged around each other, circling carefully.

"What happened?" Alice hissed at Vin, who shook his head.

"Mallory did."

"Where's Gwyn?"

"In the back, shouting at the manager, I imagine."

"Shouting? Why isn't he out here?"

"It's a long story. Quiet."

He visibly tensed as the stocky man lunged at Mallory, who dodged sideways and ducked, turning to face the other man and punching him straight in the nose. There was a horrible cracking sound and more blood hit the floor. Mallory shifted his weight and aimed his boot at the back of the man's knee, dropping him to the ground before circling him again, and Alice's stomach lurched as she saw him reaching for his gun. As his opponent tried to clear his head and haul himself upright, he looked up, and straight into the barrel of Mallory's Colt. Mallory's wings opened, fluttering in agitation, as Alice suddenly understood everything he had been trying to tell her. If this was what an angel was capable of, she wondered, what did that mean for her?

Mallory glowered at the man he had beaten. "You ever try that again and I'll take your head off, you understand?"

There was no answer, only a quiet nod. Mallory chewed his lip, and Alice saw his finger tense on the trigger. But he switched his grip, and smacked the side of the gun into the man's face, knocking him out cold. He stood over the huddled figure and sniffed, then turned abruptly and walked towards a flight of stairs at the back of the room.

Alice turned to Vin, her eyes wide. He shrugged, and pointed to the stairs. "After you."

Mallory had already disappeared through a door at the top by the time Alice and Vin had mounted the stairs.

"What was that about?" she asked.

Vin pulled a face and nodded back at the man on the floor. "That's Drial. Ignore him, he's always causing trouble."

"Is he...?"

"An Earthbound? Yeah, he is. He's kind of a gambler, starts fights, that sort of thing. He and Mallory have this running... *issue*." He put a strange emphasis on the last word, and wrinkled his nose.

Alice shook her head. "I was going to ask if he's alright. He's not moving much."

"Ah, gotcha. He'll be fine. Before he got sent down here, he was one of the angelic guard. They're the grunts: heavy lifting, minor intimidation, a bit of standing around looking pretty... you know. I wouldn't worry about him. It's not the first time he's got his nose broken." He caught her eye. "Seriously, he'll be fine. Mallory packs one cracker of a pistolwhip."

"About that..."

"Never try to cheat Mallory at cards. Not cool."

"That's all he was doing? And Mallory did... *that?*" Alice pointed to the splattered blood on the floor.

Vin laughed. "That's not all he was doing, but I'm not sticking my face into that mess. But the cheating thing, he was doing that for sure. Roped in Sari over there to help him." He gestured to a woman standing near the door, and Alice recognised her as the woman Vin had been talking to outside.

"You know her?"

"Saritiel? Sure I know her. We're the same choir: Barakiel. Thing is, her gift is more straightforward than mine. If I told you Barakiel's very handy round the card table..."

"He's lucky?"

"Something like that. You want luck, it pays to have him on your side. Saritiel's plugged right into it, so you can imagine how Mallory reacted when he realised what was going on."

"How'd he know?"

"How'd he know? I told him, that's how. And then I took Sari outside for a quiet word. It's against the rules, pulling a stunt like that."

"I wasn't sure there were any rules."

"You want to get back where you came from, sure, there are rules. Some are more easily bent than others. But those weren't the kind of rules I meant: I'm talking about the Halfway House rules. Even so, Mallory's in for a whooping for that mess."

Through the door at the top of the stairs they reached a narrow landing, barely light enough to see the end. Alice could just make out several doors leading off either side of the corridor.

"Wait," she said, catching at Vin's arm.

He stopped and looked at her. "What?"

"You said you and Saritiel are from the same choir?"

"And?"

"But I thought the choirs were all supposed to be connected. So if she's lucky, how come you turn the Fallen to stone?"

"You wait till you meet one of them in a dark alley. *Then* tell me it's not lucky." He pointed at one of the doors ahead in the gloom. "They're in there."

THE DOOR OPENED into a dingy little office with a sticky floor. Directly ahead of them, Mallory was sitting on the desk, swinging his feet. He smiled at Vin as they entered. Then his face clouded when he saw Alice.

"You're not supposed to be here. How did you find us? No, never mind. I may be daft, but I'm not daft enough to expect you to answer." He glanced over his shoulder, then back to them. "Meet Mickey," he said, gesturing to someone behind the desk. "This little toerag's about to lose his licence."

He picked up a sheaf of papers from the desk and dropped them on the floor. Alice peered down at them: there were pages of notes in that curving scrawl of Mallory's, and a handful of grainy black-and-white photos, all of the same man. She picked one up and looked at it. He was handsome, there was no denying that. Cropped dark hair and dark-ringed eyes; a black coat with the sleeves pushed up carelessly, tight black jeans tucked into expensive-looking boots. The photos had been taken outside the bar; she could just make out the swingboard in the corner of the picture.

"Look closer," Vin hissed in her ear, and tapped his wrist.

She turned back to the photo, and saw it: around his left wrist there was an unmistakable white band, bright enough to show up even in the surveillance photos. She dropped the picture. He was one of the Fallen.

She looked up to see Mallory watching her, his eyebrows raised. Then he winked, and swivelled around on the desk so he was facing the other man. "You know how we feel about the Fallen. So what I want to know is, why have you been letting one of them come and go as he damn well pleases?"

"It's not like that…" The man's voice was thin and reedy. He sounded petrified.

Mallory scooted closer to him. "It's not? Really? Then how about you go ahead and tell me how it is, Mickey. Because I'm all ears."

"He came… He said he was looking for something…"

"Aren't we all, Mickey? Aren't we all?" Mallory's voice rang with sarcasm, but it was lost on the terrified landlord, who shook his head feebly.

"Not something. Someone. He was looking for someone."

"Oh?"

"Said it would be a half-born. Newly woken. Said there were 'interested parties.' That it would be worth my while, and that if I didn't help them, they'd, well…"

"That they'd what? Rip you open and hang you by your own intestines?"

"That was about the gist of it, yes." His voice faded to a whimper, and Mallory growled.

"That's the Fallen all over for you. About as imaginative as mud. Always with the ripping and the hanging."

He half-turned towards Alice and Vin, but was distracted by Mickey, who had lunged for the desk and was rummaging around in a drawer. Mallory kicked his hand away, but not soon enough, and a sharp, loud bang echoed round the room. Alice's ears rang and she shook her head to clear them, reaching out for Vin's shoulder to support herself. As soon as she touched him, however, he leapt away, throwing her off balance and tipping her onto the floor. She looked up... and suddenly saw why he had jerked away. The shoulder of his jacket was scorched, smoking; he was staring at her with wide eyes – almost as wide as those of the landlord.

Alice's hand was burning. The fire coiled around her fingers and spun about her wrist. Just like the last time, she couldn't feel any heat or pain, only a mild tingling, like pins and needles in the very tips of her fingers. Not that that had stopped Vin's jacket from catching fire where she had touched it. She stared at her hand. Vin stared at her hand. Mickey the landlord stared at her hand and muttered a few choice words under his breath... and from the other side of the desk, Mallory groaned and stood up, shaking out his wings. The sound of moving feathers pulled Alice back to herself, clearing her head in a moment. The fire faded and she rubbed her palms together briskly, scrabbling her feet against the floor as she stood up. Mallory was staring at Mickey, his hand pressed tightly against his shoulder. Blood seeped down the front of his jacket.

"Ouch," he said. "That hurt." He pulled his hand away and looked down at it crossly, wiping it on his jeans. "I don't like getting shot. Frankly, it pisses me off." His wings stretched further out from his back as he leaned over Mickey, clamping his hands down over the arms of the chair and pinning him in place. "And you probably don't want to piss me off..."

"Mallory." Gwyn's voice made them all jump – no-one more than Mickey, whose look of terror became one of abject despair when he spotted the blond angel in the doorway.

Mallory let go of the chair and backed away. Gwyn stepped into the office, and gave Alice a dirty look. "You, I thought I locked in. You need to learn to do as you are told, Alice." He turned to Mallory. "The Fallen have been here, alright. The storeroom reeks of them. More than one, and I'd say there was one of the Twelve. Which means you," he said, pointing to Mickey, "have some explaining to do."

"I told him already. There was one. He came by, said he was…"

"Yes, yes. I'm not interested in Rimmon. Him, we know about." Gwyn waved towards the photographs on the floor. "I want to know who else paid you a visit."

"There was just him, I swear it!" His voice sounded increasingly desperate.

Gwyn sighed. "Be careful what you say next, little man. Don't forget who you're dealing with."

As he spoke, his wings snapped open, sparks hopping from feather to feather and across his fingertips. His eyes shone in the gloom and even Vin was edging away, obviously preferring to stand next to Alice and risk being set on fire again over getting too close to Gwyn.

The man in the chair looked suitably cowed, but before he could say anything, Mallory sighed. "I've had enough of this," he muttered, and without another word, he folded his wings and stormed past them, out of the room.

"I swear I don't know anything! On my soul!" Mickey called after him.

Gwyn narrowed his eyes. "I'll remember that." Like Mallory, he closed his wings and – with one last look – left the room. Alice and Vin exchanged glances and followed, pausing only for Alice to pick up one of the photographs from the floor. The same instinct she'd followed earlier told her that it might be worth hanging onto. She closed the door on the quiet sobbing coming from the office.

As she reached the foot of the staircase, she saw Mallory lope over to the angel he had beaten earlier, now hunched over a chair.

"Come here, you old fraud," he said, and tipped Drial's head back, placing his other hand on his forehead. He held him there for a moment, then with an awful cracking sound, Mallory's nose began to bleed. "You know, you don't deserve me," he said, dropping his hands and moving on, limping a little as he headed for the door.

Alice's fingers began to tingle, ever so gently, and she stuffed her hands into her pockets. She was beginning to see a pattern. Mallory shouldered his way through the crowd that had gathered around Drial and pushed through the door into the dark, ducking into an alley beside the bar.

It was raining; a light, misting drizzle. But, just as before, Mallory wasn't getting wet. Not even a little bit. It was as though the rain simply went *around* him. Just like it was doing to her.

Outside, Vin grinned at her. Mallory rolled his eyes and sniffed, rubbing at his nose. Gwyn was watching her, tapping his knuckles against his teeth.

"Vhnori?" he said.

Vin looked round. "What?"

"I'm going to ask you to do something a little... unorthodox."

"Okay...?"

"I'd like you to hit Mallory, please."

"For real?"

"Now, if you don't mind."

Mallory looked over at him. "*What?* Hit me? What for?"

"Humour me," Gwyn said and waved Vhnori on. Vin shrugged and stepped in front of Mallory, who folded his arms. "Don't you even think..." He was cut off by Vin's fist connecting with his jaw.

"*Ow.* Also, you punch like a girl."

"Eyes on Alice, please," Gwyn said, staring at her. "Alice? Take your hands out of your pockets. Your jacket is smoking."

Alice looked down. A wisp of smoke curled up from her pockets. She slowly drew out her hands, and warm light bounced off the alley walls. "It's not my jacket. It's *me*." Despite his rapidly swelling jaw, Mallory's mouth dropped open. Vin simply looked uncomfortable – although that may have been more down to the fact he was cradling his hand; Mallory obviously had a harder head than he was expecting. Gwyn was still watching as Alice held her hands out, as far away from her body as she could. She was, after a fashion, getting used to the whole fire thing, but that didn't mean she liked it. And then she could have sworn she saw him smile, and quicker than she could follow, Gwyn had knocked Vin off his feet with a sudden blow to his ribs. Vin groaned and rolled on the ground. Mallory smirked, but not for long. Gwyn turned to him and simply said: "I think he could use a little help, don't you?"

The smile faded from Mallory's face. "You what?"

"He has a broken rib, at the very least. I don't think you can leave him like that, do you?"

"How the… what the… why…" Mallory couldn't quite make it to the end of any of the sentences he started, but after a minute or two, his shoulders sagged. "How the fuck is that fair?" he said, finally. Even so, he knelt down next to Vin and, swearing under his breath, he placed his hands on the groaning angel's chest.

This time, it was immediate. The fire flared at Alice's fingertips, running up and down her arms, skimming her throat. She stood as still as she could, afraid even to breathe. Gwyn nodded. "You don't need to be afraid of it, Alice. It won't hurt you. It can't."

"That would be a lot more reassuring if I wasn't *on fire* right now."

She pressed herself against the wall, trying to edge back from the flames. The raindrops – which were going to such lengths to avoid falling on her – hissed and spat as they fell into the fire. Mallory pulled his hands away from Vin, muttering as Vin helped him up. The fire susbsided; the flames were gone.

Alice stared at Gwyn. "Happy?"

"Ecstatic."

"I don't suppose you'd like to fill me in on what the hell that was all about, would you? You know, seeing as I'm the one who seems to turn into the human torch every time someone socks Mallory..."

"What?" Mallory was leaning on the opposite wall. "What have I got to do with it?"

"Precisely," said Gwyn. "But Alice has worked it out, haven't you?"

"The first time... It was when Mallory healed my head. His headache."

"And then?"

"Upstairs."

"When our charming little friend shot him. And again when he healed Drial, and now..." Gwyn spread his hands to indicate the alley.

Mallory stared at Alice. "Every time I feel pain."

"I think so." She nodded.

Mallory stared at her for a while longer, then laughed, throwing his head back. "Then you're going to have to get used to it, because that happens a *lot*."

Vin cleared his throat. "Why him, though? What's so special about Mallory? No offence, mate, but, you know..."

"Think, Vhnori," said Gwyn.

Vin pulled a face. "Stop calling me that. No-one calls me that. Except you."

"Quite, Vhnori."

Alice knew. "It's my mother, isn't it?"

"Bingo." Gwyn nodded. "Seket was an empath. Raphael's choir, which – of course – is why Mallory is here. You connect with his pain because you are both connected. It's instinct: nothing more."

"What does that mean?"

"It means that given time, it won't just be Mallory. It could be anyone. Earthbound, human, Descended... perhaps even

Fallen." He jumped forward and snatched up her hands, turning them over in his, examining them. "Don't you see? If you can control it..."

"No." She snatched her hands back. "No. I don't want it."

"What?"

"Take it back."

"I don't understand."

"Take it back, you hear me?" She pushed past him, past Vin, to Mallory who sagged against the wall. "Take it back, please!" She held her hands out to him. "I don't want it. I don't. I can't."

She ran out of words. The rain drifted past her, around her, but the tears still ran down her face. Mallory glanced up at Gwyn, his face dark, then pulled Alice into his shoulder, wrapping his arm around her, smoothing her hair as she wept.

# CHAPTER TEN

## Gambler's Ruin

THE BAR WAS almost empty. This was good. He hadn't been able to face the Halfway, not after seeing Alice in the alleyway, so he had simply walked into the first bar he had found in the other direction. Apart from the man at the corner table who was singing quietly to what was left of a pint of beer, Mallory was the only customer. Or at least, he had been...

"Hullo, Mallory."

"You have until I count to ten to get out of my face. After that, you'll be wearing your own backwards."

"You've not lost your charm, have you?" The man from the photographs leaned against the bar next to Mallory, tapping his fingers in an irregular, irritating rhythm.

Mallory moved his glass away and started counting. "Ten. Nine. Eight..."

"Always in such a rush to throw the first punch. And when I'm here to do you a favour, too." Rimmon made a tutting noise and wagged a finger at Mallory, as though he were admonishing a naughty child.

Mallory snorted. "The only way you'd be doing me a favour is if you go and f –"

"Mallory..." Rimmon cut him off, but Mallory didn't care. He emptied his glass down his throat and gestured to the barman for a refill.

"I told you. Piss off. I'm busy."

"Look, I'm not here to fight with you."

"Shame."

"You don't like me. I get that."

"Don't like you? Rimmon, you're lucky you've still got a head. I've not exactly had an easy evening, and you've featured in that already, by the way. So right now, I'm a poster boy for self-control. Whether or not I *like* you is irrelevant."

"Alright. I get the message. You're in one of those moods."

"Stop talking like you know me. Could you just do that? That *one* thing?"

"But I do know you, Mallory. Remember?"

"Fuck off. Again."

"I could make a deal for you. I like you. I always did, despite the circumstances." Rimmon had clearly decided that charm was the way to go.

Mallory wasn't in the mood for charm, "Really? You've got a funny way of showing it, joining up with the Fallen. Landing me down here. I can see how that translates as giving a shit."

"And I feel bad about it, I do. So let me help you. They gave you, what, a hundred years? Two?"

"Five. Five hundred years as an Earthbound."

"And for what? Losing a half-born?"

"Wouldn't you just love that?" Mallory laughed. "You were only the start of a slippery, shit-covered slope that ended with Gabriel taking me to pieces. You just came under the heading 'incompetence.' My personal favourite," he said, his voice hard, "was 'questioning the status quo.' Like that means anything."

"You'd be rewarded for that with us. Promoted, not punished. Join us."

"Yeah, it's really working out well for you guys, isn't it?" Mallory said, tapping his wrist.

Rimmon looked down at his brand. "A small price to pay for freedom."

"Having Lucifer boot you out of your own head whenever he feels like taking a walk? That's not freedom. I'll serve my time, thanks."

"This isn't an offer I'll make again, Mallory."

"Frankly, I don't give a shit."

"Things are not what they seem. You think you know what you're doing, what you're getting into, but you don't. You don't even know the beginning of it."

"And you're warning me why, exactly? We're on different sides now, or have you forgotten?"

Mallory knocked back another drink, and Rimmon sighed. "It doesn't have to be like this."

"Sure it does."

"Why?"

"Because this is how it is."

"I could help, if you'd let me. If you'd ever let…"

"Thanks, but I'll pass."

"Mallory, you don't want me as your enemy. I don't have to be."

"You already are."

Rimmon's face clouded and he drew back slightly, straightening his back and pulling away from the bar. When he spoke again, his voice was chilly. "You won't win. You can't."

"Maybe, maybe not. Doesn't really matter."

"Why's that?"

"Because," said Mallory, rolling his glass in his hand, "that's the difference between you and me, Rimmon. I still have hope. What do *you* have?"

He looked down at the bar. When he looked back up, he was alone.

# CHAPTER ELEVEN

## Hallowed Ground

"Do you hear that?"

Gwyn put out his arm to stop them. They were at the end of the road, a few hundred yards from Mallory's church, when they heard it: a cracking sound. Very faint, but distinct in the quiet of the night. Alice held her breath, straining to pick it out, and Vin shuffled from foot to foot.

"I've not heard that sound in a while," he said.

"No. I would advise that you and Alice take a walk in the other direction. I'll handle this."

Gwyn's wings opened, shivering with electricity, and despite herself Alice hoped no-one was looking out of a window anywhere nearby. Her legs still felt shaky from earlier; from discovering that this spectacular new gift of hers that Gwyn was so enthused about came, ultimately, from other people's pain. Not from something good, but from something bad. Very bad indeed.

Something inside her had broken in that alley, and she felt like she had cried for hours – leaning on Mallory with the rain pouring down around her. He had taken her by the shoulders and gently drawn her away.

"Alice, you're who you always were. You're still the same person. Nothing about you has changed. You just didn't know all you were."

"But I don't want this! Why does it have to be me?"

"Because it's who you are." He had dropped his hands and stepped away – calling to Gwyn in that language they used with one another – and vanished into the darkness. All Gwyn would tell her was that Mallory needed to be alone.

And now they were here. In the dark. With the noises.

Vin looked over his shoulder, and cleared his throat. "You know what? I think we'll be sticking with you."

Alice followed his gaze down the road and saw three figures standing in the middle of the street, side by side; arms folded and watching their every move. First one, then another, then the third, unfurled tattered, jagged wings.

"I see," said Gwyn, "Well, I imagine they're back there for a reason. No doubt there's someone we're supposed to see up ahead. Let's not keep him waiting." He flapped his wings once and was airborne, rising above them.

Vin sniffed. "Show-off. Don't worry," he said, seeing the look on Alice's face, "I won't leave you."

But his voice wasn't quite as reassuring as he obviously intended it to be, and he glanced back at the three Fallen. "I think we'd better get a move on."

They hurried through the church gate, and Alice slammed it behind them.

"What are you doing?" Vin asked, pulling at her arm. "You know it's not going to make any difference to them? They're *Fallen*. They really don't give a crap about a gate."

"I know, it just seems…" They peered through the gloom of the churchyard. The trees cast long, shifting shadows: just right for monsters to hide in. A dark shape loomed out at them and Alice caught her breath. Only to realise it was only a memorial statue. A real one, this time. A sound behind her made her jump, but it was only Vin's wings, twitching in the breeze.

A deep chill washed over Alice, beginning in the pit of her stomach and spreading up through her chest and down into her arms. It felt like… fear.

But not hers.

She looked at Vin. She was feeling what *he* felt.

Still fighting to control herself, she thought back to what Gwyn had said in the alley: her mother was an empath. He had mentioned a name – Seket. Was that her mother's true name? Really? She was an empath. Mallory was an empath, which was why she connected with him... but what if she was starting to connect with others now? Like Vin?

"Vin?"

"What?" His voice was little more than a whisper.

"Can you... I don't know. Can you try and... man up a little, please?"

"You what now?"

"I can feel your fear."

"Really?"

"Really."

"Sorry."

A shadow dropped, landing just behind them. Gwyn was back.

"There's no way around this, I'm afraid," said the Descended. He swayed slightly to avoid the swing a startled Vin took at him before realising who it was.

Vin staggered, then shook his head. "That? The sneaking up? Not cool."

"Apologies. This way." Gwyn pointed ahead of them, further into the shadows. Alice gulped back another cold rush of fear, unsure whether or not it was hers.

There was no sign of the Fallen, not that that meant anything. Alice got the feeling that they were being guided (and none too gently) towards someone, and she wondered whether that was the same someone – or some*thing* – behind those horrible cracking sounds. The ones that were getting louder. She hoped Gwyn knew what he was doing.

The path looped around the church and beneath the trees; funnily enough, to exactly the same spot where Vin had caught

Lilith. And there, leaning against one of the tombs, was a huge, hulking man – not a man, judging by the scrappy wings that stuck out from his back; one of the Fallen. Alice could finally see what was making the cracking sounds, and immediately wished that she couldn't.

Piled up next to the Fallen on the tomb were long, thin bones, which she could only imagine had come from the graves around them. He was picking each up in turn, weighing them in his hands and snapping them neatly in two before lifting each section to his mouth and sucking furiously. Alice's stomach flipped as she watched him chew on the end of a bone, then toss it aside and reach for another. She found herself drawing closer to Gwyn, and she wasn't the only one. Vin had scuttled behind the taller angel and although his face was largely in shadow, she could see that he felt just as queasy as she did... in fact, she thought as another wave of nausea slapped into her, she could *feel* it too.

The Fallen raised his head a little and sniffed, loudly. He threw the bone he was holding over his shoulder and turned to face them full-on, his hands on his hips.

Gwyn stepped forward. "Batarel. I should have known by the smell. Are we interrupting your dinner?"

"He wants to speak to you."

"Does he? I'm surprised he remembers how to string two words together." Batarel's head dropped forward, and when he raised it again, his eyes were the same whiteless, lidless glowing red that Alice remembered from the Fallen who had launched himself at them in the graveyard. Batarel rolled his shoulders and neck from side to side, and when he spoke, his voice had changed. It fizzed and crackled like static on a radio. Gwyn took a step back, and gestured for Alice to stand behind him. This wasn't good, she thought, as she ducked between his wings.

"Gwyn. My brother," said the almost-Batarel, holding out his arms to Gwyn. Gwyn didn't move, and Batarel sighed. "Still holding a grudge? Aren't we a little old for that?"

"A grudge? Lucifer, if it was just a grudge, we wouldn't be having this conversation. And I am most certainly *not* your brother."

Alice peered over Gwyn's shoulder. "Lucifer?" she whispered to him, "As in...?"

She saw Gwyn nod gently. The red eyes suddenly fixed on her, the mouth below them breaking into a broad smile.

"And there she is! Well? Come along, child. Step out where I can see you."

"The half-born is under my protection, Lucifer." Gwyn's voice was stern. "*Our* protection. You know what that means."

"Which is why there's no harm in my seeing what all the fuss is about. So, hop to it." Alice felt a pull at her feet, dragging her out from behind Gwyn, who glared at her. Completely exposed to the glow of those red eyes, she felt very small and alone.

"You do look like your mother, don't you? It's really quite remarkable, the resemblance. Tell me, do you know who I am?"

"Should I?" Alice's voice managed to sound braver than she felt.

Lucifer cocked his head on one side. "I would hope so. After all, the daughter of an angel and a priest? What kind of education did you have if you don't know the Morningstar when you see him? Oh, yes. With a pedigree like that, you were theirs from the moment you were born, or that's what they'll tell you." He caught her stare and grinned. "You'll have to excuse my appearance," he said, waving down at Batarel's body. "I don't get out much these days."

"You're wrong about my father."

"Am I, now? And in what way am I wrong, precisely?"

"He wasn't a priest."

"Oh, no? Don't tell me: he didn't believe in any of it?"

"That's right."

"Perhaps that's what you remember, but it wasn't always so. I see more than you might imagine," he tapped his nose and crouched down, scooping up a handful of soil and rubbing it between his fingers. "Tell me child, if that were true, did it never occur to you to ask why he had so many books about faith on his shelves?"

"They were my mother's…"

"Were they? And, knowing what you know now, I might wonder what your mother would need to know of God that she couldn't learn by simply asking." He brushed the dirt from his hands, all the while smiling that awful smile, and stood up, looking at Gwyn. "The rules have changed, brother. The balance is tipping. And you think this scared little girl, this half-born, is the one to save you?"

"I think I've heard enough."

Gwyn raised one of his arms, opening his hand as he pointed at Lucifer. The smell of ozone filled the air and sparks raced down Gwyn's fingers, and, with an ear-splitting crack, a bolt of lightning shot from his hand and struck the Fallen angel, throwing him sideways. Alice jumped back behind Gwyn as Batarel shook his head to clear it. His eyes were no longer red: Lucifer had gone.

Batarel shook himself down. "Nice trick. Stings a bit. You got anything else?"

"Have I got anything else?" Gwyn smiled. "For you? I'll do my *very* best."

A rush of wind blew dust into Alice's eyes, and she blinked, rubbing her hand across her face. When she looked up again, Gwyn was striding towards Batarel… but he looked different. His suit had disappeared, and in its place was armour: a breastplate strapped over shining mail, and his wings out wide, sparks coursing across the feathers. It only took him a few steps to reach Batarel, whom he knocked off his feet with a single blow to his chin.

She would have stood there, rooted to the spot with her mouth open, staring at him forever, if Vin hadn't pulled at her. "Alice! The others – they're here. Move!"

So rapt had she been watching Gwyn that she had not noticed the three Fallen sliding into the shadow of the tree behind them. Vin, however, had, and he wasn't prepared to let them gain any kind of advantage. He hauled her away from the path and among the graves, feet catching in the long tufts of grass as they ran.

The churchyard was larger than Alice had first thought; it opened into a whole cemetery to the side of the church, and Vin obviously hoped to lose the Fallen in the maze of tombs. Alice's heart pounded so hard she was sure it would break through her ribs. Finally, Vin stopped.

"Thank god!" she gasped, but he held up a hand, motioning her to be quiet.

"They're still there, somewhere," he whispered.

The sound of footsteps rustling through grass and leaves to their left made them both jump, but the steps kept going, passing them by.

"That was close. Come on, we should get inside."

He peered around the side of a tomb and looked back at Alice, but didn't get any further. A large pair of hands snaked around the stone and clamped around his head, yanking him back. Alice bit down on a scream and pressed herself back against a gravestone. She could hear the sounds of a struggle from the other side: fists connecting with flesh – and what she fervently hoped was not a tearing sound – and she gradually became aware of a cold sensation in the small of her back, an almost-ache that she couldn't quite place. Her back spasmed, and somewhere in the dark Vin cried out.

Alice held up her hands. If what Gwyn had said was true, all of it, she should be able to do... well, something. She had no idea what, exactly, but that didn't seem to be the point. There was another thump, this time accompanied by a low snarling sound, and Vin yelped again. The cold spot on her spine grew, and at last, she could feel the fire inside her fingers. Taking a deep breath, she jumped up and shouted, "Hey!"

It did the trick. Not far away, she could see Vin being held (or possibly held *up*) by one of the Fallen while another threw punches into his side and ribs. Grey feathers lay scattered around their feet, and the Fallen holding Vin had blood on his hands. Vin himself was pale, his head lolling to one side. She wasn't even sure if he was still conscious, and for a second, she wondered whether that might scupper her plan, such as it was. But she had other things to worry about: both the Fallen had stopped their attack on him, and were staring at her. Their stares gradually turned to smiles, and the one who was holding Vin released him – he promptly crumpled and hit the ground, hard. Everything Alice had been feeling vanished. The pain in her back was gone, her hands appallingly normal. Vin was out cold, which meant she was too. Aware the Fallen were moving towards her with expressions she didn't want to see, she smiled and gave them a feeble wave.

"Hi!" She edged her foot behind her, feeling out the ground and getting ready to run. "So. This whole 'Fallen' thing. How's that working out for you?"

She shifted her weight and was starting to back away when the pain in her back returned with a cold flare, her fingers suddenly prickling. She looked past the Fallen and saw Vin, still flat on his back but with his arms outstretched. A fine grey mist was seeping from his palms, sliding across the grass towards the Fallen, who had stopped.

The mist wound itself about their feet and twisted around their ankles, spiraling its way further and further up their legs. They picked up their feet and tried to step out of it, doing their best to shake it off, but if anything it clung to them more closely, winding tighter and tighter with every movement they made. And then they began to scream.

Alice couldn't see what had changed at first, not until she looked down. As the mist worked its way up their bodies, it left their feet free... and their feet had been turned to stone. In fact, their whole bodies were changing beneath the mist, and by the time it had reached their necks, everything below their waists was solid rock. She watched as the grey cloud swallowed their faces, and a moment later, the screaming stopped. Vin dropped his hands, the mist vanishing. He rubbed his forehead, and Alice was dimly aware of a slight ache there too. Her fingers itched uncomfortably, but, so far, no fire. Perhaps Gwyn had been wrong; perhaps this gift wasn't what he'd thought after all.

"Alice!" Vin's shout snapped her out of her thoughts. He had propped himself up on an elbow and was struggling to get to his feet. He pointed to a spot behind her left shoulder. "Duck!"

She dropped, and felt a breeze pass over her head. Scrambling towards Vin, she could hear the footsteps closing in on her. The last of the Fallen. She had forgotten all about him. Vin was on his feet and in the air with a leap, landing behind her; she caught her foot on something and fell forward, turning over in time to see Vin knocked aside like a toy. But the Fallen wasn't moving. He was waiting.

Shaking, she stood up. She didn't run. What was the point? Between her and safety, there was at least one of the Fallen – and who knew how many more – not counting Batarel, who might have given Gwyn the slip. And *he* was someone she did not want to get any closer to than she already had.

"You looking for me?" she said, hoping she sounded more confident than she felt.

The Fallen nodded and licked his lips. He was holding a very large and very shiny knife. A very *sharp* knife. Alice remembered the sensation of something narrowly missing her head and gulped.

And without warning, something clicked inside her head, and – not knowing what she was doing, or why she was doing it – she raised her arm, holding her palm out towards the Fallen. Her hand ached, deep inside the bone. It was just like stretching a tired muscle. A plume of flame erupted from her palm, wrapping around the Fallen in a breath. He shrieked and flailed wildly, his arms burning like torches in the dark – and with a ripping sound, he was gone.

Alice stood frozen to the spot, staring at the place where he had been. Somewhere behind her, she heard the rustle of feathers and uneven footsteps. Vin was on his feet. He leaned on a stone next to her. His face was bruised, his mouth bloodied, and it looked like he'd have a beautiful black eye in the morning, but Alice was more concerned by what she could see of his wings. Clumps of feathers had been ripped out, leaving holes in his wings, which shuffled sadly against his shoulders. He followed her gaze and shrugged. "This? I've had way worse than this in my time. It's never as bad as it looks. Bugger, though: like I haven't had my wings clipped enough, right?"

Alice didn't have any words. Instead, she held out her hand as though it were a bomb that might go off. He nodded. "I saw. And to think you did that all on your own. I don't think you'll be needing me hanging around to protect you much longer, will you?"

"Don't go. Please. I don't…"

"Oh, I'm not going anywhere. Who said I don't need *you* to protect *me*?"

"Reluctant as I am to break up this little party of yours," said Gwyn's voice from the shadows, "we should leave."

He strode towards them, past the two Fallen whom Vin had turned to stone, pausing briefly to lay a hand on each of them. His fingers sparked and the statues shook, shining a hot blue as cracks raced across them, finally collapsing in a cloud of dust. "The Fallen have been in Mallory's room: they turned it upside down. Not that you could tell, apart from the scent they left over everything."

"Is Mallory…?" Alice began, but Gwyn shook his head.

"He wasn't there. I doubt he'll be pleased at the mess, but other than that I'm sure he'll be fine. But it does prove my point. They came here, looking for you, and there was nothing to stop them. We need to find somewhere else to keep you."

"Keep me? What am I: a gerbil?"

"You, Alice, are a weapon. And like all weapons, we need to make sure that you don't fall into the wrong hands." He ignored Alice's open-mouthed fury and turned to Vin. "Take her to the twins. They're expecting you."

As he turned away, Alice almost called out to him. She wanted to ask him what right he had, who he thought he was... and then she remembered the angel in his armour, and she was silent. She already knew the answer.

# CHAPTER TWELVE

## Marked

AFTER THE FIGHT at the graveyard, Gwyn had done one of his regular disappearing acts, leaving Vin to lead Alice to 'the twins.' Shivering, and beginning to feel aches which she suspected were entirely her own, Alice followed. Vin was unusually quiet, not at all himself, and Alice wondered whether he was simply tired and a little shaken up (not to mention *beaten* up) or whether Mallory had had a point. Even the Fallen had been angels once, and even the Earthbounds remembered their brothers. They didn't speak much, not until they finally reached a block of flats with plate-glass windows and tall security gates. It looked expensive: arm-and-a-leg expensive.

Vin stopped in front of the gates and sized them up, his eyes narrowing. "Alice?"

"Aren't you going to buzz them?" Alice pointed to the security call-box fixed to the wall beside the gate.

Vin cracked a lopsided grin, suddenly looking like himself again. "Are you kidding?" He gestured for her to come closer, and shook out his wings. "Let's hope I didn't lose too many feathers." He slung an arm around her shoulder and Alice was suddenly lifted off the ground and over the gates. "Uh, Vin?"

"Don't worry. They're only on the ninth floor."

"Which one's that?"

"The top one." His breathing grew a little more laboured as they rose, and by the time he had dropped them both onto a large glass-fronted balcony on the ninth floor, small beads of sweat stood out on his forehead. He leaned forward, resting his head on the balcony rail. "Clipped wings. Can't fly so much."

"When you're an Earthbound?"

"You get them back when your time's done. But in the meantime…" He fluttered his wings sadly.

"Does it hurt when they…?"

"Yes." His eyes darkened. "More than you can believe."

There was a click from the other side of the balcony door, and it slid back along its rails. A head of dark hair stuck out, shouted something Alice couldn't quite make out, and then vanished back inside. A moment later, two bodies came barreling out and launched themselves at Vin, who raised his arms slightly and staggered back. "Take it easy, guys. It's been a big night. Alice, meet the Twins."

The bodies detached themselves, and two heads swiveled to look at Alice. She found herself staring at two almost-identical faces: childlike, with large green eyes, one male, one female. They were exactly the same height, and stood in precisely the same way, with their heads tipped slightly to one side. The man, slightly more heavily built with broad shoulders and wide arms, had black hair slashed across with white, while his sister's was bright white with a black streak that fell across her eyes. She smiled and held out her hand to Alice.

"Florence. Come on in."

"Alice."

"We know. We were told you'd be coming." Florence stepped inside, and Alice was ambushed by the other twin, who threw his arms around her in a bear hug that knocked the breath from her body. Just as she thought she was going to pass out, he released her and she gasped, choking as quietly as she could. He beamed at her. "I'm Jester," he said, then turned on his heel and vanished through the doorway. Vin made an amused face, and ushered her inside.

They even gave Alice a room – a room with an honest-to-goodness *bed*, not a sagging couch full of woodlice and other unmentionables. And Alice fell into it and slept for a day and a night, waking to early morning sunshine pouring through the curtains and the smell of toast. Her bag, which she had given up for lost at Mallory's, was at the end of the bed; she pulled on clean clothes, feeling more human than she had since this all began. She opened the door, and a steaming cup was thrust at her. Blinking in surprise, she took it, and realised it was attached to Vin, who was leaning on the wall.

"Morning."

"Hi," she said, still groggy.

"There's breakfast. Are you hungry?"

"Starving." Alice couldn't remember the last time she had eaten. Whenever it was, it was most likely something Mallory had put together, which meant it would have been delivered pizza. Possibly a couple of days old. The thought of real food made her head spin. Vin steered her down the hallway and towards the kitchen.

"Word of advice," he said. "Don't let Florence cook you anything. *Anything*. Not even toast, you get me?"

"She's not good in the kitchen?"

"Girl's a disaster. Trust me. She made me scrambled eggs once and it nearly killed me. And I'm an angel. I'm hard to kill." He nudged open the door at the end of the corridor. "Look who's up!"

"Alice!" Florence looked up from a newspaper, and Jester waved a spoon at her, his mouth full of cereal. Florence stood up from the table and pointed at a large red fridge. "You want anything? I can get something together if you..."

"No!" Vin said, a little too quickly. Florence looked wounded and he patted Alice's shoulder. "She's still a bit woozy. Maybe

111

just give her a minute." He parked her on a chair at the table. "Drink the tea. Accept nothing," he whispered.

Alice settled into her chair, sipping her drink, and then she jerked away from the table; the mug falling away from her and shattering on the floor, the chair clattering against the tiles. Her hands. She held them in front of her, staring down into the palms. They had felt so hot, she had been expecting to see flames. She had been sure...

Vin's hands settled on her shoulders. "It's just the drink, Alice. It's alright. Nothing's going to happen to you. You're safe." He picked up the chair and pressed her into it, while Florence mopped up the spilled tea, scooping the broken china into her hands.

"I'm sorry," Alice said, but Florence shook her head.

"Never liked that mug anyway. Gift from one of his exes."

She raised an eyebrow at her brother, who wrinkled his nose and turned his attention back to his breakfast. Vin poured himself a coffee and wandered away to the living room, leaving Florence staring at Alice. Finally, she spoke. "So, you're the one they've been talking about, huh?"

Alice shrugged. "I... guess. I'm sorry, I don't know much..."

"Of course you don't. They don't share – not in their nature."

"You say 'they.' So you're not....?"

"Earthbounds? God, no. We're half-born, just like you. Well. Maybe not *just* like you, but you get what I mean. Vin's our Mallory. He was sent to prepare us for when the gifts started kicking in. Not that they're doing very much yet." Florence looked a little embarrassed.

"What can you... wait. *You* know Mallory?"

"*Everyone* knows Mallory. He's the closest thing the Earthbounds have to a general. He's hardcore. You're lucky." Florence sounded almost wistful.

Vin's voice drifted through from the next room. "I can hear you, you know!"

"Fortunately for Vin," Florence said, louder than was entirely necessary, "we're such good students that we never need him around for long, and he's free to piss off back to Hong Kong."

"Anything to get away from you two," Vin replied, and Florence stuck her tongue out at the door. "Don't do that. You'll stick like that if the wind changes."

"There is *no* way you saw that!"

"Nope. But I know you, Florence. Now leave me be."

"He is *so* rude," Florence said, turning back to Alice. "Sorry. He takes a bit of getting used to."

"He's fine. I'm not sure how I'd have managed without him last night... the other night."

"I heard. You took out one of the Fallen. That's really impressive. I've never heard of a half-born doing that on their own before. We don't have the strength, I guess. But you? No wonder they're making a big deal of you."

Jester dropped his spoon into his bowl and pushed it across the table. "Can we see it?" he asked, reaching towards Alice.

She frowned and drew back. "See what?"

She saw Florence shake her head slightly at Jester. "I don't think she knows yet," she hissed.

He looked taken aback, then embarrassed. "Oh. Sorry." He paused. "But now she's wondering what the hell we're talking about, so we might as well take a look, right?" He gave Alice another of his smiles, and the room felt warmer. "Gimme your hand." He took her hand, pulling it gently towards him and flipping it over, pushing back her sleeve from her wrist. A memory of white brands in the darkness flashed across her mind. "Jackpot," said Jester, pointing at a dark smudge on her wrist.

"What? Let me see!" Florence was all elbows, scrambling to look over Alice's shoulder. "No. Way."

"And we're looking at what, exactly?" Alice asked, feeling uncomfortable.

"The mark."

"And that would be..."

"Didn't Mallory tell you?"

"Apparently he's too busy being a general. *What* mark?"

"Choir mark. First time you really use your gift, it leaves a mark." Florence picked up Alice's wrist, turning it this way and that, trying to get a closer look. "It's the mark of your choir, see?" She held out her own wrist, which on closer examination had a long squiggle across the back of it, a sort of jumble of the number three, a long line and the letters v and e.

"Zadkiel. He's all about memory and the mind and stuff." she said. Alice nodded sagely, despite not having the faintest idea what Florence meant. It didn't seem to bother either of the twins, who were already bent over Alice's hand: she wished she could take it off, and leave it on the table for them to pore over.

"I'm not even going to ask," said Vin from the doorway.

Florence barely looked up, but pointed to Alice's hand. "It's coming through, look!"

"Seriously?" Vin was across the room faster than Alice had ever seen him move – even in the graveyard – and shoving the other two out of the way. Now there were three people peering at her hand.

"Can't you make it any clearer?" Jester asked. Vin sighed.

"You did not see me do this, you hear?" He placed the flat of his palm over the back of Alice's wrist, and she was aware of a tremendous pressure. She tried to pull her hand away, but Vin held it in a vice-like grip. "Don't... move," he said through gritted teeth, and then the pressure faded and he released her. She let her arm drop to the table, not noticing that Florence's endless chattering and fidgeting had stopped.

"Alice? Look." Vin pointed to her hand, and she leaned forward, somehow reluctant to move it. She was starting to want to keep a healthy distance between her hands and the rest of her. But there it was: right in the middle of her wrist, where the ashy smudge had been moments before, there was a clear mark, similar to Florence's. Only it wasn't similar; not at all. While Florence's looped and swirled, the thing on Alice's arm was jagged and hard-edged, totally alien.

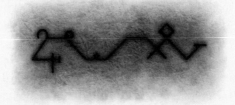

Vin let out a whistle. "Like we needed convincing."

"What is it?"

"That? That's Michael's sigil. You're his, alright." He shook his head. "Man, is Gwyn going to be *pissed*."

"Why? I'd have thought it would make him happy."

"Nope. And you know why? Because it was Mallory who was sent for you, not him. He's a passenger. When it comes to what happens to you, it's Mallory calling the shots. Gwyn might be the Descended, but Mallory's the mentor." His eyes twinkled. "And Gwyn's not going to like that one little bit."

COINCIDENTALLY – OR PERHAPS not – Gwyn turned up soon after that, knocking on the door of the flat hard enough to dent the wood. "Mallory will take care of that," he said as he strode across the threshold. "Should he ever deign to grace us with his presence."

The twins made themselves scarce. They seemed uneasy around Gwyn – not surprising, given the hushed arguments he and Vin kept having in corners, all in that language they spoke whenever they didn't want anyone human to understand them.

"It's the language of the Descendeds," Jester had whispered, when he found her eavesdropping at a door. "It's, like, some weird angel-speak. Obviously the Earthbounds speak it too, because... you know. But they say that if you Fall, the knowledge is burned out of your mind. Ouch."

He shivered comically, but Alice suspected it was true. Gwyn's little lecture about Mallory had been pretty graphic, and he didn't exactly strike her as being prone to theatrics. And that was how the next few days went: with Gwyn coming and going, Vin largely watching old horror movies and Jester and Florence doing whatever it was they did. Alice felt awkward being the reason for the invasion of the twins' home, but if either of them were unhappy about it, they did a good job of hiding it. Besides, she liked them. It was good to spend time in the company of other *people*. Fond as she'd become of Vin in a short time, he was different, somehow *other*. The same was true of Mallory. She still didn't know how she felt about Gwyn, but at least she felt she was beginning to understand him, which was a definite improvement. It didn't make him any less abrasive (or irritating) but it made him easier to forgive. And at the back of her mind, too, there was still the memory of him striding towards Batarel... Although she was reluctant to admit it, he frightened her.

There was nothing frightening about Mallory, other than how long he had been gone with no word. Everyone assured her he would show up eventually, but that hadn't stopped her from worrying, and she continued to worry until he marched through the door and draped himself across the furniture as though he had only been away for a few minutes. "What did you degenerates do to my house? It's trashed, and it smells of... You know what? I don't even want to think about what it smells of." Mallory was clearly furious.

"I'm afraid it looked like that when we got there. I assumed that was how you'd left it." Gwyn barely even looked up from the book he was reading.

"The Fallen?"

"What do you think?"

"Bastards."

Mallory rolled his leather jacket into a ball and tossed it, and his gun, on the coffee table, as he slumped back into the sofa, and ignoring Florence's indignant shout about wearing shoes indoors.

Alice was so relieved to see him that it was all she could do not to hug him, but something stopped her. He looked pale and drawn; there were dark circles under his eyes, and although his smile was as open as ever, it was hiding something. She didn't need to guess it. She could feel it – an ache somewhere in the middle of her chest that surged over her in a wave as soon as he stepped into the room. But he hurled himself down next to her, kicking off his boots when Florence howled at him, and smiled. "How you doing? Still alive, then?"

There were so many questions: where had he been, what had he been doing... why had he left her? But he wasn't going to explain any of it. And it didn't really matter. All she wanted was to feel safe, to feel normal for a while; now, with Mallory back, she did. For the time being, anyway.

# CHAPTER THIRTEEN

## Fire & Water

"THAT IS THE most ridiculous thing I've ever heard. *Ever*."

"Whatever." Jester shook his head.

Alice knew she'd made a mistake the second the words were out of her mouth. "I'd love to," she'd said. Bad idea. But she hadn't known any better. Vin might have warned her about Florence's cooking, but no-one had seen fit to wise her up to the twins' shopping habits. She was tired of being cooped up in the flat, tired of staring out of the windows, tired of pacing the hallways. Tired, and stir-crazy. And so were the twins. It was becoming increasingly apparent that they had imagined this would be some kind of elaborate sleepover... and as time passed, and it dawned on them that their role lay somewhere between prison guard and glorified babysitter, their mood changed, and the flat became even more claustrophobic.

So when they asked Alice if she wanted to run into town with them, despite all the angels' warnings about the Fallen (and an argument with Mallory which Florence appeared to have won by threatening to *cry*), she had been ridiculously glad of the change of scene. It hadn't occurred to her that it might turn into the longest afternoon of her life. After three hours with Florence trying on every *single* item of clothing in one shop, Alice was wondering whether this wasn't, in fact, hell. Now the pair of them were arguing over who had used the last of the milk, just like they had been for the last twenty minutes.

Alice slumped further back on the bench and stared at her feet. Twenty minutes and they were still going strong. How was it possible to argue about something – anything – for that long? She'd never entirely understood the inner workings of sibling relationships, not having any herself, but if these two were anything to go by it was just as well. Imagine what life would be like if you set fire to your house every time you had a fight with your sister...

Slowly, she tuned them out, their voices fading into the background. The street was busy, despite the cold wind and the threat of rain. People were hurrying here and there, scurrying about with bags in their hands and harried expressions on their faces. No-one looked like they were having fun. It was comforting: Alice wasn't having fun either. Quite apart from Jester and Florence, the warning Mallory had given her before she left still rang round her head. "Be careful, Alice. The Fallen will be everywhere. And you don't know them like we do. You won't see them coming."

"So, what happened to the 'Wherever you go, I go,' Mallory from the other day?"

"Believe me, if I could go with you, I would. But there's somewhere I have to be," he tipped his head towards Gwyn. "Vhnori too. It's important."

"And you're letting me out?"

"Reluctantly. But Florence has pointed out somewhat *forcefully* that you can't spend your life cooped up in here, and she's right. Hiding doesn't seem to be doing us much good. Besides" – he smiled – "from what I hear, you took care of yourself pretty well."

"Mallory, about that..."

"Not now. We'll talk, later. I promise." He lifted his arm, and for a second she thought he was going to ruffle her hair, but he stopped, and his hand dropped back to his side. "Be careful. They will be out there. Trust your instincts. If something feels wrong, it *is* wrong."

"What about the twins?"

"They know what to do. If anything happens, they'll take care of you until help arrives."

"You mean until you arrive, right?"

"Something like that." He glanced down at his feet. "I have to go, Alice. Stay safe. I'll see you later."

Which left Alice sitting on a bench with the wind biting into her bones, trying not to hear the twins.


AN ITCH IN her palm made her scrunch her hand tightly into her pocket as she scanned the crowded street. This suddenly didn't seem like such a good idea. For some reason, she had assumed that she would be safe amongst people. Her control of her gift was – so far – non-existent, and while the empath in her had only connected enough with Mallory and Vin to trigger it, she had thought that a street full of strangers shouldn't pose a problem. But she had underestimated the force of the crowd: stubbed toes, broken bones, trapped fingers; headaches, backaches, bellyaches... multiplied a thousand-fold and bearing down on her like a truck. The tiniest of needles jabbed at her fingers; pins danced in her palms.

The world was full of pain, and now she knew it.

She bunched her fists into her coat and stood up. Neither Jester nor Florence noticed, so busy were they bickering. The subject was obviously irrelevant, so long as they had something to fight about. Without knowing quite why, Alice took a step away from the bench, and before she knew it, she was walking away, fast. It felt... right. She knew she should stop, but something was tugging at her, pulling at her feet and asking her to follow. So she did.

She crossed the street, turned down another road and walked. She walked through the doors of a department store, she walked through the perfume hall and down the stairs, down more stairs and more; moving in a daze, she followed her feet until there were no more steps to take and the stairwell ended in a heavy door.

She was on the lowest level of the department store's car park. There were a handful of cars around her, but with no lift and a long, concrete climb up to the shopping levels, most drivers opted to sit out the wait for spaces above. Yellow security tape flapped around the edge of a large puddle, the water dripping into it from a split pipe above making a high-pitched *plink* as each drop fell.

For the first time that afternoon, Alice relaxed. Her hands felt normal; not the slightest prickle or sting. She flexed her fingers and sighed. Maybe she should try and get some alone time. It was only now, after hours of fearing her hands would give her away – that the fire would spring from nowhere, burning everything it touched but her – that the tension drained from her body. Everything she felt now was her own, the pain her own.

Somewhere, a door swung closed; the *bang* echoed through the car park. At that moment, Alice thought, she was alone. *Totally* alone. She had walked away from the twins and they hadn't see her go. The Earthbounds and Gwyn were somewhere else; they didn't even know where she was. She was *alone*. And if she was alone, she was defenceless.

Another door banged – or perhaps it was the same one – the sound bouncing off the hard floor and walls. She was defenceless, and she was exposed. Panic bolted her feet to the floor, and she suddenly wondered whether it *was* all hers. She knew it would be sensible to move – that it was important to move, not just to stand there like a fool – but somehow, she couldn't find a way to do it. There were footsteps. Where they were coming from, she couldn't say. They seemed to be everywhere, and whether there were five or fifty people suddenly in there with her... she shut her eyes. It was the only thing she could do.

"I thought you'd be taller. I'm a little disappointed." The voice was right in her ear. "And I thought they'd keep better track of you. This won't do Mallory any favours, will it? To lose you so soon, before you've even had the chance to prove yourself; it's really too bad. Oh, well."

Alice flinched as she felt breath on her cheek.

She opened her eyes.

He was almost nose to nose with her. The first thing she saw were his eyes – they were so close that they filled her world. They were blue, so very blue that she found herself thinking of Gwyn, and then she remembered that, yes, the Fallen were angels once. She was toe to toe with a Fallen, and she was alone, and she was afraid. He smiled at her and his smile split his face. It was wider than it should rightly be, and he had slightly too many teeth.

"Poor little lamb, straying from the herd," he said, turning away from her. One side of his face was scarred, old burns running from the tip of his ear to his jaw. "There's no-one here to help you now. Of course, how could you not come? Not when you're an empath. Not when we've got something that calls to you."

He clicked his fingers, and the door of a car swung open. A heap of stained clothing tumbled out, and it took Alice a moment to understand what she was seeing. It was a body. There was a scuffling sound and a small head of sandy-coloured hair appeared. A child, gagged and bound. A little boy. He was crying, choking on the cloth over his mouth.

Alice swallowed a whimper. She was supposed to be afraid, she knew that. It was what the Fallen wanted. He smiled at her.

"You can feel *that*, can't you, Alice? Feels good, doesn't it?"

He waved, and from somewhere in the shadows another of the Fallen appeared, stopping to haul the child from the car.

He dragged the boy, none too gently, across the oily concrete to the edge of the puddle. The little boy's eyes were fixed on her, fear radiating from them, blotting out everything else. The other Fallen swatted the yellow tape away and walked to the edge of the water, hoisting the child over his shoulder as though he weighed nothing. He stepped forward and into the puddle, which swallowed both of them, closing over their heads as though they had never been.

And that was when Alice screamed.

The sound rang off the steel pipes, filling the empty space, and the blue-eyed Fallen with his too-wide smile watched her, rubbing his ears as the echoes died away.

"That wasn't entirely necessary, now, was it? Loud, but not necessary?" He reached a hand towards her, and Alice suddenly found she could move. She ran.

She made for the doors, the sound of her feet swirling around her, or maybe it was the sound of his feet, following. She barely managed to stop before she hit the stairwell door. It was locked. Glancing behind her, she went for the next one, which was also locked. No wonder he wasn't following. She slumped against the door, her knees giving way as his laugh sang out.

"You came here for the child. Out of every pestilential little human out there, his fear called out the loudest. You sought it out, and it held you here because we held him. And now we hold him forever. He's ours. And he'll never feel anything but fear again, and you couldn't save him."

"Who are you?"

"Oh, you do speak, do you? Better watch that. Speaking out… well, let's just say the outspoken are always the first to Fall."

"I asked who you are."

"And I didn't answer. You could say I'm a friend of your mother's, but then, the last angels you met who said that stood by and watched as your father died, didn't they?"

"You're not an angel, though, are you?"

124

"On the contrary," his voice hissed in her ear, and she jumped. He wasn't anywhere in sight, so how... It felt as though he were leaning on her shoulder, too close, oppressive. "I'm the only kind of angel you can trust. You think you can trust the Descended? Why? He'll discard you as soon as you've served your purpose. It's what they do. You're nothing to him. And the Earthbounds? They're all half a step from damnation. Why should they help you? But me... I have nothing to lose."

"And a man with nothing to lose has nothing to hope for."

It was a new voice. A full, warm voice. A rush of cold air grazed Alice's cheek and the feeling of the Fallen leaning on her shoulder vanished. She was aware of a quiet buzzing, somewhere at the edges of her mind. The lights overhead dimmed, then flickered, and died one by one, the darkness creeping closer and closer until the only light left was the one above her. It grew brighter... then wenr out, stranding her in the gloom.

A warm breeze stirred her hair. It smelled of oil and petrol, and something else. Smoke. Woodsmoke, soft and welcoming. Safe. Alice stared into the blackness, looking for something – an emergency light, another door... anything... and then she saw it.

A tiny spark, hanging in the air. It shimmered and glittered, and she heard a cry and the scuff of feet on concrete. All the while, the light grew stronger and brighter until it filled the car park, brighter than the bulbs had been, chasing the shadows across the walls. It was so bright, so *white*, that it hurt her eyes and she blinked back tears, throwing her hand across her face, but even with her eyes closed she could still see it.

Slowly it began to dim, and she dropped her hand, opening her eyes carefully. There was a man in the midst of the light. And he was burning.

Fire spilled down his back, spun from his fingers. It ran across his chest and pooled at his feet. Beneath it all, she saw the glint of metal. He was wearing armour, just as Gwyn had been in the graveyard, and within the fire it shone white-hot. He strode forwards, and his steps made no sound. Without a word, he reached behind a parked car and hauled out the Fallen, who had scuttled behind it as soon as he realised what was coming. The Descended lifted him easily and held him up, his feet dangling several inches above the floor.

"Xaphan. Well, well, well. I should have known." He flicked his wrist and Xaphan sailed through the air, crashing into a pipe and hitting the floor. "And what, might I ask, are *you* doing here?"

"Me? Oh, nothing. A little mindless consumerism." The Fallen picked himself up and dusted his clothes down. He eyed the angel. "Just killing time. Minding my own business."

"Is that so? Always in the wrong place at the wrong time, aren't you, Xaph? The wrong place being anywhere outside hell."

A ball of flame formed above the Descended's hand and he tossed it at Xaphan – who smiled, and reached up and grabbed it out of the air. He held it for a moment, then let it fall, crushing it beneath his heel.

"Oops." He brushed his hands together. "You've forgotten where you are, you silly little angel. You're underground, and that's our turf – not yours. Too bad. Too bad for you, anyway." He snarled, his face contorting, and his spiny black wings sprang out from his back, the burned feathers rattling against one another. The Descended looked him up and down, and opened his own wings.

His wings were, like Gwyn's, white, but unlike Gwyn's they flamed. Fire shimmered across them, curling into the air at the tips. He beat his wings once… and then stopped.

Xaphan grinned again. "I told you. Under. Ground." He pointed up. "And car parks have so *little* headroom, don't you think?"

He charged the Descended, head lowered, ramming into his ribs with a ferocious speed. They both hurtled back, a spinning mess of feathers and spines and fire; the Fallen scratching at the Descended, ripping at him with claw-like nails. Alice didn't understand why he didn't just throw Xaphan off. Surely he could, simply by shaking his wings. And then she understood. The ceiling. It was too low for him to use them. The Fallen knew that. Just like he had known that she would be drawn to the helpless boy's fear, and that she would come alone. He knew too much, and he was toying with them.

The Descended let out a sudden howl, and a sharp pain speared through Alice's back. Xaphan pulled away from him, his hands full of feathers and his mouth smeared with blood.

"You can burn me all you like, but sooner or later, you're going to run out of wings." His hair was smouldering, his face scorched, but still he attacked. The other angel swatted him away, but the fire around them was fading: he was wounded.

And if he was wounded...

Alice slipped behind a column of pipes and peered round. The two angels were still tangled together: Xaphan tearing with teeth and hands; the Descended batting him away – he was stronger, but he was slipping, and the Fallen clung on to him with no regard for the flame that seared his flesh.

Alice told herself that she was not going to consider this a problem. She was just going to... well, to do something very stupid indeed. The pain in her back grew more intense as it rose, shooting from shoulder to shoulder. And as it did, she lifted her hand.

Xaphan jerked away from the Descended. She must have made a noise; he looked straight at her and straight into the wall of fire that raced towards him.

He screamed as it swallowed him. He staggered this way and that, the sound he made filling Alice's ears... and then she heard the Descended calling to her. Dragging her eyes away from the flaming Fallen, she saw the angel pointing at the middle of the car park.

"The water! Don't let him reach it!"

But it was too late. Xaphan had made it to the tape, and for a second the screaming sounded like it was laughter. He toppled face-first into the water… and was gone. Only the faintest smell of burning hair remained.

The Descended was already on his feet, peering into the dirty pool. A thin slick of oil floated on the surface. Carefully, he stretched out a finger and poked it into the water. It was barely deep enough to cover his fingernail.

"Tricky old Xaph," he muttered under his breath, then stood up and wiped his hands together, and it dawned on Alice that he had changed. The fire was gone, the wings and armour with it. Instead, she was looking at a man with a narrow face and scruffy hair, stubble across his cheeks and chin. In place of the armour was a pair of jeans and an old red t-shirt. He was barefoot. The lights were back on and she looked him up and down.

"Aren't you cold?"

"Hardly." He held out his hand, and Alice saw the smallest of flames circling his palm. "You are Alice. I am A'albiel. Michael sent me." He turned his hand over, palm-down, and Alice saw the same angular mark that had made the twins get so excited – it shone gold as though it was lit by something beneath his skin. He beamed at her. "You may call me Al."

"Umm, thanks?"

"You're welcome. We should leave." He prodded at the edge of the water with his toe. "This has been most… illuminating."

"The puddle trick?"

"Yes. The 'puddle trick,' as you call it. Xaphan is well regarded by the Fallen. He has an inventive mind. This reeks of him."

"It reeks of something. Can we, you know, go now?"

"Yes. We must find the twins. And your mentor."

"Mallory? He's not here."

"Oh?"

"He said he had somewhere to be. With Gwyn."

"I see." He looked thoughtful. "And you were here alone?"

"It was a trap. I couldn't help myself, I just sort of came here. They had a boy. They, well…" She pointed at the puddle. "They took him. In there."

"It isn't the first time. They've been taking people, like this: puddles and holes, as though the ground simply opened up and swallowed them."

"Is that… supposed to happen?"

"What do you think?"

Alice shrugged. "Hey, define what's supposed to be normal. You've got wings and I just torched a guy. Again."

"You. I like you." He led her towards the door. "You will be safe for now. Find the twins. I will speak with their mentor – they should know better than to leave you unattended." He paused. "Would you know…?"

"Vhnori. It's Vhnori."

"Ah." He frowned.

"Al…? Can I ask something?"

"You can ask. It's not certain I will answer."

"What's happening to me?"

"You are becoming all that you are." He opened the door and ushered her through it.

"All that I am? What the hell's that supposed to mean?" She asked, turning round… but he had gone, and the only thing behind her was a tiny spark in the air and the faint scent of woodsmoke.

# CHAPTER FOURTEEN

## Revelations

VIN WAS SITTING at the table with his arms folded and a face like thunder. He kicked two chairs back with his feet and glared at the twins. "You two? Sit down. I'm going to rip you a pair of new arseholes."

Alice backed out of the kitchen so quickly, she nearly tripped over her own feet.

News travelled fast. By the time she had found Jester and Florence (who were looking for her, pale-faced) and they'd made it back to their flat, both Earthbounds and Gwyn had been waiting. Gwyn had moved to strike Jester, who had the misfortune of being first through the door, but as his hand had come down, it had been caught by Mallory.

"No. This is Vhnori's business." He'd turned to Florence. "He's waiting for you in there."

He'd pointed to the kitchen, and they'd sloped inside. Seeing Vin's face, Alice thought it was time to leave, and she shut the door behind her. She was left to face Mallory.

"It's not that I blame you," he said, unscrewing his hip flask. "You wouldn't have been able to help it, and the Fallen knew that." He took a swig. "But you could have been killed. Or worse." The flask disappeared back into his pocket. "And that's my fault. I forgot that Florence was about as responsible as my left shoe."

"Mallory, I need to talk to you."

"I know. You fancy some air?" He gestured to the window, then laughed as her eyes widened. "I'm talking about a walk, Alice. Nothing else."

"Oh, good. I thought I was going to die when Vin brought me here."

"He wouldn't have dropped you." He paused, thought about it, then shrugged. "Not from *very* high up, anyway."

They took the lift, much to Alice's relief. She had definitely had enough of empty stairwells for the time being. Possibly forever.

The weather was turning colder – unseasonably so for autumn – and there was a bite in the air that made Alice shiver. Even Mallory pulled his jacket tightly around himself and stuffed his hands into his pockets.

"Let's take a walk, then."

They stepped through the security gate and turned down the road. Alice waited for him to speak. There was clearly something on his mind, but she knew better than to try and prise it out of him. If she did, he would either clam up or, worse, disappear again. They had gone at least half a mile before he spoke, and turned to look at her.

"How're you holding up?"

"I miss my dad. It's like I'm fine, and everything's normal, and then someone comes and punches me in the stomach, over and over again, and there's just this… *space* where he ought to be."

"I'm sorry."

"I don't blame *you*, you know."

"You blame Gwyn."

"Of course I blame Gwyn! I was… he…"

"Don't." Mallory cleared his throat. "Other than that?"

"Other than that? Well, I miss my life. My job. Home."

"Missing home? I can understand that," he said with a wry smile. "It's hard. I know."

132

"I'm trying not to think about it. Not unless someone pokes at me with a load of questions."

"Class-A denial. Fair enough. If it's working for you."

"What else am I supposed to do?"

"Embrace it."

"I don't even know what *it* is! Quite apart from you dropping into my living room, nothing's exactly clear, is it? It's all half-whispers: rumours, hints and veiled comments dropped to me by fallen bloody angels. And cryptic messages from other angels who catch fire and then bugger off again. So maybe – just maybe – if you want me to embrace anything, someone's going to have to tell me what the hell's going on!" She stopped, seeing Mallory looking at her with a mixture of amusement and bafflement. "What?" she asked. He shook his head.

"You're so like her. You really are."

"My mother."

"Your mother."

"You said, when I met you – when you came to the house – that you knew her. You knew her better than you've let me think, didn't you?"

"We were friends. Same choir. It's inevitable."

"You weren't just friends, though, were you?"

Mallory didn't answer the question. Instead, he stared at the pavement and started walking again. When he spoke, his voice was artificially cheery. "I'm a little jealous, you know. Michael sent A'albiel for you. That's a big deal."

"You know him?"

"Know him? No – I told you before, I've never even *met* one of Michael's choir. There aren't many of them, and they're the big guns. They stick together, but you knew that already, what with the sign and all."

"Mallory?"

"Yep?"

"Who, exactly, are you jealous of. Me, or him?"

"Ain't that the question. I'll let you know when I work that one out myself." He suddenly changed course, and walked through a narrow gap in a row of metal railings.

"When was the last time you sat on a swing?" he called back to her.

She shrugged. "When I was a kid. You know, before I grew out of it!"

But he either didn't hear her or pretended not to. He was jogging now, heading towards a small playground full of rusty equipment. By the time she caught up with him, he was already sitting on a swing, his feet stretched out in front of him. The chain creaked a little too loudly as he rocked backwards and forwards on his heels.

"Where were you?"

"Somewhere else."

"I needed you."

"No, you didn't."

"You *are* jealous."

"I had somewhere I needed to be, Alice. Let it go."

"Where?"

"You really want to know? Really? Fine. I was at Council, justifying the fact that I'm still here. Defending every last thing I've said and done since the last time I had to do it. Which, if you ask me, is far too often. Hoping that Gwyn wouldn't shaft me and that Gabriel doesn't pick today to decide he's had enough of me and take my wings once and for all." He glared at his feet. "That good enough for you?"

"Like a parole hearing?"

"But worse. Much worse."

"Why didn't you tell me?"

"It's none of your business."

"You said I could trust you."

"You can."

"Prove it. You owe me answers."

"I don't owe you a thing."

"You know what, Mallory? You're right. Maybe you don't. But you know something else? I'm willing to bet that if I shout loudly enough, there'll be someone out there who will give me answers. I can't seem to throw a rock in the air without it coming down on one of the Fallen, and they're all telling me more than you are, so…"

"No." There was a clatter of metal, and Mallory was on his feet, the swing now lying several feet away from its frame. "You think you'll get answers from them? All you'll get is a messy death, stretched over forever. They'll smile with their faces while they slit your throat with their nails. And don't forget: they're everywhere. Even the Twelve are watching – and don't make the mistake of thinking that just because you've not seen much of them, they aren't a threat. So you promise me here and now that whatever happens, you *will not* go to the Fallen. Promise me, Alice."

"Then start talking."

She was shocked by the force of his reaction. Surely he knew she wasn't serious? To be fair, she *had* forgotten about the Twelve. After so much talk, they didn't seem to be causing the trouble she had expected. In fact, she was rather beginning to hope they might simply have gone away. Clearly not.

"Three years ago, a woman named Iris Roberts woke up one morning and found a hellmouth in her garden. She and her family were taken. They were the first. Since then, thousands have been stolen away. All by the Fallen."

"Excuse me, but what? A hellmouth?"

"You saw one in that garage: the water that opened for the Fallen to escape? And in the graveyard too. Hellmouths are any way into hell, except a few of these have been a bit more literal. The one that swallowed Iris and her family had teeth."

"Eww."

"It's a little more than 'Eww.' The balance is starting to tip."

"Wait." She held up a hand. "I've heard that, somewhere." She frowned, trying to remember. It had been almost the exact same phrase... a chill ran down her spine. "Lucifer."

"What?" Mallory's eyes opened wide.

"The night you left: when we were attacked in the churchyard, and the Fallen did some weird possessed trance thing, and Lucifer said, 'the balance is tipping.' He asked Gwyn if I was supposed to be the one to save you... Him... Oh, you know."

"Then there's little point in trying to hide it any longer, is there?" Mallory sighed. "What's the first word you think of when I say 'angel'?"

"I don't know. Guns." She shrugged, and Mallory laughed and shook his head.

"That's my girl. Alright, what's the first word *most* people would think of when I say 'angel'?"

"Guardian. Salvation. Heaven. God. Pick one..."

"Right. And wrong. Remember what I told you before: angels are soldiers. That's all we do. Why would we care about human salvation?"

"Because... because... well, you're angels. That's what you *do*."

"I told you what I do. Think, Alice."

She screwed her eyes shut, picturing the room when he had told her. "You said the Fallen want to get out, and it's your job to keep them down. By any means necessary."

"That's right. Angels aren't here to save you, any of you. You have to do that all by yourselves. What we're here for is to make sure you get a fair chance at that. The Fallen don't play fair. All we do is level the playing field. They pop their heads out of the pit, we kick them right back down."

"You kill them."

"After everything you've seen, and everything we've told you, do you really think you can kill the Fallen? In theory, of course, it shouldn't be that way, but theory rarely works in practice and they've found a loophole. Hell keeps them alive, whatever we do. So, in practical terms, they're just as tough as we are. All we do is send them back to where they belong, and take the wind out of their sails."

"But they can just come back... how's that fair?"

"Bingo. It's a fight we can't win, and a war we've been fighting forever. We have to be lucky all the time – they only have to be lucky once."

"Then how come they haven't won? If the odds are that bad?"

"Because we're good at it. Even the Earthbounds. Might not look like it, but we fight just as hard as the Descendeds. Harder, maybe, because there's not a single one of us who doesn't want to earn his wings back. Take Vin: you look at him and you see some guy with a quick mouth. But that's not all he is. Whatever he says, whatever he does, he's an angel before he's anything else. He might be stuck down here and his wings might be clipped, but he's one of us. We keep the balance, whatever the cost."

"Then what's all this about the balance tipping?"

"That's the problem. Somehow the Fallen have found a way to weight things in their favour. I don't know how, but I'll wager anything Xaphan's behind it, he usually is." Mallory stared at his boots. "The thing is, these hellmouths – in the simplest of terms, they're using them to kidnap people."

"What's the point of that?"

"Again, simply put? They're taking them because faith is the same as hope – and there is no hope in hell."

"Ouch. You should have warned me before you got all metaphysical."

"Hey, you asked. The bottom line is that they're suddenly edging ahead, and every living soul down there only makes it easier. The balance is tipping in their favour, and we need to tip it back. Which is where you come in."

"See, this is the bit I don't like."

"Alice. You are a weapon. A perfect, perfect weapon. On the one hand, somehow – and no-one quite knows how – you've ended up with a gift that knocks all of ours into the shade. That fire? Once you get control of it…" He blew out a long breath. "And on the other, you're an empath. Your power comes from pain. There's plenty of that in hell. Who else could we send?"

Vin was still shouting at the twins when the hallway exploded.

The force of the blast threw all three of them to the floor of the kitchen, knocking Jester's head against the tiles with a *crack*. Coughing, Vin pulled himself up, wiping plaster from his eyes and hair. The room was full of smoke and dust: fine, white, settling like snow. Florence was shaking her head to clear it, the sound of the explosion ringing in her ears as much as it was his. He waved for her to stay down.

Other than the high-pitched whine inside his head, there was no sound in the flat. Nothing. And that was… suspicious. He edged around the scattered furniture towards the door – what was left of it. A few splinters of wood clung to the hinges. The hallway was wrecked: the front door replaced by a gaping hole into the landing, the walls blackened, the doors leading off it reduced to matchsticks. There was no sign of Gwyn, nor Mallory and Alice. Was it too much to hope they were out? Sliding around the doorframe and into the hall, keeping his back pressed against the wall, he crept towards the door to the living room, and walked straight into a fist. The room slipped away and faded to nothing.

When he woke up, he was sitting on a chair in the living room. Actually, he discovered when he tried to move, he was *tied* to a chair. It was not a promising start. Nor was the black case lying open on the table in front of him, prominently displaying a wide selection of sharp objects in a dazzling array of shapes and sizes. There was no-one else in the room, but that case belonged to someone, and Vin was pretty sure it wasn't him.

"Look, guys, I get that you're trying to be all dramatic and everything, but seriously? That's a bit bling, isn't it? You pussies."

"Meeow," said the Fallen, sliding into the room.

Vin smiled coldly at him. "I'd shake your hand, but you know…" He spread his hands as well as he could under the ropes, but for once even Vin's bravado was failing him. It wasn't just any Fallen who had walked into the room: it was Purson.

"If you're wondering where your precious little half-breeds are, you might as well stop. You won't be seeing them again any time soon, so forget about them. I don't want you distracted."

"Don't worry. You'll be getting my full attention when I take you to pieces. Let's see if you're smiling then." It was an empty threat, and he knew it. Worse, so did Purson. Of all the Fallen – of all the Twelve, even – why did it have to be him? Vin cursed silently, and wished that Barakiel's luck was a little more literal sometimes. This was not good. Not good at all.

Purson sidled up to him and tugged on the ropes binding his hands. They didn't give, and he nodded in satisfaction. "Don't want you wriggling out and giving me one of your little party tricks now, do we? Jeqon and Goap send their regards, by the way."

"They're talking again? Already? I must be losing my touch." And as soon as the words were out of his mouth, he knew he'd made a mistake. After the incident with Lilith, he wondered whether he actually *was*… He tried to shove the thought to the back of his mind, but it was too late.

A smile spread thickly over Purson's face "Maybe you are. After all, Lilith got away from you, didn't she?"

"Did she? Really? Huh. I must have missed that. I guess it was all the dust blowing in my eyes – you know, from when Mallory blew her away."

"You should show some respect. Remember who you're talking about." Purson's fingers were walking across the knives. Vin tried not to look.

"We are talking about the same Lilith, right? Not all that bright, bit of a sulker... and, let's face it, she's not exactly statuesque, is she? Oh, whoops. Poor choice of words there. My bad."

"You just can't help yourself, can you? All this talk. It spills from your lips like lava. I wonder what will happen when I take your tongue?"

"Mate, I'm sorry. I got totally the wrong end of the stick. I had no idea: you and her... *wow*. Now I get it. You guys – completely made for each other." Vin paused and took a deep breath, tensing every muscle. "You're both as stupid as each other, and frankly, the only person who could love a face like Lilith's is the poor bastard with a worse one."

Even though he was expecting it, the knife hurt. Purson drove it between his ribs and twisted it – first one way, then another. The blade was hot and cold and felt like forever. The Fallen didn't bother to remove it, instead holding up his hands and pointing to the case.

"You can keep that one. I've got plenty."

The next knife grazed his collarbone, and Vin felt the bone snap as the metal forced its way through. The third almost cost him an eye. The room began to mist, but Purson slapped him awake.

"No, you don't. I've got lots of treats in store for you – don't want you to miss a thing."

It was going to be a very, very long evening.

"You want me to go *down* there? Seriously?"

"Yes."

"You know what? At this point, that doesn't even surprise me," Alice said.

Mallory shrugged. "Of course it doesn't. You've known all along that's what you would have to do."

"Some of my old tutors would agree with you. Mr Thomas always told me I was headed straight for hell. Express train, no waiting."

"And what did Mr Thomas teach?"

"Religious studies. According to which, you should be sitting on a cloud strumming a harp and playing frisbee with your halo."

"In which case I don't think we need to take his word as gospel, do we?"

"I see what you did there. Clever."

"I can be, on occasion. But I meant it, Alice. You're necessary."

"You're not going to tell me it's my destiny or something, are you? Because, honestly, I don't think I can take that. I might have to go and throw up."

She looked so serious that Mallory couldn't stop himself from smiling. He shook his head. "There's no such thing as destiny, Alice. The Fallen will tell you otherwise, because they want you to feel helpless; same for everyone. It's where their power comes from. But there's no stone tablet engraved with your future, no sand-timer to tell you when your number's up. There's only the choices *you* make."

"So I have to choose to walk into hell?"

"Yes."

"And why would I be insane enough to do that?"

"In time you'll understand, Alice. In time."

Mallory lifted his flask to his lips and gulped down what must have been half its contents. Alice raised an eyebrow at him, but said nothing.

The light was fading. In the distance, the streetlights glowed deep orange; the cars' headlights sparkled and bumped their way down the road. The wind smelled of leaves, of moss and bonfires – and Alice felt her heart skip. But it was only the wind. There were no angels there, and it frightened her when she realised that she was almost disappointed. Maybe she would be mad enough to do it; to walk into hell unbidden and unbound... after all, everything else around her seemed to be falling into madness. And she didn't care. In fact, she wasn't sure that she didn't like it.

As they approached the twins' building, she found her feet dragging, something slowing her pace. An itch somewhere behind her eyes, a crawling sensation beneath her skin. Something was wrong.

"Mallory?"

"What is it?" He stopped, just ahead of her, his gun in his hand. It shone like fire in the artificial light.

"I don't... there's just..." She couldn't finish the words. Her skin had suddenly grown several sizes too small, catching her and crushing her...

The sound of shattering windows made them both look up, and Mallory swept her to the ground, leaning over her and covering her with his body as they were showered with glass and metal. It rained down on them for what could only have been moments – it felt like eternity – and as he helped her to her feet, he pointed up.

"Look."

Smoke was pouring from the top-floor flat, oozing over the balconies and out of the broken windows – and someone was standing outside, just behind the balcony rail and looking down at them. Whoever it was, the figure hefted something heavy and large to shoulder height, and then tossed it over the edge. A handful of dirty-grey feathers fluttered over the rail after it.

It fell, and it landed with a sound Alice never wanted to hear again. And then her world exploded.

The pain was so vicious it knocked her to her knees, shook the breath from her body. Fire raged up and down her limbs, over her shoulders and back; flames lapped at her throat and chin in waves. Everything was red – inside, outside, the whole world. It bled and it burned and it *hurt*.

She could sense Mallory standing beside her and she threw out her arm, feeling along the pavement for him. There was a sudden smell of melting tar; a sound of cracking concrete. "Help him. Please."

He left her side, and through the blur she saw him crouch beside Vin's body. If she hadn't been able to feel it, she would have thought he was dead. But there was no mistaking this. From very far away, she heard Mallory's voice and saw him shifting around Vin, who slowly lifted his head. It was working, but the pain didn't recede. The fire showed no sign of burning itself out, and it was only as Mallory slumped to the ground himself that she remembered. Mallory would feel that same pain that Vin had... and so would she, all over again.

Every inch of her blazed: with pain, with fire and smoke and heat. It swallowed her whole, buried itself in her mind and took control. There was nothing beyond it, not the pavement, not the building, not the angel who stood over her, driven back by the flames. She opened her mouth to cry out, but only sparks came, drifting away on the darkening air. And then there were two of them beside her, both the Earthbounds, their hands on her shoulders, lifting her... and the fire was gone. As quickly as it had overrun her, the pain was gone. In its place, there was a hollowness and a faint ringing in her ears. The streetlight arced above her and cool hands pulled her down into darkness.

# CHAPTER FIFTEEN

## Bullseye

SHE COULD TELL where she was from the smell alone. Opening one eye, she saw the damp-stained ceiling, and opening the other, she saw Mallory sitting on a chair not far away, rifling through the pile of papers on his lap and smiling at her wanly.

"Wotcher," he said, touching his hand to his temple in mock-salute. He sat back and crossed one leg over the other, dropping the pages on the floor beside him. "This is getting to be a habit, isn't it?"

"I don't know," she said, sitting up. The sofa was back-achingly familiar. "There was the time I woke up in a bed. With sheets and a pillow and everything." Her arms felt sore; the skin tender and bruised. "What happened?"

"What do you remember?"

"Not much. We were outside the gate and I just felt... odd. Then the windows blew out, I think, and there was... something. Falling."

"That would be Vin."

"Vin?"

"He had a run-in with one of the Twelve."

"Is he alright?"

"He is now. But he wasn't exactly in the best shape. Not surprising, given that he was tortured half to death and then dropped out of a ninth-storey window."

"Jesus." Alice's hand flew to her mouth.

"He's fine, Alice. Nothing that couldn't be fixed. We're tougher than we look, remember – but he was in a lot of pain. Which brings us to you."

"Did I?"

"And then some. I think the best word would be 'exploded.' You melted the road. I was actually pretty impressed." He smiled, but his face clouded again. "It made me realise something though: we need to think about getting you some control over it. Can't have you spending the rest of your life burning up every time someone breaks a leg…. What?" He tailed off, seeing the expression on her face. She was frowning at him, her ams folded across her body.

"I thought you'd be more worried about making sure I can do whatever it is I'm supposed to be doing."

"Alice, what do you think I am?" He scooted forward and crouched in front of the sofa. "I told you: you're necessary. Whether you like it or not, you're in the middle of this and there's no getting away from it. But there's a bigger picture – there's always a bigger picture – and that's how you live with this gift. You have to make your peace with who you are, and accept what it means. Otherwise, whatever happens, you'll never be able to get on with the rest of your life."

"Assuming I have a life, right? I thought there was some kind of cosmic bullseye on my back?"

"You're just a bag of sunshine, aren't you?"

"I'm not sure I understand what I'm supposed to do."

"You have to be willing to take control of it, to own it – *all of it*." He placed a curious emphasis on the last three words, and Alice stared blankly at him. He met her eyes, then suddenly looked away. "And I know just the place to start." His gun was lying on the table in front of her, and he picked it up, spinning it around his palm.

It was only then that Alice noticed what was missing: people.

146

There was no sign of Gwyn, of Jester and Florence or Vin. It was just the two of them.

"Where are they all? What happened to the twins? Were they in there?"

"You don't need to think about it, Alice. There's other things that need your attention."

"What *happened* to them?"

"I don't know," he sighed, pulling the slider of the Colt back and peering at it. "Vin's gone looking for them. He thinks they were taken – provided they lived."

"And Gwyn?"

"Oh, he's around. A little tied up at the moment, but he'll be back and breathing down my neck again before you know it. Enjoy the break." His gun went back under his jacket and the hip flask came out. Alice cleared her throat. "Is that wise?"

"Is what wise?" he asked, the flask pausing on its way to his lips. She nodded at it, and he glanced down, then laughed flatly, downing the contents. "Probably not," he said as he screwed the lid back on and dropped it into his pocket. "This is where it gets hard."

"And you said I'm being cheerful? Great. What now?"

"Now you start learning how to stay alive."


"YOU WON'T LIKE this," he warned her as they rounded the corner.

They were at the far end of the cemetery, fields, trees and graves the only things around them. Mallory seemed edgy, passing his gun from hand to hand as he walked. Alice followed, numbly. Something in her had changed. She had lied to him, of course. She remembered the fire; how it had burned the world around her down to a small, bright sphere of pain. The memory of it itched inside her flesh. Mallory was talking, but his voice floated past unnoticed. She had felt Vin's pain –

not at a distance, not filtered and faded, but as sharp and clear as if it were her own. It turned her stomach, even now. And the flames... so fast and hard and hungry. She shrugged the thought away, then stopped dead in her tracks.

Ahead of them was a large tree. It was obviously old. One of the first trees to be planted in the cemetery, maybe, or maybe it was there first, the graves slotted in around it. You didn't tend to argue with trees that size. If you did, you couldn't expect it to end well. And tied to it, his arms stretched back around the mass of the trunk, was a man. He looked familiar, and Alice's mind jumped back to the Halfway to Heaven, the grainy photographs there, and then she caught sight of a flash of white at his wrist and she knew. Not a man: a Fallen.

"His name's Rimmon," Mallory said, dropping to one knee beneath the tree. He tugged on a rope. Not only had he bound Rimmon to the tree itself, he had tied his ankles to sturdy iron stakes planted hard into the ground. Satisfied, he stood up and brushed the dirt from his hands and knees, ruffling Rimmon's hair before walking back to Alice. "He's not one of the Twelve, before you ask. He's a lackey, nothing more exciting than that. Quite the charmer, when he wants to be."

"Fuck you, Mallory," Rimmon mumbled, just loud enough to be certain he was heard.

Mallory stopped, his head tilting to one side. Without a word, he turned and leapt at Rimmon, his wings opening and lifting him clear of the ground with one easy beat. His boot slammed into the side of Rimmon's jaw, and the Fallen's head snapped to the side with the force of the blow. He spat blood at Mallory, who landed several feet away, adjusting his cuffs and moving back towards Alice. "You feel that?"

"Feel what?" she asked.

"Come on, Alice."

"No, honestly. Feel what?"

She was lying. Of course she was lying. As soon as Mallory's feet had left the ground, she felt a spike of fear that wasn't hers: cold, sharp and hard. And as Mallory's boot met Rimmon's face, there had been a dull ache and the familiar crawling under the skin of her palms. She buried it, and she lied.

Mallory shook his head and ran his hand back through his hair. "Alright. You win."

Suddenly the gun was in his hand... and so very casually, he pointed it at Rimmon, who froze. His eyes widened as he stared at Mallory over the barrel, and Alice felt the wash of his fear again. It didn't even fade when Mallory lowered the gun – and when the bullet hit Rimmon's foot, it only grew more insistent, almost drowning out the pain she felt in her own. Almost, but not quite. Mallory looked across at her. "How about that?"

"No."

"Really?" He turned back to Rimmon. "Lucky I brought *lots* of bullets, hey?" He fired again – this time into the Fallen's other foot. Alice flinched.

Another bullet hit Rimmon's shoulder; yet another, his thigh. And Mallory was about to take aim again when Alice couldn't hold it back any longer. With a sigh, she felt something inside her give, and the fire ran across her skin like quicksilver. The pain was gone, and with it, the icicle ache of Rimmon's fear. In its place was warmth and light and flame. And it was hungry. Mallory lowered the gun and nodded approvingly.

"There you go. That wasn't so hard, now, was it?"

"You have to stop. This isn't right."

"I'll be the judge of that, Alice."

Mallory tucked the gun away and strode over to Rimmon, now sagging against the ropes that bound him. He was bleeding heavily, sticky redness soaking through his black coat and making it shine like tar. Mallory leaned close to him, their faces almost touching. "You forgot: war is what I do. You try bringing the battle to me, and you better be sure you're going to win. You tell that to Lucifer next time you see him."

"Tell him yourself." Rimmon's head lolled, and his voice was thick with the blood running down his chin. "You remember, when they're cutting you to pieces. You remember that I tried to help you." He rolled his head to the side and looked right at Mallory, who smiled and punched him in the face.

He was still awake. Alice could feel him somewhere inside her mind, scrabbling for purchase on his fear. She was dimly aware of the pain the gunshots caused him, but it was no longer hers. She felt calm, suddenly at ease with the flames that boiled the air around her, with the sparks that kicked from her hair. She closed her eyes, and she was lost in the blaze.

When she opened them again, Mallory was watching her. "Let it go, Alice."

"Let what go?"

"You're holding on to it. Let it go."

"I don't..."

"Let it go."

He stepped back, his wings spread behind him, and Alice wondered what he had looked like before he was Earthbound. Whether Mallory, with his battered jeans and tattered wings, had worn armour that shone like the sun... and as she thought it, she felt the heart of the fire; knew what it wanted. It flared around her, brighter than she thought she could bear. And she let it go.

The flames raced to her fingertips and spilled out, pouring off her skin and into the air until she stood behind a wall of fire. It hung in front of her, shifting, waiting – then it rushed towards the tree. Rimmon saw it coming and he screamed, suddenly finding the strength to pull against the ropes that held him. The fire wrapped around him like another skin, winding itself about him, into his mouth and eyes and nose. He was lost inside it, and for a moment, Alice thought she saw something else beneath the flames, a flash of red that came and went. He burned and he burned and he burned, until, with a tearing, sucking sound, the flames disappeared and took him with them, leaving only a few charred ropes wrapped around the tree.

There was silence. A single spark danced across Alice's face and she brushed it away. "That was wrong."

"Oh, really?"

"You tied him up, Mallory. And you tortured him. *We* tortured him. How's that right?"

"Because it's what needed to be done."

"I don't see why."

"You don't, do you?" Mallory was angry, she could see it in the way he moved, hear it in his voice: a rage that bubbled through her blood, too. "You never will, either. That's why you have me. So that you can keep your precious human morals. So that you can keep your humanity."

"Listen to yourself. Saying it like that's a bad thing."

"Sometimes, it is. You lack clarity. It can't be helped."

"I'd rather that than be cruel, because that's what *that* was." She jabbed a finger at the still-smoking ropes. "That was no better than what they did to Vin, and you know it. Are you as much of a monster as they are?"

"Of course I am, Alice. I have to be. I'm an angel." Mallory's voice broke her heart. She watched as he beat his wings – once, twice – and was gone, leaving her in the cemetery.

She stared at the sky and screamed until her throat was raw.

HE WASN'T GONE long. She knew he wouldn't be. He slouched his way out of a small copse a few minutes later. "Have you finished venting?"

"Yes." She felt a little embarrassed. The screaming might have been a little over-the-top, maybe, but it had been necessary. *Something* had been necessary, otherwise her head would have exploded. Probably. He patted her shoulder. "You did just fine. I'm proud of you."

"Doesn't mean it was right."

"Alice, you listen to me. What do you think would have happened if you had been in the flat when Purson got there? I'll tell you. It would have been you in that chair, and you I was peeling off the concrete, and you wouldn't have made it. That would have been it: game over. For you, for me, for all of us."

"Purson?"

"Nice chap. Hell's tracker – hell's torturer, for that matter. He wouldn't have thought twice before taking you to pieces, and you know what? He'd have enjoyed every second of it. All of them would. So don't even think about showing them any mercy. Do not pity them. They won't return the favour."

"That's not the speech you gave me before. I liked that one. The brothers one."

"They were. Don't you see? That's why there's no space for doubt. A second is all they need. The slightest hesitation and you're lost. They made their choices, and now they must live with them. All of them."

"What did this one – Rimmon – mean? When he said he was trying to help you?"

"None of your business," Mallory said sharply.

Alice put her hands on her hips. "You don't get to say that to me. Not again. It *is* my business. You ask me to trust you? I do. You tell me what to do, and by and large, I've done it. I've asked you for answers before, and if you want me to carry on being a good little girl, *you* need to trust *me*."

"Do I?" he laughed. "And what should I be trusting you with?"

"I don't know, do I? That's just it." She planted her feet and stood firm. "You could tell me what the drinking's about, for a start."

"Do I really need to explain to you why people drink, Alice? You, of all people?" His voice was light, but there was no escaping his meaning.

A chill curled around Alice's spine. "Why do you say that?"

"Because I *know*, Alice. I know everything about you. Including that."

"It was a long time ago…"

"No, it wasn't. It was a couple of years. To me, that's a heartbeat."

"I really don't want to talk about it."

"No, you don't, do you? And that's why they had to force you to go back to therapy, isn't it? Because – and I think I've got this right – 'talking won't help.' Have I got the sum of it there?"

"How do you know all this?"

"I told you, Alice. I *know* you. You think we'd leave you unprotected all these years? There's always been someone watching over you. Your junior school teacher, Esther Charles? A half-born. Eddie North, your college lecturer? An Earthbound. Your therapist…"

"You're telling me that Dr Grove is an angel? Seriously?"

"No, I was going to tell you he owed me money. But that's not the point. The point is that you have never been alone – however much you might have felt it – not really. Not since your mother left."

"Left?" The chill crept up her back and through her chest. Mallory was always careful with his words, and he was being particularly careful now. Alice's knees shook. "Mallory. You said angels were hard to kill. And my mother was an angel… and she's dead."

"Alice," Mallory's dark eyes met hers, and they were shining in a way she had never seen before.

A tear slid down Mallory's face.

"About that. Your mother… she isn't dead."

# CHAPTER SIXTEEN
## Real Estate

THE HOUSE HAD been empty for several months – yet another victim of the slump. It shouldn't have been, of course. It had light, airy rooms and a garden that was larger than most in the street, but the tenants just didn't seem to stick. There were a hundred reasons why tenants broke their contracts or simply did a bunk – and by now he'd heard them all – but none of the usual suspects seemed to fit the bill here.

The door creaked as he opened it, and he swung it back and forth, checking for warping or signs of damp. Nothing. Just as well: shifting an empty house from the books is one thing; shifting a *damp* empty house is quite another. They can always smell it, tenants, as soon as they step foot through the door. Of course, then they do nothing about it and complain when the plaster drops off. He sighed, and he sniffed. No, no damp. Dust, mostly.

He plodded from room to room, flicking on light switches and staring at the ceilings, touching his hand to radiators and peering into cupboards. All was well. A quick clamber into the attic told him that, yes, the wasp nest was still there, but it was abandoned. He made a note to call the exterminator to come and deal with it in the week. In the kitchen, the boiler chugged obligingly when he tweaked the thermostat a couple of degrees higher; with the weather turning cold, it could do with the heating running a little hotter. Didn't take long for a cold house to become a damp house, and then you're right back with the sniffy-tenant problem.

Only the basement remained.

The last people to live here for any length of time had complained, once, about the basement. They said it was cold: colder than it should be. He had, of course, explained to them that the basement was unheated, uninsulated and – obviously – several feet underground. It was natural for it to be chilly. No, they said, you don't understand. It's *cold*. There was some nonsense about withholding their rent until the issue was resolved, so he had booked a maintenance visit for the next week and told them to keep the door shut. When the agency's maintenance man turned up, they had gone. No word of warning, no phone call... nothing. Just gone, like they'd never been there at all.

The girls in the office liked to joke that the house was haunted after that – which was all well and good between the strip-lights and carpet tiles, sitting at the desk with a cup of coffee and a pile of paperwork, but not so much fun when you're alone in the gathering dark, with the rain beating on the windows of a house that wants to be left alone.

He straightened his tie and cleared his throat, momentarily angry at himself, and reached for the handle of the door to the basement stairs... then snapped his hand away as his fingers brushed the knob.

It was cold. Searingly cold; cold enough to have left a red welt on the tips of his fingers where they touched the metal. He held his hand up, peering at his skin – and saw his breath in front of him. He backed away – or tried to. Instead, he found himself slipping sideways, his feet fighting for grip on a floor that had suddenly become like glass. The ice was spreading out and across the floor, away from the door... which swung on its hinges and stood, open, inviting.

It wasn't that he wanted to step through it. Far from it, a good portion of his mind was telling him to get out now, as fast as he could, and not to come back – to throw the keys in the nearest hedge and to lose the memory of this house. But it was the other part of him that was winning.

He took a heavy half-step forward, skated the rest, grabbed at the doorframe for support. His hands stuck to the ice that crawled up the wood and he had to pull himself free. Here, at least, his shoes gripped the bare concrete of the floor. A bulb hung from the ceiling. It was already lit, the glass misted with cold. The stairs dropped away ahead of him, bounded by the wall on one side and a black iron banister on the other. Icicles hung from the rail, trails of frost etched across its surface. His suit felt very thin.

The stair-treads crunched under his weight, but thankfully his feet held steady – more so than his knees, which shook violently with every step – and yet he could not bring himself to turn around. A chill breeze shifted his hair and gooseflesh rose on his arms. A few more steps…

The basement was empty. It was cold, yes, and it was small, but it was empty. There was nothing there except for a lightbulb hanging from the roof, a few cobwebs and a very frightened estate agent, desperately trying to choke down the heart that seemed to be beating in his mouth. It was strange, but clearly not (and he paused before he turned the word over in his mind) supernatural. He stood for a moment, trying to pull himself together, and that was when he noticed the keyhole.

Set into the wall at shoulder height, just across from him. It was brass, old-fashioned, and dulled by frost. And it was lit. He wouldn't have seen it otherwise. Who would look for a keyhole in a brick wall, never mind one in a basement? But there it was. A blue light spilled out, drawing him closer. He pulled his jacket closer around him and moved towards it, holding his hand in front of it, watching the light on his palm. He ducked his head, lowered his shoulders and edged up to it until he was near enough to look through.

An eye looked back at him.

The ground shivered as he fell back, his arms and legs moving in different directions at once – all as eager as each other to get themselves far, far away from *this*, whatever it was.

The ground shivered, and the world shook, and the bricks pulled themselves from the walls and spun through the air, and he was screaming.

And the man on the other side of the wall just smiled.

# CHAPTER SEVENTEEN

## Genesis

MALLORY HAD KNOWN he would have to do this. And now it was time.

"There's another kind of angel: they're known as Travelers. They're almost always from Raphael's choir: empaths, usually. They choose to be down here. Not as an exile, but as a visitor. It's temporary; a passing state. The thing is, up there, you're disconnected. You can see the world – all of it – but you feel so little. It's why the Descendeds seem so cold. It's not that they're cruel or that they don't care, it's just that they don't understand. And that can make it hard to *connect*. So the Travelers live as humans for a while, they *become* human, and then they try to pass on everything they've learned. It keeps us from forgetting what we're fighting for, reminds us why we make the sacrifices we do.

"The thing is, the Travelers never know how long they've got. They live as humans, among humans. They build up lives, friendships, relationships, families, but they have to return when they're called. It's the only binding put on them when they leave – that they will heed the call. Whatever lives they had, whoever they were, everything gets left behind. But sometimes, they don't listen."

He hoped his voice was still holding steady. It didn't feel like it, but he couldn't stop.

"It's a nice idea: the voice comes down from on high and says hey, go on a field trip. Come back and share your findings with the class. Maybe it'll concentrate their minds a little, but it's not so easy. Not really. To unpick the fabric of a life? To disentangle months – years, maybe – of hopes and dreams? To just up and leave? How easy is that? And for an empath, who will feel the pain chasing them with every step they take towards home?

"Travelers cause complications. Descendeds forget – angels forget – how much of a problem we are. Humans and angels, we don't mix. We're not supposed to. Their minds aren't built for it. Doesn't matter how much faith they might have… faith's just that. It's a belief, trust in something. So when you out-and-out prove it, it opens boxes that are meant to stay closed. It changes things.

"Your father loved you, Alice. He did. He loved your mother too. He didn't know to begin with, not even when you were born. She always hoped she would never have to tell him, I think, and when she did, she…"

He stopped, frowning, and took a deep drink from his flask.

"You remember the day Gwyn and I came for you? You found it easy to trust me, didn't you? Not him – and I don't blame you for that, because he *is* Gwyn, after all – but me, you felt safe with. Surprised even yourself. And you know why? It's because we'd met before. You won't remember it, you were too young the first time. Five, maybe. I came to see Seket, your mother. She'd refused the call, and I tried to talk her out of it, tried to make her change her mind. I tried to persuade her to leave. Raphael was willing to give her another chance – he always did have a soft spot for her – and I thought, I thought if I… I don't know what I thought. Maybe I thought that if anyone could get through to her, it would be me. Well, that was wrong, wasn't it? All she did was throw me out. She said I couldn't understand. Me. Not understand *her*. Maybe she was right. After all, I didn't. I told her she should answer the call, go home while there was still time, while she still had a chance. You know what she said? She looked at me, and she laid a hand on my arm and she said, "Mallory, this *is* home."

"That was the last time I spoke to her.

"Your father knew, of course. By then, he knew everything. He was broken. I've never seen a man with such a hole in his soul. And *you* could feel it – even then, you could feel it. You were a little older, but your world had just fallen in on itself and you paid no mind to yet another pair of visitors to the house. Richard was... let's say he was *uncertain* when it came to the future, and we couldn't be having that. Not with you in the picture. So Gwyn made him swear; made him swear on things that not so long before were only *ideas* to him, that he would keep you safe. That when you were ready, when it was time, he would call us. And then he could be free. Of course, things changed: the Fallen found a way to tip the balance and they found you. I don't entirely understand how those things fit together, and I don't need to. My job is to keep the Fallen down, and part of that is keeping you safe until you can do it yourself. You're almost there. You just need to remember, Alice.

"You need to remember who you are.

"You need to remember what you saw."

# CHAPTER EIGHTEEN
## Deja Vu

ALICE HAD HAD the dream before. Many times.

She was standing at the top of a hill, in the street she grew up on. Across from her, a crescent of houses stretched away down the slope, curling round on itself at the bottom. It was noon, but the sky was heavy, gloomy with a coming storm.

The paving slabs sucked at her feet as she started to move. They slowed her, pulled at her, holding her back from where she needed to be. She had to reach the end of the road. Tugging her feet up from the pavement, she walked... and it was only that desperate need to move, to be where she had to be, that got her past the eagle.

It was always there, the eagle. And once she saw it, she always knew she was dreaming, always knew that none of this was real – not that it helped her. She was still fighting her way down the incline, fighting to drag down the too-thin air. And there it was, hunched on the roof, watching her. A giant of a bird, bigger than anything she had ever seen, and when it spread its wings, they blotted out the sky.

Alice walked. Alone and afraid, she walked.

The corner was close now, and already she could see past the bend to the figure waiting there: waiting for *her*. Her mother, her hand shading her eyes despite the dark as she looked for her daughter, a breeze catching her hair and swirling it up and around her face.

Someone was with her, behind her. A man. She could make out the line of his shoulder as he placed his hands on her mother's arms. Her hair spun in the air, whipping back and forth as the wind built and the sky darkened to midnight.

Alice saw her mother reach for her, call out, but her words were lost between them, and although the stranger's grip held firm, she did not seem to struggle... and Alice stopped.

The paving slabs were hinging on themselves, swinging up like a trapdoor between them, and she could no longer make out her mother's face through the wind and the dust and the dark.

Her voice was gone, and although the ground had freed her feet, they would not move. She was frozen and rooted, silent, and her mother walked through the gale to the trapdoor. She paused a moment, that unknown man still only two steps behind her, then her shoulders sagged and she stepped back into his embrace.

Somewhere overhead, thunder roared and the eagle was airborne, and beneath a sudden flash of lightning, the paving slammed down again, and Alice's mother and the stranger were gone, leaving Alice alone in the storm.

"YOU NEED TO remember who you are. You need to remember what you saw."

ALICE IS SIX years old, and barefoot.

She has slipped out of the front door – her father in the garden, busy with the lawnmower, has no idea that his daughter is running down the street after her mother, who has forgotten her wallet. Alice knows she shouldn't be outside on her own, but how far can her mother have got in five minutes? She knows the route she takes when she walks into town: they've walked it together so often. She turns the corner into the top of the Crescent – and there, right at the bottom of the hill, is her mother.

But something is wrong. Her mother is no longer walking. She has stopped, and is looking around, wrapping her arms around her body, her hair blowing in the wind. The man walking towards her... Alice didn't see him before; where did he come from? One of the houses? Does he know her mother? From the way she steps back, away from him, it almost looks like she's afraid. And still he comes closer. He moves oddly, like he is too large for his own body, and the bright sunlight glints from something on his face. Glasses.

The wind is still rising, and Alice's own hair is blowing now, into her eyes and her mouth. She tucks it behind her ears, but it whips free again, flipping around her like a halo.

A cloud passes in front of the sun; a shadow falls across the pavement.

And she sees him. He lands near the end of the road, just ahead of her – swoops in on wings white as teeth, feathers shifting against one another as he moves. Small sparks speckle the feathers and he folds them behind him, striding towards her mother. She cannot see his face, but she knows it will not be kind.

Now Alice's mother is caught between the two: the man and the angel. She looks from one to the other, and that's when she sees her daughter on the hill. She calls out and the angel stiffens slightly but he does not turn, nor does he stop. Instead, he advances on her, one arm raised, and spreads his wings, hiding them all from Alice's sight. Feathers fill her world. There's a cry, hard and harsh and fearful, and the street is awash with light and flame. Lightning courses down the road as the cry builds to a scream that echoes off the houses. The angel lowers his wings and Alice's mother is ablaze with a hungry white fire.

The light fades and she seems unharmed. She sways a little on her feet, staggers first forward then back, then forward again, and falls. The angel flaps his wings, once, twice, and rises above them all. He does not leave, but perches on a rooftop where he folds his wings about him, watching. Waiting.

Alice is no longer thinking. She is running, or trying to. Because a hand is on her shoulder, holding her back. She looks around and sees another man, yet another stranger, his brown eyes fixed on the road ahead.

"You don't want to do that, Alice. You want to stay right here," he says, his voice warm but distant, and she obeys.

She watches as the man with the glasses lifts her mother from the ground. She feels the earth shake, and watches as it opens… she watches as her mother is carried into hell, and watches as the ground closes over her.

Alice is six years old, and barefoot, and shaking. Without a word, Mallory gathers her in his arms and turns away, towards home. She buries her face in his chest, smelling leather and incense and candlewax. He carries her back to her father, standing ashen at the end of the drive, who takes her into his own arms and smoothes her hair, pulling her close. He, too, is shaking, his body shivering in spite of him. There are no words, and then there are only the two of them – alone with each other in the sunlight.

# CHAPTER NINETEEN
## Nor Are We Out of It

"THAT DREAM..." SAID Alice.

"It wasn't a dream, no." Mallory shook his head.

"And you were there."

"I was."

"You knew. You've known all along. Everyone knew."

"Alice..."

"I was six years old, Mallory. I was six years old, and I watched my mother burn, and I watched her Fall. And in all the years that came afterwards, all the times I had that nightmare; in all the times I dreamt it, no-one thought to tell me that it was okay? No-one thought it might be appropriate to tell me I wasn't going mad? Did it cross anybody's mind to mention this when they took me out of school and put me in a *hospital*?"

"What, Alice? What could anyone say? That you were reliving the memory of your angel mother Falling, of seeing her carried down to hell? Imagine what would have happened to your father if he had tried."

"Do you know what they *did* to me? I was a *child*. Do you have any idea what my life was like in there?"

"You want to talk to me about being kept somewhere against your will? Somewhere you don't belong? Somewhere that makes you ache for home every time you breathe? You want to go there? With *me*?" There was an anger in Mallory's voice that Alice had rarely heard. Not just anger, but a bitterness, and a sorrow. It wasn't enough.

"A year in hospital. Two years with a shrink. Four years with a therapist. Six years of medication…"

"I know."

"No, you don't. All this time, I thought it was my mother dying that messed everything up. She died, and something was wrong with me. I just couldn't cope with it. I looked around and saw other kids who'd lost their mums or dads, and I wondered why I couldn't be like them, why I was so weak. And now, after all this, you come along and tell me that it was *you* who ruined my life. You and all the other goddamn angels."

Mallory's slap stung her cheek, forcing her to take a step back. She steadied herself and glared at him. His face was stern, his wings extended and twitching in agitation.

"There is a line, Alice, across which you do not want to step. You want to blame me for everything that might have gone wrong in your life? Fine. If that makes you feel better, you go ahead and do it. But don't you dare stand there and tell me that your life is so very much worse than a thousand, a million – a billion – others. You want pity? You won't get it from me. That's not what I am, and I warn you now, feeling sorry for yourself is a faster way into hell than anything Xaphan could ever conjure up. But you know that already, don't you?"

"Excuse me?"

"You think I don't see you flinch every time?" He whipped out his silver flask and waved it at her, and Alice found herself pulling away. "You see?" he said. "I *know* you, Alice. I know what you've done, who you've been, how you've spent your time on this earth, so don't even bother trying to convince me you're something you aren't."

"Oh, right. And maybe if you weren't so fucking obscure all the time, I might feel a little more inclined to believe you."

"You want clarity? Sure. Here it is. Your mother, Alice, your mother was one of the most extraordinary of Raphael's choir. I know that, because she, of all the angels, was the one I chose to love. I loved her, and she left me. She chose to leave me – to leave all of us – and she chose damnation. And now, here I am: trying to explain to her daughter, who looks so *very* like her, why I have to send her into hell itself. Why she has to walk in there willingly and alone, and why she might never come out again. All in the name of a war we can never win. How's that for you?" He uncapped the flask and took a long draught, then wiped the neck with his sleeve and held it out to her. "Now, are you sure I can't tempt you?"

"Funny." The ground felt soft beneath Alice's feet, uneven and unstable. "I…"

"It's alright." He pocketed the flask and sighed. "You're doing well, you know. For what it's worth, I'm proud of you."

"Thanks?"

"I mean it. But we're out of time, and you're not ready. You're a long way from ready. You can't control yourself and you're not strong enough."

"Wait… alone?"

"Sorry. I should have mentioned that sooner. It's in the rules. I'm doing my best, but…"

"Alone. I have to go in there alone."

"Yes." He had the good grace to look uncomfortable.

"And what…" – she choked on her words, but somehow they found a way out – "what am I supposed to do when I get there?"

"You remember those people I told you about? The ones who've been stolen? They're the reason the balance is tipping. You have to make sure no more are taken."

"But how am I supposed to do that?"

"Xaphan. It has to be Xaphan. He's found a way of opening these hellmouths – you have to stop him. Stop whatever it is he's doing."

"Why me?"

"Because you're you. And because I know you can."

"How? How the hell do you know that?"

"It's called faith, Alice. You should try it sometime."

"You don't want to put your faith in me, Mallory. I'll let you down. I let everyone down, in the end."

"Alice…"

"No, it's true. I do. I just…"

"Alice?"

"This is all too big; it's too much. I can't…"

"Alice!"

"What?"

"It's snowing." And, sure enough, the sky was filled with swirling white specks. They spun and drifted down to the ground, settling softly around them as they stared upwards. Just like the rain, it left the two of them untouched, collecting around their feet, but never once landing on them – dancing past them in languid spirals. "It's beautiful," she whispered.

"It's not," said Mallory, shaking his head.

She frowned at him. "How can you say that? Look at it!" She held out her hand, trying to catch one of the flakes, but still, they darted away from her.

Mallory stared at her. "What month is it, Alice?"

"What month? It's…" She paused. "It's October."

"It's snowing. In October. Here." He folded his arms, and Alice understood.

"Hell's cold, isn't it?"

"Colder than anything you've ever imagined. It'll freeze your soul." He gestured to the snow that thickened the sky overhead. "This? This is just the beginning."

"It's snowing," said Gwyn when they walked into Mallory's room. He was sitting, reading a newspaper. The front page headline seemed to be about a celebrity scandal: Alice could only assume that he was catching up.

"Snowing? No shit," Mallory slammed the door behind them. If anything, it was actually colder inside than it was outside.

Gwyn barely even looked up. "You should know by now that I am absolutely immune to sarcasm."

"It makes me feel better."

"This is not necessarily a good thing." Gwyn dropped the paper on the floor. "I took the liberty of having the place cleaned a little. Not completely, of course. I can't work miracles, can I?"

"You've... moved things," Mallory said, poking at a pile of books on the floor.

Gwyn frowned. "If by 'moved' you mean disposed of, and by 'things' you mean three years' worth of rubbish, then yes, I have 'moved things.' No need to thank me, but I really would like to discuss that. Out there." He pointed to the window.

"It's too soon, isn't it?"

"Yes. We thought we had more time." Gwyn folded his arms. "Everything is in place. Is she ready?"

"Umm..." Alice raised her hand and cleared her throat. "*She's* right here, you know."

"Of course you are, Alice," Gwyn said, fixing her with a blue-eyed stare, then turning straight back to Mallory. "Well? Is she?"

"Nowhere near."

"And does she know?"

"About my mother?" she cut in. "Yes, thanks. I know. Not before time, either..." She bit back her words as Mallory placed a firm hand on her arm.

Gwyn looked at her oddly. "About Seket? I rather assumed you would have worked that out for yourself by now. You saw it, after all."

Out of the corner of her eye, Alice saw Mallory's free hand rub his forehead. His grip on her arm tightened. "Timing, Gwyn."

"Oh?"

Alice's head hurt. It suddenly felt too small, as though everything inside it would force her mind open and seep out through her ears. There was more. Of course there was more. How could she have expected that to be the end of it? Would there ever be an end to it?

Gwyn shrugged. "She needs to be ready, Mallory."

Mallory glared at him, then started to speak, but Alice couldn't understand any of it. It rolled and twisted and fell from his tongue, the language of the angels. He kept going, too: for what felt like hours, he kept on speaking – never once pausing for breath or for Gwyn to answer. And whatever it was he was saying, Gwyn didn't like it one bit. His face grew darker and darker, his eyes stonier... until at last he snapped a hand up, pointing at Mallory. Sparks fizzed from the tip of his finger and Mallory fell silent.

"Enough. If you are not able to prepare her, then I will. Perhaps it would be better if I assumed responsibility now, rather than at the last minute when you have failed?"

"I will *not* fail, Gwyn. Not you, and not her."

"Maybe you will, maybe you won't. I have to say there are some who think you a most unwise choice, given your... emotions."

"You listen to me, Descended. You may not like me, and you may not believe me, but I am the best choice for her. The only choice. You disagree? Then speak to Raphael. If you dare."

"Oh, Raphael has his hands full. They all do. Heaven itself is in a state of panic, Mallory. The Fallen have never drawn so far ahead, not since the beginning. Much further, and we may never be able to defeat them."

"I thought," said Alice, quietly, "that was the point. That there was no winning, on either side. That there's a balance, and it has to hold. So why would you need to worry about beating them?"

"It's a manner of speaking, Alice," Gwyn snapped. "If we hold them in check, we win. If we don't, we lose. We cannot afford to lose."

"That's why I'm here. Just tell me what I need to do."

Mallory's hand dropped from her arm. "It's not that simple, Alice. There's things… you can't imagine. It's *hell*."

"So, what? You spend all this time convincing me I need to go down there, and now you change your mind?"

"Hardly. I just want you to be sure. To know what you're getting into."

"You get me ready, and I'll get it done, whatever it is I'm supposed to do. Like I said, that's what I'm here for, isn't it? It's what I've always been here for."

"No. Remember what I told you. Destiny… it doesn't exist. There's no prophecy, no seers steering your course. There's only you. You are free to do as you choose. You always have been."

"Then I choose hell."

A sudden gust of wind rattled the window, and a pane of glass fell, shattering on the floor and making all of them jump. Snowflakes tumbled in after it. Gwyn eyed Alice, then nodded in approval.

"Good. The choirs will be pleased. We have found a way in. It won't be easy, but we can get you to the first hellmouth, and you will have a guide to take you through the upper levels."

"A guide? I thought I had to be alone."

"It won't be one of us, Alice." Mallory's voice was solemn. "It will be one of the Fallen."

"Oh. How?"

"It's complicated, and we don't have time to go into it now. There's too much to do." He frowned at Gwyn. "When?"

"Three days."

"Three days? That's not enough time."

"It's the time you have." Already the light in the room was growing brighter. Gwyn was leaving. "Whether she's ready or not, she goes in in three days."

# CHAPTER TWENTY

## Cry Wolf

BALBERITH COULD HEAR dripping, somewhere behind him. It was irritating. The others either hadn't noticed, or didn't care – neither would surprise him. Half of them were too bone-deaf to hear it, and the other half too stupid to care about noises in the dark.

He cared.

Years of planning, of preparation, of experiments and corrections and failures... the very thought of them made his ribs ache. Failure does not go unpunished in hell, and *boy*, had there been failures. Years of effort and care. A plan set in motion at precisely the right moment... and then, somehow, Heaven had scooped the half-born. You might even call it a miracle – if you believed in that sort of thing which, naturally, he didn't. Balberith believed in order, in lists and – on occasion – in the Dewey Decimal System. He most certainly did not believe in the rubbish about fate that Forfax had taken to spouting, and he couldn't decide what was more annoying: listening to it, or watching the others nod their heads sagely.

The dripping continued.

"Look, can we just stop?" he said. "Is no-one else bothered by that? Honestly? Because I can barely hear myself think." He folded his arms as the other eyes in the room fixed on him. "I'm just saying. It's distracting."

"Fine," Purson heaved himself up from his chair and disappeared into the gloom of the warehouse. There was a heavy clanking sound, then a soft metallic whisper, and a sudden scream. The dripping stopped and Purson strode back to his chair, wiping his hands. "Happy?"

"Ecstatic." Balberith gave him a sour look and adjusted his glasses.

"When the two of you have quite finished?" Xaphan stepped out of the shadows. "Things are not going to plan. Now, I wouldn't have thought that I needed to remind you of this, but apparently I do: this is seen as a Problem. And Problems, as we all know, tend to have Solutions, where Lucifer is involved. And *that* I'm certain I don't have to remind you of. So, to recap, where are we?"

"They say the angels have found the half-breed a way in. She'll be alone. And she still can't control her gift."

"Ah. On that last point, I beg to differ." The light caught the scar tissue on the side of his face, making it shine. "She has control. It may well not be *enough*, but she has control. And she has one other thing." He paused for effect. "Mallory."

Mallory's name launched a wave of grumbles around the room. Every one of the Twelve – every one of the Fallen – knew Mallory, and every last one of them hated him.

Xaphan smiled, waved them to silence. "Of course, it may be that Mallory will be less of a problem than we've always assumed. There's so much more to this girl than we'd ever hoped. So much potential. She may not be that hard to break after all, in which case, the Earthbound becomes little more than a fly to be swatted..."

"How so?" That was Balberith.

Xaphan rolled his eyes. He disliked Balberith – more, even, than he disliked the other Fallen – but he forced himself to smile. "I'm afraid that's a little above your pay grade, old chap," he said, flashing his teeth a little wider than was necessary. Balberith blinked, once, twice... then looked down at his lap.

"I told you you could leave Mallory to me, you know." Purson was, unsurprisingly, cleaning his nails with a large knife.

"Hardly," said Xaphan. "You didn't exactly cover yourself in glory with the way you handled Vhnori, did you?"

"Look, like I told the boss, he was dead when I left him..."

"No, he was not! He was *almost* dead. Which, when you have one of Raphael's little healers on hand, is no use whatsoever!"

The shattered glass in the window jangled as the pieces shifted against one another and Xaphan cleared his throat.

"The angels are sending the girl in underprepared. They know this. We know this. They're desperate. And that's precisely why they're going to lose." He spread his ruined wings, and began to laugh.

# CHAPTER TWENTY-ONE

## The Surest Way Forward is to Stop Looking Back

ALICE HAD BRUISES. Alice's *bruises* had bruises. She ached every time she moved, and it didn't seem to be getting any better. Nor, in a move she thought particularly unfair, would Mallory help. So not only had he put her through what she could only describe – ironically – as hell, he wouldn't fix her either.

"Look at it as a warm-up. This is how they'd kiss you hello in hell."

Three days.

Three days of being thrown around in a graveyard; of learning to duck, to sidestep, to not fall over her own feet.

Three days of shivering in the endless cold, of falling into snowdrifts, of being knocked down and picked up, just to do it all over again. She had been pushed and pulled and thrown like a ragdoll, and still Mallory came back at her with more.

There had been a point, halfway through the first day, when she had landed face down in the snow, bleeding and broken and begging Mallory just to let her rest. And he stood over her and folded his arms. "No. Get up."

"No."

"Get up, Alice."

"You can't make me."

"Watch me. I can do whatever I want, including breaking every bone in your body if that's what it takes. And then I'll just put you back together and start all over again."

"Why?" She spat out a mouthful of bloodstained snow.

He shrugged. "Because the harder it is now, the easier it'll be then."

He leaned forwards and gripped her shoulders, hauling her to her feet. She swayed a little, looking up at the sky. The snow kept on coming – it hadn't once stopped.

"What happens if I fail?"

"You won't." He had his back to her, his wings folded around his shoulders as if to keep himself warm.

"What happens?"

"I don't know." He turned towards her and his face was serious. "We've never been this close before. Maybe nothing. Maybe everything."

"That's cheering."

"You want me to lie to you?"

"Not... *lie*, exactly..."

"Alice, I've told you before: the most important thing is that you get out alive."

"You mean I'm not supposed to sacrifice myself for the greater good?" she said, only half-seriously.

Mallory raised an eyebrow. "Not if you can help it. That's an angel's job. You're half-human." He fluttered his wings, and the snow swirled around them. "You find whatever it is Xaphan has rigged down there to open the hellmouths, you destroy it and you get out as fast as you can."

"And everyone down there, the ones the Fallen are holding?"

"You aren't to concern yourself with them. You make sure you get out. That's all."

It was at that moment that Alice understood what Mallory had not been saying. All this talk of risk, of choice, of the possibility she might not come back... of the future.

"This doesn't end it, does it?"

"No." He smiled sadly. "It's a war we can never win. All we can do is keep the balance."

"I thought you weren't going to lie to me, Mallory."

"Who's lying?"

"Can you try – just once – not to be so damn literal? And just tell me whatever it is you're leaving out?"

"I can't."

"I see…"

"You don't understand. I *can't*. I'm gagged. Forbidden."

"Gwyn?"

"Gwyn."

"Is there any way to…"

"*Technically*," Mallory said with a sly smile, "you belong to a higher choir. So if you were to *ask* me, I may not be able to tell you directly, but I might be able to give you a yes or no."

"Fine." She sighed. "Is it important I get out of hell alive?"

"Yes."

"To whom?"

Mallory gave her a withering look. Alice rolled her eyes and tried again. "The Descendeds want me to come back out?"

"Yes."

"The Archangels?"

"Yes."

"They're never going to let me go, are they?"

"No." Mallory's chin dropped. "I'm sorry, Alice."

"And that's it? I'm now the angels' pet? I go where I'm told, do as I'm told?"

"You're valuable."

"What if I don't come back out?"

"Then you'll be dead. Or worse." He wrapped his jacket more tightly about him. Even in the snow, he was still wearing the same beaten-up clothes. Alice had never seen him in anything else. "And they'll just start looking for the next half-born."

"It never ends."

"It never ends."

They were silent for a moment, the snow eddying around them. It struck Alice that there were no other sounds, anywhere. No cars. No kids playing in the snow. Not even the birds. The world was hiding – it just didn't know what it was hiding from. She did. And it was enough to make her take a deep breath and square up to the angel in front of her. Again.

"I suppose I should be grateful you've fixed the shower?"

"It might be nice. I suggest you sit under it." Mallory's voice was muffled by the bathroom door, but she could still hear the amusement in it. "But I'm warning you now that I'm not coming in there to get you out if you seize up."

"You're a real prince among men, aren't you?"

"Actually, yes. Don't bother with the cold tap. It still doesn't work."

The idea of a shower had come as a surprise. Somehow, she had assumed that just like the rain and the snow, the water would simply go round her, but when she mentioned this to Mallory, he gave her one of his looks. The ones that made you feel like you were five years old and had just been caught stealing a biscuit. Apparently, only "the weather" did that. Obviously.

Her fingers were so cold she could barely unbutton her shirt. The chill had crept so far inside her bones that she was beginning to wonder if it wasn't fear. Because, she thought as the pipes groaned, that nagging fear that had followed her around since this began was now so thick that she could taste it, could feel it settling on her shoulders like a cloak. She could smell it: a sour, cloudy echo that followed her wherever she went. She clambered stiffly into the shower and felt the water run over her, over the bruises and the grazes and the cuts and the soon-to-be-scars, and she gave in. She let the fear wash over her with the water. It clambered inside and stretched itself out into her hands and her fingers; it choked its way into her lungs and suddenly her palms were burning. Burning. With actual fire. In the shower.

"Uh.. Mallory?"

"Mmm?"

"Why am I on fire?"

"Are you?"

"No. Because I joke about this sort of thing all the time. Of course I bloody am!"

"Huh. That's interesting."

"No, it's incredibly inconvenient!" She held out her arm and watched as the water turned to steam when it touched her skin, evaporating into the flame. "Whatever you're doing, can you stop it?"

"Not me. You figure it out." He sounded remarkably calm. "We talked about this, remember."

They had. All part of the patented Mallory crash-course: How To Stop Being On Fire. Yes. Alice closed her eyes and tried to concentrate – which was, admittedly, hard, given the fire skipping up and down her arms – and breathe. Breathing helped.

Ten minutes later, she was dressed again, and standing in the bathroom doorway, glaring at Mallory, who was slouched on his sofa, reading one of his notebooks filled with scrawled symbols.

"You want to explain what that was?" she asked, tapping her foot in irritation.

He didn't look up. "Not really."

"Where did that come from? There's no-one here; no-one in pain…"

"There's you."

"Fair enough, but I've been aching like this for…"

"There's more than one kind of pain, Alice."

"*What?*" She stared at him. "Do you talk like this just to drive me crazy?"

"Your gift. What triggers it?"

"Pain. What am I missing, or am I just being thick? No, wait. Don't answer that."

"The thought never crossed my mind," he said, trying to hide his smirk behind the notebook. He glanced over at her and coughed, dropping the book and swinging around to look at her properly. "And you think pain's only a physical thing, right?"

"No. Yes. Maybe?"

"It's alright, Alice. It means we've done it."

"We've done what?"

"We've got you to a point where you stand a chance. You've got control. Not just the part of you that's governed by your empathy. You own it. All of it."

"Yay?"

"And just listen to you. You're giving me attitude. You weren't a couple of days ago, were you?"

"No, but..."

"No. And you know why? It's because you're not afraid any more, isn't it?"

He raised his eyebrows at her, and she opened her mouth to reply... but stopped. He was right. She wasn't. The fear that had crawled inside her was gone. Almost like it had been... burned away.

Mallory nodded. "You took it all – the fear, the pain, all of it: all the things you've been carrying round your whole life – and you turned it into fuel. You let it in, and you let it feed you... and you beat it." He was up from the sofa, dropping the book on the floor and pacing up and down the small room. "All you have to remember to do is to let it in, and you'll be fine."

"Let *what* in, exactly?"

"Everything."

"Oh, that's helpful." Alice turned on her heel and disappeared back into the bathroom, slamming the door behind her. From the other side, she heard Mallory say, "You're welcome."

\*     \*     \*

THE LIGHT WAS fading as they left. Someone had scraped the snow off the path from the church, and it occurred to Alice that although there were footprints, clear signs of life coming and going, she had never seen anyone other than the angels – or the Fallen – around it.

Mallory simply shrugged. "Just because you don't see something, it doesn't mean it isn't there, does it?"

"That's what Gwyn said. About your wings."

"We have a script."

"Funny."

He had given her a coat. It was long, and it was red and warm: warmer than anything else she owned. He had passed it to her across the table, wrapped in dark tissue paper. "You'll need it. You've heard the phrase: 'when hell freezes over'? Well, it already did."

"A snowball's chance in hell?"

"No-one said the Fallen didn't appreciate irony."

The door closing behind them made an awful, final sound.

THE HOUSE WAS small, neat, suburban. Not unlike the house Alice used to live in; the street almost identical even down to the boxy front gardens and the makes of the cars parked along the kerb. There was little to mark this house out as different, except for the blankness of the windows. It wasn't just that the house was empty: it was *soulless*. This was a house that knew it had been abandoned, and it wore that knowledge like a shroud.

Mallory pushed his way past an overgrown shrub to a gate standing shoulder-high at the side of the house. He reached over it and unbolted it, raising an eyebrow at Alice. "What?"

"Well, you've got wings. You could, you know... fly."

"There are some things, Alice, which need to be done *right*. You'll see."

He lifted the latch and the gate swung open. It led to a wide passage that ran alongside the garage. There were pots here, the plants in them long since dead, and weeds had pushed their way between the paving stones. A tangle of bindweed slumped out of what once must have been a child's sandpit, now filled with muddied slush and snow. Ahead of her, Alice spotted a half-rotten football in a border and her stomach heaved. This was the house that had once belonged to Iris: most likely, it still did, provided Iris and her family were still alive. This was the first of the hellmouths.

They rounded the corner of the garage and there, ahead of them on the lawn, she saw it. She couldn't stop herself. "Jesus wept."

"Most probably. I know I did." Mallory's voice, behind her, was gruff.

"It's not what I was expecting."

"Why ever not? Hell. Mouth. Description's pretty accurate."

It was. *Terrifyingly* accurate. Up ahead, only just visible in the near-dark, a circle of enormous teeth had forced its way up through the ground. They loomed over the figures waiting for her, their wings whispering in the breeze. Gwyn was the first to step forward, looking over her shoulder and nodding a greeting to Mallory. "You're ready."

"I guess so…"

"It wasn't a question."

"Oh."

"I'm proud of you, Alice. You have done well."

"Thanks?"

She shuffled from one foot to the other. If she was entirely honest, she was hoping she wouldn't have to see Gwyn here – although, if she really *was* being honest, she knew it was unavoidable. She could never quite put her finger on it, but there was still something about him she couldn't trust. Maybe it was just his distance. Maybe it was something else... like the fact he'd let the Fallen break her father's neck. Yes. That would probably do it. He was looking her up and down thoughtfully. "You know, I was almost afraid, when we met."

"Afraid? Of what?"

"That you would be a disappointment. After your mother... well. You can't blame me for thinking it, can you?"

"I'm not sure I see your point."

Alice clenched her fists, trying to ignore the flash of sensation in her palms. Gwyn shook his head. "So many thought you would turn to the Fallen. So many. They thought you would let us down; that you couldn't help it." He smiled. "I told them, 'Have faith.' And here you are." He spread his hands beatifically.

"Bullshit."

It was thinly disguised as a cough, and it came from the shadows to Gwyn's left. Gwyn's head whipped round, and Alice followed the line of his gaze. There, half-hidden beside a tree, was Vin – and a few steps behind him was Jester. He waved. Alice stared at him open-mouthed. "How... I thought...?"

"Yeah. Me too," said Vin. "Turns out he finally got the hang of his gift and managed to give Purson the slip. Of course, he left me behind to get *tortured*, and to then spend two days tearing my hair out trying to find him... but what can I say? I'm obviously a natural teacher."

"More like I'm a natural talent," Jester said with a smile. "Apparently, I can make you see whatever I want. Who knew?"

"So when he didn't want to be found... Well. I tell you, this kid is going to be *golden*." Vin patted him on the shoulder, and pulled his sunglasses out of his pocket, pausing with them halfway to his face. "Toast a few Fallen for me."

"Vin. It's dark. You can leave the sunglasses."

"It's a look. Shut up." He sniffed, and Alice laughed. There was no sign of Florence, and no-one mentioned her. Alice considered asking, but thought better of it.

She caught the scent of woodsmoke and spun round. In the shadows beside the house, she could just make out three figures talking: Mallory, Gwyn and... someone else. Mallory's head was lowered and he looked uncomfortable, fidgeting as he spoke. No, not uncomfortable: uncertain. She breathed in the scent on the air, trying to remember it. It was familiar, she knew that much. It was safety. It was A'albiel, the Descended who had rescued her from Xaphan. No wonder Mallory was uncomfortable – hadn't he said he'd never met one of Michael's choir before? Still, there was a first time for everything.

Alice peered at the hellmouth. It didn't help. It still looked just as ugly, and just as scary. Nor was the farewell party helping. It all seemed a little final – like the thud of Mallory's door closing behind them, this was a little too much. She scuffed at one of the teeth with her shoe. It felt solid enough, and the bloody great hole that dropped away into the earth behind it looked deep enough. She stared down into the dark.

It really *was* dark.

Something across the hellmouth caught her eye and she dropped to a crouch, slinging an arm around the closest tooth for balance and leaning out a little. As she'd thought: stairs. Someone had carved a staircase into the hellmouth – into what looked exactly like the flesh of a throat. Fighting back a shudder, Alice wondered what you had to do to get that particular duty on hell's rota. It can't have been good. But still, *stairs?*

She stood up, wiping her hands and turned to face the others. Gwyn was right behind her, making her jump. "You should go."

"I thought I was going to have to jump or something. You didn't tell me there were stairs! And there I was, worrying about how I'd get out..."

"The steps won't bring you back up," Gwyn said with a calm smile. "They will only take you down."

"One-way stairs? That's ridiculous."

"That's the Fallen."

"No, really. That's impossible. Stairs can't only work one way. They're... *stairs*."

"Try it. When you reach the third step, try to turn back. But I warn you, Alice: you won't be able to." His expression was carefully, infuriatingly blank.

She sighed. "You know something? You guys are weird."

Mallory snorted, and Gwyn shot him a look of disapproval before placing his palms flat on Alice's shoulders. "I have to ask you, Alice: do you enter of your own free will?"

"What?"

"You're supposed to say yes," hissed Vin from under the tree, and it was his turn to get a dirty look from Gwyn.

Alice rolled her eyes. "Haven't we already done this?"

Gwyn's chilly ozone-scent filled her mind. "And you understand the consequences, should you fail?"

"Oh, god, no. Don't want to think about it. Don't need to. I won't fail."

Gwyn opened his mouth, paused, then closed it again. Apparently there wasn't an answer to that. And that was good enough for her. Taking a deep breath, she walked around the circle of teeth, around the mouth, and stopped at the top of the steps. There she was, standing at the jaws of hell and hoping that no-one could see her shaking.

She stepped down.

They were all watching her.

She stepped down again, and again.

Out of curiosity, on the third step she turned and stepped back up... and found herself standing on the third step again. She tried again, and once more she realised she was stepping back onto the third step. "Wow. That's a headfuck."

A'albiel was at the edge, looking down. "We will not abandon you, Alice."

She turned her face away from the sky, away from the angels, and began the walk down into darkness. The last thing she heard from above her was a warm, familiar voice saying, "Have faith."

# CHAPTER TWENTY-TWO
## Down the Rabbithole

THE FURTHER SHE walked, the darker it got, and soon she couldn't see her hand in front of her face. While this didn't exactly make her happy, given the stairs she was climbing down opened on one side to a bottomless pit, she had no choice but to keep going. Fun as the only-forward stairs were, Alice was sure the novelty would wear off pretty quickly. She kept one hand on the wall, allowing it to guide her round and ignoring just how *sticky* it felt. It gave her something to concentrate on; something – anything – other than where she was going.

Mallory hadn't helped, standing on the other side of the table and staring at her with his sad eyes, saying, "There will be people you know, Alice. People you trusted. Remember how I told you that we have always been watching you? Well, so have the Fallen. And just as we had you surrounded, so did they."

"You had to tell me that now?"

"I thought you should be prepared."

Like anyone could be prepared for this. She misjudged her footing and tripped, grabbing at the wall to help regain her balance. Her fingers sank into the wall up to the knuckle.

"Alright," she said to no-one in particular, pulling her hand free with a revolting squelch, "That? That's just about the worst thing ever."

The whole thing was impossible. She had caught herself that

time, but she had no idea how much further there was to go, and it was inevitable she would slip again in this darkness.

She closed her eyes, not that it made much of a difference, and listened to the panicked pounding of her heart… and suddenly there was light. She held her hand ahead of her and the flame in her palm was barely the size of a tennis ball, but it gave her a chance to look around. It wouldn't take long to burn itself out. She had come to realise that using her own emotions was a little like running on reserve power – just enough to get out of trouble, but never enough to do anything constructive – so she tried to commit as much as she could to memory.

The stairs kept on sweeping round and down, always down, further than she could see. That was either extremely encouraging or incredibly depressing; she wasn't sure which. Nor could she stop herself from looking at the wall her hand rested against. She wished she hadn't. It was definitely not earth, although she'd known that. It was softer. And were those made by… fingernails? Three long parallel gouges that swept past her at shoulder height, then abruptly cut off.

The fire burned out.

On the plus side, it had burned up the jolt of fear she felt, and she was calm again as she set off into the blackness.

HER LEGS WERE aching by the time she realised she could see again – not clearly, but there was definitely a faint light coming from somewhere, edging her world with a sickly blue sheen. At this point, though, she'd take grey over pitch black. She peered down the central pit. It certainly looked like it was lighter down there, but whether that was a good thing remained to be seen. What it did mean was that she could pick up the pace a little, and despite her protesting muscles, she skipped down the stairs two at a time.

"You'd think I was in a hurry to get into hell. That's my life now."

There was no answer. There was no-one *to* answer her. She missed Mallory.


THE FLOOR, WHEN it came, was stone, for which she was grateful. After the teeth and the suspiciously fleshy wall, she'd had a horrible feeling that she was going to find herself in the middle of a medieval painting, all flying livers and god only knows what else. But no, it was stone. Boring, grey stone. Still, it *was* hell, and her feet didn't seem to want to move from that last step. Her breath billowed out of her, thick as an ash-cloud. It was cold down here. Really cold.

"Your guide will meet you at the gate," Mallory had said. So where was he? Was this it, and Mallory was just being poetic, or should she be looking for an actual *gate*? And what, Alice wondered, would it look like? Her stomach flipped quietly and she decided it was safer not to give that too much consideration. She stepped down.

The floor made an alarming cracking sound and she threw out her arms for balance, half-expecting to be tipped sideways, but nothing happened and, feeling slightly foolish, she adjusted her coat and drew it closer around her. At least there hadn't been anyone to see that. First impressions and everything. The stairs were at the end of a corridor hollowed through the same bland grey stone, which swept away around a tight bend. The pale blue light that had seeped up the steps was stronger here; it seemed to be coming from somewhere further along the passageway. There was something about it that made her uncomfortable, as though her eyes were constantly being pushed sideways. Huddled into her coat, she started around the corridor.

It curled around itself, dropping away more steeply the further she went. The blue light grew brighter as she turned a corner and spotted a large sconce bolted to the wall. It burned with a chilly blue flame; dark drips ran down the wall beneath it and there was a sticky black puddle on the floor. Alice had never seen anything like it. She lifted her hand, wanting to see if the flame was as cold as it looked, but as her fingers drew close, it shivered and drew away. The fire flattened against the wall, smearing itself across the stone, then pulled back to its original shape as she lowered her arm. She tried again, and exactly the same thing happened. The flame was *avoiding* her. And it cast no shadows.

"Well, that's just *odd*."

There was a sound from down the corridor and Alice froze. Just because she hadn't seen anyone so far didn't mean that she was alone. On the other hand, it could well be that her guide was waiting for her. She walked towards the noise.

The passageway ended, opening up into an enormous cavern: the roof soared up and away, arching further than she could see. And towering over her, their tops lost in the height above, were the gates of hell. Alice's eyes still felt like they were being squeezed inside out by the peculiar light, but she stared anyway, panning down the front of the gates. Higher than a cathedral, broader than an ocean liner... they were vast.

Between her and the gates, there was a man. He had his back to her, the collar of his jacket turned up. There was something horribly familiar about the way he was standing; the way he held his shoulders, his hands jammed into his coat pockets. She took a step back, suddenly uncertain, but as she did so he turned his head slightly, and sniffed.

"You're late," said her ex-boyfriend, turning to face her with an icy smile.

# CHAPTER TWENTY-THREE

## The Devil You Know

"You?" SHE SAID. *"You?"*

"No need to be rude. You could at least pretend to be pleased to see me, for old times' sake."

"Why?! The last time I saw you, I told you to..."

"...to go to hell. Fair enough. Did that, and yet here you are. Anyone would think you were following me."

"Oh, you're funny." Alice brushed her hair away from her face and looked Rob up and down. "So. You're my guide."

"Unless you want to go alone? But I'm telling you, you won't get far." He nodded in the direction of the gates. They really were very big.

"Wait. You don't really think I'm just going to waltz into hell with one of the Fallen, do you? Because that's what you are, isn't it?"

"Sure. I'll just go get one of the others. Who'd you prefer? Purson? He's a big fan of your new friends – I'm sure he'd be thrilled to see you. Or what about Xaph...?" He smiled as she recoiled at Xaphan's name. "Of course. You two have met already, haven't you? I forgot." He folded his arms. "Because that's the problem, isn't it? It's not that you've got to rely on one of us for help – and I know that's got to hurt, right, princess? – it's that you've got to rely on *me*. So let's just get this out the way now. Give me your best shot."

"You'd love that, wouldn't you? If I made this all about you?"

"Fine. Have it your way."

He turned away, apparently unconcerned, and Alice's anger, so well controlled until then, exploded out of her.

"And that's all you have to say for yourself? I should have known. I mean, I always thought you were just stupid, selfish... pick a personality trait. It never once occurred to me that you were actually out-and-out *evil*."

"Evil? Look at me, Alice. Do I really look evil to you?"

He held out his arms and spun slowly round. He did have a point. Rob had never looked particularly menacing. He was as tall and just as skinny as Alice remembered, with a face that could have been handsome were it not so pinched, rather like all the Fallen that Alice had met. Maybe it was a family resemblance. But suddenly, knowing what he was – what he *really* was – made a lot of sense. He watched her eyeing him. "Let me be clear: I never made you do anything you didn't already want to do. I couldn't. Still can't. That's not how it works. Think of us as... enablers. We just help people to make the choice that benefits us the most. Don't take it personally. It's just business."

"'Just business'. I bet you say that to all the girls."

"Actually..."

"Say another word and I'll kill you," she snapped, holding up a hand. "Seriously."

"I'd like to see you try." There was a taunt in his voice, and she screwed her hands into tight fists, refusing to rise to it. It must have shown in her face, because after a moment, he made a dismissive sound and sniffed. "Whatever. Look, you need me and I'm supposed to help you. So let's just get on with this, alright? I'm not the bad guy – whatever they've told you. Whatever you think you know." He pointed at the gate ahead of them. "You think this is where I wanted to spend forever?"

"Not the bad guy? Quite apart from being an unutterable

shit, are you telling me that you Fell by mistake? All this, it's just a great big misunderstanding?" Her voice rose and she lunged forward, grabbing his wrist and pulling back his sleeve. She was looking for the brand, but what she saw stopped her in her tracks. "Jesus Christ."

The ground heaved beneath them, pitching her into him and sending them both sprawling on the frost-covered rock.

"You want to watch what you say down here," said Rob as he stood up and brushed himself down.

Alice simply sat on the ground and watched as the surface of the stone rippled like water around her. It might have been her imagination, but for a second she could have sworn she saw *something* there: the shape of a face pressing up from beneath. Either way, it was gone and the rock settled. It was just rock. She pointed at Rob's arm. "What happened to you?"

"This? Nothing." He cradled his arm, rubbing at the wrist, but Alice was dragging at his sleeve again.

"Nothing? That's not nothing." She jabbed at the place where the brand should be, and which was instead covered by a tangled web of scar tissue. The top of his wrist was swollen, puffed out to two or three times its original size, and blackened, scabbed. The underside of his hand was no better; worse still, an untidy hole had punched through his flesh there, as though a spike had been forced out from under the skin.

He yanked his arm back, pulling his sleeve down to cover as much of it as possible. "Leave it, Alice."

"I want to know what..." she said, reaching for him again, but he cut her off, drawing sharply away, his eyes narrowed.

"Take your hands off me, half-breed."

His voice echoed off the gate, off the floor, off the corridor behind her, and she realised he wasn't Rob-the-ex any longer. He never had been. He was one of the Fallen, and everything had been a lie.

Somehow, it helped.

"Half-breed? That's really nice. That the kind of man you are?"

"You forget: I'm not a man."

"No, you're not, are you. So who are you? Really?"

"Abbadona..." He opened his wings and rattled them at her as if to prove his point. Wings that, she realised, must have been there all along, hidden from her, just like they were hidden from the rest of the world. But now she could *see*...

"...And here's the deal: I take you in, you do what you need to do and get out. When you report back to whoever-it-is that's pulling your strings, you tell them I held up my end. That's it. You see, you're my ticket out of here."

"Am I, now? Pleased to meet you."

She held out her hand and he laughed. It wasn't a particularly kind laugh, but it died away when he saw the sigil on the back of her wrist, glimmering and glittering and flashing like fire, even in the cold blue of hell.

"So. You want to get out? Then you'd better take me in."

And she walked past him, straight towards the gate.


"You know, people aren't normally so keen to get in here," he said, loping after her. He stopped just behind her and she looked up at the gate. And up. And up.

"It does stop, right?" she asked over her shoulder.

He shrugged. "Beats me. Certainly doesn't open."

"It doesn't open? Then how..."

"Magic," he whispered in her ear. She felt his breath roll across her cheek and she recoiled.

"You're not remotely amusing. How?"

"I told you: magic." He pointed ahead to a spot at the side of the gate, where rock met... Alice felt her stomach churn... where rock met bone. The gate was built of bones: thousands of them; hundreds of thousands, stacked one upon another as high as she could see and bound together with rope that oozed unpleasantly. To the right of them – where he was pointing – the rockface was covered in a thick sheet of ice. Although, as they drew closer to it, it looked more and more like it was nothing *but* ice...

Alice's jaw dropped. She was looking at a waterfall: a frozen waterfall, and the ice was moving – slowly, yes, but it was definitely moving; flowing down into a crack in the rock in front of her. "That's the way in?"

"Tell me, Alice, what do you think the gate there is for?"

"To keep the Fallen... to keep you in."

"Then it doesn't do a very good job, does it? Who do you think built it?"

"I don't know." She fidgeted uncomfortably. She had a nasty feeling she did actually know, but she didn't want to put the thought that was rattling round her head into words. If she did *that*, it made this an even worse idea.

"Did it ever occur to you that we might have made the Bone-Built Gate ourselves? And that rather than keeping us in, the whole point of it is to keep the Descendeds *out?*"

"Not really, no."

She'd been right: hearing it out loud definitely made things worse. Luckily, he was too busy feeling pleased with himself to notice, running his hand over what looked a little too much like a thigh bone at the edge of the gate.

"The Bone-Built Gate can only be opened by Lucifer, in the flesh, from the inside. And the only way to get inside is through here."

He nodded towards the waterfall, and as he did, the creeping flow of the ice shifted and pressed towards him. Alice stared as the ice bulged, then began to shape itself into two arms; arms which reached out for the Fallen. It was familiar, too familiar, and Alice felt fear rising in her throat. The arms. Her father's death. She bit her lip, hoping Rob couldn't tell what was going through her mind, but he seemed far too interested in watching the hands coming towards him. He let them get almost close enough to touch him, then stepped aside, shaking his head.

"She never gives up. Don't let her get hold of you."

"Why?"

"Because she won't let go again, and then it's curtains for you" – he drew a finger across his neck – "unless, of course, you can breathe ice."

He tossed something towards Alice and she automatically caught it. It was a coin. Small, silver. It had obviously once been stamped with something, but the design had long worn off and now the surface was almost smooth.

"What's this?"

"Pays for your passage." He threw his own coin into the gap into the rock, and the frozen waterfall peeled away like a curtain. "Should keep her happy."

He vanished into the ice and it closed behind him, leaving Alice behind. She turned the coin over in her hand.

"This is such a bad idea," she muttered to herself as she flipped it into the gap.

Just as it had done for Rob – Abbadona – whatever it was he called himself now – the ice opened up in front of her. It looked dark inside, and it was cold; she could feel the chill rolling towards her in waves. As she stepped into it, it snapped shut behind her. There was little light, and what there was was washed-out, dim, but she could just make out a pathway ahead. A step at a time, she edged through the passage, turning slightly to avoid the walls. It was barely wide enough for her to walk through, and the ice creaked alarmingly overhead. She had lost count of the steps she had taken – and there was still no end or exit in sight – when it occurred to her that this could be a trap. After all, she had no idea where she was going and no guarantee she would be safe... but then she remembered the scars where his brand should be. What had happened to him? And what had happened to his brand? It was almost like it had been burned away...

A sudden sensation of deep, deep cold made her turn around, and then leap back. A hand was stretching out of the ice towards her, the fingers curling as if to grab at her hair. Alice squealed and ducked, narrowly avoiding the other hand coming at her from the side. Now on her hands and knees, fingers stinging from the chill of the freezing stone, she slid along the floor, and found herself tumbling out through a gap in the ice and into the light again.

Abbadona leaned over her. "Nearly catch you, did she?"

"You knew that would happen?" Alice scraped herself off the floor.

He shrugged. "I did warn you she never gave up. Charon's not fond of angels, not even half-breeds."

"You're an arsehole."

"Really?" He shot an amused glance over at her, and scratched his nose. "You're going to have to do better than that. This is hell, sweetheart. I get called worse things than that before breakfast. Now get yourself together. Where we're headed, Charon is the least of your worries."

# CHAPTER TWENTY-FOUR

## The Plains of the Damned

ALICE'S BREATH CLOUDED out of her and hung, a little disconcertingly, above her head, like a halo. It was cold here, so very cold, and her eyes prickled as they started to freeze over. She blinked hard, and tried her best to ignore the quiet crackling sound.

"Of course. This is hell. Why wouldn't your eyes freeze open?" she muttered under her breath.

Abbadona raised an eyebrow at her. "When you're done?"

"What? It's just... It's so cold."

"That's because it's hell. As opposed to, say, Maui." He watched as she pulled her coat closer around her, wrapping it as tightly as it would go. "It won't do any good, you know."

"What won't?"

"Your pretty little jacket. This cold, the hell-chill, it'll get into your bones. Get into your soul, if you let it. The longer you're down here... well. But they didn't warn you about that, did they?"

"Would you just shut up? Where are you supposed to be taking me, anyway – seeing as you're the one with the plan?"

"Down there." He pointed ahead of them.

They were standing at the top of a cliff that jutted out into an enormous cavern. The revolting bone gateway was some distance behind them, and Alice couldn't even begin to see where the passage they had taken ended. The tops of the gates were still lost in the space above them and there was no sign of the roof or of the side walls – just the cliff on which they stood and then endless blackness. Except...

She took a few steps closer to the edge of the cliff and peered over. Immediately wishing she hadn't, she stepped back and tried to clear her head. The drop was staggering – but that wasn't the whole of it. She had looked at what was down there, and she had seen it. Really *seen* it. More than that, she had felt it.

Below was the floor of the cavern. It stretched away into the distance and, as far as she could see, it was covered with people. At first, she didn't know what they were, the shapes on the rock: they ran the length and breadth of the plateau, thousands of them in regimented lines. Hundreds of thousands of them, frozen bolt-straight like an army of the dead. But they weren't dead, not really. They were alive, and they *hurt*. For the first time since Mallory's little boot-camp, Alice's skin burned. She could feel the fire scratching away inside her, looking for a way out... She could control it now, though; she knew she could. Hoped she could.

"Plains of the Damned," said Abbadona, leaning over her shoulder. "They go on forever."

"Who are they?"

"Who aren't they? All human life is here. Everyone who's ever ended up in hell – bar a few illustrious exceptions, of course – is here. All getting the five-star treatment. No expense spared."

"What does that mean?"

"Come on down and take a closer look. I'll show you."

Alice shivered again, and she told herself it was just the place, the temperature; the relentless, numbing cold. But it wasn't, and she knew it: it was his smile. It was the look behind his eyes. It was the way he smiled when he looked at the people below.

She was afraid of him. And worse, he knew it.

"The ones who were taken..."

"They're here too. Where else would they be? They're just as damned as the rest of them. All did it to themselves, you know."

"But you *took* them. They shouldn't even be here!"

"Now, you're assuming that they wouldn't have ended up here anyway. Which is a mistake." He sniffed. "Never assume. Didn't your little angel friends teach you that?"

There were steps. More steps. She couldn't stop the groan escaping, but he either didn't hear or he chose to ignore her. *He's enjoying this*, she thought, and if it wasn't for the fact that his brand had been burned off, she might have been even more unhappy about the position she found herself in. But she had agreed – had, in fact, chosen to do this – and he was hoping to get *something* from her – or from the angels, anyway – in exchange. So she followed.

The stairway was shorter than it had at first appeared. From the cliff, the Plains seemed to start far below, and yet it took a surprisingly short time to reach them. Knowing how tricky the Fallen could be – after all, wasn't that why she was there? – Alice decided to accept that somewhere, there was an illusion happening, and that for the moment she didn't need to know exactly what it was and where it might be. It would only make her head hurt, and she was already having to concentrate hard enough on not catching fire. The closer she got to the Plains, the more insistent the itching in her skin became and the more she had to concentrate on not noticing it, on balling her hands into fists and biting her lip and breathing, above all, *breathing*.

She hesitated on the last step. Abbadona turned and flashed that smile of his at her. "What's wrong, Alice? Worried you're in a little over your head?"

"Not exactly."

Her words came out through gritted teeth as she fought to keep control. The ends of her hair sparked gently and she could almost smell the fire. Her head hurt, her body hurt...

even her teeth hurt, and there were suddenly voices in her head, chattering in a hundred languages.

"I can't wait all day. Well, theoretically I *can*, but I won't."

"Really? I thought you were just about made of time." She swallowed the heat and the pain back down and stepped onto the Plains.

"It's not time that's the killer. Not down here, not right now. It's the others, if you're seen, and if Lucifer finds out about this" – he lifted his damaged wrist – "you can't even imagine what he'll do."

"I can. I'm picturing it right now, actually," she smiled sweetly at him.

"Nice."

"For me, yes. For you? Not so much."

She batted her eyelashes at him, all the while remembering the red eyes that looked out of Batarel's face in the churchyard. Abbadona stared at her, and then something seemed to occur to him.

"Wait... you've met him, haven't you? You've met the Morningstar. He spoke to you, didn't he?"

"Sort of. I think it was more an opportunity to size me up. I used to have a form-teacher at school who looked at me like that. Mrs Evans. Everyone said she was probably the devil. Maybe she was."

"Fascinating as this little detour down memory lane is, don't you think you're missing something?"

"Probably. If I knew that, I wouldn't be missing it, would I?"

"Ha-bloody-ha. Try this: why didn't he kill you?"

"What?"

"Why didn't he kill you? All he's wanted – and I do mean *all* he's wanted – for years, centuries: it's been to defeat the Descendeds. To break them. To *end* them. You're the best chance they've had yet to stop him, and you're telling me that you just walked up to him and he had a clear shot at you... then he let you walk *away*? Why?"

"Gwyn...?"

"Gwyn? Lucifer's not afraid of him; don't you go relying on that. Lucifer's not afraid of any of them. Except Mallory, perhaps. You'd have to be entirely mad not to be afraid of Mallory."

This was news to Alice. "Why?"

"Because he's insane. That's why. What do you think got him exiled in the first..." He tailed off. "You don't know what he did, do you?"

"Should I?"

"Ha!" His laugh this time was sharp. Triumphant. His wings shivered behind him as he shook his head. "Looks like your guardian angels aren't telling you everything. I wonder, has it crossed your mind what else they might not be sharing?"

He was still laughing as he walked on ahead of her, towards the frozen figures.

They stretched on, endlessly: their eyes open and iced over, staring into nowhere. Row upon row upon row of them. She stepped between the first two rows, her head feeling increasingly crowded and uncomfortable. It wasn't just that she could feel them, the people around her, it was that they looked as though they could move at any moment. just snap out of it and step away. Of course, it wasn't *likely*, but still...

The man to her left had red hair and a short, untidy beard. Lumberjack shirt, blue jeans. Barefoot. A gold ring hung around his neck on a chain and Alice found herself reaching for it. She stopped, pulling her hand back, but Abbadona nodded.

"He won't wake up, you know. He doesn't care."

He sidled off to peer at a nearby woman and Alice caught the ring between her fingers, drawing it closer. The outside was scratched and dented, the inside worn smooth. A woman's name was engraved around it, just visible, and Alice wondered where she was – whether she was here, whether she was missing him. She looked at the woman on her right: could that be her? It didn't seem likely, however hard she tried to picture them together. This one looked like she might be a bit too high-maintenance for him – designer clothes, for sure, and haircuts like that didn't come cheap. But she, too, was barefoot and her toes curled in on themselves against the cold. Her eyes were open and blank like all the others, and her make-up had been smudged; smeared, even. Just behind her stood another woman, younger, her hair tied back from her face and her brightly-coloured raincoat looking horribly out of place. A dog lead dangled from her hand, an empty collar still attached. None of them were exactly the kind of people Alice had expected to find in hell, but then it wasn't quite the hell she had expected, either.

Alice had never given much thought to hell, but she had a few ideas about it. Pitchforks sprang to mind, and horns, and fire. Somehow, heat had become an integral part of this vague mental image. But the cold? The cold was worse. Whenever she thought she was getting used to it, she breathed a little too deeply and felt it creep inside her, making her eyes water and her lungs burn. And it stayed there, the cold – twisted itself through her ribs like a weed, rooting somewhere she couldn't reach. She hoped this plan worked, and soon. Hanging around too long didn't seem like a good idea.

Something moved at the edge of her vision and she jumped, whirling towards it.

There was nothing there, just the endless rows of bodies.

Maybe she had imagined it. She was, after all, in just about the creepiest environment imaginable with no idea how she was going to get back and only a Fallen angel for a guide. It didn't exactly make for a relaxing day out. But no, there it was again: a movement at the very corner of her eye, barely seen, and this time, she *heard* it. It was a whispering, whimpering sound: almost inaudible, barely human. For the first time since she had walked into hell, Alice cracked, and taking a deep breath, she opened her hand. The flame was there in an instant: shifting across her palm and rolling around her fingers. It felt good, like release. The only sign Alice had that these bodies were still occupied was the pain rolling off them, the terror. They were all so frightened, and despite their numbers, they were all so alone – and Alice was standing there, soaking in it. Drowning in it. Letting even the slightest portion of it out meant she had space inside to breathe again, to think.

There was a rattle of wings behind her and she looked round to see Abbadona nose-to-nose with the redheaded man. Without taking his eyes off him, he said, "It's only the Ghasts. They're nothing." He blinked, and was about to turn away when he spotted the fire boiling inside Alice's hand, and his eyebrows shot up. "Fuck me. Look at you now. Really are one of them, aren't you?" And he took a step back, apparently measuring her up.

Just like that, their own personal balance tipped, and while she was still afraid of him, now he was almost certainly afraid of her too.

"Here's a suggestion," he said, his voice suddenly wheedling. "How about you point that somewhere else, and I'll take you on past the Ghasts?"

"Ghasts?"

"They're…" he paused, considering his answer. "Well, once upon a time, they were you."

He beckoned to her, and hurried through the lines of people, weaving in and out, back and forth, then stopping so sharply that she almost piled into him, getting a mouthful of spiny feathers into the bargain. She spat the taste out of her mouth: soot and oil and dust. Peering past his wings, she saw what he was talking about.

It was a figure, of sorts; hunched over and lurching between the ranks ahead of them. It was grey, all over – its clothing, its hair… even its skin. As Alice watched, it stopped in front of a man in a torn suit and ran its hand across his face, skimming his eyes and brow with its fingertips. Abbadona leaned back slightly and whispered to her through his wings. "The Ghasts keep an eye on the Damned. They tend their dreams, make sure things are running smoothly."

"But what *are* they?"

"I told you: they used to be you. They're half-borns. Only they work for us."

"They joined the Fallen?"

"What? Everyone's entitled to make a choice. I promise you, there's plenty of people who'd rather die than be stuck with Gwyn."

"Can't imagine why," she said quietly. Then, to him, "And you'd be able to help with that, no doubt."

"Not exactly. You see, the problem is the Ghasts are trapped here, just like we are. They're only half-borns, so they don't last long. What you're looking at is a Ghast who's been down here a while. You remember what I said about the hell-chill? *That's* what it does to a half-born." He nodded towards the shuffling figure, which must have heard him, because it suddenly turned to look at them. Or at least, turned its face towards them, as Alice realised it couldn't see them, however hard it tried. Its features were ruined: the mouth twisted, the cheeks sunken, and where its eyes should be were two bloody balls of ice. It stared at them with its empty eyes, then as suddenly as it had turned, it looked away. Abbadona shivered. "Give me the creeps, they do. But you stay down here long enough…"

"That's what it'll do to me?" Her voice felt thick and claggy, and the cold sensation that settled in her stomach had nothing to do with the temperature.

"Eventually. Not the eyes, though. The Descendeds did that."

"Wait, the *angels?* The angels put out their eyes? Not the Fallen?"

"What can I tell you? They don't like it when people don't want to play on their team. And you can always rely on Gabriel for a bit of old-school wrath and vengeance." He watched as the Ghast ambled on down the line, stopping here and there to peer at one of the faces it passed. "We should try and avoid running into too many of them," he whispered. "Just like everyone else down here, they've got a direct line to Lucifer. He doesn't generally listen to them, but if enough of them start chirping up, we're going to have a problem. Or you are, anyway. I'm only taking you through a couple of levels. After that, you're on your own. That's the Twelve's turf down there, and I'm just not that stupid."

"Gentleman, aren't you?"

"I try my best." He dropped into a mock-bow and stalked off.

Alice stared after him, past the people crowded onto the Plains. Even as they dreamed, their fear spilled out around them. It inched its way towards her like dark smoke, and the single consolation she had was that the fire busily raging inside her kept the hell-chill at bay. Most of it, anyway. She followed Abbadona, who – despite everything he had said about keeping a low profile – looked for all the world as though he was out for an afternoon stroll; his hands deep in his pockets, his shoulders back, and... "Are you *seriously* whistling?"

"Just as demanding as you always were, aren't you?" He spun on his heel and jabbed his finger towards her. "You remember, Alice, you're on my ground now. I know the rules down here, and you don't. All it takes is one word from me..."

"And what? I'm willing to bet that you've got a lot more to lose than I have. Who do you think would be more valuable to Lucifer: a half-born from Michael's choir, or one little Fallen who's snuck out and done a deal with the angels? He's got hundreds of you, but as you say, there's only one of me."

Abbadona's mouth opened, then closed again and he scowled at her. "You want to be careful talking like that. Dangerous road to start down. It's that kind of attitude that lands you somewhere like this."

"Thanks for the advice. You understand why I don't believe a single thing you say, right?"

"Believe me or not; doesn't make it any less true," he said. "But whatever. I'm done standing around chatting. Besides, the next level's my favourite. That's the really *fun* one. This is just the warm-up." His eyes twinkled at her, and it struck her that he meant it. He didn't want to get out of hell because it was hell. He *liked* it. He just didn't like everything that came with it.

"You're a monster." The words caught in her throat. The world spun, and it was full of lies; of pain and loss and hate and fear. He pulled a face, pouting. Mocking her.

"Monster? Really? I haven't even shown you where we keep the kids yet."

# CHAPTER TWENTY-FIVE
## Knock, Knock

VIN STARED UP at the Bone-Built Gate and let out a low whistle. "If I didn't know better, I'd think they didn't want to see us. I'm actually kind of hurt." His head tipped back as he tried to follow it all the way to the top, but he quickly gave up. "They might as well have just hung a big sign out the front that says 'Fuck off.'"

"I think they did," said Mallory, running his hand across one of the bones. He sat down in front of the gate and stared at it, glumly, one hand reaching under his jacket for his flask.

Vin paced up and down behind him. "I thought we weren't supposed to be here: those rules you mentioned...?"

"Screw the rules." The cold had even crept into Mallory's drink, making him shiver as it went down. He didn't enjoy the feeling. And no, they weren't supposed to be there, but it didn't exactly seem as though the Descendeds were playing by the rules any more, either.


"YOU'RE NEEDED."

"Am I, now?" Mallory had not been surprised by Gwyn's voice coming from the other side of his room, nor by the lack of warning before his appearance... or even a simple greeting. What did surprise him when he looked up from his book was that Gwyn was in armour, his wings bristling with sparks. "What's this? Suit at the cleaners?"

"I said you're needed."

"And I heard you. What you didn't tell me is where, or why." He folded his arms.

"Are you challenging me?"

"No, I'm just waiting for you to tell me what you want. You could start by explaining... that." He pointed at the armour. "Off to war, are we?"

"Yes."

"What?" Mallory paled. "Are you saying what I think you're saying?"

"She's on her way, Mallory. It won't be long before someone notices her. They'll all be watching."

"And you know how thrilled I am about that."

"You say you have faith in her? Good. Then you don't need to worry about her. You're confident Alice can complete her task, and if you are, then so am I. But that alone is not enough. This was always going to be a two-pronged attack. With Alice on the inside, we have the perfect opportunity..."

"We can't destroy hell, Gwyn. It's impossible. Lucifer's too deeply embedded."

"Maybe not. But we can certainly inflict enough damage to keep them occupied licking their wounds for a while."

"This was supposed to be about the balance; about restoring things to the way they should be, not trying to tip it in our favour. It can't be done."

"Yes, it can. Don't you see? *Now*, it can. Think, Mallory. Think what we could do!"

"No."

"No?"

"I won't have any part in this. It's wrong. You *know* it is." Mallory picked up his book again, but Gwyn clicked his fingers and it crumbled to dust in his hands. Mallory sighed. "Great.

Now I'm never going to know if they get together at the end."
He brushed his palms together and stood up, looking Gwyn up
and down. "I don't know what you're thinking, Gwyn, but I'm
asking you not to do this. Please."

"The orders come from Gabriel."

"Of course they do. There's no-one else stupid enough to
come up with a full-on assault on hell. Except you, maybe. You
don't think they'll be expecting us?"

"Knowing there's a half-born running around inside hell
should focus their attention elsewhere relatively quickly. And
believe me, Mallory, they *will* know. However careful she is,
Lucifer will sniff her out. The rest is up to her." He narrowed
his eyes at the Earthbound. "So I hope you trained her well."
He paused, examining his fingernails. Against his armour, the
gesture looked absurd. "If you have a problem, of course, you
can always take it up with Gabriel…"

"That won't be necessary." Mallory picked up his gun, tucking
it into his belt. Even across the room, he could feel Gwyn's
satisfaction. "Tell me, Gwyn: you want to take the war to
hell, *into* hell? What happens to the ones who die down there?
Because you know the Fallen won't be kind. They don't even
have to work at it to kill us, if we go in there. It doesn't matter
if we're Earthbound, Descended or even Archangel. And then
there's the rest of it: get stuck down there and death would be
a blessing, so what happens to the ones who get left behind?"

"They get left behind. But if we take the Gate, we even the
odds. They will have no shelter."

"Neither will we."

"You're not listening. In hell, we have no shelter. If they kill
us, we die. But destroy the Gate…"

"The same thing happens to them. No reboots, no do-overs."

"Quite."

"But they'll be desperate. And there's a lot of them – the
damage they could do…"

"Collateral damage. Acceptable losses, given the stakes. And if you're weak enough to let the Fallen take you, I'd argue that you deserve everything you get."

"That seems a little... cruel."

"Remind me, Mallory: isn't it you that's always talking about duty; about your job as a soldier? Yes? So here's a suggestion: go do it, before I take your wings for good."

"So, err, how are we going to do this, then?" Vin had wrapped his wings around himself as best he could. Anything to keep out the cold. The tips of the feathers were slowly turning brittle with frost.

Mallory sat and stared at the Gate, cradling his gun in his lap. "I have no idea."

# CHAPTER TWENTY-SIX

## Other People

"OH, LOOK. MORE steps. Goody!"

"I'm sorry. If you'd called ahead, we'd have had lifts installed."

"Wait. You hear that sound? That's my sides, splitting."

Alice rolled her eyes. She was bored with Abbadona's barbed comments, she was tired and she was cold. She had no idea where she was going, what she was going to do when she got there, or even what kind of place 'there' might be. It was all starting to feel a little...

"Hopeless?" he said, glancing back over his shoulder at her. "That's the angel juju wearing off. You see, you spend long enough with them and the world gets all shiny. Anything's possible when you see it through an angel's eyes, and you're an empath, aren't you? So you get a double-dose. And now you're down *here*..."

"Nothing seems possible. I get it, thanks. I'm just sick of all these sodding *steps*." She peered over the edge of the staircase. "How much further?"

"Not far now."

"I can't see anything down there,"

"I know. I told you this level's fun."

"What?"

"You'll see. Sort of."

He chuckled, and turned his back on her again.

\*    \*    \*

HE WAS RIGHT, though: she had felt so confident, so sure of herself. They had told her she could do this, and she'd believed them. Mallory had made her believe them. But the further she went, the colder she got, and the more uncertain she became. What if they had been wrong? It was possible, wasn't it? What if, for all their talk, she was just Alice, and there was nothing special about her at all? What if she failed?

The stairway ended abruptly, and she found herself standing on another sheet of rock. Abbadona was staring ahead, looking for something – although what, Alice couldn't make out. She couldn't make *anything* out, as it happened. Ahead of them, there was nothing but blackness. Just complete, total and utter dark.

"I told you this would be fun," he said.

"What am I looking at, exactly?"

"You ever heard the phrase 'dark night of the soul'?"

"Vaguely."

"Come off it, Alice. Of course you have. I remember your living room. All those books. You grew up with theology coming out of your ears."

"So? What's that got to do with anything?"

"This is it."

"It's dark."

"Precisely. And you have to go through it."

"That's stupid."

"I don't make the rules." He shrugged. "I'll be a few steps ahead of you. There's a path that cuts through to the next level, but you'll have to stay close. If you get lost, you're staying lost. And before you even think about lighting up," he pointed to her hands, "don't. Just don't."

"I think I can handle a little bit of dark. I'm not four, you know."

"Let's see how you feel when you get to the other side. *If* you make it to the other side."

He sounded entirely too smug, and Alice found herself weighing the possibility of setting fire to him against that of punching him in the face. Both felt like they would be equally satisfying, but instead she gritted her teeth and curled her fingers tightly against her palms.

The first few steps were fine; a little unsteady, perhaps, but fine. As soon as her foot touched the floor for the next, however, it was as though a curtain fell around her, boxing her into a dark so thick she could almost touch it. Nor was it just an *absence* of light; this was a visible darkness, with a presence all its own. Quite without realising it, she stopped walking.

Hearing a whispering sound behind her, she spun round. There was nothing there, just more of the same darkness. Again, there was a noise at her back and she turned again... and again... and again – until, with a horrible crawling sensation, she realised she had no idea which way she was facing. She opened her mouth to call for Abbadona, but no sound came out. She could *feel* the dark rushing into her mouth and throat, clogging it with velvet. She retched, and forced her mouth shut.

The whispers in the dark continued. Ghasts, she thought. It must be Ghasts; although, given closer consideration, that wasn't such a comforting idea. The noises swirled about her, a current of sounds, and the more she listened to them, the more she thought she could make the voices out, pick out the words. "Disappointed," said one. "Disappointed, disappointed, disappointed..."

"...Not responding to the treatment as well as we'd hoped..."

"...Let me down. What would your mother say?"

She would have known that last voice anywhere. It was her father's.

Suddenly, she was nineteen – no, twenty – again. He'd had the grace to wait until just after midnight; sitting in the back room, her head in her hands. Her clothes were crumpled and smelled dirty, and there was grime under her fingernails. He paced up and down in front of her, saying things she barely heard and barely cared about. All she was interested in was making her headache go away. Possibly after she'd found a way to stop the churning in her stomach, or the shaking in her hands. Or both.

"...So much potential, Alice. If only you'd *focus*..."

"...Not what I was hoping for..."

"...Just look at yourself...."

"...Trying our best to help, but you need to let us..."

"...Given you everything, and all you've done is thrown it back in my face..."

"...Ungrateful... Ashamed..."

"...Recommend another course, a different medication..."

THE VOICES WERE coming thick and fast. No longer whispers, they filled Alice's ears, filled her head. There was nothing now except for the storm that raged around her in the thick, silky darkness.

"...Don't even recognise you any more..."

She braced herself for what she knew was coming. It wouldn't be long now.

"...Give anything, *anything* to trade you for her... Don't understand why they took her away and left me with *you*..."

Alice sank to the floor, burning like a comet, and she was lost.

AND THEN A hand reached through the fire and the darkness and took hold of her wrist, pulling her to her feet. The voices were gone and the only thing left was a wispy strand of black mist that caught at Alice's ankles. Abbadona shook his hand up and down, looking wounded; already the fresh burns on his hand were turning into great shining welts. "Fun, huh?"

Alice coughed. "You've got a weird idea of fun."

"Welcome to the Dark House. It's always been my favourite."

He waved an arm behind him, and Alice saw huddled figures slumped on the ground, scattered here and there across the floor of hell, just as she had been. Some of them were bone-thin, the skin stretched across their faces and limbs, their mouths ripped open in mute despair. "All in their own private little rooms, just like you were," he said. "I did warn you to stay close, but you don't listen. You *never* listen, and now you've gone and attracted attention to *us*, what with that little flame-up, and it won't be long before one of the Twelve puts two and two together. Let's just hope it's Jeqon: he's thick as shit, so he's bound to make fourteen."

"If you'd at least warned me..."

"If I'd warned you, it wouldn't have been nearly so entertaining. But you better learn to put a stopper in that fire of yours, or we're never getting out of here. Not in the same number of pieces we came in, anyway. You coming, or what?"

# CHAPTER TWENTY-SEVEN
## Blood of Angels

THE DARK HOUSE, as Abbadona called it, had left Alice feeling distinctly uneasy – although, she thought, she had probably got off lightly. She didn't dare ask how long the people she had seen there had been trapped on that level, or whether they would ever leave. How did hell work, anyway? Did you just get put somewhere, and that was it, or did you get shifted round on some kind of awful conveyor belt system? She stopped walking.

"You know, I get the feeling something's gone a bit wrong in my life."

"Talk about stating the obvious." Abbadona appeared to be chewing gum. Alice fervently hoped it was gum.

"You are, as ever, the fount of sanity. I mean that I've actually started to think about how this place works. That's not... well, it's not *normal*, thinking like that, is it?"

"Hardly. But then you're not exactly normal, are you, sweet pea?"

"Don't call me that."

"Oh, come on. I'm just trying to have a little fun."

"See, there's that word again."

"What word?"

"Fun. You keep saying it. How can you think any of this is 'fun'? Did you see those people back there? Any of them? What did they do, exactly, to deserve this?"

"Uhh, hello? Hell? What do you think?" He snapped his fingers and a hazy white shape appeared in the air in front of them. Alice raised an eyebrow. "What's that? Hell's version of CCTV?"

"Shut up."

A blurred face had formed in the centre of the square, its eyes closed as though in sleep. Abbadona peered at it, then shook his head and made a hard flicking gesture with his left hand, so hard that Alice was sure she heard a bone pop. The face zipped away, only to be replaced by a new one... still apparently unsatisfied, he flicked that away too. And the one after, and the one after that, until he had scrolled through what must have been hundreds. Finally, he settled on a face that belonged to an old man, eyes closed as before but frowning.

"This is Adam. Not *that* Adam, obviously. He's one of the residents of the Dark House, and he will be for a very long time to come. Looks harmless, doesn't he? Someone's granddad, I'll bet. Used to bounce the kids on his knee, then fall asleep on the sofa and snore on a Sunday afternoon. Lost his glasses a lot, and could whistle Beethoven."

"You're going somewhere with this, aren't you? I can tell."

"You catch on quick. Well, lovely old Adam here started off small: the odd squirrel, a rabbit, the neighbour's cat. Next it was dogs: stray ones, then stolen ones, then ones he went out and bought for the purpose. He carried on like that for years, mildly unhappy but – like all of humanity – destined to keep plodding along in the same old rut, until he came across a kid, maybe fifteen or so, sleeping rough one winter. He bought her a couple of hot drinks, made sure she got the occasional meal... just a kind old man looking out for a little girl. And then, one night while she was asleep, he came for her, didn't he?"

"I don't really want to hear..."

"But you asked, Alice. You asked what someone like him might be doing in hell, what right we have to punish him. He butchered that girl, just like he butchered the three that came after her. And then he thought he could just put it all away: tuck everything he'd done – everything he'd ever been – inside a big box, put a lid on it and become someone new. Become someone's grandfather, maybe. But, you see, we don't worry about who you are when you come to us. We're more interested in who you *were*. And he, I'm afraid to say, was not a very nice man."

"So what happened to her? That first girl?"

"Oh, she's here somewhere too. Heroin addict. We don't like them at *all*."

Abbadona smiled broadly and snapped his fingers again. The image vanished. Alice only wished the ones in her head were as easy to forget.

"You're going to need these." He handed her two small balls of something. They were sticky and left dark oily streaks on her palm.

"Now I feel bad I didn't get you anything. Not when you've given me this lovely" – she peered at it – "earwax?"

"You must be feeling better. Don't worry: that won't last long."

He pulled another lump of the stuff out of his pocket and split it in half, rolling it into two small balls. Alice looked at the stuff in her hand, cautiously. She'd seen it before, somewhere down here, or something very like it. She vaguely remembered something about a lamp... actually, it was *very* vague. Which was odd, because it hadn't been that long ago, had it? She shook off the thought, and watched with curiosity as Abbadona continued to roll the balls around his hand, then stuck one in each of his ears. And she was about to ask what he was doing, when she saw the first spider-thin thread creep out of his left ear. It hinged its way out from deep inside, lengthening all the time, and felt its way around the edge of his jaw. Finally, it latched onto his skin, burrowing in as another thread shot out of his ear and followed it... then another, and another until his whole ear was covered by a solid-looking black web.

Alice gulped. He nodded towards her hands. "Your turn."

"You want me to put this" – she held it up – "in my ears? In. My. Ears. My actual ears. You want me to put the spiderwax in my ears and let them get all sealed up?"

"Basically."

"What for?"

"It's going to get a little... noisy. Stopping up your ears will protect you."

"Doesn't seem to be doing much for you. You can still hear me, can't you?"

"Pardon?"

"You're not funny."

"Look, Alice. You can come at this two ways. Either I'm lying, and if you put those in, you'll lose your hearing – or I'm telling the truth, and if you don't put them in, you'll lose your mind. It's your choice." He stuck his hands in his pockets. Alice frowned, then shrugged.

"When you put it like that..."

IT WASN'T A pleasant sensation. The little balls somehow wriggled further down inside her ears than she could ever have pushed them, and her mind flashed with panic as she realised she was never going to be able to get them out. She felt the threads weave together and anchor into her jaw: a series of tugs and sickly popping sounds, and then it was done. Resisting the urge to touch the sides of her face, she glared at Abbadona.

"I'm not happy about this."

"I know. That's what makes it perfect."

"And how come I can still hear you?"

"Don't worry about it. I could explain, but... well, frankly, you wouldn't understand. So let's stick with saying it works and you'll be just fine."

She couldn't resist any longer, and poked at her ear. As the tip of her finger touched the surface of the web, it moved, and she retched.

"*Really* not happy."

"You'll thank me when it stops your brain from running out your ears. Just don't ask me what it is."

"What is it?"

"You're so predictable."

"Seriously. What is it?"

"Blood. Mix it up with naphtha, and it's pretty much what makes everything run down here."

"You can stop now." She held up her hand. "Before I throw up all over you."

"Wouldn't be the first time," he said with a sniff.

Ahead of them was a door; just a door, standing on its own with nothing to the sides of it, and apparently nothing behind. It was painted a cheerful sort of yellow. The doorknob had a daisy on it. Alice walked around it.

"Through the door, right?"

"You're catching on." He laid his hand on the doorknob and she saw him suck in a deep breath.

The blast that hit her as he opened the door knocked the air out of her, and forced her back a step as though someone had swung a tremendous weight directly at her chest. There was no sound, just pressure. Immense pressure, all of it coming through the yellow door.

Alice did not like the look of this at all.


"Now, don't you say I never take you places," Abbadona said, peeling the black web from his ear.

Alice cleared her own ears and sagged to the ground next to him. Whatever that had been, it hadn't been fun. Every step had been like walking through a hurricane full of hammers, and her whole body ached. Her eyes felt loose in their sockets, as though they might roll out if she moved too quickly, and her ribs seemed to be knocking against each other. She resolved not to move at all for the foreseeable future, and instead settled down to listen to the gentle thumping that had started inside her head. If she kept still enough and lay down, closed her eyes, it almost didn't hurt at all. *Almost.*

It was surprisingly comfortable on the rock, and at least the strange flat light that was everywhere in hell wasn't still making her feel like her eyeballs were being turned inside out. She had even got used to the cold. Not before time, either, she thought. After all, she had been down here... And she paused, scratching around in her memory. How long *had* she been down here? Had she slept? There didn't seem to be any night or day, just that endless pale light, filling the caverns of hell. She hadn't eaten, either, and she wasn't hungry, so it couldn't have been that long, could it?

Alice's eyes snapped open as she sat up. She was supposed to be doing something, but she suddenly couldn't remember what. There had been something important, she knew that much. It was important, and she had promised she would do it; promised she *could* do it, and now it was gone like ash on the air. Where her memories should be, there was only fog: a grey blanket that threatened to smother her if she poked around underneath it. Puzzlement gave way to panic, and then – slowly – to confusion. Perhaps it hadn't been all that important after all. If it had, surely she couldn't have forgotten it, could she?

"It's got you, hasn't it?"

"Got me?"

"The hell-chill. It makes you forget. You having a hard time keeping your head on straight? Remembering things?"

"I'm fine. It's just... there's something..."

"Something you're supposed to be doing. I'll say. But you've lasted longer than I thought you would, I'll give you that." He stood back with his arms folded and stared at her. "It wears off once you get across the river."

"What does?"

"Oh, you're going to be a bundle of chuckles the rest of the way, aren't you?" He dropped down to a crouch and leaned in close. "Alice, do you remember?"

"I... I don't know. There's a thing, I know that. A thing I should do, should remember to do. I..." She looked up at him blankly. "Help me?"

"You had to go and ask, didn't you?" he said with a sigh, rocking back on his heels. "I'm only taking you as far as the river. After that, no deal. Besides, you'll be fine once you're on the other side." Alice had no idea what he was talking about, but he carried on anyway. "It'd be stupid to take you further than that. Worse, it'd be suicide. They'll *all* be watching for you. All of them. And if they see me with you..." He watched her rubbing at her temples and frowning. "You don't understand a thing I'm saying, do you?"

"There was something I had to do."

"Yes, yes. I know. But right now, I need you to stand up. You can do that, right?"

"But I'm comfortable."

"I know. That's the problem. If you don't get up now, you won't. Ever. That's it. Game over. Done. You're *this* close." He held his finger and thumb a hair's breadth apart. "Hell's got her hooks in you, and unless you get up and you get moving, you'll never be free. So get up. Now."

"I... I... don't...." Her eyelids were growing heavy.

"Oh, for..." he tailed off with a growl. "I swore I was over doing this." Leaning close to her, he slung her arms around his neck and picked her up, holding her tightly against his chest, his wings held out as a counterbalance. "Just so we're clear, you'd better make sure those angels of yours hold up their end of the bargain, or I'm personally going to see to it that you wish I'd left you here to rot."

\*   \*   \*

ALICE OPENED HER eyes.

She was in a boat.

This was mildly unexpected.

Alice closed her eyes again.


"ARE YOU AWAKE?" Something sharp nudged her ribs.

"I am now," she said, sitting up with a groan. The boat rocked alarmingly, and she clutched at the sides. "I feel like someone scraped out the inside of my head with a trowel."

"Close enough. Bad case of 'forgetting what you came for.' Don't look surprised. It's something of a specialty round here, and to be honest I'm surprised you lasted as long as you did. You've got some pretty good mojo working for you. But when you went down, you went like a stone. And now here we are, on the river. Or more specifically, here *I* am, taking you to the worst place I could possibly be going."

"Which is where, exactly?"

"Right smack into the middle of hell. Look."

Alice peered over the edge of the rowing boat. They were on a wide river, flowing between two almost-identical rock plateaux. She looked from one to the other, and back again, but still couldn't work out which one they had come from and which they were going to. The boat didn't seem to be moving anywhere quickly, which wasn't particularly helpful, but if she was forced to pick, Alice would have said they had come from the one on the right, and were going to the one on the left. Or maybe the other way round. While she was debating the near-imperceptible difference between the two, she let her hand drop over the side, trailing absently into the water. It prickled her skin, sending an itch shivering up the underside of her arm and into her spine. Her bones felt hot. She swallowed the feeling back down.

"I wouldn't do that if I were you," said Abbadona, and she snatched her hand back up, just as something lunged out of the water after it. She tried very hard not to pay too much attention, but whatever it was, it was dark, slimy and had a *lot* of teeth. Even that, however, didn't worry her nearly as much as the colour of the water. She held up her fingers and stared at them as they dripped thickly, darkly, redly into the boat.

"You know," she said without taking her eyes off them, "I think I can see why the angels don't like you lot."

"Every angel who ever died. Fallen. Earthbound. Descended. They've made this river what it is."

"But what's the point?"

"What?" He was staring at her, his eyes wide and his mouth twisted. "What's the *point*? The point, half-breed, is to remind you what sacrifices have been made. Some by us, some by them. The *point* is that you've been dangling your dainty little fingers in the blood of my brothers. The point is that this is what keeps hell moving, what keeps it working. Sacrifice. Sacrifice. And pain."

Staring at the river, she reached her hand towards it – and the fire was there, sparking across her fingernails. As the tips of her fingers brushed the surface, flames sprang up to meet them: four tiny pools of light that rose and fell on the darkness of the river, and Alice suddenly felt the wind on her face, felt a light settle on her. She caught the scent of the ice, of the cold and everything hidden inside it; she felt the fear and the pain and the loss and the anger, felt it boiling around her like a thunderstorm. And then, as Abbadona scrambled past her in the boat, cursing and trying to put out the still-burning spots on the river with his hands, Alice knew Mallory had been right: who else could the angels possibly have sent?

THE BOAT CAME to rest against the shore. Alice had come through the forgetfulness. She had come through the fields of hell, through the past and the cold; through the ice and the doubt and the fear, and for the first time, she felt ready. She felt *sure*.

"This is it," Abbadona said, tying the boat to an iron post. "For the record, I don't want to be here. Wasn't part of the plan, wasn't part of the deal."

"Then why are you?" she asked, turning to face him.

He met her gaze, then looked down at his feet. "Because I can't let you go alone."

"Growing a conscience?"

"Not exactly."

"What, then? You've held up your side of the bargain, haven't you?"

"And then some. You're not exactly an easy passenger, you know."

"Then...?"

"Let's just say I think I'm finally starting to see the big picture."

"You're Fallen."

"Alice, even the damned can wish for hope. You: pulling this off, getting out of here – you're mine. My last hope. You don't just abandon your hopes on the riverbank."

"Coming from anyone else, that might be deep."

"I have hidden shallows."

He skipped out of the boat and stood on the shore. "They'll be coming for you, for both of us. As soon as you set foot on the rock. They already know you're here, they just don't know where. But this is their ground. They own it. They built it. There's nowhere to hide."

"So?" Alice stepped out of the boat. For a moment, she felt nothing. Just the cold and empty darkness, but then...

It began with a single pinprick on the back of her neck. Just one, like a mosquito bite – and for a second, she was afraid she had made a mistake. But then she felt the warmth of the fire as it wrapped her in a second skin, smelled the flames as they spun around her... with every step she took, it burned brighter;

hotter and higher, her feet leaving blazing marks in the stone as she walked.

Abbadona jumped back, his face whiter than she had ever seen it.

Behind them, the river of blood burst into flame, and Alice walked on.

# CHAPTER TWENTY-EIGHT

## New Golgotha

MALLORY RAISED HIS head. "You feel that?"

"Feel what?"

"That. Something... changed." He watched a veil of dust skitter down the Gate.

"Cold. I feel cold. And I'm getting sick of the death-stare whatsherface over there is giving me."

Vin pointed at Charon, who was watching them from inside the frozen waterfall with an expression that had settled somewhere between 'cautious distrust' and 'total hatred.'

Mallory glanced over at her and she scowled, retreating further back into the ice. He laughed. "I don't think she's very keen on our being here."

"Well, she's going to really have something to complain about in a minute," said Vin, smugly. "I made a couple of calls." From somewhere nearby there came the sound of feathers moving against one another. *Lots* of feathers. "Really good reception down here, by the way."

"Is that so?" Mallory raised an eyebrow and hauled himself off the ground, turning to look at the passageway they had come through earlier.

It was full of angels.

"A couple of calls, you say?"

"I had some spare minutes," Vin shrugged. "And besides, nobody wants to miss this."

"Miss what, exactly?"

"Come off it. We all know what's going on. She works from the inside, you work from the outside... bam! We take them down."

"Well, I'm glad you're so sure of that. If you come up with a way to do any of it, you'll let me know, won't you?" He flapped his wings, and wandered towards the crowd of angels making their way towards them.

"Now, you I wasn't expecting to see here," he said to the first angel he reached.

Saritiel brushed her hair back behind her ears. "It takes more than brute strength to breach the walls of hell. It takes luck."

"So does poker. Wouldn't you be better off making a nuisance of yourself at someone's card game?"

"I'm not here for *you*, Mallory," she said.

Mallory winked, and patted her shoulder as he walked on. "Don't I know it..."

THEY KEPT COMING; hundreds of them. Every Earthbound he had ever met seemed to be pouring through the opening and into the cavern, and it wasn't long before the vast space began to feel quite crowded. It was noisy, too: the sound of a thousand angels; all jostling each other, calling to one another – shouting, laughing, swearing... an army of them. An apocalypse of them.

They smiled at him as they passed, one after another; called his name, slapped him on the back, tugged at the feathers of his wings... each and every one of them knew him, and they were all there for the same thing.

"A couple of calls," he muttered under his breath, but suddenly, he had hope again. It filled his head, his heart, until his chest felt altogether too small to contain it.

"Choirs! Fall in!"

Mallory's voice echoed around the cavern, loud enough to make the Earthbounds nearest to him jump. The chatter that had filled the space died down immediately, replaced by a quiet shuffling. Angels filed past one another in silence, looking for other members of their choirs and falling into practiced rows. By the time Mallory had walked back to the Gate, with the exception of Vin, who stood in front of the Gate itself, every other angel stood somewhere in a neat column; silent, watching. Mallory stared at them all – then he heard a quiet voice behind him.

"Just out of curiosity: now that you've got an audience, what are you going to say?" Vin asked.

"Nothing as good as I might have done if I'd had a little notice."

"What does that mean?"

"It means I haven't the faintest idea."

They were still waiting. He sighed, and beat his wings, lifting him above their heads. Their eyes followed, fixed on him.

"I haven't seen some of you in a long time. A *long* time. Too long. Except you, Brieus," he said, pointing at an angel with a shaved head. "I'm not sure forever's long enough not to see you." He winked, and there was muffled laughter, as someone elbowed the other angel in the ribs. Mallory waved his arm towards the Gate. "But you're here now. You know who's through there. You know *what's* through there, and there isn't a single one of you who needs me to tell you how this will go. If you cross to the other side, you might not come back. Some of you won't. I don't want that on my head. This isn't a fight we can win; it isn't a fight we should even start, but it's Gabriel's party, not mine." A ripple of complaint spread back through the ranks at the mention of Gabriel, but Mallory shook his head. "I won't, *can't*, order you to follow me. I won't even ask you to. But one thing I will say to you is this: I know why I'm here. Do you?"

There was a stunned silence, and he dropped back to the ground with his wings folded behind him. Vin stared at him with wide eyes.

"What was that?" he asked, quietly enough for only Mallory to hear.

Mallory shook his head and half-smiled. "Just wait."

"Wait for what? Everyone to piss off again? If that was your idea of rallying the troops, mate, I hate to say it, but you really suck."

"You'll see." He went back to studying the Gate.

THERE WERE VOICES behind him now: urgent voices, whispering voices, arguing quietly amongst themselves. And then one voice carried clearly over the crowd, from somewhere at the back.

"What, sit this one out? And miss all the fun? Not bloody likely!" There were shouts of agreement and, suddenly, all the angels were cheering. The sound echoed off the Gate and filled the cavern like a cathedral.

Mallory kept his back to them, and raised his eyebrows pointedly at Vin. "Told you."

"Bit of a gamble, wasn't it?"

"Call it an exercise in free will." He stared up at the Gate again, taking another long gulp from his hipflask, which, if anything, had got even colder, turning the contents slow and syrupy. "Now we've just got to get through the Gate."

"About that... how exactly are you going to bring it down?"

"I'm not," Mallory said, pocketing his flask. "You are." And without another word, he walked past Vin and was lost in the crowd.

Inside her waterfall, Charon sneered, and vanished.

\*    \*    \*

"LOOK AT IT! A bullet'll never get through that. They're not stupid."

"We're talking about the Fallen. Of *course* they're stupid," Brieus peered into the eye-sockets of a skull. "This guy must've been a looker, just get a load of those cheekbones."

"That's a woman's skull, Brieus."

"Even better. Hellooo."

"Do you think you might like to... I don't know, *focus*, perhaps?" Mallory said.

Brieus rolled his eyes and walked back to the others. "Says mister 'I-can't-ask-you-to-come-with-me.' Nice touch, by the way. Couldn't have done a better job myself."

"You're right. You couldn't."

Mallory slotted a new magazine into his Colt and aimed it at the middle of the Gate. Casually, he squeezed the trigger... over and over and over again until the entrance to hell rang with gunfire, and his gun finally made an empty clicking sound. "Go check if you want: it won't even have nicked the paintwork. Like I said, not stupid."

"That's not possible," said Vin, and he hurried over to the Gate. Mallory and Brieus watched him as he hesitated, then ran his hands over the bones. When he turned back to face them, he looked disappointed, and a little sick. "First of all, that thing is grim. Just grim. I know they're twisted and everything, but..."

"We get it. Move on."

"Not a scratch. How's that even work?"

"I told you: they're not stupid. They built it to keep us out, remember."

"Out of bones. *Bones*."

"Yes, Vin. Out of bones."

"Lots of them."

"Which should prove that they're determined, if nothing else." Mallory looked thoughtful. "And it's the bones that are doing it."

"How so?" Brieus asked, slapping Vin – whose face had turned an interesting shade of greenish grey – on the back.

Mallory shrugged, tucking his gun back under his jacket. "No idea. But it has to be the bones. Just look at it. They could have built it out of ice, out of rock... anything. They don't use it to go in and out. It has no *purpose* other than to stand between us and the Fallen. If they've used bones, they've used them for a reason."

"Maybe it's just to give the willies to the more... sensitive among us." Brieus laughed, and Vin pulled a face. He followed it with an obscene gesture, which both Mallory and Brieus chose to ignore.

"If you ask me, you're spending too long on the wrong question. Who cares why it's made of bone? Your gun doesn't even dent it, fine. So what will?"

"It's not the wrong question, Brieus. You're just not looking at it the right way. It's not a case of asking what will break the bone. It's a case of asking what happens if it isn't built of bone any longer?"

Brieus stared back at Mallory, then took a slow step back.

"At the moment, what I'm really wondering is whether all that drink hasn't finally gone to your head. You can't *change* it, Mallory. It is what it is. Unless you've got some way to turn it to marshmallow and have us all waltz right through. Which would be sticky, to say the least."

"It doesn't matter what it is, though, does it? It only matters what it *isn't*."

"Which is still completely irrelevant, because you..." Brieus tailed off as he followed Mallory's gaze. He was looking at Vin, now sitting on his heels but looking a little less ill. "Oh. *Ohh*."

"Now do you see?"

"That's not possible."

"Says who?"

"It'll never work."

"And if it doesn't, then you have my full permission to say 'I told you so.' But I don't think you'll get the chance." He crouched down next to Vin. "What do you say?"

Vin looked back over his shoulder at the Gate. "How far up do you think it goes?"

"I can take a look, if you want…"

"Nah. It's fine." He stood up and stretched, cricking his neck first one way then another and opening his wings. "I'll go." He shuddered theatrically, and with a flap of his wings he was gone, soaring up above them.

Brieus was watching Mallory carefully. "It could kill him."

"It could. It won't."

"Even so…"

"Vhnori is perfectly capable of making his own choices, Brieus."

"But it's your judgement he's trusting. Which is more than some of us would in his place."

"Do you have a problem, Brieus? Because if you do, I'm happy to settle it right here. Now."

Mallory's voice was cold as he stripped off his jacket and dropped it by his feet, rolling up his sleeves.

Brieus jumped back to a spot he thought was out of reach. "Look, Mallory, I'm on your side, alright? I wouldn't be here if I wasn't. None of us would. All I'm saying is that you'd better be sure, because if this is what it boils down to, and it goes wrong…" He left the sentence hanging in mid-air. They both knew what that would mean.

Mallory scooped up his jacket and slipped it back over his shoulders, hiding a shiver. "If this goes wrong, taking care of Vhnori will be the least of my problems."

VIN LANDED WITH a thump, several minutes later. He had gone as high as he dared and got precisely nowhere. The top of the

Gate was still far out of sight by the time his wings gave out. It wasn't often that he missed his old wings, but this was one of those times. Of course, what they could really have done with was a Descended – even Gwyn, if absolutely necessary – but they were keeping themselves predictably clear of the whole business. Once the Gate was down, it would be another story. Then, he wondered whether even the Archangels would make an appearance... once it was done, and ready for the taking. He sighed. Same old story. Still, if this didn't count towards getting back into their good graces, he didn't know what would. And besides, he was sure he'd seen Saritiel somewhere in the crowd earlier.

"Well?" said Mallory, not looking up from his notebook.

Vin rolled his wings back behind his shoulders. "Well, what? There's not much to say. I went, I looked, I saw pretty much fuck-all of any use."

"Think you can do it?"

"Who knows? It's pretty big..."

"I never had you down for understatement."

"Me all over. Understated. Cool. Collected." He made a sliding motion with his hand, and managed to hit Saritiel in the shoulder, not realising she was walking up behind him. "Ouch."

"Shit. Sorry. I... err, didn't see you."

"Clearly." Saritiel narrowed her eyes at him, then turned to Mallory. "I came to see if there's anything I can do."

Mallory made a strangled squeaking sound in response, his whole body shaking with suppressed laughter as Vin blushed furiously.

Sari sighed. "I see I've caught you boys at a bad time. I'll come back later." She spun on her heel and stalked off, leaving Vin waving forlornly after her.

Mallory roared with laughter. "Understated. Cool. Collected. *Absolutely.*"

"Piss off, Mallory." By this point even Vin was smiling. "You're not helping."

"Sorry. It's just…" His face crumpled into a laugh again. "It's really not your day, is it?"

"No. It's not…" Vin suddenly turned and looked back over his shoulder at the Bone-Built Gate. "You know what? I reckon I *can* help you out with that. But I'm going to need something."

"What's that?"

"A serious amount of luck. Give me an hour, and I'll meet you back here."

Mallory watched him go, then turned his attention back to the Gate, running a hand over the bones that had been lashed together to build it. It didn't make him feel any better than it did Vin, but there was something admirable about the sheer bloody-minded effort that had gone into it. Say what you want about the Fallen, but they never did things by halves. Something moved at the corner of his vision, drawing his eyes to the ice. Charon was back, staring out at him in open hostility, and he blew her a kiss before raising his fingers to draw a pattern in the air, which he then flicked in her direction. She opened her mouth in a frozen hiss and retreated into the cascade of ice, but not before he saw the figure behind her who ducked aside as she sank deeper, obviously just as keen to keep out of her way as he was to avoid being seen by the angels. Looking out was a man with cropped hair and dark-ringed eyes, and Mallory's blood pounded in his ears.

"Rimmon."

# CHAPTER TWENTY-NINE

## If You Can't See the Woods for the Trees, What You Really Need is a Chainsaw

"I THINK WE should've turned left by that fruit tree."

"You *think?*"

"Hey. Don't get snitty with me, I'm just following you!"

"Now why in the world would you do that?"

"Err... because you're supposed to know where you're going, maybe?" Alice poked Abbadona's shoulder, hard enough to make him flinch.

He gave her a dirty look. "Only on the top levels, which is where I agreed to be your guide, princess. Not down here. No way. This is the Twelve's patch. This is where the *crazy* people come."

Alice was reluctant to admit it, but there was definitely something in what he was saying. Since they had crossed the river, things had been both easier and harder. Easier in that all those nagging doubts had evaporated and she felt clear, focused. Sober. She still didn't know exactly what she was looking for in hell – something of Xaphan's, yes, but *what*? – but Xaphan was one of the Twelve, and that meant she was on the right track. This side of the river frightened Abbadona too, and he was now putting more of his energy into getting out alive than he was into being unpleasant. This could only be a good thing. In fact, it had been a while since she had imagined setting him on fire. Perhaps she was just getting used to him again.

The landscape was changing around them as they walked, or not so much *walked* as stumbled blindly, occasionally bickering about the direction they should be going. Alice was exhausted – bone-tired and soul-cold – but still she kept going. Her companion didn't look like he was doing much better. So from that point of view, it was getting harder. *Much* harder.

The bare rock of the upper levels of hell had given way to a forest, albeit the most unsettling one Alice had ever seen. There were still no real shadows; just the same grey-blue light, making the trees appear somehow false, like the painted backdrop of a stage. She had imagined that if she touched one, it would be smooth and flat. Despite this conviction, she couldn't quite bring herself to actually reach out and lay her hand on one of the trunks. They were awful-looking things with knotted branches twisted quite out of shape, the roots ripping back out of the ground and threatening to catch hold of her feet as she passed. The leaves, too – such as they had – were black and frost-burned, the edges curled in on themselves, and the whole thing was nicely set off by the vicious thorns that jutted out of the wood at all angles. It was a place she was keen to leave as soon as possible, and she deeply regretted not having taken the other path (or what there was of one) earlier. But that had been before the forest.

"Alright," she groaned, sitting down heavily, "so you have any idea where we are? At all?"

"Sure. I told you: where the crazy people come." He sat down beside her and stretched his legs out, shoving a tree root to one side with his boot. It bounced back and he scuffed at it, swearing.

"That's not helpful."

"Doesn't make it any less true, though, does it? See these trees?" He leaned back and grabbed hold of a small branch, oblivious to the thorns that pricked his skin. With a sudden burst of effort, he tugged on it and it snapped clean off the tree, and a high-pitched scream rang out, making Alice sit bolt upright, her eyes wide. As the scream faded, a soft moaning rose up around them as though in answer. It, too, died down and left them in silence. Abbadona held up the branch. "The trees don't like it when you do that."

"What *are* they?"

"Used to be people." He dropped the wood and rubbed his palms together, wiping the blood from his hands. Alice stared at the branch he had discarded and reached for it, but he slapped her hand away. "I wouldn't do that if I were you. They might not like having the odd branch pulled off, but just imagine how they'd feel about a forest fire."

Alice promptly put her hands in her pockets. He had a point. "So if they used to be people, what did they do to end up here?"

"No idea." He twisted a piece of root that had caught on his jacket, and there was another shriek from the tree. "Like I say, I don't come here, so don't expect me to know all the rules, but I'm telling you, it can't have been good." The tree shrieked again, and he swore at it. "Well, let go of my fucking coat then, would you?" he said, pulling at the root, which clung on all the more stubbornly.

Alice edged away. "Don't you think you should stop doing that? If it… hurts it?"

"Hello? Fallen. Not supposed to be *nice*."

"Clearly."


SHE WATCHED AS man took on tree, and lost. Repeatedly. The swearing got louder. The shrieking got louder still, and the moaning with it. Eventually, Alice couldn't take it any more and leapt forward, forcibly hauling Abbadona to his feet and away.

And let go immediately.

She hadn't just felt it; she had *seen* it.

Abbadona, beaten and bloody, and tied to a wheel. It spun, slowly. So slowly. And it burned with a black fire that chewed at his flesh without ever consuming him. It just kept on burning.

Her ears rang and her breath caught in her throat. There were stars floating across her vision, pinwheeling past her.

She was seeing what had happened to him when he'd come back to hell.

"This is because of me. I did this."

"No." His voice was surprisingly gentle. "Purson did that. The wheel's one of Xaphan's greatest hits."

"It hurt…"

"Oh, yeah. It hurt. A lot. And for a long time. Every once in a while, Lucifer would pop into my head, just to make sure I wasn't lying about just how *much* pain I was in. He's nice like that." He helped her to her feet, steadying her as she staggered slightly. "I should thank you, really. I guess that was the point I decided I'd had enough." He held up his burned wrist, rubbing at it thoughtfully. "I've never minded it down here as much as some of the others. We have a purpose, you know? The Plains… the Dark House… it makes sense after a while. Even *you* get that," he said. "But this? What Lucifer's done, there's always someone else in your head, and after a while, you can't even be sure that what you're thinking is actually *you*, and that really is hell, Alice."

"And that's why you've come this far? Because you feel like you owe me?"

"Piss off. No. I've come this far with you because I'm done down here, and you're really my best option. My only option. So I'm helping you, and if we get caught, then god help us both."

Alice was about to answer, but heard a rustling, shuffling sound behind her and turned. At first, she saw nothing, just the cold, empty forest, but then a pair of black-tipped ears appeared from behind a fallen tree, then two round yellow eyes and a long, pointed muzzle.

"Look at that," she said, watching as it crept out further, eyeing the two of them. Abbadona was busy examining a hole in his jacket – the result of his epic battle with the tree – and didn't look up. "What?"

"It's a fox. I think he's watching us."

"A what?" he dropped the hem of his jacket and peered over her shoulder.

"A fox. Look! There."

"Alice." Abbadona's voice was quiet, calm, but urgent. "There aren't any foxes in hell."

"But…"

"Run!" he grabbed her hand, ignoring the fire that flashed up between them, and he dragged her with him – and they were running through the forest, ducking the low-hanging branches, jumping the roots that stuck out of the ground like iron spikes. The thorns tore at Alice's hair, at her skin and her coat as they raced past; her heart pounded and her muscles burned. The air stung her face and her eyes streamed, but it was not the cold that chilled her even as she ran: it was the single question which hung in her mind. Because if that had not been a fox….

Behind them, the fox hopped down from the fallen limb of the tree and blinked, watching as they disappeared into the forest. It scratched behind one ear and yawned lazily… but as it yawned, its mouth opened wider and wider, stretching further and further open, until its whole head seemed to disappear behind its jaws – and still it yawned, becoming a thing of teeth and throat and little else. And suddenly, there was a man standing in its place. A man with too many teeth and a badly-scarred face, smoothing down his hair and smiling as he spread his burned wings.

# CHAPTER THIRTY
## Oriflamme

"You BRING YOUR whole choir with you, or what?" Mallory eyed the Earthbounds who were following Vin and lining themselves up in a semi-circle around the Gate.

Vin shrugged. "Everyone I could find."

"Will it be enough?"

"One way to find out." He shook his wings free with a flourish, opening them wide. "Hold these," he said, passing Mallory his sunglasses. "And look after them, would you? Those are my babies. You break them, I break you." On that note, he turned and stalked away.

Mallory looked down at the glasses and shook his head. "Muppet."

"I heard that!" said Vin's retreating back.

THERE WERE FEWER Earthbounds from Barakiel's choir than he had hoped. This meant one of two things: either his peers had decided to sit this one out, or Barakiel's boys and girls tended to be much better-behaved than the other Archangels' and there were simply fewer of them in exile. Thinking back to the time before he was banished, Vin strongly suspected the latter. Still, fifty was a good enough number, particularly when one of them looked like Saritiel. She had taken a position directly in front of the Gate, right behind where he would need to stand – and sure, maybe he could argue it was for purely practical reasons, her gift being one of the strongest, the luckiest, in the whole choir. But equally, he could convince himself quite happily that, really, it was because she wanted to be close to him. *Needed* to be. Yes. That sounded a whole lot better.

He stopped in front of the Gate, staring at it like he hoped that would be enough to bring it down. It wouldn't, but it was always worth a go. The truth was that he had no idea whether this would work. Nor what it could do to him if it didn't.

"Alright, then. Let's do this."

He rolled his shoulders and took a deep breath. As one, the other angels opened their wings; heads tipped back, eyes closed. Vin blew out the breath he had been holding and turned his hands over, palms up, tipping them towards the Gate. Grey fog tumbled from his hands, spilling through his fingers and sliding over the rock towards the bones. It crept up the vertical surface of the Gate, clinging like dust to everything it touched: thin tendrils of mist weaving around the curves of skulls and hips wedged side-by-side. Inch by inch, the bleached white of old bone darkened to grey, mottled with age and moss.

Sweat beaded on Vin's forehead as the stone rose up the Gate, far beyond his head and out of sight – rushing now towards the vanished roof – and for the first time, his hands shook. Really shook, uncontrollably. His body ached. His head throbbed and the cold, which he had been doing his best to ignore, drilled into his heart. There was something else, too: a dull ache in his bones; a heavy slowness that was binding to him somewhere deep inside, but he pushed it away. He knew what it was, and that was enough. The Gate must fall.

He could feel the stone now, feel the weight of it pulling on his hands and drawing him towards it. He pulled back to hold his ground. It was so nearly done, so close. Just. A. Little. More.

Somewhere high above, stone met bone met rock and, with a groan, it was over. Vin was vaguely aware of the voices behind him: the angels of his choir opening their eyes to see what it was that he had done.

The Bone-Built Gate was no longer bone. No less solid, it could have been cut from a mountain and dropped into hell. It had worked. A cheer went up from the Earthbounds huddled behind the ring of Barakiel's choir just as Vin's strength gave out. His legs folded in on themselves and, suddenly, there were hands on his shoulders.

"Vhnori?"


MALLORY WATCHED AS the Gate changed, slowly at first, but then with alarming speed. He saw Vin sag as his hands dropped, saw Saritiel rush to his side. The cheer echoed around the entrance to hell: a thousand angels spoiling for a fight, and they were just the beginning. Mallory knew what would happen as soon as the Gate was down. The Fallen had broken the rules, and the full wrath of the angels was about to land on them. He almost felt sorry for them. *Almost*, because Alice was still in there.

Without realising it, he had been shouldering his way through the crowd towards the Gate, checking his gun and reloading it as he went. He stopped automatically beside Vin as Saritiel helped him to his feet. "Not bad."

"You're welcome."

"Want these back?" Mallory held out the sunglasses, and Vin took them, a little shakily.

"What happens now?" he asked as he dropped them into his pocket, first giving them a quick once-over. He caught Mallory staring at him and shrugged defensively. "They weren't cheap, alright?"

"Hmmph. Now," said Mallory, turning his gun over in his hands, "we see what's through door number one."

He let out a long, loud whistle and the angels who had crowded around the Gate, touching it as though they couldn't quite believe what they were seeing, suddenly parted like a sea, clearing a path between Mallory and the Gate. They stood stock-still, just watching. Waiting.

Mallory was running. His wings snapped open, and he was in the air, racing towards the Gate. Rolling in mid-air, he brought up the gun and pointed it at the centre of the Gate, unloading every round he had and firing until the chamber was empty. At first, nothing happened, and his heart sank. Then he heard it: a quiet cracking sound, almost too low to notice.

"Clear the Gate!" he shouted, and suddenly the air was full of angels massing behind him, their wings beating in time. Spinning towards the Gate, Mallory offered up the closest thing he had to a prayer that he was right, that the stone would give, just as his boot crashed through it.

The cracks spiderwebbed out through the Gate; the broken edges of the stone grinding against one another as they shifted. Fragments shook loose and rained down, shattering into dust as the remaining angels took to the air – even Vin, exhausted but in no hurry to be crushed by falling rock. The Gate was crumbling, and the angels drew back as the pieces grew larger and fell faster, from higher and higher.

A huge dust-cloud rose from beneath the pieces as they fell, mushrooming up and around them and swirling through the currents made by the beating wings of the angels. The air grew thick with it: a dusty, musty, choking fog that shut out everything beyond it and cloaked them in silence. The only sound was of feathers.

Transformed, the Gate had lost the power of the bones which had held it in place for so long. Without that, the sheer weight of the stone had collapsed in on itself, as Mallory had known it would, leaving a pile of rubble and an empty space between the ice cliffs. All it had taken was a push in the right direction.

Hell was open to the angels.

And the Fallen were waiting.


THEY WERE THERE, on the other side, in a single line. There were hundreds of them, their eyes all fixed on the angels. Mallory landed on a tumbled heap of stone and dust, scanning the line. There was no sign of Rimmon this time, but a shimmering blue figure caught his eye, far to the left of the line. Charon. Beside her was a tall, broad-shouldered man in blackened armour; his shoulders and helmet almost completely covered by a pale, stiff cloak. He carried a standard and banner with him, its high pole topped with a human hand, shriveled and twisted with age. Mallory sighed. The standard and the cloak of human skin could only mean one thing: that Azazel had been promoted. If there was one of the Fallen he hadn't wanted to see acting as standard-bearer, it was him. What Azazel lacked in intelligence, he more than made up for with sheer brute force and, worse, obedience. If Lucifer told him to jump, he not only asked how high, but who he should land on when he came back down. More worryingly, even at this distance Mallory could see the bright red glow of his eyes. Azazel wasn't alone in his head.

The rubble shifted abruptly beneath him and Mallory was forced to jump clear, his wings slowing his fall. Behind him, the rocks continued to move and judder apart, leaving a hole where he had been standing. He edged closer to it and found himself peering into a void, which gaped back up at him, dropping away to an ice-laden river far below.

"Really rolling out the welcome mat," said a voice behind him. Vin sounded tired, strained, but at least he was standing. He leaned around Mallory and stared down into the gap. "That's a seriously big hole."

"Isn't it? Red-carpet treatment. You see him?" Mallory nodded towards Azazel, and Vin's eyes met Lucifer's.

"No. Way."

"Worst possible combination. Lucifer riding Azazel. Still, now we're here it'd be rude to keep them all waiting. Especially when they've cranked out the standard."

Mallory stared across the cliff-top at hell's battle-flag. It had been a long time since he'd seen it – a *very* long time – and the years didn't seem to have done it any favours. He remembered it being ragged, but now there was more hole to it than cloth. A scorch-mark ran across the top of the fabric; a souvenir from Michael. Mallory couldn't recall which particular member of the Fallen had been the standard-bearer that time, but it didn't really matter. He hadn't lasted long.

"What do you see?" he asked Vin.

There was a pause, and Vin sniffed. "Purson playing stick-pin with my liver. Nice. You?"

"You don't want to know."

The standard showed you your fears, your nightmares, the very *worst* of your memories; everything you thought you'd boxed up and hidden away in the darkness, running to meet you. When you fought hell, you didn't just fight the Fallen. You fought yourself.

"Got something for you." Vin sounded subdued, which was not altogether surprising, given what he'd just managed to do.

Mallory looked round at him and folded his arms. "Oh?"

"Here." Vin held out a small, L-shaped packet, wrapped in a carrier bag.

Mallory took it and turned it over in his hands, knowing full well what it was. "That's a lot of effort you've put into the presentation." He scrunched the bag up and tucked it into the pocket of his jacket then held the gun out at arm's length, testing the weight and the feel of it in his hand. "What's this in aid of?"

"In aid of? It's in aid of maybe getting out of here alive. That and my being an exceptionally nice guy. Besides, I like you and

I don't really want to have to scrape you off the floor and carry you out of here. It'd ruin my coat."

"I see." Mallory held the two Colts – his, and Vin's gift – side by side in silent gratitude. "An Uzi might have been nice."

"Don't like you *that* much..." Vin laughed, but his laugh tailed off as he looked out at the rows of the Fallen.

They were still there, waiting. And Lucifer's red eyes still shone out from beneath the shifting standard, the flag writhing like a serpent. Vin opened his mouth to speak, to ask Mallory how they could possibly get out of this, but the other Earthbound was already striding away from him, back towards the massed ranks of angels. They were no longer a crowd. They had instinctively fallen into lines, columns, battalions. Heads raised and eyes forward, wings spread – they were ready for war. A single Earthbound stood to attention at the head of each column, waiting for their orders. Mallory stopped in front of Brieus, who grinned at him. "I take it that face means we're not just going to be able to stroll in."

"Hardly. Would you like the bad news, the worse news or the real kick-in-the-face news?"

"Hit me with it. But quietly." Brieus glanced over his shoulder to make sure they were far enough from the first row of angels to avoid being overheard.

"There's a whole army of them waiting, Brieus. They've brought out the standard – which, by the way, *Azazel* is carrying – and, as if that's not enough, it looks like Lucifer's come out to play."

"Who's he in?"

"Who do you think?"

"Well, *that's* not exactly cheering, is it?"

"No."

"You're sure it's the standard?"

"Of course I'm sure. What else do you think it's likely to be?"

"I don't know, Lucifer's washing?" Brieus hissed, obviously aware that his voice had been rising. He stared at the ground for a moment, and when he looked up, his eyes were darker, emptier. "The standard. No quarter."

"No quarter. They're serious."

"We should wait for the Descendeds. The Gate's down, they'll be coming soon."

"Not soon enough."

"Mallory..."

"I can't make you go in, Brieus. I can't make any of you, and I was very clear on that. If you want to change your mind, you can leave. But if you stay, you fight, or you die. Maybe both."

"You know something, Mallory? Sometimes, I really don't like you," said Brieus, but he remained at attention, his eyes fixed on Mallory as he walked the line, his wings beating slow as a heartbeat. And it was the sound of Mallory's wings which muffled his answer to Brieus, whispered soft and low.

"Neither do I."

"I DON'T DO speeches," Mallory said to the Earthbound in front of him: one he vaguely recognised, but whose name he had either forgotten or never known. "I'm not going to stand up front and give orders. But you listen to me, and you make sure you pass this on. The Fallen have raised hell's standard. They will show us no mercy. You die down here, that's it. Game's over. There's no coming back from it. But now the Gate's down, the same applies to them. They have nowhere to run, nowhere to hide while they heal. Nowhere to limp back to and lick their wounds. If you kill a Fallen here, now, they stay dead. And they know that. So they're going to fight like they mean it." He paused, watching the angel in front of him turn pale, his shoulders sagging slightly. "Spread the word."

He walked back to the breached Gate, his wings carrying him easily to the top of the rubble where Vin was still standing. "Any change?"

"Lucifer and Charon have been having an... *animated* discussion, but other than that..." said Vin, pointing at them.

They had been standing side by side earlier, but they now stood slightly apart; Charon had her back towards Lucifer, her arms crossed and her chin in the air.

"Is she *sulking*?" Mallory asked.

Vin pulled a face. "Looks that way, doesn't it? I tell you what, though: I wouldn't turn my back on him."

"We already did. That's why we're here."

Mallory lifted his silver flask to his lips and threw his head back to drain it, but as he did, it was snatched away. Startled, he straightened up to see Vin lean forward and lob it into the chasm beneath the rock and the rubble. It glittered as it fell, blue in the cold hell-glow, looking for all the world like a falling star as it spun towards the river far below. Too shocked to speak, Mallory gave Vin a murderous look and slowly pulled out one of his guns. He checked the magazine, the chamber, then flicked the safety off and aimed the barrel very carefully at a spot between Vin's eyes.

Vin blinked back at him. "You're going to shoot me over that? Go ahead."

He lifted his chin slightly, keeping his eyes on Mallory's. His wings bristled behind him. Still Mallory said nothing. Instead, he stared down the gun at Vin, who stared defiantly back.

The deadlock could have gone on, but a sudden roar from inside the shattered Gate made them both jerk their heads round to look at the Fallen. Not quite a cheer, not quite a battle-call, it was the sound of a thousand lost voices, maybe more, all crying out in fear and pain and hatred. Above all, hatred. It rushed past them, over them – *through* them – and Mallory lowered his gun, still glaring at Vin.

Vin glared back. "Don't you give me that look! You want to take it out on someone, how about you start with them?" He waved his hand at the massed Fallen, but Mallory narrowed his eyes, and still he said nothing.

The noise was rising; individual shouts broke through, some in the language of the angels, some in human languages, and some barely more than feral howls. And with the wave of sound came the smoke. Thick, black and oily, it clung to the voices like a parasite, carried across the Gate. Deep in the ranks of the Fallen, blue torches sprang to life, one by one, floating above the sea of broken angels.

Mallory's face clouded further. "They brought hellfire. Oh, *goody*." He jumped lightly down from the heap of rubble and started towards the ranks of Earthbounds, still patiently standing to attention. But after a few steps, he stopped and turned back to Vin. "Try not to die, alright?"

"That an order?"

"Would it make a difference if it was?"

"Nah."

"Then consider it a request by a friend."

"We're alright, then? After, you know, me and the throwing…?"

"You brought me a gun, Vin. We're alright." Mallory winked and turned away again, leaving Vin on the pile of stone, staring out at the Fallen and trying to ignore the fact that even his wings were shivering.

# CHAPTER THIRTY-ONE

## Ixion

ALICE'S BREATH CAME in ragged gasps; her face was numb from pushing through the cold air as they ran. Her lungs were full of nails and the path was a river of swords beneath her feet. And Abbadona was still running.

She stumbled and caught herself, but her knees gave beneath her and she sank to the ground. "I can't."

"Alice, you have to get up. He could be right behind us. All of them could."

"So? If the Twelve know I'm here, and they know you're helping me, then we're both screwed. And whether we're screwed here or, I don't know, a mile further down the road, we're still screwed. But I can't run any more."

Abbadona sagged, and blew out a long, frustrated breath. "Fine. But that's on your head, not mine."

"As long as it's not on my *feet*," she groaned.

He sat down beside her and ran his hands back through his hair so hard that strands fell out, floating down to the floor. "Shit. Shit. Shit."

"You knew this would happen, Rob." She didn't even notice his old name, his false name, slipping out until it was too late. Either he missed it, or he didn't care. All he did was stare at his feet, pulling at his hair and swearing under his breath. "Like that's going to help? Get a grip."

"Excuse me?" He stopped pulling at his hair and looked sideways at her.

"You're seriously telling me you thought you, we, could pull this off without being found out?"

"In case you hadn't noticed, Alice, it's a pretty fundamental part of the plan. I can't take on the Twelve. No, scratch that. I can take on the Twelve. I'll just *lose*. And die. Painfully."

"You're forgetting something."

"What?"

"Me." As she spoke, Alice picked up a small stone that lay next to her feet. It was rough, and it was cold in her hand. She tossed it lightly into the air, where it promptly burst into flames. A spiral of white smoke coiled up and away, and all that came back down was pale ash. It wasn't entirely unexpected – after all, if she didn't think *something* would happen, there would have been no point in trying it – but even so, the little flurry of ash made her uncomfortable and short of breath. Out of the corner of her eye, she could see Abbadona; his eyes wide, his mouth even wider. She patted his knee. "Close your mouth, would you? Something'll fly in."

"How did you know it would do that?"

"I didn't *know*, exactly. I just thought, you know, that it would."

"You know something, Alice? You scare me."

"If it helps, you're not the only one."

They both stared ahead of them, past the settling ash and back down the path they had come. Now they weren't running, she could hear how quiet hell was. Or, rather, *not* hear it. Before, there had always been something: the noises of the other levels – creaking ice, or the whispering of the Plain; the scratching and moaning of the forest, and the voices of the Dark House. The voices. She would never forget those voices. But here, hell was quiet. Silent. The only sound was Abbadona's breathing. Everything else was empty, cold and still.

A hand settled on her shoulder and she swiped it away. "Look, just because we're able to have something approaching a civilised conversation right now, it doesn't mean I want you touching me, alright?" She turned towards him angrily. Things were complicated enough without *that*. But as she turned, she saw his hands in his lap; saw his face, waxy and pale as he stared past her to a spot somewhere behind her. She saw the dark eyes behind him, and the sharp, shining steel at his throat.

The hand lifted from her shoulder, then casually, insultingly, it patted her head.

"You don't scare me, Alice," said Xaphan. "Nice display. But before you even think about trying any of your tricks, I should warn you: you'd better be sure you can finish me off. Purson over there too. Otherwise we'll cut your little friend here into pieces in front of you."

"What's that to me?" She swallowed hard. There were sparks beneath her skin, scratching to get out. "He lied to me. He made me believe he was something he could never be. Why should he mean anything to me? He's a Fallen."

"But you're not, are you?"

Xaphan stepped around to where she could see him, and gestured to Purson, who grinned and dug the blade he was holding into Abbadona's neck. Blood spilled from the wound, but Abbadona did not flinch. He stared ahead, blankly. Alice, however, *did* flinch, and Xaphan saw it.

"I wonder, is it that you're still fond of him, or is it that you're just too human? The angels have great plans for you, but I wonder whether there's angel enough in there to do what is necessary. There's too much of your father in you, I suspect, and not enough fire." He nodded to Purson again, who dragged his knife across Abbadona's throat. It left a fine line like a necklace, oozing redly, and Alice turned her face away. "I thought as much," he laughed as he leaned closer.

With so little distance between them, she could see the sweep of scar tissue that covered one side of his face: there were faint lines that ran across his cheek like a roadmap, and shiny knots of burn-tissue, some of it old, some of it fresh and angry. He blinked at her.

"So now I suppose the question is what we do with you..." Xaphan tailed off, his head tipping to one side as though he was listening to something a long way off.

Alice shivered. Not something, *someone*. Lucifer. She looked quickly towards Abbadona. Purson still had his knife at his throat, but although his chin was raised, his head tipping back, his eyes were fixed on her.

Whatever Lucifer had said, Xaphan was smiling. The scars on his face bulged and his teeth glittered and Alice fought to keep control of the fire that tore and scratched at her insides, looking for a way out. She could let it, she thought; let it out and it would burn them all. Including Abbadona. Could she let him die? More to the point, could she kill him? What would that make her? She squeezed her eyes shut and pictured the flames, and saw herself lost and alone in the middle of hell. Forever. Xaphan stepped around her and over to Abbadona, hauling him to his feet by the lapels of his jacket. Purson's blade followed and still Abbadona kept his eyes on Alice. Xaphan stood in front of him and sighed.

"I really did expect more from you. We all did. *He* certainly did. And after all that time we spent together, after everything we talked about, I was absolutely convinced that we understood one another, and then you go and do something like this." He snatched at Abbadona's wrist, pulling the sleeve back and exposing the burned-off brand. "Clever. Clever, clever boy. Of course, Gabriel wouldn't be dealing with a Fallen. And, no offence, dear chap, but if he did, it wouldn't be one as insignificant as *you*. And none of his Earthbounds would risk it, which leaves his Descendeds. And that *is* interesting." He rubbed his chin thoughtfully. "Not that it helps you much. You see, you've rather over-extended our patience, and that's not good news for you. Not good at all."

"'Our?'" snarled Abbadona, finally taking his eyes off Alice and meeting Xaphan's gaze. "You're getting ideas above your station again. I know he's not in there, so just give it a rest. You don't scare me." He spat at Xaphan's feet.

Xaphan frowned. "I thought you might say that. Still, it doesn't make any difference. I've had my orders. It's back on the Wheel with you, and this time you're staying there."

Alice saw Abbadona sag, just slightly. Xaphan had already turned away. "And you, Alice? You get to watch."

She knew what they would do to Abbadona. She'd seen it already, and knew as well as he did what this meant. If she did it, if she turned the fire loose on all of them, it would be a mercy, as far as he was concerned. But he would still die, and he would die at her hands. And no matter what there had been between them, no matter whether he had lied, no matter what he was... he did not deserve to die in this place, and not through her. He had told her that she was his hope, and she could not let his hope be the one to destroy him. Besides, there was still time...

She felt a sudden chill, and a pain somewhere behind her – not quite a part of her, and distant. There was a lurch of vertigo, a flash of light and then, nothing.

THERE WAS SOUND before anything else. Voices seeped in at the edges of Alice's mind, muffled and distant at first, but growing clearer, louder, more certain.

She opened an eye. Outside, was nothing but searing light, and inside it was dark, and warm, and peaceful. She had a nagging feeling that there was something she was meant to be doing. It was important. It was important and it made her angry. Or perhaps they were both the same thing? It didn't seem to matter so much in here, in the dark. Maybe she would just stay here for a while...

"Alice. Alice. Aaalice..." The voice calling her name wasn't one she knew. No – that wasn't quite true. It wasn't one she *liked*.

"Alice. I know you're awake. There's no point trying to pretend."

"Time to get up and play, Alice." Another voice; this one sharp, all edges and points.

Someone poked her hard in the ribs and she rolled over, curling into a ball. Another poke, this time to her back, and harder still.

"Get up, Alice. I'm getting terribly bored of waiting. And, besides, there's someone here who's just *dying* to see you again."

No. She really didn't like that voice. It reminded her of something: a feeling, more than anything else. Of feeling tired, of feeling cold. Of feeling frightened.

Xaphan. It was Xaphan, and suddenly her eyes were open.


"THERE YOU ARE. I knew you were in there somewhere. You have very pretty eyes, Alice. It would be such a shame to keep them closed any longer. Or to let Purson have them."

He glanced over his shoulder towards the dark-eyed Fallen standing a few paces behind him, then turned back to Alice. "He's very impatient, you know. Between you and me, it's exhausting keeping up with him. *Exhausting*." He looked back again and rolled his eyes. "But the thing is, he's very useful. Not to mention well-connected." He lowered his voice and leaned closer. "I think he's something of a favourite at the moment. Not that *that* ever lasts for long. We all have our moment in the sun, of course." He drew away from her again, and Alice automatically tried to follow, but banged her forehead on something cold and solid.

She shook her head to clear it, and it was only as she did this that she saw the bars in front of her.

She was in a cage.

Xaphan watched her register this with great amusement.

"What, you thought you could simply stroll around? Like I'd let that happen. No angel – Descended *or* Earthbound – has ever set foot on my level, never mind in my lab. A half-breed's bad enough... But then we all have our orders, don't we? I have mine, you have yours and *he* has his." He stepped neatly to one side, but even before he did, Alice knew what she would see.

To call it a room would be unfair. It was a space, a workspace: a lab, lit by the same sickly light as the rest of hell. A workbench ran the length of the opposite wall, littered with books, broken glass and strange, twisted tools. A flask sat above a blue-flamed burner; its contents bubbled and shrieked. Where the bench thrust from the rock wall, there was a wheel. Eight feet across, it was built of steel-bolted bone. Broad leather straps hung from its edges; another from its hub, and dark stains spread patchily across it. She knew what this wheel was. She had seen it in Abbadona's memory. Even from here she could feel it weeping pain like a wound. And even from here she could feel his fear, as he stood beside it with his head bowed in defeat, Purson gripping him tightly and forcing his burned wrist into the first of the straps.

She didn't realise that the shout was hers until he looked up at her with sad eyes. She didn't realise that her hands were wrapped around the bars of the cage until the cold-iron froze her palms. She didn't realise that she was pulling on them, shaking at them, hauling at them with all her strength until her shoulders ached, and even then, she didn't stop. And all the while, Purson methodically fastened the buckles on the straps.

Alice's throat was dry and sore but still she couldn't stop screaming, because everything else was falling away, all the angels; all the fire and the pain; all the blood and the death and the horror... and all that was left was Alice, watching a man she had once thought she loved bound to the wheel where he would die.

He held her gaze, and it no longer mattered that he had never been who she thought he was. It didn't matter that he had been little more than a spy, nor that he had lied. She was about to watch his execution, and they both knew it.

Purson stepped away from the wheel. The straps held Abbadona – *Rob*, the name such a trivial matter now – stretched out across the wheel. Still his eyes were locked to hers.

"Alice?"

There was a new voice – a woman's voice. Young. Familiar. Alice tore herself away from the wheel, and looked for it, her grip on the bars slipping, her arms hanging heavily by her sides. There was no-one else there: just Xaphan, Purson and Abbadona, tied to the damned wheel. Waiting.

Waiting for what?

The air around Xaphan began to shimmer, to shiver ever so gently, and then dropped as though everything behind him had been an illusion, a curtain which had been allowed to fall.

Suddenly, there was someone standing beside him. Green eyes, and a streak of black against bright white hair.

"Alice, I'm sorry."

"No, Florence. You're not." Alice's voice was cracked, but still managed to sound angry, angry enough that Florence took half a step behind Xaphan for protection. "How can you be sorry? You're on the wrong side of the damn bars."

"I never... I didn't..."

"Yes, you did."

"If you'd just let me explain..."

"Explain what? Why you let everyone think you were dead? Why you left your brother? Why you left Vhnori to the Fallen? And this, what about *this*? You've got an explanation for this?" Alice banged on the bars.

"Because Xaphan asked me to." Florence's voice was low, her eyes on the ground.

From the wheel, Abbadona began to laugh. "You love him? You're out of your fucking mind, sister."

"No one asked you," snapped Xaphan, taking his eyes off Alice for the first time.

Abbadona snorted. "You got me on the Wheel already, Xaph. What else are you going to do to me? Talk me to death?"

Alice was staring at Florence, her face dark, and Florence shook her head in frustration. "If anyone was going to understand, I would have thought it would be you. We're the same..."

"No, I really don't think we are."

"So you never loved him, then?"

"It doesn't matter, does it?"

"Alice," Florence was at the cage now, her fingers twining around the bars, resting on Alice's. "I didn't mean it to end like this. You were never meant to... it shouldn't have been you. They told me it would be an Earthbound..."

"How long?" asked Alice. It seemed to matter.

"Since the beginning," said Florence. "Since the first hellmouth."

"She's been making people *choose*, Alice. They have to make a choice, remember. Xaphan's been using her." Abbadona was still laughing. "They see what they want, and they jump right in."

"Ah, not entirely true," Xaphan cut in smoothly. "We needed to use a degree of... persuasion at the beginning, yes. But in time..."

"...the balance started tipping," Alice finished his sentence for him. "And then you could just take them."

"Well, now. Mallory *has* been busy teaching you, hasn't he?" Xaphan raised an eyebrow, but managed to look no less smug. "You're quite right. Once the balance passes the tipping point, we don't need people to make a choice. We *prefer* it, of course, but it's no longer necessary." He opened his arms expansively.

"It's over, Alice. The angels have failed. We have control. And all humanity will Fall, whether they choose to or not."

"You're a pompous old goat, you know that?" Abbadona's wrists strained against the leather straps. "You felt it earlier, just like I did. The Gate's down. The angels are coming, and you think it's just going to be the Earthbounds? They've got into hell, Xaphan. The Descendeds, the Archangels... they're all coming. And they're all coming after *you*."

"Me? I think not. After all, that's what *you're* here for, isn't it? To help the little half-breed destroy the hellmouth machine?" He half-looked to his left, caught himself and stopped, grinning. "Nice trick, Abe. But not nice enough. By the time the angels find you, and realise you failed, it'll be too late. And I'll be long gone."

"Too late? Too late for what?" asked Alice, her attention suddenly snapping away from the touch of Florence's fingers. Her skin was warm. Alice felt like she hadn't been warm in years. Not since all of this began.

"Hey!" Florence yelped in pain and pulled her hands away, backing up towards Xaphan.

Alice looked down. Her hands were burning. Flames boiled up the bars, licking at the metal, but it stayed as cold as ever.

Xaphan ushered Florence behind him and stepped forward to stroke the cage. "That's not going to help you, little girl. I forged those bars myself. No amount of angel fire's going to get you out. Who are you really angry with, I wonder? Us, or yourself? All that confusion, all that emotion. You were so busy thinking, you forgot to fight back! It made my job much easier; I should thank you. I never imagined we'd take you so easily. Perhaps I overestimated you? Still, burn all you like. It won't make a difference here. Not for you."

Alice heard the challenge in his voice and let the fire burn anyway. It cleared her head. "Have you seen the Ghasts, Florence?" she said, enjoying the feel of Florence's fear.

"Of course I have."

"You know they were like us, once. Half-borns. Maybe more like you: half-borns who Fell. You know what happened to them?"

"You mean their eyes? Sure I know. It's not like I've only just got here. But Xaph, he won't let that happen. Not to me."

"You keep your eyes open, Florence. Next time you see me, one way or another, it'll be the *last* thing you see."

A flame slid between the bars of the cage and towards Florence, weaving through the air, reaching for her.

"And that's quite enough of that," snapped Xaphan. He whistled to Purson, who took hold of the edge of the wheel with both his hands and pulled down, hard. There was a low rolling sound like thunder, a scrape of steel on stone, and the wheel began to turn.

An oily smell filled the air, a burning blackness, and dark flames sprang up along the rim of the wheel. Small at first, they skipped around the edges and down the spokes. Abbadona's eyes widened a little; his jaw set as the fire found him. Purson stood in front of the wheel, watching with satisfaction, and slowly raised his arm. He was holding a metal bar. He struck out with it, hitting Abbadona's leg with a terrible crunching sound. He waited for some kind of cry: none came. He struck again, and again there was nothing from Abbadona, but as the wheel turned and brought his face level with Alice, he looked out at her. Pain in his eyes, fear in his face, he looked at her and he said: "Sorry, princess. I did my best."

The black flames covered him, and Purson struck blindly into them, over and over and over again. But Abbadona made no more sounds, and still the wheel turned.

ALL THIS TIME, Xaphan had eyes for nothing else: only the burning wheel. Abbadona would be causing no more trouble, that was certain, not now the Gate was broken and hell was breached. That was a problem in itself, of course, but at least it wouldn't be his.

Satisfied, he turned towards the cage... just in time to see Alice go nuclear.

# CHAPTER THIRTY-TWO

## Catharsis

XAPHAN DIVED FOR cover beneath the workbench, dragging Florence with him, pulling her on top of him in the process. Florence's heart hammered against his ribs, her breath hot on his neck as she huddled closer. It made him feel vaguely sick.

"What happened?" Her voice was muffled by his chest.

"That," he said, wriggling away from her, "is how you find out which side a half-born comes down on: angel, or human." He had almost managed to slide himself out from under her when her fingers clamped around the lapels of his coat. She blinked at him tearily. "Thank you."

"For what?"

"If you hadn't pulled me down with you…"

"Oh, I wouldn't worry about it. I needed to get to cover. You just happened to be in the way."

"But I…"

"Spare me, Florence. Just tell me if she's still out there."

"I can't tell."

"Well, how about you stand up and take a look?"

"You heard what she said before. What if she meant it?"

"Then you'd better hope you see her before she sees you, hadn't you?" And with that he gave her a shove, sliding her along the floor and into the open.

\* \* \*

"ALL YOU HAVE to remember to do is to let it in, and you'll be fine."

It had sounded so easy when Mallory said it. And back then, it had been. Then, hell had been an idea, a premise – a possibility. But now it was real. It was real and it was here and it was now. And Alice had seen, and she had felt...

The fire burned brighter, hotter.

There was just too much of it. Too much of it outside. Too much pain, too much fear.

There was too much of it inside. Too much to hold.

The wheel was still turning slowly. Still burning blackly. It was just a wheel now: *he* was long gone. His pain was gone, but it still echoed in her head.

There was too much pain, and too much death, and there was no space left.

Too much to hold, and it was all piling up, piling up, piling up.

Alice felt something give, deep inside.

The world went white.

FLORENCE EDGED FORWARD, still crouching, and peered around the edge of a stool that lay on its side. Xaphan's lab was almost unrecognisable: charred papers littered the floor – some still smouldering – and broken glass glittered in the wall where it had been embedded by the blast. The wheel where Purson had tied Abbadona was still spinning, although not as quickly and certainly not as evenly. There was no sign of Purson, for which Florence was grateful. More than any of the others, he gave her the creeps. More, even, than Lucifer.

She had met Lucifer only once, and it wasn't an experience she wanted to repeat. It was the day Xaphan had brought her to the Gate; the day he had brought her to hell. Charon barred their way, and suddenly Xaph wasn't Xaph any more. It wasn't just the red eyes: everything about him had been different, even down to the way he moved. Lucifer had walked around her, looking her up and down – examining her – and when he spoke, although it was still Xaphan's voice, he sounded like a stranger. He *was* a stranger.

"Do you know what you're doing, girl? This isn't a game. And I warn you, eleventh-hour repentance is not something I have much patience for."

"I understand. Xaphan said you need me. That's why I'm here."

"He did, did he? That's Xaphan for you. He'll say anything to get a girl." He drew closer, running a finger down her cheek. "And I do mean *anything*." He smiled at her. "Are you curious to hear what he really thinks of you? I can tell you, you know. Everything that goes on up here" – he tapped the side of his head, Xaphan's head – "belongs to me, just like everything beyond that Gate does. It's mine, all of it." He stepped back again and narrowed his eyes. "Do you understand *that*?"

"Yes." She looked at the floor. Anything not to meet his gaze. Whether this was the right response, she couldn't say, but it seemed to be enough. Lucifer nodded.

"He hasn't lied to you. Which, for Xaphan, is new. But he's wrong about the Brand. He thinks he'll let you take it, but he won't, and with good reason."

"Can I ask what that is?"

"You can. Of course, I wouldn't normally answer, but in your case, it amuses me not to. Whether or not he lets you is largely irrelevant, because I will not permit it." He folded his arms, enjoying the shock on her face.

"But without it…"

"Yes, yes. Without it, you'll fade; become a Ghast. I'm afraid it's inevitable. But you see, a branded half-born loses her gift, and what good are you to me then? You're just another half-breed, as worthless as the rest."

"Xaph said there were exceptions."

"Did he, now?" Another smile. "One. *One* exception. And one is quite enough. You make your choice, Florence. And if you choose us, I suggest you keep an eye on the angels. They don't take kindly to coming second." He pointed at his eyes and laughed. "I've enjoyed our chat," he said, looking her up and down again, slower this time. "I'm already looking forward to the next one. Until then..." His eyes closed, and when they opened again, Xaphan was back. He had a strange look on his face – a mixture of anger and fear – but he said nothing. Instead, he took her hand and led her towards the Gate.

FLORENCE STOOD IN the ruined lab, with just two thoughts in her head. The first was: "What happened to Alice?" The second was: "What if I chose the wrong side?"

THE CAGE WAS gone. Just gone. In its place was a ball of flame that flickered and swayed, and at the heart of the fire stood Alice. Molten metal bubbled around her feet. She stared ahead, not registering Florence ducking back behind the stool and out of sight.

The fire dimmed and shrank back until all that remained was a bracelet of flame around each of Alice's wrists, and still she stared emptily ahead of her. She took a step forward, out of the puddle of iron, and she paused. She turned her head from side to side, like an animal searching for a scent, and then she started to walk, leaving a trail of blazing footprints behind her.

Florence shrank further behind the stool and held her breath as she passed, not entirely trusting that Alice would see an empty lab.

It wasn't the fire that followed in Alice's footsteps that made Florence so keen to avoid attracting her attention, nor was it the fact she had just melted bars of solid cold-iron into nothing. It wasn't even the threat Alice had made before Abbadona died.

It was Alice's eyes, and the fire that spiralled deep in the darkness behind them.

"WELL?" XAPHAN'S VOICE sounded rougher than she remembered. She nodded, mutely.

"Florence? Are you *there?*" He hauled himself out from under the bench, dusting his clothes off as he straightened up. "Did you see which way she went?"

"That way," Florence managed, with a squeak. She pointed in the direction Alice had gone, but her hand shook so wildly she might as well have been waving. Xaphan tugged a slightly warped cupboard door open and produced a large bag, slinging it over his shoulder. "Good. Then we go *this* way." He took Florence's hand and pulled her gently towards another door.

"What are you doing?"

"Running. We're running."

"Running where?"

"Out. You heard Abbadona. The Gate's down, the angels are coming, and we don't want to still be around when they get here."

"What about Alice?"

"She's following orders. She's been told to find my little toy and make sure it can't open any more hellmouths. So that's what she's going to do."

"Shouldn't we stop her?"

"You want to get in her way, do you?" He let out a long whistle. "It doesn't matter whether she destroys it or not. It's done its job, and we've done ours. So now we get gone."

"Wait... I don't understand. I thought the plan was to catch her, to hold her here."

"If it was as simple as that, do you really think Lucifer would have left it to me? Anyone could have done that. Even Purson, who I see has made himself scarce." He led her out into a steeply-sloping corridor. "All we had to do was to push her buttons."

"By killing the ex-boyfriend?"

"Something like that." He was walking faster now, towing her along. "You see, you may not realise this, but Alice has a lot of *issues*. Issues like those, they generate all kinds of emotions, very few of them positive. I just gave her somewhere to focus them. Since the angels found her, her whole world has changed. She's lost everything she cared about. *Everything*. And then there's that gift of hers, which she can barely control. Trust me. I've been doing this a long time, and I'm very, very good at it. When someone's on that narrow a ledge, all it takes is a little nudge."

From somewhere far above, there was a sound like a shout; a cheer. Xaphan broke into a run, his fingers still around her wrist.

"Alice's world has fallen apart, Florence. And it all began with the angels. So, tell me: who do you think she's going to blame?"

# CHAPTER THIRTY-THREE

## The Shadow of Death

WHEN THE DESCENDEDS came, they brought the shadows with them.

Mallory couldn't remember who had begun the charge, or how, only that he had been running towards the Fallen, just as they were running towards him. It was a scrappy beginning, but it beat waiting any longer. His guns were in his hands and his wings were open, and suddenly he was sailing over the heads of the Fallen.

He understood war. He always had. It was simple. There were two sides: yours, and theirs. If you wanted to stay alive, it was important your side won. Raphael knew this about Mallory. It was why he had been promoted as rapidly as he had. He might have a healer's gift, but he was a fighter by nature, and the Fallen were afraid of him while the ranks respected him. It was Raphael who had saved his wings when Gabriel wanted to take them.

He fired into the Fallen below, massed so thickly that he didn't even need to aim. Another beat of his wings and he was down among them, shooting, kicking, punching. The Colts clicked, the magazines empty, and he dropped into a crouch to reload. By now, other Earthbounds were barreling into the fray, cutting their way through the Fallen towards one another; regrouping just as they always did in battle. Something at the edge of his sight made Mallory look up: one of the Fallen had spotted him and was charging towards him with a jagged knife held high, so intent on his attack that he had forgotten one crucial thing. Mallory's wings, which snapped open again, sweeping him aside; muscle and bone and feather meeting flesh and knocking him to the ground as Mallory spun on his heel. He looked down into the face of the Fallen below him and met his gaze as he aimed the barrel of a gun at his heart and pulled the trigger. He was gone before the Fallen's eyes closed.

Knots of Earthbounds were forming amongst the Fallen, who fought alone and with little regard for strategy. They were disorganised, chaotic. Azazel might be carrying the standard, but he was far forward and no real focus for the morass the angels were sweeping through. The Earthbounds, however, were drawn to other members of theirs choir, both by instinct and by years of training. They clustered together, turning outwards to protect each others' backs – the most basic of their battle tactics. Any Fallen who came close was cut down.

Mallory, however, moved alone. He ducked a clumsy swing from a Fallen and came back up with an elbow aimed into his face. The Fallen dropped and Mallory forged on. It was easy, this. No thought, no emotion. Just movement; constant motion. Keep going, never look back. Only forward. Only ever forward.

The noise was rising now. Cries and shouts echoed off the rocks around them, and the ground was becoming slippery underfoot. A horrible crackling sound followed by a scream somewhere off to his left told him that a clutch of Gabriel's choir had found each other and were hard at work even as he kicked the feet out from beneath a dark-haired Fallen who rushed him with a flail.

It really was very simple. Your side, or theirs.

\* \* \*

ACROSS THE FIELD, Vin slipped through the battle like a mist. He brushed past the Fallen, laying his hand on a shoulder here, an arm there; sliding his fingers around a wrist or across the back of a neck and moving on. And each of them that he touched found their movements slowed, their reactions dragging. By the time they noticed the grey fog creeping along their limbs, it was too late. On he went, deeper and deeper through the fight – never stopping, never waiting.

He had lost Mallory early on. He was glad of it, in a way. To keep up with Mallory's dervish-like dash through the Fallen would probably kill him quicker than the Fallen could. He caught sight of him every once in a while, and he could still hear his guns; it was enough to reassure him that the Earthbound was still alive.

One of the Fallen felt Vin's hand on his back and spun round, lunging at him with a nasty-looking blade. Vin leapt upwards, trusting his wings to lift him clear, but the Fallen grabbed hold of his arm and dug his nails into the flesh. Letting out a yelp, Vin tried to prise the hand off his arm, with little success. The Fallen locked his other hand around his free arm and held on with a steely grip. His wings straining to hold them both, Vin looked around him desperately, and spotted a narrow outcrop of rock, jutting from the side of the cavern wall. He stopped fighting off the Fallen, who was now holding on less in an effort to bring him down, and more in an attempt not to fall into the midst of the battle – and flew. The outcrop came closer, closer still, and with what felt like the last strength he had, as the rock came within reach, he swept sharply upwards, swinging his arms out as he did so. The Fallen smacked into the side of the rock with a thick crunching sound, releasing his grip and dropping away.

Suddenly lighter, Vin soared up the rockface until he saw a small ledge. His wings aching, his blood pounding in his ears and throat, he settled there and looked down and out across the battlefield.

From here, he saw why the Fallen had assembled where they had. The rock walls of the cavern protected their flanks, forcing the Earthbounds to meet them in a head-on assault. It was a simple, but effective, defensive tactic. Azazel might even have come up with that one all by himself. But they had positioned themselves in front of a cliff: the plateau was relatively narrow, and all it would take was a push from the angels to drive them back over it – not to mention that more and more of the Earthbounds were, like him, using their wings and taking to the air. Perhaps the Fallen had underestimated the amount the Earthbounds could fly, but that didn't seem likely. After all, the Fallen and the Earthbounds had been fighting for centuries. Just not here. So why, when they had the perfect opportunity, would the Fallen waste a home advantage?

Vin stared ahead of him. Something didn't fit. Even Azazel wasn't that stupid. Probably. And if he really was in charge, what was Charon doing beside him, not to mention Lucifer? He scanned the field, tracking the Fallen below him, watching the way they moved. The hairs on the back of his neck rose even as he hurled himself forward, dropping back to the field with a single word on his lips.

"Nets."

THERE WERE THREE Earthbounds in the air around Mallory when he heard Vin's voice, faintly, from somewhere close by. He couldn't quite make it out – there was too much noise, too many indistinct sounds screaming together into one. Ahead of him, a Fallen had pinned an Earthbound to the ground and was about to cut his throat, and that, thought Mallory, would not do. His guns vanished into his belt, and quicker than a heartbeat he was behind the Fallen, his hands around its neck and twisting. There was a snapping sound, and Mallory drew out his guns again as the Fallen toppled sideways, the other angel nodding thanks.

What happened next took even Mallory by surprise.

From somewhere far away, he heard a noise like glass breaking, but colder and harder and sharper and angrier. And then silence. Complete silence. It wasn't just that the Fallen were quiet, nor that the other Earthbounds had all stopped to listen, too. It was more like the air had suddenly been pulled away, leaving them all in a vacuum.

Just as suddenly as the silence, the sound came back in a rush. It rang in his ears and in his head, achingly loud. Screams and cries and shouts and dark, wet noises. And before he could wonder what had just taken place, the first angel landed at his feet.

It was Domiel, his face empty, his body tightly curled in on itself. His wings were shredded. Blood oozed from the broken feathers, mottling the grey with heavy red. He was dead, and tangled all around him was a wicked blue net, woven from ice and anger and sharp shards that shone jaggedly out at Mallory. For a moment, all he could do was stare at the angel – but then he was reaching for the net, his fingers digging around the bonds even as they cut into him. It was useless; Mallory was powerless to help him, or even to try. The net didn't break; didn't slacken, and with another dreadfully solid sound, another angel was brought down.

The Fallen, it seemed, had come up with something new.


AT THE HEAD of the army, Azazel held tightly to the standard. He tried his best not to look at it: like most of the Fallen, his fears were darker than any Earthbound's. He knew precisely what he would see across hell's battle flag, and it was something he could *really* do without. He was alone now, in his head, at least. Lucifer was long-gone. By now busy bouncing from head to head, looking for an unguarded back, an exposed throat, an opportunity to do some damage. He had left Azazel with instructions, and company. Or a babysitter. Despite his insistence that Azazel carry the standard, it didn't appear that he actually trusted him with it, which was why Charon was circling him, slashing and slicing at anyone who happened to come close (Earthbound *or* Fallen, which confused him more than a little) with a blade cut from ice. Some would consider the role of glorified flagpole during the greatest battle since the Fall to be slightly undignified. Azazel, ever-aware of the presence of someone else in his head, made sure it wasn't a thought that ever crossed his mind.

He had his orders.

He waited.

THERE IS NO time in hell. With no day, no night, no season other than the bitter bone-cold of endless winter, there is no way to mark the passing of ages, other than in heartbeats, in battles lost or won, in blood spilled and wounds healed.

In hell, nothing changes.

Except for when it does.

Somewhere in hell, an iron sconce bolted to the wall burned with a cold, thin blue light. Beneath it, a sticky black puddle had collected on the stone, reflecting everything above it. It reflected the flickering of the hellfire, reflected it shivering and shuddering in a sudden draught that sprang from the end of the corridor; it reflected the flame as it tried to break free, to run from something it feared. And it reflected the darkness as the shadows raced through the passageways, as the Descendeds flooded into hell.

CHARON'S HEAD SNAPPED up. Azazel watched as she dropped her blade and vanished in a cloud of ice-cold air.

They were here.

The torches dotted through the Fallens' ranks flared, then blinked out, one by one.

He lifted the standard high above the crowd of Fallen that had formed in front of him, driven back by the Earthbounds' attacks, and balanced it on his hip, freeing up one of his hands. Keeping his eyes on the breached Gate, he fumbled behind his back until he found the small tube strapped between his wings. No more waiting.

The tube unclipped easily and dropped into the palm of his hand. He snapped his arm round just as the first shadow spilled from the rubble of the Gate, leeching across the rock towards them. He lifted his arm and fired just as the darkness overtook him.

All was noise and confusion and impossible, visible darkness, and at first he thought he had misjudged it, left it too late. But as he braced the standard, braced himself for the attack, his flare burned into life above, casting a strobing blue light across the field. One by one, the other torchbearers fired their own flares, and there was at least a kind of light to fight by. If the angels thought that snuffing out hell's lights would help them, they were going to get a surprise. He smiled, and nodded to the closest of his comrades, who had caught his eye. "Let's see what they do now," he said smugly.

"How about this?" whispered the voice beside him, and all he saw was a flash of metal as the other Fallen melted away before his eyes.

Azazel dropped the standard, and drew his knife.


ALL WAS NOISE and confusion and darkness, and Mallory knew that somewhere – *somewhere* – just ahead of him was the Fallen he had been hoping to see. The sheer gut-force of his hatred still surprised him, even now. Cropped dark hair, and those clothes... the Fallen weren't exactly known for their dress sense. It could only be Rimmon. And this time, when Mallory caught up with him, he was going to *stay* dead.

He knew that he wouldn't be able to stay away, just as he hadn't been able to keep away from the Gate. Just as he hadn't been able to keep away from the Halfway when news of Alice started to spread. Of course he would be there, somewhere on the field, if only to be sure that Mallory would see him. Obviously, he hadn't taken the hint, not even when Mallory tied him to the tree and shot holes in him. He was an itch that couldn't be scratched, a fly that couldn't be swatted. A splinter in the soul that dug in deeper with every attempt to remove it. Mallory had long accepted that Rimmon was just another part of his punishment, but he was also beginning to think that this was the one part he could do something about. It wasn't revenge. Not really...

He had only caught a glimpse – a fraction of a moment – but it was enough. The battle melted around him.

And then the shadows came.

It could only mean one thing, and for that he was glad. It was time the Descendeds put in an appearance. But in the darkness, he lost his prey, and although he forced his way forward using his elbows, his fists and his boots, by the time the Fallen had lit their torches, Rimmon was gone. He scanned the faces, searching for him, but there was no sign.

So intent was he on his search that he didn't notice the Fallen with a scar down one side of his face, one eye long gone, who saw him and grinned. He had a long knife in his hand, its blade cut with jagged teeth and notches, and he raised it as he stepped behind Mallory, the point aimed for the back of his neck. And all the while, Mallory was still, his eyes tearing the battle apart as the Fallen struck.


THERE WAS A sound of the air splitting in two, and the faint smell of ozone, and Mallory spun around as Gwyn, armour-clad, tossed the bleeding Fallen aside.

"You, of all people, I expected to watch your back."

"You took your time."

"On the contrary. My timing, as ever, was impeccable." Gwyn sniffed, smoothing his hair back. "You can thank me later."

"I had him. I *had* him, Gwyn."

"Hardly. He almost got you killed, and he didn't have to lift a finger to do it. He's fitting right in, isn't he?"

"Don't you have something better to do?" Mallory raised a gun and, for an instant, Gwyn wondered if he was going to shoot him. Mallory abruptly adjusted his aim and fired twice, hitting both the Fallen who were charging towards them.

Gwyn scowled at him. "Status?"

"Unknown. They're chaotic: every man for himself. And there's a lot of them. They're using the walls to protect their flanks – no way round, unless we go airborne, which brings me to the nets."

"Nets?" Gwyn's eyes snapped open as wide as they would go. "Tell me about the nets."

"Like nothing I've seen before. They won't just bring you down; they kill. They wait until there's a handful of us in the air and then…" Mallory stopped, glancing all around him; taking stock. "I can't see where they're deploying from. Maybe they're firing them from down here, maybe they've got something up above." He nodded upwards, and Gwyn followed his gaze past the pale blue flares hanging high above. "And don't even get me started on those lights."

"So, in short, you know nothing?"

"That's pretty much the sum of it." Mallory gave the closest thing he dared to a shrug.

Gwyn sighed. "And Alice?"

"I don't know. I thought…"

"As far as we're aware, the device is still running. The hellmouths are holding. Perhaps she's failed. Perhaps she's…"

"Not Alice. She won't fail, Gwyn. Give her time."

"There *is* no more time." Gwyn looked distracted, then flicked his fingers towards something on his left. Electricity arced past Mallory's ear, and there was a horrible cry behind him.

"I'm not having this discussion again, Gwyn. In case you haven't noticed, I'm a little… busy." Mallory fed more bullets into one of his guns. "You wanted to bring the fight to the Fallen? Here we are. And so much for their attention being focused elsewhere. They were ready. *More* than ready."

"And how many of the Twelve have you seen out here, Mallory? You tell me that." Gwyn didn't wait for an answer. He spread his wings, showering the ground with white sparks, and, nets or no nets, he soared overhead.

In the middle of the battle, Mallory was suddenly still. He had seen Azazel, yes. He had even seen Charon. But the rest of the Twelve… where *were* they? They should be here. The Gate had never been breached before. Why were the Twelve not defending it? Mallory didn't believe for a second that Alice's presence was a distraction. If anything, he would have expected *this* to be the diversion, and a grand one at that.

His fingers twitched slightly. There was something happening that he didn't understand, and he didn't like it. Not one bit. But it didn't change the fact that he was a soldier, and he was standing at the heart of a war. He loaded his guns, and was moving again.

# CHAPTER THIRTY-FOUR

## Wheels Within Wheels

ALICE DIDN'T KNOW where she was going. It wasn't that she was lost, exactly, more that someone else seemed to be in charge of where she put her feet. They moved entirely of their own accord, following a path she couldn't see. She was just a passenger, along for the ride.

Left, right. Left, right. Down corridors and passageways. Through doorways. Under archways. Past a long row of metal bars set back from the wall, separating her from the space beyond. A space where something squeaked and gibbered and made unspeakable sounds.

There were other noises too: distant shouts and cries. Metal on metal, and every once in a while, something like an explosion. It was far above, and far removed, and didn't seem to matter. Only one thing mattered. She just wasn't sure what that *was*, exactly. Still, her feet seemed to know.

She stopped abruptly in front of a small door. A hatch, cut into the rock. And as she reached for the handle, Alice was surprised to see the fire that jumped from her fingers and into the lock, burning it from the inside out so that the door sprang open.

*I didn't do that*, she thought, but if she hadn't, then who had? The idea of someone else being in charge of the fire did *not* make her happy. She tried raising her hand, and nothing happened. *Not liking this*, she thought. She tried again, and although it felt as though she was pushing against water – a whole *lot* of water – there was give in it, and she felt it. She tried once more, begging her body to listen… and with a dizzying rush, she was herself, and in control again.

"Well, that was… odd," she said, surprised at how hoarse she sounded. Her head felt heavy and damp and unfamiliar, and she wondered what had happened to her. There had been pain, and fire – a lot of both, come to think of it – and then a warm, white fuzziness which had wrapped itself around her like wool. She could remember everything that had just happened, and she bit down against an unexpected spike of pain as she did, but it almost felt like it had happened to someone *else*. Shock, perhaps. It did things like that, didn't it?

So how had she wound up here? And where was *here*, anyway?

She ducked her head and stepped through the hatch.

Beyond it was a low-ceilinged passageway which she had to stoop even further to walk down. It wound away into the rock ahead of her and she bumped along it, scraping her head, her back, her arms as she went. The further she went, the smaller it seemed to become, and the further it seemed to go on; with each step it felt as though the walls might suddenly collapse in on her and bury her or crush her. She fought the urge to scream, fought the panic rising in her throat, fought the telltale pricking of her fingers, and she breathed.

It was a trick, a disguise. Just as the angels hid their wings in plain sight, so this was hiding something. It wasn't real; not at all.

She closed her eyes tightly, shoving the choking claustrophobia to the back of her brain, and then opened them again, slowly.

She was standing in a doorway. There was no passage, no sharp stone walls beyond. Just a room with some surprisingly shiny wood panelling, given this *was* still hell. A few details aside, it was the kind of room which wouldn't look out of place in an old boys' club: dark wooden walls, a polished floor covered in worn rugs. A desk, topped with green leather. A few chairs – old, and well-used. A roaring fire in the fireplace.

Of course, the devil's in the details, and they weren't exactly minor. The room was octagonal; the pictures on the walls not oils of landscapes and gentry but of men and women torn to pieces by wild beasts and savage machines. The fire crackling cheerily in the fireplace burned cold, its flames copper-green. And in the middle of it, half-shrouded by the fire, was Xaphan's device. A part of her knew what it was and where she would find it before she even stepped into the room. The same part that had led her here, taking charge and guiding her – *pushing* her – this way. And that part of her, the angel part, apparently didn't think to share what it knew with the rest of her.

She crouched down and peered at. It was a flat disc, cut from a metal like brass – not the cold-iron she had seen so much of already in hell. But the disc had been sliced again and again into pieces, into rings and sections of rings, all spinning within one another on their own axes. Faster and faster they spun, around and above and beneath each other – *through* each other, sometimes, and it seemed impossible that this could be it. That this could be the thing she had been sent to find. That something so small could have led to all of *that*.

She stretched her fingers towards it, and the flames backed away from her. Such a small thing. She could pull it apart with her fingers, burn it to ash, crush it beneath her heel. It didn't matter how she did it. All that mattered was that it was done.

The metal was cold to the touch, of course. What wasn't, in hell? But as her fingers brushed it, she saw in her mind's eye a flash of red, and she understood too late that she had made a mistake. Too late, she realised that this, the tricky little corridor, it was all the same thing. It was all a trap. And as the pain of every soul lured into hell against their better judgement and against their will washed over her, she threw back her head and screamed.

The room filled with fire. The papers curled on the desk, their edges smoking and tanning. The oil melted from the paintings on the wall, the colours sliding down the panelling to the floor. The smell of sulphur filled the air as chair-leather cracked and popped in the heat. It went on forever, until it was just another level of Alice's own personal hell. It forced her to her knees, and she fought to take control of the fire, of herself; throwing her will up against it harder and harder while it battled her back. And slowly, so slowly, she drew it all back inside herself until there was nothing but Alice left.

Nothing but Alice, who lay on the floor in a pool of sweat and tears and blood.

She had done as they asked.

She had done her best, and perhaps they had doubted it would be enough, but she had done it.

Like everyone else, *everyone* else, she had done her best.

And now she was angry.

# CHAPTER THIRTY-FIVE

## Dust & Ashes

BALBERITH WAS RUNNING. He wasn't built for it, but he was sprinting headlong for the closest way out of hell that he knew, even dropping his bag of precious ledgers on the way. It seemed the only thing to do. After all, if they were to catch him, everything afterwards would be an irrelevance. He glanced over his shoulder, and ran faster.

A fleck of grey settled on his glasses and he brushed it away, feeling it smear between his fingers. Another landed, and another, and soon he was running through a thick grey snow. Before he had gone a hundred yards, he was ankle-deep in it, and he could feel the heat at his back.

He rounded a corner, and his legs gave way beneath him. The doorway… the stairs for which he had so desperately striven… it was sealed. It wasn't even the angels who had done it – it could only have been one of the Fallen, one of the Twelve. Xaphan, more likely than not. All out to save their own skins, as always.

All was lost.

He turned to face his fate.


IN THE DISTANCE, like flood water rushing down a bore, he saw a wave of boiling flame. Lightning flashed at its edges, the fire churning across it as it rolled into hell.

The Archangels.

# CHAPTER THIRTY-SIX

## A Woman Scorned

"You hear that?" Mallory shouted across to Vin.

"Which bit, in particular?" he shouted back, narrowing his eyes as though it would save his ears.

The noise was louder now than ever. Particularly now the Fallen had started launching their mortars.

Like the nets, they had caught the angels by surprise. One moment, they had been fighting the Fallen on the ground – even the Descendeds having abandoned the air, thanks to the nets – and the next, burning naphtha was raining down on them. There was no shelter, and no respite. Mallory had seen one of Zadkiel's choir take a direct hit. It was not something he wished to see again. Not long after, he had found Vin. It hadn't been hard; he simply followed the trail of broken stone.

"Still alive?"

"You know me. Some people are just *born* lucky."

"And some have me to look out for them," said Mallory, knocking Vin off his feet and shooting the Fallen behind him in the face. "Thanks for the gun, by the way." He waved it, still-smoking, at Vin as he helped him to his feet.

Vin shrugged. "Knew it would come in handy."

"Any idea where they're firing those from?" Mallory ducked as another mortar exploded somewhere overhead, raising his wings as though they would shield him.

Vin shook his head, his hands clamped over his ears. "Can't get in the air long enough to see. And I've tried. We've all tried."

"*All* of you?"

"You can't ask her to, Mallory. No way."

"I don't need to ask her, Vhnori. She knows what needs to be done, and she's the best one to do it."

"Mallory," Vin laid his hand on his friend's arm. "Please."

"I'm sorry." Mallory patted Vin's hand once, then shook him off. "Find me Saritiel. That's an order."

THE FALLEN HAD their mortars, but Gabriel's choir had their lightning. It arced over the battlefield, never striking the same spot twice. Unlike the mortars, however, the angels had nothing to fear from it. While it bounced unpredictably through the air, it never came even close to hitting an Earthbound or Descended, simply forking around them as it grounded. It was the only advantage the Fallen had not managed to counter, and as a result they were putting their heads together and seeking out any and all of Gabriel's choir.

The Descendeds had assumed control of the field, issuing commands to Earthbounds within their choirs – but all orders came from Gwyn, and all of those orders went through Mallory. And that was why every single one of Gabriel's choir had a guard of at least a half-dozen other angels watching their backs, and when one fell, another angel took his place. It was hard and it was bloody and it was cold, but it was working. If only they could get rid of the mortars, they actually stood a chance.

VIN CAME SCRAMBLING back to Mallory, Saritiel right behind him. She was dusty and bruised; a dirty cut ran the width of her forehead and her wings were missing a good handful of feathers.

"It's no use, Mallory. I tried."

"What did you see?"

"Nothing. They're everywhere. There's no artillery, no stands; they could be coming from thin air, for all I can tell. I'm sorry." She hung her head, and Mallory sighed. Another mortar exploded above, making them all flinch.

"There's one thing," she said as the echo died down. "There was talk of driving them back, of pushing them towards the cliff, did I hear that right?"

"Yes. With the walls flanking them, there's nowhere for them to go. If we push hard enough, we could force them up to the edge. It's not a plan I like, though." He shook his head.

Saritiel and Vin exchanged glances as she leaned closer. "We can't. The cliff? It isn't a cliff."

"What?"

"It *moves.*"

"I'm not sure I understand…"

"Look where we're standing!" She pointed to the rocks rising above them. "This is where they started out. We *have* driven them back, but they're not running out of ground…"

"…And they won't. *Lucifer.*" Mallory kicked out at the rock beside him. Lucifer was changing the layout of hell, extending his will into the earth around them and altering it to protect his own. "Alright. That's good to know."

"Hardly," said Vin with a dry laugh. "If you ask me, it's pretty shitty to know, but hey."

"At least we can count out the plan where we force them back over the edge," Mallory said. "I need to get this back to Gwyn. Whether he *listens*, of course, is another matter."

He ducked away from them, cutting his way through the fight. One of the Fallen came at him with a knife, but he knocked it away, following closely with a kick to the chest that dropped the Fallen where he stood. Gwyn was some way off, but he could see him, the light of the flares bouncing off his armour, his sword crackling as he swung it left and right. He was taking the Fallen to pieces, but still they kept on coming. Either they were more desperate than Mallory had believed, or they were a sight braver than he had ever realised. Probably something between the two. Gwyn's sword flashed hypnotically, the smell of lightning slicing the air as Mallory drew closer.

Mallory was aware of a tremendous pressure at his back; of an unexpected heat, and the sensation of sudden weightlessness. Sure enough, he was being lifted off his feet, a thermal beneath his wings picking him up and dragging him aside and ever higher, however hard he fought it. This was not a good place to be. Biting his lip, he closed his wings and dropped like a rock.

GWYN SAW MALLORY tossed aside. He saw the fire coming closer, a step at a time. He felt the heat of it on his face, and for a moment, he welcomed it. It drove out the hellchill, which by now had caught even him. He assumed it was A'albiel.

He was wrong.

ALICE MOVED THROUGH the battle with purpose, not hearing the crack of the lightning or the crash of the mortars. She looked neither left nor right, but made her way steadily towards the heart of the fight. There he stood, his sword in his hand, looking for all the world like an avenging angel should. Except the funny thing was that that was *her*. With every step, the fire dug deeper into the rock beneath her, putting down roots and burrowing further into hell, finding more pain, more fuel. More fire.

She had done what they asked, and now it was over.

It had begun with a stranger, silhouetted against the gloom of a rainy day, and it would end with him.

It would end now.

\* \* \*

MALLORY STUMBLED TOWARDS them: Gwyn, motionless in the face of the fire that came for him, and Alice, serene, but burning like he had never seen. He hadn't though it possible to burn like that – half-born, Earthbound, Descended, *anyone* – and to live. Even from where he stood... the heat. The heat of it. And Alice was *in there*. He tried to call out to her, but the air scorched his throat and no sound came. He was vaguely aware of angels scattering around him, of Fallen running.

There was a hand on his shoulder, holding him back. It was, even by his standards, not the kind of hand you argued with, and he looked round to find himself staring at A'albiel, who shook his head. "You need to stay here, Mallory. Just go with me on this."

"I need to get to her. I can help."

"No. The only thing you'd do in there is burn."

His grip on Mallory's shoulder tightened.

ALICE STOPPED IN front of Gwyn, who was frozen, his sword unmoving in his hand. He did not flinch when the ring of fire sprang up around him, locking him inside the burning circle with her, nor when the flames snaked upwards and inwards, seeking each other out and meeting at a point above his head.

INSIDE THE CAGE, everything was quiet. Alice met Gwyn's astonished stare. "All of this. It's because of you."

"All of what, Alice? Hell? Hardly."

"You think I care about hell? Seriously?"

"It's in your nature."

"Screw my nature."

"You want to blame me for what you are, Alice? You're looking to the wrong angel."

"What's that supposed to mean?"

"You forget, Alice, that this began long before you and I met. It began when an angel chose a human over her duty."

"You should be very, very careful what you say about my mother, Gwyn." Alice's hand bloomed into flame.

"And you should remember that you're a half-born, nothing more. You don't want to cross me, Alice. You'll regret it more than you know." He raised his sword, electricity crackling up and down the length of it. "You really don't know who you're dealing with, do you?" He made a small gesture with his left hand and a shower of white sparks fell from his fingers, damping the flames. He stepped forward just as Alice hurled the ball of fire she had been holding straight at his head. He ducked, and took another step forward.

"You think you'll find her down here? That's why you came, isn't it – that's the truth. You can tell yourself this was all down to me, all down to Mallory, all down to any of the others, but it was your choice. You couldn't help yourself." He swung his sword at her. It made a sound like sheet metal tearing. "You think you'll recognise her, Alice? After all this time? You even think she'll *remember* you? And who's to say she wants to? I hate to break it to you, but given the choice between staying with you or Falling, she picked hell. She *chose* it, Alice. She chose to Fall. Anything to get away from you."

"You're lying."

"I don't need to. You know it's true, don't you? Deep inside, where it's dark and quiet – in that little place you like to pretend doesn't exist? The place you tried in so many ways to forget that you knew? But whatever it is you do; drown it, bury it, *burn* it… That's the place that will tell you over and over again that your mother's one of them now."

"You're lying!"

The bars of the fiery cage wavered slightly, and for a moment Gwyn thought they might fall, but with a roar, another row of bars soared up inside them, bringing the fire just that little bit closer. The tips of his wings began to prickle as the feathers curled in the heat. He swung his sword again, harder this time, and far closer to her, forcing her to duck beneath it. She answered with a dart of fire he had to jump sideways to avoid.

His patience ran out and he lunged forward with a growl. Sparks crackled in his hair, lightning bled from his eyes... and he found himself striking at thin air.


OUTSIDE, MALLORY CRANED his neck. He saw sparks, and flames, and little else beyond the fire. But A'albiel looked through it, past it and straight at Alice. He was muttering something under his breath.

"I can't say I find that very reassuring, Al."

"It's nothing... It's just. Oh. Oh, shit."

"What?"

"Look."

Mallory looked harder, until the fire burned itself into his eyes and he was sure he would never see anything but flames again. And the harder he looked, the harder it got, but just when he thought he would have to look away, he saw something else moving inside the cage with them.

"Who... who's in there?"

"Who do you think?"

# CHAPTER THIRTY-SEVEN

## Choirmaster

SOMEONE WAS PULLING Alice in several directions at once. It wasn't unpleasant, exactly, but it was peculiar; like being weightless and heavy all at once. Like flying. Like falling. A feeling she'd had before.

The sensation that a single set of eyes was watching her, and that they saw everything she was.

Everything she was, and everything she ever could be.

THE MAN SITTING across the room was half in shadow, the light catching the contours of his face; dark hair brushed back from a broad forehead and eyes full of spinning fire. He was resting his elbow on the arm of the chair and studying her carefully, his chin leaning against his hand.

Alice found herself taking an involuntary step backwards. "Are you who I think you are?"

He didn't answer. Just kept on staring at her.

"You're Michael."

"Marshall of the Armies of the Heavens. General of the Angels. Leader of the Hosts, Master of the Fires."

He laid both his hands on the arms of the chair and stood, slowly. A heat-haze shimmered about his shoulders as he straightened, then faded as he shrugged and folded his arms across his chest.

"I'll answer to any of them, but to be honest they're a bit of a mouthful. The angels tend to call me the Choirmaster. Of course," he said, lowering his voice, "they don't know that *I* know that, so don't let on, will you?" He winked at her and, quite unexpectedly, Alice felt a pressing need to sit down. Quickly. And on the floor. She stared as his wings unfolded: vast swathes of feather and flame.

"*You're* Michael?"

"You sound disappointed. It's the shirt, isn't it? You were expecting something... dressier."

Alice felt her mouth opening and closing, but no sound came out. Especially not once she saw the burning golden sigil on his forearm. He followed her eyes. "Look familiar?" He watched her hand move to her wrist and beamed at her. "Oh, I know what you're thinking." He tapped the side of his head. "Can't keep me out, I'm afraid. You're one of mine."

"You can read my mind?"

"Only if I want to. Which – and let's be clear about this – most of the time I don't. I've got quite enough thoughts of my own in my head without adding an entire choir's worth. As you can imagine, it gets rather cramped in there if I start listening in."

"But you can't..."

"Take over?" His face darkened slightly. "No, Alice. I think you're confusing me with someone else." He held out a hand, pulling her to her feet and indicating two armchairs. "Sit with me a while? I believe there are some things we need to discuss."

"Where are we?"

"Balberith's study. He won't be needing it any longer."

"Balberith?"

"Clerk. Hell's record-keeper. Pedantic like you wouldn't believe, sorry. 'Detail-oriented,'" he said, spotting her smirk. "Every soul that ever came down here, human or angel, he noted them all in those books of his." He pointed to the shelves across the room, lined with row upon row of books. "And before you ask, no. You may not look. You won't like what you see."

"About my mother?"

"About any of it. In case you hadn't noticed, hell isn't exactly a holiday camp, and generally speaking it's full of not very likeable people."

"And my mother?"

"You really are *persistent*, aren't you? Here I am. Michael. Archangel; commander of the choirs of angels. And you insist on questioning me about a silly little Fallen." He ignored Alice's gasp. "You honestly expect me to think of her as something more? She Fell. And, to put it bluntly, the only kind of Fallen I'm interested in is a dead one. That includes your mother."

"But I thought... I mean..."

"You want to know how a child born to a human and one of Raphael's pets ends up in my choir? Of course you do." He leaned back into the chair and the leather creaked under his weight. "Simple. She asked me for a favour."

"She what?"

"She asked me for a favour. Specifically, she asked me to strip your gift. The whole empathy *thing*. I can't say I blame her. It must be terribly tedious, always knowing how everyone *feels*. Quite bad enough when you're dealing with thoughts: at least there's usually some reason in there. But *emotions?* What a mess."

"You didn't, though, did you?"

"Didn't what? Strip your gift? No. Not exactly. I told her I would take you under my protection and order Raphael to remove it."

"Which you never did."

"No. It must have slipped my mind."

He lowered his chin, his eyes still fixed on her. The spirals of fire in his eyes were hypnotic, and she could almost believe him. *Almost.*

"So, why?"

"Because I saw a chance. A chance that was too good to miss. I already knew what your gift was: pure empathy, just like your mother's. I could see it, even while you were still a baby. She laid you in my arms, and you looked up at me, and I could see it. I could *taste* it, Alice." He leaned forward. "You could feel others' pain. Really feel it, in your bones. And I thought, in the right hands, in the right place – in the right time – a gift like that would be more than a mere gift. It would be a blessing. A weapon."

"A weapon. You looked at a baby, and you saw a weapon?"

"I'm a soldier, child. A very good one. And I was right. Because look at you: I had to pull you away from one of Gabriel's favourites before you took off his head! Quite remarkable."

"Right. Look at me. Some angel you turned out to be." Alice's fingers were digging into the leather of the chair. It was smouldering around them.

Michael banged his hands on the arms of his chair, and it burst into flames.

"You will respect me, Alice. You may find you don't like me, but you *will* respect me. I will not be spoken to in that tone. Not by any man, not by any angel. You remember what you are, Alice. One of my dogs, one of the hounds of heaven. And remember this, too: if needs be, I will muzzle you." His face softened slightly, the flames behind him disappearing back into the chair. "But I forget. You have done well. You have made all the choices I hoped you would make, and they have led you here. If I had planned your course myself, I couldn't have laid it better."

"You didn't exactly give me a choice, though, did you?"

"Choice? Have you learned *nothing?* You've had nothing *but* choices; a dazzling, shining multitude of them. You are absolutely unique. A glorious experiment. I had no way of knowing what you could become. What you *have* become."

Alice stared at her hands. It was too dangerous to look him in the eye. Every time she did, she found herself agreeing with him. He sighed. "I haven't done this right, have I?" He sagged back into the seat and drummed his fingers on the chair. "Mallory is so very much better at it than I am. You will forgive me, I hope?"

She didn't answer.

"In time, you will understand. This is new to you, and it is hard. I know that. But you *must* understand, Alice. There is more at stake than the happiness of a half-born, and your mother knew that. At least, she did, before she took complete leave of her senses."

"You're saying my mother knew what you would do? And what, that she offered me up like a... like some kind of...?" Alice snapped, looking up.

But she was talking to an empty room. Michael had vanished, leaving nothing behind but the smell of woodsmoke.

# CHAPTER THIRTY-EIGHT

## Pennies From Heaven, Dropping Like Rain

"WHERE'D SHE GO?" Mallory watched the cage of fire collapse into ash around Gwyn. There was no sign of Alice, just an angry angel with sparks spitting from his armour. On any other day, it might have made Mallory laugh.

"Al? Where did Alice go?" he turned to A'albiel, who was scowling.

"Michael took her."

"Michael? As in, you know, *Michael?*"

"That one."

"Well, that's just swell, isn't it? Where did he take her?"

"How should I know?"

"Al?" Mallory's voice hardened. A'albiel was being evasive, and he wasn't in the mood for it. "I'll ask you again. And this is the last time I'll ask nicely. Where... did... Michael... take... Alice?" He scratched his temple with the barrel of one of the Colts, and A'albiel raised an eyebrow at him.

"Are you trying to threaten me?"

"Why? Is it working?"

"Not exactly. But I understand your concern. He won't harm her, you know."

"Gosh, that's reassuring. You'll forgive me if I take that with a pinch of the proverbial, won't you?"

"What?"

"Never mind."

It was difficult for Mallory to miss the look Al was giving him. He tended to forget that most Descendeds had enough trouble getting their heads around any language that wasn't Enochian, let alone sarcasm. Still, seeing a Descended completely and totally flummoxed was worth the effort. Even if he did like this one. He sighed, and checked the field behind them.

Unsurprisingly, the arrival of first the Archangels and then Alice had cleared the ground. Mortars still broke overhead and the rock ran redder than ever, but the Fallen were starting to thin. Some had fled the Archangels, some had been cut down. Some had surrendered. Mallory didn't think it would take long before they wished they hadn't. If he was less cynical, he might have believed they had won. But with the gates of hell broken, the Fallen fleeing and – as Gwyn had so succinctly pointed out – none of the Twelve on the field, it felt far less like victory than it did defeat.

"Mallory?"

"Hmm?" He started slightly. He had completely forgotten that A'albiel was still beside him. In an attempt to recover his dignity, he turned his twitch into a casual roll of his shoulders.

"May I ask you something? I don't wish to appear... indelicate?"

"You see, you open a question with that and I'm already picturing how many different ways this conversation could go bad."

"Does that mean...?"

"Ask away."

"You haven't been with Gwyn long, have you?"

"Relatively speaking, no." Mallory glanced up at Gwyn, who had regained his composure enough to corner a small group of Fallen. Blood-soaked and bone-tired, by the look of them, they huddled into the rock as he dispatched them, and Mallory found himself reaching for his flask. His pocket was empty, and he silently cursed Vin. "I was assigned to him after Nathanael was killed." He fidgeted with his guns. It was a subject which still made him uncomfortable. "Meresin did it, on the Hill."

"The Hill? But that was less than a year ago. I'm surprised you could be re-assigned to another so soon. Usually, these things take time. Particularly when Gabriel's involved." Al shook his head, lowering his voice conspiratorially. "Or so I've heard."

"He as much of an arsehole as the rest of his choir?"

"I couldn't possibly say. It isn't my place. But I thought you and Nathanael…?"

"We got along. He understood me, which is a sight more than I can say for Gwyn. If I didn't know how much Gabriel hated me, I'd think Gwyn volunteered for the job just to piss me off."

"Maybe he did. But Mallory, there's something which troubles me, and while I don't wish to speak out of turn…"

"Would you just spit it out, already? What is it with you lot? Gabriel's boys are all psychopaths, and Michael's choir are all worried about hurting someone's feelings?"

"Hardly." Al drew himself upright, which made him several inches taller. Mallory hadn't realised he'd been slouching. He fought the urge to stand on tiptoe. Al continued: "It's just… well, there's something that doesn't quite sit right."

"Again: spit it out?"

"I was at the Hill, Mallory. Nathanael was not there."

"That's impossible. He died there. It was Meresin. He grabbed him from behind and…"

"No, Mallory. *He was not there.*"

"Maybe you didn't see him. I heard it was untidy. To say the least."

"You were absent?"

"Long story."

"So you did not see it yourself?"

"You think I'd be this relaxed about it if I had?" His hand was moving back to his inside pocket again. The next time he saw Vin, he was going to kick him till he bled. Even if he fixed him afterwards, the point remained.

"Believe me, Mallory. I would have known if Nathanael had been with us on the Hill. I would have welcomed it, and perhaps things would have turned out differently. But he did not fight. He was not there."

"I don't get it. Why would he tell me that Nat died... that he died with honour? How could...?"

"Who? Who told you?"

"Who do you think? Gwyn, of course.... *Oh*."

GWYN DID NOT understand. As he cut his way through the backs of fleeing Fallen – his sword a blur of flashing light and his wings blazing blue – he found himself wondering where it had begun to unravel.

Like all the best plans, at its heart it had been an overwhelmingly simple idea: to be the angel who led the charge on hell.

Overwhelmingly simple; overwhelmingly, completely and utterly impossible.

Unless, of course, you were in the right place at the right time. Or could arrange to be.

Everyone remembered Seket. The Traveler who Fell, who got nothing more than she deserved.

But not everyone had remembered her daughter.

And not *everyone* had chanced to overhear a conversation between Seket and Michael – of all the angels, *Michael* – which had turned out to be very interesting indeed.

At the time, of course, what Gwyn had heard had little relevance. He was just another soldier. But he was a solider with ambition, and he knew that all information is useful in the right circumstances. So he filed it away and returned to his duties.

It was years before he had reason to think about Seket again, years in which he had worked hard and served well and advanced further than he had ever imagined possible. Gabriel himself had shown an interest in him; had suggested that, in time, there might be a place for him amongst the higher ranks.

In time.

Gwyn did not care for 'in time.'

And so he had listened at doors and in stairways. He made it his business to hear everything that was said or whispered, to know everything that was left unsaid... to understand the silences between the words, the quietness underneath them.

Then the hellmouths had opened, and the war had escalated beyond all imagining.

As with so much else, it had been chance that led him to hear about Nathanael's assignment. It was political, of course. These things always were. All half-borns were assigned an Earthbound as their mentor, and the Earthbound in turn answered to a Descended, always from another choir. That was how it worked. Seket being – having been – one of Raphael's, he had insisted that Mallory be her daughter's mentor. This had caused no little consternation amongst Gabriel's choir. After all, angels' memories are long, and no-one had quite forgotten how Mallory had lost Rimmon to the Fallen. The thought of another loss, under their watch, was too much to bear. Nathanael vouched for Mallory; persuaded Gabriel that he could be trusted, that he would be the right choice, and at last it was arranged.

Except that Gwyn had arrangements of his own.

It HAD NOT been hard to draw Nathanael away from the host on the Hill before the enemy had even broken ranks. Nathanael was a good solider, a loyal soldier. It only took the mention of Gabriel's name...

The battle was bloody and no-one thought twice when they saw Gwyn, stained with the stuff. No-one thought to question whose blood it might be, and when they found Nathanael's broken body, it only took a whisper to confirm what they feared: that the Fallen had finally bested one of their own. In the confusion, few had even noticed his absence, and Gwyn felt satisfied. Proud, even.

But someone *had* noticed: A'albiel.

WITH EACH SUCCESS, Gwyn's confidence grew. He had placed himself in the perfect position. He followed Alice's progress, he monitored Mallory, Vhnori, even A'albiel. Anyone who might influence her. He dragged the spy Abbadona back out of hell by his heels, screaming, and offered him a deal he did not have the power to keep – confident in the knowledge that Gabriel, once all this was done, would reward him. With a well-placed word, he had even persuaded Gabriel that the time was right to attack, and now it was all coming down around his ears.

He had forgotten to watch the girl. Not Alice – the *other one*. Florence. It had never occurred to him, not once, that she would side with the Fallen. He could see why they found her so attractive, naturally, but even so. When he had realised, he had set about ensuring the blame fell squarely where it deserved to. On Vhnori.

Everything was unravelling. How could Gwyn have known that Xaphan would catch both Alice and Abbadona? And how could Gwyn have known that she would turn on him... him, of all the possible choices? Not Michael, not Mallory, but *him*? How could he have known that there was a bigger plan than his at work: greater than a single angel's plan for advancement and more powerful than his own ambition.

He raised his sword, and one of the Fallen dropped to his knees with white fire pouring from his mouth.

Victory was all that mattered now.

# CHAPTER THIRTY-NINE

## Cocytus

ALICE DROPPED HER head into her hands with a sigh. "What *is* it with this lot?" she asked no-one in particular.

She had been waiting – not long, admittedly, but long enough – to see if Michael came back. She sat in Balberith's study, listening to the faint explosions from above, staring blankly at the spines of the ledgers. Once or twice she had even walked over to the shelves to run her fingers along the leather, watching the sparks that jumped from her nails.

It would only take a moment to find it.

A moment to see everything she already knew to be true, laid out on paper in front of her.

She stared the books down, and she turned her back on them.

She wasn't exactly sure what she had expected from Michael. Perhaps she had expected him to be like Mallory, only, somehow, *more so*. Clearly, she couldn't have got that more wrong. And while the simple fact that Michael had been a disappointment didn't bother her as much as it could have, there was something else...

What if she was wrong about her mother?

All her life, Alice had carried memories of her mother; bone-deep, stone-solid memories. They were all she had of her. And although the things Mallory had told her had made her faith

315

in them waver slightly, they still held up. Or at least, they had until now.

But what if she was wrong. What if everything she had believed in, everything she remembered, was a lie?

THE DOOR CREAKED, and Alice whipped round to look at it – half in hope, half in fear. But angels didn't tend to hide in hell's half-open doorways, and there was no sign of anyone. Still, had the door really been *that* far open? She stared at it, but it didn't move. There was something odd, though, something about the floor, about the way it caught the light. It was shining. Ice.

Alice was across the room and throwing open the door in a heartbeat, looking out and down the corridor. It was empty, stretching away out of sight. Shadows dripped down the walls, pooling on the floor. Hell was collapsing under the force of the angels and she wondered idly whether this was how people felt as their ships sank, as their cars spun and left the road, as their planes crashed: the pressure of slow, aching inevitability. The flat black space left when all hope has gone.

Her foot slid out from beneath her, throwing her into the wall, and she realised there was ice out here, too – and not everywhere, but snaking its way along the corridor. A pathway. There was no way of telling where it went, but what did she have to lose?

The ice creaked beneath her, and the uneven surface sent her slipping sideways, first one way, then the other, but still she was running. The rough walls on either side of her bruised her as she hit them, scraped and cut her, and soon her arms and hips were red and raw. Blood dripped from her fingertips, where sparks danced. Still she was running, following the path that had been left for her.

The corridor sloped sharply downwards and she almost lost her footing altogether. Clinging to the walls, she edged forward, onward, downward. The drop grew steeper and soon the floor turned into steps, all coated in a layer of ice. And still she followed it, even as the shadows thickened, and the world shook around her.

Even for hell, it was cold here, and she could have sworn she could feel the wind on her face.

The corridor turned abruptly back on itself, and ended in a solid wall of ice. Or at least, it appeared to. Alice took a deep breath and slapped her hand against the wall.

"Charon!"

Nothing.

"Charon! I know you're here."

A faint whispering sound, somewhere inside the ice.

"Charon, come out, before I burn you out."

"Look at you," Charon was still buried in the ice, but Alice could see her clearly, blocking her path. Their eyes met, and Charon gave her a sly smile. Just like all the others, she had too many teeth. Far too many teeth. "Look what the angels have done to you, child. Turned you into their toy. Are you here for them, or for you? Do you even know?"

"I don't see that it's any of your business."

"Hell's business is my business. I keep the Gate. I keep order here."

"Seriously? I kind of hate to break it to you, but you're *really* bad at it. And – I'd guess – out of a job."

"You didn't answer my question."

"Not going to. So we could stand here…" Alice stopped, knowing how absurd it sounded, and laughed. "You know what? You brought me down here. You *wanted* me down here, and don't for a second think I don't know who's pulling the strings. Open the damned door."

"As you wish." Charon moved aside and the ice opened like a curtain, peeling back to leave an empty space. A blast of cold, stale air wrapped around Alice as she stared into the darkness, and she heard Charon whisper something behind her.

"And that was what, exactly?"

"Nothing that you would understand, half-breed."

"That's it. Screw you. I'm sick of this. I'm tired. I'm so incredibly fucking tired, and I'm cold." With that, she rounded on Charon, plunging her hand into the ice behind her and doing her best to shut out the biting, blinding cold. And then Alice's fingers closed around Charon's wrist, and she smiled at her. "Like I said: out of a job."

She watched Charon's wide smile fade and turn to horror as she realised what was about to happen, as fire slid around her wrist and bubbled up her arm, as she screamed inside the ice-wall as it started to boil, and all the time, Alice held her there, watching her burn.

With Charon's scream still ringing in her ears, she turned and started down the stairway into the darkness.

THE STAIRS FELT like they went on forever, and with every step, it grew colder and darker, as though the shadows were filling hell from its roots. The breeze she had felt on her face was stronger here, moving her hair and forcing her to pull her coat tighter just to keep from freezing.

Each step took her further, deeper, into the cold, and she was afraid now, really afraid, but unable to stop.

And with no warning, the stairs ended at a narrow, arched doorway. Beyond, everything was cold and blue.

Alice stepped through the archway.

SHE WAS STANDING on the edge of a frozen lake, the doorway at her back. The shadows were gone here: everything was the same flat blue that made her eyes itch and burn. She thought she'd got used to it, but somehow, here it seemed flatter. Bluer. Colder.

Something moved under the ice and she dropped into a crouch, rubbing her hand across the surface to clear it of frost, to see beneath. A face loomed out of the deep, eyes open but unseeing. Scars ran down the cheeks; the skin was blistered and dead-white. Feathers floated in the water around it, and just as suddenly as it had appeared, it was gone. Below, the shadow-shapes of wings, of war-torn limbs and broken bodies, drifted, lost beneath the ice.

Alice wrapped her arms around her chest and stared into the light. There was something ahead of her, on the ice, although she couldn't quite make it out at this distance. It was solid-looking. A block, resting on the surface of the ice, perhaps? And there was something in front of it, something darker. It almost looked like a figure. Just... sitting.

Not sitting.

Waiting.

Suddenly, her legs were moving, her feet running, pounding the ice. She did not hear the cracking of the ice, nor feel the cold wind as it blasted her. She did not see the fingers, the hands, the arms which reached up from beneath the ice – forever frozen there, hopeless and helpless. She did not see them, and her feet moved past them.

ALICE WAS SIX years old, and barefoot

Alice watched her mother die

Alice watched an angel Fall.

The wind is still rising, and Alice's hair is blowing now, into her eyes and her mouth. She tucks it behind her ears, but it whips free again, flipping around her like a halo.

Alice is six, and twenty, and twenty-three. Everything she has ever been, everything she ever could be, is coming together now. Now, on the lowest level of hell, here on the frozen lake where her mother has always been waiting for her.

# CHAPTER FORTY
## We All Go to Hell

SOMEONE HAD FASTENED a tight band around Alice's chest and was twisting it harder and harder, until it was impossible to breathe. The ice she stood on was thick, she knew that, she did – but it still felt spongy and far-off beneath her feet.

Her feet had run towards the thing on the lake of their own accord, and now they had stopped all by themselves. It was still a little way off, but Alice could see it more clearly: a great slab of ice. And inside it was a man.

Not a man: an angel. From here, she could see his wings, outstretched and shackled and buried in the ice.

Not an angel. Lucifer.

This was the heart of hell, and the ice was his prison.

She understood then: the Gate, the Fallen, the brands. Everything about hell was designed to protect him. He was vulnerable, both buried and exposed, and he had found a way to bend not just the Fallen to his will, but hell itself. It answered only to him. A sudden memory flashed through her mind – a memory of a face pushing up through the rock, of a face *made* of the rock beneath her as she stood on the wrong side of the Bone-Built Gate. The *right* side, if you thought about it.

He had been watching her all along.

*　　*　　*

THE WOMAN IN front of Lucifer's cell was sitting, hunched over, her head down. Long grey-streaked hair fell over her face and shoulders. The burned ruins of wings stuck out uncomfortably from her back, the bones at odd angles to one another; the feathers stripped to little more than spines. She showed no sign of noticing Alice when she stopped in front of her, but instead rocked to and fro, humming something under her breath.

Alice felt a stab of raw emotion as she recognised the lullaby.

"Mum? *Mum?*"

Still the angel rocked to and fro, back and forth, humming softly to herself.

"Mum? It's me. It's Alice. Can you hear me?"

Nothing, although Alice could have sworn that the humming stopped, just for a second, then continued.

"It's Alice, Mum. Alice. Do you... do you remember?" She bit her lip. What if she didn't remember her, didn't know her? Would that be worse than the other things she had been so desperately fearing?

"Mum. Mum." Alice knelt beside her and reached forward, hesitantly, laying her fingertips on her shoulders.

The hand that slapped her away moved too fast to see. Anger boiled up inside Alice and her palms itched and ached, but she swallowed the rising fire even as it choked her. She reached forward again, her voice steadier this time. "Mum...?" She shook her head. It was hopeless. "I guess you don't remember me. Do you remember who you were, before you were here? Your name was Kate..."

"Haven't been Kate for a long time." The voice was an echo, a shade. But it was her mother's. "I was, once. I dreamed a life. But it was only a dream, I think."

"It wasn't a dream. Look at me. You did have a life. Your name was Kate. You were married, his name was Richard. You had a daughter, Alice. Me."

322

"Alice. No. I would remember. I would remember a daughter. I have no daughter."

The words were like a blow to the face. Fire flared in Alice's hands before she could stop it, and the Fallen angel's head jerked up.

"Fire. Fire bad. Burning, burning." She skittered backwards, hands scrabbling for purchase on the ice, trying to get as far away from Alice as she could.

"No!" Alice clamped her hands together. "No, no. I won't hurt you. I promise. I just want you to remember."

"Nothing to remember. Only cold. And dreams. So many dreams." She lifted her head and her hair fell away from her face.

Alice found herself looking at her mother. Older than she knew it, and thinner, greyer, but it was her mother's face. Her mother's eyes.

"What do you remember?"

"Flying. I dream of flying. Of stars. Of the sun and the moon and the seas. Of light. Of warmth. Of hope." Her eyes met Alice's, and she blinked. "I dream of hope."

"You used to have another name. Before. Do you remember that?"

"Names are all the same. All useless here. We are legion, we are nameless. We are Fallen."

"Seket. Your name was Seket. Your *real* name, I suppose."

Alice saw something shift behind her mother's eyes: a spark that had not been there a moment ago.

"Seket." She frowned. "Yes. That name. I... I know it. I can feel it. It feels like sunshine. Like summer rain."

"I guess?" Alice found herself shuffling uncomfortably. This was... well, *strange*. Even allowing for the fact she was talking to her not-actually-dead-after-all mother in hell, this was strange. "You remember?"

"I do, I think. I was not always here. Not always cold. I had... I was..."

Seket raised her hands, turning them over as though seeing them for the first time. One of her wrists flashed white in the icy light, and Alice flinched. Of course her mother was branded. She had known she would be, and yet... to see it. It shocked her.

"Alice?"

"What?" Alice looked up. Her mother looked back at her. It was not just her mother's *face*, but her mother, all of her, looking out from behind her eyes.

"Alice."

"Mum?"

"I remember. I remember, Alice. Everything."

"I thought..."

"How could I forget you, Alice?" Seket was standing now, slowly, unfolding herself, holding her hands out to her daughter.

"I thought I'd lost you."

"You did. I lost myself. That's what happens here. That's why it's hell."

"You left. You left us. You left me."

"I know."

"How could you do that?" Alice snatched her hands back. "How could you *choose* to do that? It's not even that you let it happen. You *chose* it."

"And you're angry with me. I understand."

"No, you don't."

"You're forgetting, Alice. You're forgetting that I am more than you think I am. I am more than just Kate, mother to Alice and wife to Richard. I am Seket, once of Raphael's choir."

"Don't."

"Don't you see? I understand what you feel, because I feel it too. I feel it because you do..."

"But I don't *know* what I'm feeling! I just... can't." The words tumbled out of Alice's mouth. And it was true. She didn't know.

Since Mallory had told her that her mother was still alive, still there, somewhere, Alice had imagined what it would be like to see her again. To speak to her. To *rescue* her. It was the reason she had walked into hell without a second thought, despite the fear and the cold and the horror. It had kept her going through the darkness, through the noise, even through the rage and the fire and the pain. And now, after all the years without her – after everything that had changed – she was faced with a stranger. A stranger who was both more and less than her mother. Or at least, her mother as she remembered her.

Seket nodded, as though she heard everything Alice thought.

"How else could you feel, Alice? What do you expect? I am who I always was, but you did not ever know me, not truly. You could not. And you... look at you. You were a child. My child." She broke off, looking down at her feet. Alice followed her gaze. She was barefoot. Seket cleared her throat. "Don't you see? I never chose to leave you. How could I? Never." Her hands crept towards Alice's face, hesitated, then continued, smoothing down her hair. "It was because I didn't want to leave you. Because I wanted to protect you. I was ready to run forever, to outrun the angels. And I could have. I know I could have... except..." She tailed off and Alice pulled away.

"Except what?"

"Except that I knew, Alice, when you were born. I knew what you would be, and I didn't want you to carry that, to carry the burden. I went to Michael. I called him, and he came. But Gabriel, he heard my call too. He followed, and he found me."

"So why didn't you just run?"

"I told you. I couldn't let you..."

"Then why not let me choose? Why not just run, and let me decide for myself?"

"Because that's not how it works."

"So instead of one – what did you call it? – 'burden,' you decided to leave me with another one?"

"I don't understand. Everything... your emotions are so confused. What is it you're asking me?"

"I'm asking why you couldn't just stay alive."

"Ah." Seket shook her head. "I tried. I trusted Michael."

"Well," said Alice, shoving her hands into her pockets, "that was your first mistake, wasn't it?"

"You've met him?" Seket seemed surprised.

"Oh, yes. He's lovely. If you like sociopaths. We had a nice chat earlier."

"He's here?"

"They're all here. *All* of them. I came looking for you."

"Alice…" Seket looked around her uneasily. "Alice, how did you find me? This is the lowest level of hell. You can't have come this far on your own. Where are the angels?"

"As far as I know, they're picking holes in the Fallen somewhere by the Gate. It's a warzone."

"It always has been a warzone. You just couldn't see it. But who is with you? Who led you here?"

"Long story. Mallory, mostly." She watched Seket's eyes widen involuntarily, and pretended not to notice. "And there's Gwyn, although between you and me, I'm not sure he's talking to me any more. Especially since I just tried to kill him. Down here, I had a guide called Abbadona. I used to date him a few years ago, but we realised it wasn't going anywhere, what with him being one of the damned and everything."

"I can't tell if you're joking."

"You've been gone a while."

"This is important, Alice. Who brought you here? To me. Now. *How did you find the way?*"

"I just did."

"No, you didn't. You were led. By whom?"

"Charon, maybe. I followed the ice. It came here."

"Charon?" Seket drew back with a hiss. "Alice, you need to leave. Now."

"Absolutely. And you're coming with me." Alice leaned forward, trying to take Seket's hand, but she pulled away, shaking her head. "No, Alice. You need to leave. Leave me. Just go."

"What?"

"Go!"

"I've come all this way, and you think I can just go?"

"It can't be helped. Go. Go to the angels."

"Come on. We'll go together. We can find Michael; talk to him."

"No time. Alice. Go." Seket's voice was cracking and with each word she drew further back despite Alice's pleading. Suddenly, she sucked in a great breath of air and turned away. "Too late," she whispered.

"Mum?" Alice laid her hand on her mother's arm, but there was no response. "We should go."

"Oh, Alice." There was something sharper about her voice, something slicker and altogether colder as she turned her head back towards Alice. And although the voice was still Seket's, the words were not. "You think all this makes you special, don't you? Everything you've been through. All this... *loss*. I'm afraid it doesn't. Careless, perhaps, but special? Hardly. It's all just part of life's grand pageant. People live, people die. Just accept it. Let it go. Move on."

"Get out of my mother."

"Make me." Lucifer's eyes shone red in Seket's face. "Go on. Make me. If you can."

"You're threatening me, but you're not going to follow through on it, are you? So what do you want?"

"Listen to you! Give you a little taste of your own ability and suddenly you're staring down the devil. It's fighting talk. I like it. Shows spirit. I could use that." Lucifer took a step closer. Alice took a step back.

"I could have killed you a hundred times over since you set foot inside the Gate. Just so we're clear. Why would I go to all the trouble of bringing you all this way just to kill you now? Do think about it for a second, would you? And relax. You asked me what I want. It's simple. I have a proposition for you."

"No."

"You haven't even heard what I have to say."

"Don't need to."

"Now, really. I'm disappointed in you. How can you make an informed decision if you won't even listen to your options? How can you *choose*, Alice?"

"Oh, piss off."

"Now, now." Lucifer's tone grew darker. "It's a long way from here back to the surface. You have no idea what I could do to you between here and there, so don't test my patience. I've been more than reasonable so far – heroically so, given that you just killed my gatekeeper. That was, by the way, entirely unnecessary, not to mention inconvenient. So I suggest you hear me out."

"And then what?"

"And then, you choose. Simple."

"'Simple.' Of course."

"You should hear what I have to offer. I'm asking for so little. And in return, I'm prepared to give you everything you ever wanted."

"And what's that, exactly?" Alice folded her arms.

Lucifer shrugged. "Your family."

"My family. Right. Gotcha."

"Would I lie to you? Now? Why would I do that? Why would I go to the trouble to bring you here, to *lead* you here? Consider that."

"My family's gone."

"Hardly. Your mother is, well, a little occupied at the moment, but she's still here."

"And my father?"

"You don't think I can arrange for one man, one simple,

pointless little man, to be released? Me?" He made a tutting sound. "You really don't think very much of me, do you?"

"Wait – released?"

"You didn't know?" Lucifer's smile split her mother's face like a wound. "You didn't know. Ah, angels. They're tricky things, aren't they?"

"What do you mean?"

"Your father had an agreement with them, made it a long time ago. When your mother... well. He didn't want to go on, found living too much of a struggle. Who wouldn't, when they had shared their life with an angel? But the angels, they knew about you. They knew what you could be, and they wanted to keep you for themselves. So he was offered a bargain: that he would raise you, would keep going day after day after day, and when you were ready, when the time came, he would be released. He would be released, and could join your mother." Lucifer paused, batting his red eyes at Alice. "Of course, the angels neglected to mention where your mother *was*."

"That's not true. You're lying."

"Am I? *Am* I? Are you sure?"

"They wouldn't. None of them would..."

"You'd be surprised what a little ambition can do. For someone who shares blood with the angels, you don't seem to know an awful lot about them, do you? They're not so different from you – just as vain, just as self-centred. All scrabbling to be the best at doing what they're told, just so they can earn the right to be told what to do by someone slightly higher up the food chain. I see they've worked their magic on *you*.

"I'm offering you something else, Alice. I'm offering something *in return*. And all I'm asking is that you serve me instead. I can show you how to take that gift of yours and turn it into something special; something truly extraordinary. That alone is worth serious consideration, let alone the rest of my offer."

Alice found herself sitting on the ice, looking up at Lucifer while he wore her mother's body like a suit. And still he kept talking, pacing backwards and forwards, absorbed in his own words.

"I had hoped that with a little encouragement you might come to see things my way. That once Xaphan showed you what you could *be*, you might be willing to hear me out."

"Xaphan... Rob. All of that..."

"Was for this, yes. And it might have amounted to something if Michael hadn't stuck his nose in."

"He pulled me away. From Gwyn."

"Didn't he just? Meddling, meddling. Always meddling."

"If he hadn't... he said something about my hurting Gwyn."

"Hurting him? My dear girl, you would have torn him to pieces, and then we wouldn't be having this conversation. Not at all. Gabriel would have seen to that."

"But Michael stopped me." Something clicked into place in Alice's head. "He made sure I had a choice."

"Who knows what goes on in *his* head? I stopped trying to keep up centuries ago." He rolled his eyes. At least, it looked like he was rolling his eyes. In truth, it was impossible to tell. "So. There's my offer. I trust you find it acceptable?"

"And if I don't?"

"I could start by splitting you in half while you're still breathing. Or burying you headfirst in the ice here. Or maybe I'd just throw you back into the Dark House. I gather you're familiar with it?" His eyes narrowed at her.

And then a peculiar thing happened. Lucifer twitched. His whole body – Seket's body – jerked violently, and the red eyes dimmed. Not by much, but enough. "Alice? Alice. I don't have long."

"Mum? You're free?"

"Hardly. Listen to me. You can't help me. I know you want to, but you can't. You can't."

330

"I have to. I came here for you. I came all this way."

"I know, and I love you for it. But you have to go. If he comes back… when he comes back… I…" Seket's voice was straining. If there was a fight for control of her body, she was losing it. Of course she was.

"Alice, he's coming. He's coming, and he wants an answer. Promise me you won't give one to him. Hold on. Promise me you'll hold on." Her voice was fading now, even as she backed away from her daughter.

Alice shook her head. "I don't understand."

"Just… Hold on." Their eyes met, and for a moment Alice saw something there, something that had not been there before. Something almost like hope. "Have faith," Seket whispered and closed her eyes. When they opened again, they were red from lid to lid.

# CHAPTER FORTY-ONE

## Keep the Faith

"I CAN'T ABIDE being interrupted. And just as we were getting to the interesting part, too. You have an answer for me?"

"No."

"No, you don't have an answer, or no you'd really rather like to see just how many ways you can hurt?"

"The first one. Obviously."

"Ah, then we're getting somewhere. You're clearly not as stupid as you look," he said with another broad smile. He hastily added, "No offence intended, of course."

Alice smiled back at him coldly, and recoiled as he sat down beside her. "So," he said, "at least you're considering my offer. Don't get me wrong: I'm delighted. But I was hoping for something a little more... *concrete*."

"Big decision. Can't be rushed." Her mother had said hold on. Hold on for *what*? Until *when*?

Lucifer nodded. "True, quite true. But I'm going to need an answer from you now." Before she could blink, he had snapped out a hand, and grabbed hold of her wrist. His fingers burned where they touched her skin. He stood up, dragging her to her feet. "You see, I'm stretched rather thin at the moment. We're not used to quite so many visitors, you understand, and keeping things the way I like them is becoming quite a strain on my attention. I'm a perfectionist; what can I say?

And it seems our guests are quite determined to outstay their welcome."

"You mean you're losing."

"Look at it as a strategic sacrifice."

"Oh, right. That's totally what it sounded like when I was up there. Really strategic. You must be so proud of those henchmen of yours. They're doing a grand job of running away, screaming like little girls."

"Henchmen? You mean the Twelve?" Lucifer held her at arm's length, staring at her. And then he started to laugh. "Child, the Twelve are long gone. As I said: a strategic sacrifice. Where would the strategy be in sending my best soldiers to slaughter?"

"All of that, everything up there..." Images flooded through Alice's mind. A rocky field that ran red with blood. Angels who fell from the air. The Fallen running, hopelessly. "All of that..."

"All of that? I needed to make sure the Twelve were on their way. And that we had time to have our little talk, and fun as it's been, I'm going to need to press you for an answer."

"No."

"No answer, or...?"

"No. The answer is no. Actually, the answer is to tell you to..."

"And that's quite enough of that." Without batting an eyelid, Lucifer tightened his grip on her arm and lifted her off her feet, swinging her upwards. She was flying and she was falling, falling fast and the ice was rushing up to meet her. Alice landed heavily enough to feel her teeth rattle. The back of her head smacked down into the ice and stars spun above her. Her hair felt wet, sticky, and her left arm throbbed. She tried to sit up, but a wave of nausea forced her back down and she groaned. There were footsteps coming towards her. Lucifer. She rolled over onto her stomach, tried to crawl, but before she could move, a foot connected with her side, lifting her into the air again. This time, she didn't even notice coming back down. It all hurt too much.

But there was no fire.

Nothing.

There was another kick, and another. She was hauled to her feet and shaken, then knocked down again; thrown about like a toy.

And still there was no fire.

He must have known what she was thinking, must have felt her rising panic, because he crouched down next to her and stroked her hair.

"Is that the best you can do? I was hoping for so much more. If this is all you have... well. Perhaps I don't need you after all." He patted her head as she coughed and tried to wipe the blood from her eyes and nose. "A shame. I could have taught you so much. So much more than they can." He sighed. "Mind you, given time, you'd have learned. They're all the same, the angels. They *will* fail you."

"Not *all* of us." The voice came from across the lake. It was soft, and it was warm, and it was familiar. And it was angry.

Mallory.

"Ah, there you are. I was beginning to wonder when you'd turn up," said Lucifer, without bothering to look round. "How did you like my mortars?"

Alice's vantage point wasn't exactly up to much, but she still saw Mallory flinch, saw a shadow pass across his face. And although she hadn't dared to hope for it, she felt something spark at the tips of her fingers.

Mallory opened his wings, sailing across the ice towards them. She heard the rustling of the wind through his feathers; smelled the blood and naphtha covering his clothes. He looked Lucifer up and down as he landed.

"The mortars? They're great. *Loved* them. Brought you one." In one fluid motion, he reached into his jacket and pulled out a thin, club-shaped object, hurling it towards the block of ice. Lucifer screeched and dived after it. There was a loud roar;

the world shook and Mallory ducked, clutching his ears and arching his wings above his head to shield himself. He scuttled across to Alice.

"You know, for a guy who's not used his body in a few hundred years, he's pretty prissy about it."

"He's..." Alice rolled onto her side. That hurt more, and she couldn't make the words stick together. "It's..."

"Alice, I'm Earthbound, not stupid." He paused to consider this, tipping his head to one side. "Well, not *that* stupid. I know who he's riding."

"Riding?"

"Technical term."

"Oh."

"Come on, Alice. Work with me here. Last time I saw you, you were about to incinerate a Descended. So you tell me, do we need to talk about that?"

"He's still alive, isn't he?"

"Point taken." He held out his hand, and gently pulled her upright. "This is going to hurt."

"You, or me?"

"You're funny."

"Apparently."

"Never mind. Let's get you fixed up before he puts out that fire."

As it happened, Lucifer was busy doing just that, protecting his ice-bound body from the mortar blast. Mallory held out his hands to her, and looked her up and down. "I'm not going to like this, am I?" he asked.

Alice gave the closest thing she could to a shrug. "If it's any consolation, I'm not either."

He laughed and closed his hands around hers, and she felt the familiar warmth spread through her body, the same jabbing pins growing stronger and stronger, and then stopping all at once.

He let his hands drop, staggering slightly, and spat out a mouthful of blood, then shook his head sadly. "He did a number and a half on you, didn't he?"

"Is that a technical term too?" Alice shook off the echoes of the beating she'd taken.

Mallory smiled. "If you like. I'm proud of you, you know."

"Whatever." Alice wasn't watching Mallory. She was watching Lucifer squatting, toad-like, in her mother's body as he put out the last of the flames. Mallory followed her gaze, pulling his guns out from beneath his jacket and checking them over. Alice looked appalled.

"You're going to shoot him?"

"If I get a chance to, yes."

"But... my mother..."

"You're not exactly *helping*, Alice."

"And where did you get the second one from, anyway? I thought you only had one."

"Vin. I know," he said, watching her mouth drop open, "I was as surprised as you. But then he threw my drink in the river, so I can only imagine he was going for shock and awe."

"Huh." Alice looked back over at Lucifer. He had turned to face them, and stood with folded arms in the middle of the ice. He was smiling. Of course he was smiling. "You know I won't let you shoot my mother."

"And I won't let you stop me. There's more at stake than your mother. She Fell, years ago. That was her decision."

"You sound like Michael. The only good Fallen is a dead one, right?"

"Something like that." Mallory narrowed his eyes at Lucifer and stepped in front of Alice, between them. He raised one of his guns, slowly. Lucifer just smiled at him.

"No," said Alice, quietly. Mallory took no notice.

"No," she said, louder this time, and although he hesitated, he brought his gun up higher.

"I said no!" Alice grabbed at his elbow, just as he pulled the trigger. The bullet smacked into the rocky roof of the cavern.

Mallory rounded on her. "Do you think this is easy for me, Alice? Do you? Haven't you listened to a single word I've said? This is about more than you. It's about more than me. It's…"

"Don't tell me. It's your duty, is that it?"

He was silent for a moment, then simply said, "Yes."

"I won't let you kill my mother."

"She's in hell, Alice. Your mother – the mother you knew – she's already dead. Let her go."

"No."

"Alice, I can't…"

He didn't get to finish. Instead, he was sent sprawling by a kick from behind. So distracted had they been arguing with one another, neither had thought to keep an eye on Lucifer, and he had crept up on them, knocking Mallory halfway across the ice with a single blow. Alice watched in horror as Mallory skidded across the lake, crashed into a wall, and lay motionless.

"You see, child," Lucifer said, "the angels are not on your side. The angels are on their own side. You are either with them, or against them. And if you dare to stand in their way, well…" He opened his arms.

High above them, deep in the rock, something groaned and shook, and a light shower of dust and snow settled on Alice's shoulders.

"Ask yourself: what would your mother want for you, hmm? What would she tell her little girl, do you think? No. Wait. Better still: let me ask her for you." He tipped his head back, as though listening to a far-off voice, and then snapped back to Alice. "She doesn't want to die, Alice. Not at all. She doesn't understand why you've brought them to kill her. She's afraid – afraid of them, afraid of you. Afraid that you will judge her. After all, who are you to judge an angel?"

"And who," growled Mallory, pushing himself to his feet,

"are you to hold one hostage?" He was limping, and he was bleeding. Again.

Lucifer shrugged. "I've never pretended to be something I'm not, Mallory. Unlike you."

The rockfall came from nowhere. One moment, Mallory was standing, the next he was half-buried in stone and ice and dust while Lucifer looked on with blazing eyes.

"And let's just think about you, shall we? On the one hand, you're a healer, aren't you? That's what you *do*, isn't it, when you're one of Raphael's. That's all you do. But here – well, *there*" – he pointed upwards – "as an Earthbound, you're something. You're special. They look up to you, don't they? They treat you differently. They think you're wise, you're brave, but the sad little truth of it is that you're damaged goods, aren't you? You'll never make it home because you drink, and you drink because you'll never make it home. You were given a chance with a half-breed and you lost him. You lost him to me. And so you slide and you slide and you slide, burying yourself in all the wrong things, until you become what you are: a man with nothing, absolutely nothing to lose. Which is why you're here. Because you not sure that you can keep hoping any longer. You're afraid that you'll lose it." There was an ominous rumble overhead. "And without hope, there can be no faith. And without faith... well." He clapped his hands together and a tumble of stone and dirt cascaded over Mallory, smashing against his wings, his arms, his face.

Alice watched Mallory sag under the weight of the rock. Blood ran down the side of his face and one of his wings was twisted back on itself. The feathers fluttered feebly. But Lucifer had not finished.

There was a sound like nails on a blackboard and a great sheet of ice lifted from the surface of the lake, tilting and tipping, spinning on its end... then slowly it slid towards Mallory. He eyed it carefully, and with a grunt of effort, he beat his free wing and sent rubble and stones flying, pulling himself loose and rolling clear of the ice sheet just as it smashed across the pile where he had been trapped. He dropped into a crouch, looking up at Lucifer.

"Is that the best you've got?"

"Was that a rhetorical question?"

The wind howled around Lucifer, still in Seket's body, and Alice could see everything Mallory was thinking. It was why Lucifer had been so calm when he showed up, why he had made no attempt to attack her. It was the same reason she was out of ammunition, out of fire. He knew neither of them could do it. Neither of them could really kill him or, rather, kill the body he was in.

He had them both.

He had won, and she wished the ground would open and swallow her – again. Anything to get it over with quickly. Alice understood that he had won, and she despaired.

And Lucifer must have known, somehow, because he turned and gave her a smile that made her skin crawl.

It was all Mallory needed.

He leapt at Lucifer, knocking him flat and pinning him to the ice. Mallory straightened up, his boot on Lucifer's throat, and before Alice could even breathe, he had fired a bullet neatly through his shoulder. Through Seket's shoulder. Alice screamed, and Lucifer just laughed.

"Go on, Earthbound. Finish the job."

Mallory raised his gun, ever so slightly. It was now in line with Lucifer's forehead, aiming straight between his eyes.

Words were tumbling out of Alice's mouth. Angry words, frightened words, any words she could get to stick together. Mallory heard them, but still he stared down the barrel of his gun into Lucifer's bright red eyes.

"You can shoot me. I won't hold it against you. Well, not much."

"Fuck off, Lucifer."

"Listen to you. Never were very much for words, were you? Why use your head when a fist works so much better?"

"But funnily enough, you're the one stuck in hell. Explain to me how that works?"

"Oh, you're in hell already, Mallory. You just didn't Fall. So shoot me. Shoot *her*. Make it perfect."

Mallory's hand shook. His whole arm shook. He was looking at Seket's face, a face he hadn't seen in so long: it was drawn, and lined, and not to put too fine a point on it, looked like she'd been through hell. Which was fair enough. But in the middle of that face, in the place of the soft eyes he had always known, there was Lucifer looking out at him. He had his boot on Lucifer's throat, but it wasn't Lucifer's throat, was it? It was Seket's. She would be the one who died, not Lucifer. He would just hop on over to another of the Fallen. And that was the way it was.

But Lucifer had kept Seket here, kept her in this chamber, alone, all these years. Why? Was she worth something to him?

Alice.

It was all for Alice.

Mallory's grip on his gun tightened.

Lucifer wanted Alice. He had known about her, and he had her right where he wanted her. He had played them all, or even engineered it himself. Mallory couldn't be sure which, and wasn't certain he wanted to be. Somehow Lucifer had found the perfect opportunity to get to Alice.

"Always were an opportunist, weren't you?" said Mallory.

Below him, Lucifer batted his eyes in mock innocence. "I have no idea what you mean."

"You're forgetting. I know you. I know how you work. And I know Alice."

"Do you? Are you sure? Do you trust her, Mallory? Tell me that. More importantly, does she trust you? Think what she's been through: what you, the angels, all of you, have put her through. And now, at the end of it all, she gets her reward: a chance to see her mother, to be with her. You should never underestimate the power of grief."

"You know what?" Mallory rolled his eyes. "You're an arse. You always were. You've not changed." He cocked the gun.

Lucifer simply carried on smiling. "And you," he said, "apparently still have too much faith."

Alice's punch hit Mallory squarely in the jaw, knocking him sideways. "Get away from my mother."

"Alice." Mallory staggered slightly as he tried to regain his equilibrium. "That's not your mother."

"I don't care." Alice was standing between them, between him and Lucifer, her face dark.

"Alice…"

"No." She raised her left hand, and already he could see the flames around her wrist; a hot, shining bracelet. He followed her gaze… and saw the smear of blood from Lucifer's shoulder on the ice, and he cursed himself for being so stupid.

"Alice, he's using you. He's using *her*. He always has been."

"Doesn't matter." She took a step towards him, and behind her, Lucifer flashed his appalling smile. Overhead, the rocks groaned.

"Alice. If you stand in my way, I only have one choice."

"You don't make choices. You follow orders."

"Because I choose to."

"Because you have to."

"You want to get into the semantics of it with me? Fine. Step out of my way. Let me finish this."

"No." She took another step forward, and Mallory could see it in her eyes: she was going to kill him, and hand Lucifer even more than he could ever have dreamed.

"Alice. I'm not going to warn you again." He raised the gun; leveled it at her.

They stared each other down, and there they would have stayed, had it not been for the quiet voice carried on the wind, saying just two words.

"Mallory. Please."

"Seket?" Mallory's mouth dropped open.

Behind Alice, Seket nodded. It was her.

"Is he gone?"

"No. And he won't ever leave, Mallory. Take her. Get her away." Her eyes settled on Alice, still frozen between them, apparently unable to hear her. Another creak came from the ceiling of the cavern, and the ice shifted beneath their feet. Seket shook her head. "He can't hold it. Hell will collapse, starting with this cave. You have to get her out of here."

"She won't go."

"She must."

"Seket, I can't…"

"You will, Mallory. You can't win here, now, but there will be a time and a place that you can. All you have to do is find it. And be ready." She frowned. "I can't stay. He's too strong." Her eyes flashed red, and back again, and Mallory felt his heart cracking inside him. "Tell her I gave her the only thing I had left," said Seket, and then Lucifer's voice chimed out of her:

"What's that?" he sneered. "Love?"

"No," Seket answered. "Pain."


ALICE HEARD IT coming for her. It roared, breaking over her like a tide. She was swimming in it, drowning in it, and even as it washed over her, through her, she felt the fire rushing to meet it. It burned away everything in its path, everything that Seket had felt in the coldest, hardest part of hell.

And Alice knew what would happen next.

She couldn't control it, couldn't even begin to. There was just too much of it. There was nothing but pain.

Fire ripped through the ice around them, punching holes in the sheet they stood on, knocking them off their feet as blocks of ice tore free from one another. The frozen lake was burning.

Ice floes loomed over them as they tipped in the water, sliding against one another, and Alice looked from Mallory to Seket in panic. The ice lurched alarmingly, throwing her towards Mallory, who caught her and locked his arms around her, pulling her close to him where he knelt. "You stay with me."

"No. Mum!" she called, seeing her mother struggle to her feet, but when Seket looked around, her eyes were flashing red and back. Lucifer was trying to take over again, and she was fighting him.

"Not for much longer," said Lucifer's voice, but even as he said it, he lost control and the red glow faded. Seket smiled at Alice, and their eyes met, and then she turned, throwing herself forwards and on to the jagged shard of ice that rose to meet her.

The flames boiled around them, climbing higher as Alice screamed. She watched Seket's body tense, impaled on the ice, and then relax. She saw blood seeping out – obscenely red against the cold blue – and dripping down into the water and fire. She felt Mallory's arms tighten about her... and she turned her head to look at him.

"You can help her! Before it's too late. You could heal her!"

"Maybe I could."

"Then go! Go help her!"

"No."

"What? But that's what you do! You heal people. She's hurt, she's dying. She's dying. You could save her."

"No."

"Why?"

"Because that was her choice." His voice was flat; rough, sad.

Alice realised he was crying, and it was only a moment later that she realised she was too.

There was a groan overhead, and a shower of rocks fell from

the cavern roof. The ice shuddered, and Seket's body slid slowly into the lake. Alice screwed her eyes shut and wished that she could be somewhere else. Anywhere else. Any*one* else.

Mallory's grip on her shifted. He released her and he was taking her hand, pulling her to her feet.

"We have to go, Alice." Another shower of loose stones and frost fell from above them. *"Now."*

They ran. The ice slipped beneath their feet and fissures opened ahead of them, throwing fire up into their paths. They jumped from ice-sheet to ice-sheet as the pieces tipped and tilted and rolled across the water. Twice, they fell, scrambling back up again and moving, and the door to the stairs was forever away.

Behind them, on the centre of the lake, Lucifer's body stood imprisoned on its own ice sheet, ringed by fire, his empty eyes watching them go.

# CHAPTER FORTY-TWO

## Heaven Help Us

THE STAIRS SEEMED narrower on the way back up; longer, too, and even colder and darker. Mallory kept hold of her hand. She felt as though a hand had simply reached inside her and torn out everything that could feel.

She had found her mother, and she had lost her again. And this time, she was gone. There would be no more chances.

"Mallory?" Her voice felt small. "Why did she do that?"

"Because she knew it was the only way."

"She could have come with us. We could have…"

"Could have what? Saved her?"

"Yes."

"No. She knew what was right, Alice. Trust in that. She would always have been your weakness, and mine." Ahead of her, in the darkness, he sniffed.

"I let her down. I let you down, Mallory. I'm sorry. I'm so sorry."

"Let me down? Bollocks. You listen to me, Alice, and you listen carefully. You might be a half-born, but you know what that makes you? Half-human. You remember that. It makes you better than us, even better than your mother. It makes you… more complete."

"Right. Because that makes sense."

"The greatest wisdom is usually the most impenetrable. Just look at fortune cookies."

"You eat those?"

"Only the cookie. I find the fortunes tend to get stuck on the way down." He coughed theatrically and, despite herself, Alice laughed.

The blackness of the stairway was paling to grey. Somewhere beyond it, there was light, of a sort, and they stumbled out into a passageway.

"I never thought I'd be so pleased to be back in the middle of hell," Mallory muttered. He looked tired, thought Alice, as he turned towards her. Tired and stretched. "You alright?"

"No. I'm not alright."

"But you will be, and that's what matters, Alice. You *will* be."

"What happened to Lucifer?"

"Who knows?" Mallory blew out a long, frustrated breath. "But don't for a second think that he's gone. He'll be back."

"She won't, though, will she?"

"She won't, and I'm sorry for that. But it couldn't have gone any differently."

"If I…"

"No," he said, taking her by her shoulders and looking into her eyes. "You couldn't." He held her gaze, then released her. "Know that. Remember that."

A rumbling sound echoed out from the stairwell, and Mallory pointed down the corridor.

"We need to go. Do you remember the way you came?"

"Not even remotely."

"Just as well I do then, isn't it?" He rolled his shoulders, checking his wings over. The damaged one flapped weakly.

"Does it hurt?" asked Alice.

Mallory gave her a wry smile. "You could say that. It'll mend soon enough. But it means we're on foot, so best get moving. Goodness only knows what's going on up there."

\*　　\*　　\*

ON THE PLATEAU behind the remains of the Bone-Built Gate, the battle was over. The Fallen had either been killed or had fled, and Raphael's choir were moving across the field, looking for their own wounded. Following them through the carnage was a curly-haired figure with a satchel slung over his shoulder, his wings tucked neatly behind him as he bent to examine each of the injured. Slowly and carefully, the Archangel Raphael picked his way through the dying and the dead, and he wept.

From a rock to the side of the shattered Gate, Michael surveyed the ground. What he saw did not please him. There were too few of the Fallen, too many of the angels. The attack had been sloppy, too soft. More to the point, it had been a trap. One into which Gabriel had allowed his army – *Michael's* army – to march ill-prepared and unaware. The Twelve had escaped. If they had even been there at all. He doubted that they had. Lucifer was an opportunist, and he was heartless, but he was no fool.

The damage had been done. Someone would have to pay.

"Brieus?" Michael half-turned to the angel standing behind him, and Brieus snapped to attention, lowering the standard he had captured. His face was still stained with Azazel's blood, and his hands were sore and bruised. And when hell's flag fell, the battle had turned. Of course, the arrival of the Archangels might have had something to do with it, but the way Brieus saw things, it had been *all* about the flag.

Michael motioned to him, and he stepped forward. "Go and find Gabriel. Now. I want to know what he's doing."

"Gabriel? You want me to bring him to you?"

Michael considered Brieus's suggestion, then shook his head. "No, no. I think perhaps not. Find him, and report back to me." He paused, waiting for Brieus to leave. He did not, and Michael sighed. "Now!"

With a flap of his wings, Brieus was gone.

\*　　\*　　\*

FAR ACROSS THE field, Gabriel was pacing up and down, incandescent with rage. His wings lit up the shadows as he barked orders and insults at the massed ranks of his choir. This should have been his moment of triumph: the moment he had broken the heart of hell. Instead, the Twelve had fled, there was no sign of Lucifer and Michael was nowhere to be seen. It was a mess. He kept on pacing, lightning crackling across his breastplate and through his hair. So furious was he that he didn't notice Brieus sailing overhead. Nor did he see the Earthbound as he wheeled in the air, his wings carrying him back towards Michael.

Instead, Gabriel shook his head and gestured to the front rank of his choir, who drew aside. In the midst of them, his chin raised defiantly, stood Vin. Like many of the others, his face and hands were stained with blood, his clothes torn. His usually dark hair was a mottled grey, thick with dust from the battle. Gabriel glared at him.

"All this. All *this*," he said, waving his hand towards the plateau, "is because of you."

Vin said nothing, but glared straight back at him, unmoving.

Gabriel shook his head. "You disgust me. Foolish Earthbounds, believing you can make a difference, when you can barely control your own charges."

"That's rich, coming from you."

"You watch your tone when you speak to me." Gabriel leaned forward, his nose almost touching Vin's, but still Vin did not move.

Instead, he blinked, then smiled. "You should hear what they're saying, Gabriel. Earthbounds, Descendeds... even the other Archangels."

"Oh? Tell me, then, what it is that they say."

"That you're a fool. That you've become proud. That you sheltered a killer in search of glory. That Gabriel, the great Gabriel, is finished. You're *done*."

"Is that all?" Gabriel laughed. "Small words, from a small mind. No-one will miss you."

"Miss me?"

"No." Gabriel smiled coldly, and looked across the ranks of his angels. "Adriel!"

A shiver ran through the choir. Few of them had ever seen Adriel, but all of them knew who he was.

Adriel was the angel of death.

Adriel was the angel all the other angels feared.

Gabriel wasn't just going to punish Vin. He was going to make an example of him.

BEHIND THE CROWD, a quiet man was leaning alone against the rock walls. Hearing his name, he straightened up, smoothing his jacket and stepping forward.

Unlike the angels ahead of him, he wore an undertaker's morning suit, and his wings, as he opened them, were black. The feathers whispered against each other as he moved, sounding almost like voices, long-lost to time. But as he made his way out of the shadow and towards the massed angels, he found his path blocked by a firm hand on his chest. Michael shook his head and raised a finger to his lips, then backed away, wrapping the darkness about him. The only sign he was there were the tiny drops of fire that fell from nowhere and turned to ash as they landed, as Michael made hell itself weep.

Adriel nodded once, and faded back into the shadows.

WHEN HE REALISED Adriel was not answering his call, Gabriel snarled in irritation. He drummed his fingers on the hilt of his sword, then drew it with a flourish, turning away from Vin. "I see I must take care of this myself."

There was, from behind him, the faintest of clicking sounds.

He turned back, and looked straight into not one, but two guns. Fire circled the ends of the barrels.

Vin was still staring him down, but he did so from between Mallory and Alice, who stood on either side of him.

"Now, if you want to do that, you're going to have to kill me first," said Mallory. "And I'm not going quietly."

"You..." Gabriel hissed, his hand tightening on his sword, but he was forced to step back as a fine line of fire drew itself between him and the three of them, licking at his toes as it went. He scowled at Alice. "And you... You wait until Michael hears of this. You think you know what pain is?"

"Has it occurred to you," said a voice in the darkness, "that I might already have heard, Gabriel?"

Michael threw off the shadows and stepped into view. Not far behind him, A'albiel was hauling Gwyn, stumbling and bloodied, through the ranks of Gabriel's choir. With a muffled murmur, they shuffled apart to let them through, and watched as Al threw Gwyn down in a heap at Gabriel's feet.

Michael snapped his fingers and the fire died. "Enough, Alice. And you, Mallory. Stand down." He waved them away and turned back to Gabriel.

"You think you can blame all of this on one little Earthbound? Why, because he couldn't see that his charge had slipped, was with the Fallen?"

Michael heard Vin's gasp, and tapped the side of his head with a meaningful look at Alice. She looked away, but not quickly enough to hide the anger in her eyes, and Michael smiled, turning his attention back to Gabriel. "I know it all, Gabriel. I *know*. Ambition denied can drive us all to madness, but ambition such as I have seen here – overreaching, measureless ambition – leads only to disobedience, to false endeavour and to this." He pointed back to the battlefield. "There is no glory there. No victory. There is only death and destruction."

"Michael, you cannot..."

"Enough." Michael waved wearily. "Gabriel, I'll deal with you later. When my temper's cooled and I'm less likely to do something I regret. Until then, consider yourself Earthbound." He drew a complicated shape in the air with his fingers, and before he had finished, chains of fire were winding their way up Gabriel's legs and across his body. His wings stretched open of their own accord and his mouth opened in a scream as the fire rushed through the feathers, burning the tips away. "Count yourself lucky, Gabe," said Michael.

HIS SWORD WAS in his hand, and he laid it casually across his shoulders, ducking his neck away from the blade as he paced back and forth along the line of angels. "You, on the other hand," he said, stopping in front of Gwyn, "I'm going to deal with *now*."

Gwyn was on his knees, head bowed. Michael leaned forward and, grabbing a handful of the Descended's hair, pulled his head up to look at him. "Do you realise what you could have done, boy? Do you?"

"I'm sorry. I..."

"You're sorry. And you think that's enough?"

"All I wanted..."

"I know what you wanted. You saw an opportunity, and you thought you were good enough to take it. I should lock you in a cage until the stars burn black, but I'm not that kind." He swung his sword down from behind his neck. "Open them."

"No... no! Please... not Earth!"

"Earth? Who said anything about your being Earthbound? I'm not that kind, either." He whispered into Gwyn's ear, "You thought you could better us. You were proud. And you know what they say about pride, angel..."

"No. No..." But Gwyn was on his knees, and his wings were open, and the fire was raging in Michael's eyes. "Goodbye, Gwyn."

Michael swung his sword and it scythed down through Gwyn's wings, through feather and flesh and bone. It burned as it cut; the feathers glowed and sparked as it touched them, bursting into flame. Gwyn's screams echoed around them all, bouncing endlessly off the rocks and filling Alice's head, but Michael was still damping her gift, and all she could do was listen to Gwyn's cries and feel the pain of wings she didn't have as they burned, smelling the feathers as they scorched and crumbled into nothing. She glanced at Mallory: he was staring ahead of him, his mouth set into a hard line. Vin's eyes were fixed on the floor. Only Michael was watching Gwyn as he writhed and collapsed, and inside the spinning wheels of fire in his eyes, Alice saw something cold and dark, and she was afraid.

"What are you all looking at?" Michael's voice was firm, and suddenly every one of the angels who had been transfixed by Gwyn's pain remembered they had somewhere else to be, urgently. In moments, they had all scrambled away. There were only a handful of them left: Mallory, Vin, Michael, Gabriel and Gwyn, huddled on the ground.

Another angel was approaching them: one she did not know, but she could feel the warmth he brought with him, smell the scent of spice in the air. And without looking, she knew Mallory was smiling, and she knew who it was, walking across the battlefield. Raphael.

He paused when he reached Gabriel, stooping down to lay his hand on the newly-Earthbound angel's forehead, pointedly ignoring Michael's irritated cough. His face was kind, friendly, and his curly hair made him look gently childlike. Cherubic. Alice fought back a laugh, and Raphael smiled up at her.

"You do look like her," he said, and although the words were kindly meant, they cut. He stood, and laid his hand on her shoulder. "I can take it away, you know. Let me do that, at least."

"No. Thank you, but no."

"Alright. I understand, better than you think." He patted her shoulder, and turned to Mallory. "You've done well."

"I did my best."

"You did. Isn't that all I ever asked? Isn't that the most any of us can ask? And you did not fail me. Now it's time to come home. Be whole, brother, and come home."

There was a flash of light so bright that Alice had to turn her head, sure that it would blind her. It flickered across the inside of her eyelids in shades of purple and red, in gold and blue. And it was only when she heard Mallory's voice that she opened her eyes again.

She wasn't sure what she had been expecting: perhaps for him to be miraculously transformed, but he was still Mallory. Still in his battered jacket and torn jeans, still stained by the battle. But the careworn expression had gone from his face, and as he shook out his wings, her mouth dropped open. They were no longer a dirty shade of grey; no longer the same odd proportions. Now they spread out from his shoulders, restored to their full length, the feathers glowing from within. And as they shifted, settling beside one another, she smelled incense and ginger, and safety. He winked at her. "Not bad, huh?"

"It's going to take some getting used to." Alice shrugged. "What does it mean?"

"It means I get to go home," said Mallory. He whispered something to Raphael, who shook his head.

Whatever it was, Michael had obviously heard it, because his eyebrow shot up and he looked at Vin. "Vhnori?"

"Mmph?" Vin fidgeted under Michael's gaze.

"You have done well. Very well. You almost redeemed yourself, I think, but the fact remains that you failed to notice that one of your half-borns was... how to put this? Screwing a Fallen?"

"I'm sorry. I am."

"I know you are, and for that alone, I could perhaps have forgiven you. However, you lost a half-born, and one with a valuable gift. Without her mind-tricks, the Fallen would not have been able to gain such a hold, would not have been so easily able to tip the balance in their favour. And this leaves me with no choice but to punish you."

"I understand." All the fight had gone from Vin, who now stared at the ground in front of Michael.

"You will remain Earthbound, and you will serve out the remainder of your original term. But I will not extend that term, and I will not sanction you." Michael was smiling now, and Vin looked up from the ground.

"That's it?"

"That's it. I like you. You've got spirit. Once your time's done, come and find me. I can always find a place for someone like you. And in the meantime, I'll be watching. As for you," he said, turning to Alice, "I will give you some time. A rest, a chance to think about your priorities, your place in the world. But sooner or later, I will come for you. And you had better be prepared."

Alice's eyes met Michael's, and she saw everything inside them, and felt him see everything inside hers. He searched her face, her mind, her heart... she could feel him creeping inside her like smoke. Then the corner of his mouth twitched into a half-smile, and in a swirl of flame, he was gone.


RAPHAEL TOUCHED MALLORY'S arm. "We should leave. We don't belong here. Will you come?"

"Not yet. I made a promise."

"I see." He frowned. "You remember the way?"

"Are you kidding me?"

"Then I will see you in your own time. But don't wait too long, there is much to do, and much at stake."

"I promised, Rafa."

"Then do as you must." Raphael smiled at Mallory, and turned to Alice. "She was proud of you. She still is." He paused, then nodded. "I will see you again, soon." He spread his wings, and lightly stepped into the air, soaring away and vanishing in a flash of light.

They watched him go, exhausted and bruised and punch-drunk.

Alice spoke first. "Is that it? Is it over?"

"Over?" said Vin. "Nah. It's never over. This is just another fight. There'll be more."

"And this is how you live?"

"Sucks, doesn't it?" But he was grinning as he said it, and he landed a friendly punch on her arm. "Admit it, you *love* it."

"'Love' isn't *exactly* the word I'd use..."

"It so is."

"It so isn't."

"Is."

"Isn't."

"Can you two just leave it? I feel like someone's dad. I don't like it; it makes me feel old and responsible, and like I need a drink. Which I can't have because someone threw mine in the river." Mallory sounded like he was only half-joking. "Besides, we need to get out of here."

"Yeah, this place is totally dead," said Vin, shoving his hands in his pockets. Mallory shook his head, muttering something under his breath.

Alice looked around them. "Gwyn. Where did he go?" she asked. There was no sign of him, nothing at all. He had simply vanished. "Should we try to help him?"

Mallory shrugged. "It's not our concern."

"But he's..."

"He's one of the Fallen now, Alice. And he doesn't deserve your sympathy, nor your pity."

"And to think, when we first met, you were giving me the whole 'brothers' spiel. What happened to that, by the way?"

"Fuck it." Mallory kicked a stone that lay in his path, and

watched it bounce along the rock. "That was clearly my charming naivety speaking. It won't happen again. In the meantime, I suggest we find a way out."

# CHAPTER FORTY-THREE

## If You Want to Get to Heaven, You Have to Go Through Hell

THE SUN WAS setting as Jester dialed a number on his phone. The snow had stopped, and already the air was feeling warmer. Whatever had happened down there, whatever they had done, it had obviously worked. The world went on unknowing, but the angels had broken hell's hold – for now, at least.

"I've got him," he said into the mouthpiece, slapping the large wooden packing crate he was sitting on. A muffled shout came from inside. "He ran straight into it, just like we planned."

He paused, listening to the voice on the other end of the line.

"No, no-one. He popped up all on his lonesome at the other end of town. No trouble at all."

A pause.

"Would you just let me handle this? It's the least I can... No. Alright, alright. Whenever you're ready, he's all yours."

He snapped his phone shut and slid down from the top of the crate. It was large enough to hold a man – just – and built of thick wood, reinforced with steel plates. A small grille was set into each side to allow air to flow through, and it was next to this that he crouched.

"You hear that, Purson? Enjoy your time in your little box, won't you? Because the next time that lid opens, you're going to wish you were back in hell."

359

\*     \*     \*

ALICE HAULED HERSELF up through the cave after Mallory. Her arms ached from the climb and her fingers were sore, adding to the bruises, the cuts and the utter, utter exhaustion she already felt. But above her was daylight. Well, she told herself, *twilight*. She didn't care if it was pitch black up there. It was the world. The real world.

It wasn't hell, and however imperfect it was, she would take that.

"Come *on*," she called over her shoulder to Vin, who was whispering urgently to himself. Risking a glance back over her shoulder, she realised he was talking into a phone. "*How* has he managed to get reception down here?"

"You're forgetting: the Fallen are all about technology. Xaphan," said Mallory from somewhere above. There was a shower of soil, and his hand reached back down for hers. "We're there."

She let him haul her up, and she found herself in a field, lying flat on her back in deep snow, staring up at stars. "You know, compared to hell, this feels positively balmy," she said, sitting up and brushing snow from her hair. She shuffled out of the way as Vin's hand clamped around the edge of the hole and Mallory helped him out.

"You're not even out of hell, and you're on the phone already? Unbelievable."

"Some of us have social lives to maintain." Vin brushed the snow from his hands. "Of course, not that you'd know anything about that."

"Wow... Seriously. Who was it?"

"No-one. Really." He turned his phone over in his hands, and was about to drop it into his jacket pocket when it chirped. "See? Mister popular. Right here," he said, scanning the screen. His face brightened. "That's what I'm saying. Guess who's got a date?"

"You're expecting us to believe that there's someone out there who would *voluntarily* spend time with you?" asked Mallory, his head tipped back.

Vin pulled a face. "Sari wants to get a drink sometime."

"She must have got hit on the head." Mallory stretched his wings out and sighed happily. "Poor kid."

"Piss off," said Vin. Alice laughed, and looked up at the sky. It looked no different from any other clear night she had seen, with the stars glittering high above them.

It looked no different, because it was no different.

The only thing that had changed was her.

She watched as the two angels, Descended and Earthbound, set off across the field ahead of her. They were still bickering, occasionally swatting at each other. She looked back down the hole they had clambered out of; through caves and tunnels, through blood and fire and ice. Through hell.

Mallory stopped, turned. "You coming, or what?"

And then she wrapped her coat about her, and hurried after them.

IN THE SHADOWS behind them, a pair of dark-rimmed eyes flashed red, and watched them go.

# CODA

"YOU'VE HEARD THAT Lucifer's body has been captured?"

"And what good is that, Adriel? With most of the Twelve still loose, and Lucifer able to ride any one of the Fallen?"

"It's something."

"It's nothing. Worse than nothing."

Michael watched the last of his choir moving among the motionless figures on the Plains; watched them moving slowly and methodically through them, killing the Ghasts they found. From high above, it almost looked as though they were taking up positions on a grid.

Beside him, Adriel looked down over the edge. "And what about *them*? The ones the Fallen took?"

"What about them indeed?" said Michael thoughtfully, then shook his head. "Hell has enlarged herself, and that cannot be. If we leave things like this, balance is... unsustainable."

"But the taken... they're innocents."

"In my experience, Adriel, no-one is an innocent."

Michael's angels had stopped moving. One by one, they raised their arms and fire flared in the palms of their hands: tiny orange stars casting a hot glow across the Plains of the Damned.

"This isn't the way."

"That's for me to decide. This is my army."

"Is it? Are you sure about that?" Adriel spoke softly, and Michael showed no sign of having heard him.

"Michael?"

"Not a single one worth saving," said Michael, balancing a ball of flame between his hands.

He tossed it over the edge of the cliff, and turned away as his angels began to retreat, fire spinning behind his eyes.

"Let them burn."

# About the Author

BORN IN WALES in the UK, Lou Morgan grew up in a house with an attic full of spiders and now lives on the south coast of England with her husband, son and the obligatory cat.

Her short fiction has been published by the British Fantasy Society, *Hub Fiction* and *Morpheus Tales*, and most recently her story "At the Sign of the Black Dove" appeared in the *Pandemonium: Stories of the Apocalypse* anthology.

She drinks a lot of tea, is very mouthy about archery and likes cathedrals, comics and Christopher Nolan movies. And probably things beginning with other letters of the alphabet, too.

She can be found online at loumorgan.co.uk, or – far too often – wasting time on Twitter as @LouMorgan.

*Blood and Feathers* is her first novel.

# Acknowledgements

THERE ARE SO many people I should mention here that they could almost fill a book by themselves – and even then I'm sure I'd manage to leave someone out. That being said, these are the people who would inflict actual physical pain on me if I forgot them. So.

My deepest thanks to Jon Oliver: editor, friend and all-round good guy, for taking a leap of faith; and to the team at Solaris – Ben Smith, David Moore and Michael Molcher – for making me feel like a part of the family.

Pye Parr for beautiful artwork and for generally just being very cool. *Someone's* got to do it...

"Team Angel": Adele Wearing, Ro Smith and Jenny Barber, for feeding (and occasionally slapping) The Ego.

Rob Shearman, Tom Pollock, Lizzie Barrett, Jenni Hill, Fiona Higgins, Gary McMahon, Sarah Pinborough, Guy Adams, Mike Shevdon and Michael Marshall Smith, for a thousand kindnesses.

Sonja, for Milton and Marlowe and so many other things.

Will, for friendship, support and endless patience & encouragement. I owe you.

Vinny, for letting me borrow your name and maintaining a sense of humour even when I dropped it off the top of a nine-storey building. You're the best kind of angel.

Tesna, for being a better friend than I ever deserved, and for being the devil on my shoulder.

My dad, and my mother – who once asked me what I was doing this for. I miss you, and I hope this answers your question.

My husband and my son. You already know why.

And to you, reading this – whoever you are, wherever you are. Thank you.

# Blood and Feathers Playlist

THESE ARE THE tracks I was listening to while I wrote *Blood and Feathers*. Some of them go with specific scenes, some are kind of attached to characters – Vin, for instance has his own little theme tune hidden away in here, and so does Mallory. Which song goes where... I leave you to decide for yourself.

*All the Right Moves*: OneRepublic
*Make Me Wanna Die*: The Pretty Reckless
*Believe Me*: Fort Minor
*Slip Out the Back*: Fort Minor
*It's Not the End of the World*: LostProphets
*Only Man (Jakwob Remix)*: Audio Bullys
*Burning in the Skies*: Linkin Park
*When They Come For Me*: Linkin Park
*New Divide*: Linkin Park
*Dreamcatcher*: Unicorn Kid
*The Island, Pt I (Dawn) & Pt 2 (Dusk)*: Pendulum
*Witchcraft (Rob Swire's Drum-step Mix)*: Pendulum
*Ich Tu Dir Weh*: Rammstein
*Bulletproof Heart*: My Chemical Romance
*The Only Hope For Me is You*: My Chemical Romance
*Teeth*: Lady Gaga
*Walking in Circles*: Dead by Sunrise
*Dead Reckoning*: Clint Mansell
*End Credits*: Chase & Status with Plan B

## Angelic Sigils

THE ANGELIC SIGILS which appear in *Blood & Feathers* are, technically, "real"... that is to say, these are some of the sigils historically used by alchemists and others as part of rituals to invoke or conjure angels: the most famous (or infamous) practitioner being John Dee.

Along with Edward Kelley, Dee devised (or "received," as he claimed) an angelic language and alphabet which he recorded in his journals, and which later became known as Enochian.

The sigils for the five Choirs in the *Blood & Feathers* world are show below.

### Barakiel
"If I told you Barakiel's very handy round the card table..."

**Gabriel**
"You can always rely on Gabriel for a bit of
old-school wrath and vengeance."

**Michael**
"I've never even *met* one of Michael's choir. There aren't
many of them, and they're the big guns."

**Raphael**

"You're a healer, aren't you? That's what you *do*, isn't it,
when you're one of Raphael's. That's all you do."

**Zadkiel**

"Zadkiel. He's all about memory and the mind and stuff."

The angelic war has spread out of control,
and violence erupts across the globe as the Fallen's
influence grows.

As the Twelve walk the Earth, the Archangel Michael
is determined to destroy Lucifer once and for all,
whatever the cost – and Alice, Mallory and Vin will
be called on to sacrifice more than they ever
imagined possible.

The Fallen will rise.

Trust will be betrayed.

And all hell will break loose...

# BLOOD AND FEATHERS: REBELLION

**Coming August 2013**

**SOLARIS**

'difficult to put down... a thoroughly entertaining novel that I would recommend to those looking for a summer blockbuster'
*Sacramento Book Review* on *Age of Odin*

*New York Times* Best Selling Author
**JAMES LOVEGROVE**

UK ISBN: 978 1 907992 04 9 • US ISBN: 978 1 907992 05 6 • £7.99/$7.99

## POLICING THE DAMNED

They live among us, abhorred, marginalised, despised. They are vampires, known politely as the Sunless. The job of policing their community falls to the men and women of SHADE: the Sunless Housing and Disclosure Executive. Captain John Redlaw is London's most feared and respected SHADE officer, a living legend.

But when the vampires start rioting in their ghettos, and angry humans respond with violence of their own, even Redlaw may not be able to keep the peace. Especially when political forces are aligning to introduce a radical answer to the Sunless problem, one that will resolve the situation once and for all...

 **WWW.SOLARISBOOKS.COM**

*Follow us on Twitter! www.twitter.com/solarisbooks*

Cover TBC

New York Times Best Selling Author
**JAMES LOVEGROVE**

*UK ISBN: 978 1 78108 049 8 • US ISBN: 978 1 78108 050 4 • £7.99/$8.99*

## BLOOD ON THE EASTERN SEABOARD

The east coast of the USA is experiencing the worst winter weather in living memory, and John Redlaw is in the cold white thick of it. He's come to America to investigate a series of vicious attacks on vampire immigrants – targeted kills that can't simply be the work of amateur vigilantes. Dogging his footsteps is Tina "Tick" Checkley, a wannabe TV journalist with an eye on the big time.

The conspiracy Redlaw uncovers could give Tina the career break she's been looking for. It could also spell death for Redlaw.

### OCTOBER 2012

 **WWW.SOLARISBOOKS.COM**

*Follow us on Twitter! www.twitter.com/solarisbooks*

UK ISBN: 978 1 907519 62 8 • US ISBN: 978 1 907519 63 5 • £7.99/$7.99

Jordan helps kids on the run find their way back home. He's good at that. He should be - he's a runaway himself. Sometimes he helps the kids in other, stranger, ways. He looks like a regular teenager, but he's not. He acts like he's not exactly human, but he is. He treads the line between mundane reality and the world of the supernatural. Ben McCallan's urban fantasy debut takes you on a teffifying journey.

BEN MACALLAN

PANDAEMONIUM

'Smart, witty, and full of surprises, it grips until the very last shock.'
– Suzanne McLeod, best-selling author of *Spellcrackers.com*

UK ISBN: 978 1 78108 051 1 • US ISBN: 978 1 78108 052 8 • £7.99/$8.99

Desdaemona's done a bad, bad thing.

A thing so, so terrible that she has to run away from the consequences. Again. Where better to look for shelter than with the boy she was running from before?

But trouble follows. And if it's not Jacey's parents who sent the deadly crow-men, the Twa Corbies, in chase of her, then who is it? Deep under London, among the lost and rejected of two worlds, answers begin to emerge from Desi's hidden past. Answers that send her north in a flight that turns to a hunt, with strange companions and stranger prey. Dangers lie ahead and behind; inconvenient passion lays traps for her, just when she needs a clear head; at the last, even Desi has to beg for help. From one who has more cause than most to want her dead...

 **WWW.SOLARISBOOKS.COM**

*Follow us on Twitter! www.twitter.com/solarisbooks*

UK ISBN: 978 1 907992 37 7 • US ISBN: 978 1 907992 38 4 • £7.99/$8.99

Babylon Steel, ex-sword-for-hire, ex... other things, runs The Red Lantern, the best brothel in the city. She's got elves using sex magic upstairs, S&M in the basement and a large green troll cooking breakfast in the kitchen. She'd love you to visit, except...

She's not having a good week. The Vessels of Purity are protesting against brothels, girls are disappearing, and if she can't pay her taxes, Babylon's going to lose the Lantern. She'd given up the mercenary life, but when the mysterious Darask Fain pays her to find a missing heiress, she has to take the job. And then her past starts to catch up with her in other, more dangerous ways.

Witty and fresh, Sebold delivers the most exciting fantasy debut in years.

 **WWW.SOLARISBOOKS.COM**

*Follow us on Twitter! www.twitter.com/solarisbooks*